Nashborough

Nashborough

A Novel

Elsie Burch Donald

HarperCollins*Publishers*

HarperCollins books may be purchased for educational, business, or sales promotional use. For information, please write: Special Markets Department, HarperCollins Publishers Inc., 10 East 53rd Street, New York, NY 10022.

FIRST EDITION

Excerpt from "Ancient Tragedy" in *The Complete Poems of Cavafy*, Copyright © 1961 and renewed 1989 by Rae Dalvin, reprinted by permission of Harcourt, Inc.

Designed by Elina D. Nudelman

Printed on acid-free paper

Library of Congress Cataloging-in-Publication Data

Donald, Elsie Burch.
    Nashborough / by Elsie Burch Donald.—1st ed.
      p. cm.
    ISBN 0-06-018633-X
    1. Upper class—Fiction. 2. Tennessee—Fiction. I. Title.

PS3554.O46782 N37 2001
813'.54—dc21o
                                       00-065463

00 01 02 03 04 RRD 10 9 8 7 6 5 4 3 2 1

In Memory of Lucia

Where are you going, Gilgamesh?
The immortality you seek you will not find.
When the gods created man, they allotted death,
Keeping immortality for themselves.
Eat and drink, Gilgamesh; dance, be merry,
Bathe in clear water and put on fresh clothes;
Cherish the little child that holds your hand
And let your wife find love in your bosom;
For these are the joys of mankind.

GILGAMESH, Sumerian, 2000 B.C.

Motionless and reverent, the air, the earth, and the sea
guarded the tranquillity of the great gods.
And sometimes an echo from on high came to them,
an ethereal bouquet of a few verses breathed
"Well done, well done," the blended trimeters of the gods.
And the air kept saying to the earth and the aged earth to the sea:
"Silence, silence, let us hear. Within the heavenly theater
they are giving a performance of Antigone.*"*

"ANCIENT TRAGEDY," C. P. Cavafy
translated by Rae Dalvin

Who's Who

in the 1920s, when the story begins:

The Nashes of Cottoncrop

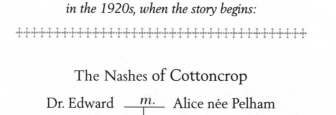

Dr. Edward —*m.*— Alice née Pelham

Seneca —*m.*— Dartania Douglas

The Douglases of Timbuctoo

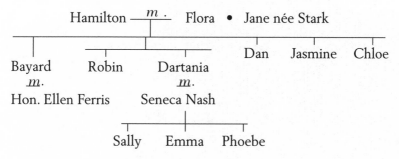

Hamilton —*m.*— Flora • Jane née Stark

Bayard · Robin · Dartania · Dan · Jasmine · Chloe

Bayard
m.
Hon. Ellen Ferris

Dartania
m.
Seneca Nash

Sally · Emma · Phoebe

For a full list of characters, see back of book.

Nashborough

The Indian Summer

╬╬╬╬╬╬╬╬╬╬╬╬╬╬╬╬╬╬╬╬╬╬╬╬╬╬╬╬╬╬╬╬╬╬╬╬╬╬

1

Even in the attic rooms that morning, blurred and intermittent noises of activity could be heard. Floorboards creaked and scraped as furniture was removed from storage and other pieces carefully put away for the day. The house's elevator, an open-work cage, droned continuously like an imprisoned bumblebee, while on the floors below, muted girlish giggles floated at intervals along the corridors, mingling with the fast-clipped tread of many purposeful feet. The commotion extended to—perhaps originated in—the garden, from which occasional feminine voices murmuring directions drifted in through the open windows.

But the dozing brain of Robin Douglas shut everything out. He simply turned over in the old half-tester bed, the bed he had been born in twenty-seven years ago that summer, and stuffed a pillow over his muzzy head. Neither the sunlight filtering through the drawn shades as through parchment nor the delightful little breezes scooting underneath the shades and puffing their ends out into the room succeeded in arousing consciousness. On he dozed, dreaming and daydreaming, until finally one particular vision cornered his imagination: Margaret Elsworthy, her honey-colored hair fluffed out like a halo (not at all the fashion), her clear gray eyes gazing on him with a serene intelligence, and her full bosom and rounded hips (not at all the fashion either) blooming voluptuously. And he believed that almost certainly he'd made up his mind. Sufficiently at any rate that when, a few minutes later, he set himself the habitual morning question, What am I going to do for happiness today? he was able to answer speedily and with resolution: a proposal of marriage; and that settled, he might have drifted into somnolence again had not the door clicked and, peering out from under the pillow, he glimpsed the silver flash of a coffeepot.

"Mornin, Mr. Robin."

"Mornin, Cal."

Robin divested himself of the pillow, put it behind him and sat up, rubbing his bony Douglas nose. "Didn't expect to see you stompin about so early in the morning."

"Ain't early." The old man set the breakfast tray down on a hassock in front of the low armchair. "Miss Chloe up. Miss Jasmine. Mr. Dan. Whole town up today."

"Good God." Robin shook his head as if this single masterful effort might regroup the contents. "Chloe's wedding!" And having registered the impending order of events, he began stuffing himself into the brown paisley dressing gown the old man had laid on the bed. No wonder marriage had taken such a hold on his mind, and now, its being someone else's, provoked a confused pleasure springing, or so it seemed to Robin, out of a mutually shared condition.

Raising the shades so that sunlight flooded the room, Calvin looked down into the garden. "Bout time it somebody's," he declared accusingly, concentrating his gaze on the activity below.

Wooden folding chairs were being set out in rows on either side of two long pieces of string tied to stakes that had been hammered into the ground at either end, temporarily marking an aisle. Down it two men in overalls struggled to transport a boxlike frame that draped and decorated was destined to become an altar.

Robin pulled his long, thin frame upright and, barefoot and squinting against the light, gingerly joined the old man at the window. "As a matter of fact," he told him, clearing his throat a little and standing up straight, "I have this very morning been contemplating a matrimonial tie myself."

"Thinkin ain't doin," the old man observed, still looking down into the garden.

"True." Robin raised his finger like the angel in an annunciation picture. "It is however the prelude to a successful enterprise. I go into action today."

"That be Miss Margaret," said Calvin, somewhere between a statement and a question.

"She's nice, isn't she?"

"Yessir, a nice lady; and do she deserve you?" he cryptically inquired.

"Maybe she won't take me." Robin smiled his thin-lipped smile; the gaiety in his face was in and around the eyes, in their gray-blue sparkle and paper-crinkly surrounds; but an uneasiness, impossible to pinpoint, shadowed the overall expression of a kind face and an intelligent one.

"Maybe she won't," the old man agreed, though privately it was not the conclusion he anticipated. "Some things don't ever happen, some do, and ain't no reason on earth why it be so." He had felt his side as he spoke, leaning forward slightly onto his hand.

"Something the matter, Cal?" Robin, more than a head the taller of the two, looked down at the old man with alarm.

"Nothin cept the Lord done give me a little poke. Remind me ever now and then he got me on his list," he chuckled philosophically.

Putting an arm around the old man's shoulders, Robin squeezed. "Hang on for a bit longer," he implored him gently. "If you can." And he patted the narrow, stooping shoulder in impotent reassurance.

"I going to try," said Calvin, giving a firm nod to which was affixed a somewhat wistful smile. "I going to try."

From the garden a woman's voice was calling anxiously. "Oh stop, don't put the aisle cloth down *yet*. Leave it till last, so it's spotless." It was the caterer.

"Pure bedlam," pronounced Robin, sitting down in front of the breakfast tray and pouring himself a cup of strong coffee. But in truth he was beginning to feel elated—as much as the effects of last night would permit.

"Sho is. An I nearly forgot." Calvin reached inside the pocket of his white jacket and removed a bulky envelope. "Yo brother Mr. Bayard here, half past nine this morning; left this for you, one for Mr. Dan; want you to sign em this morning and a messenger gon pick em up at noon."

"Just stick it on the bureau," Robin said, and went on eating his breakfast.

"Ask to see yo dad."

"Bayard did?"

"You know Mr. Ham don't see nobody fore twelve o'clock, I say. And Miz Douglas she say he better come back later, if he can. It business, he say. An she say, surely business can wait, an you know we got a wedding here today. But it can't wait, he say." Calvin's watery eyes twinkled with amusement. "And without no nevermind, off he go, straight into the lion's den."

His mouth full, Robin widened his eyes in bemused acknowledgment, aware that Bayard must be hatching some new deal and needed to get the family bank behind him. That explained the envelopes.

Robin admired his brother's cool head and brilliant intellect, his ability to ride astride in the financial world with the seasoned skill of a top jockey; but he failed utterly to understand how the business bug could bite someone who wasn't hungry, and he had decided some time ago that he didn't understand his elder brother at all: Seven years and a stillborn child between them had created a generation gulf.

As soon as he had finished breakfast, Robin opened the brown envelope, ruffled through the document to the last page, and signed beside the penciled X. Then, having conducted all the business necessary on so uncommonly festive a day, he poured another cup of coffee and turned his mind toward the wedding and, specifically, toward Margaret Elsworthy. Where better to propose a marriage than at one! And going over to the window again, he inspected the preparations taking place in the garden with a view to selecting a suitable venue.

Dotted about the lawn, men were standing on ladders tying Japanese lanterns to tree branches and tall, shepherdlike crooks planted in the ground, from which the lanterns drooped like swollen blossoms. Behind the improvised altar being covered in close-fitting white brocade, the dome of the summerhouse rose, its marble columns twined with yellow climbing roses. And despite the clichéd presence of summerhouse trysts in sentimental novels, Robin decided that probably it would do. At least it would provide some privacy. He suspected too it was the kind of thing women liked, since why else did summerhouses figure so prominently in romances?

He examined the sky. Fat little clouds like cotton pads floated, barely moving. That would keep it from becoming too hot, that and chilled bubbling glasses of champagne, smuggled at who knew what expense from France. Then, later, when the lanterns had been lit, and fireflies were sparkling on the lawn like falling stars, he would give Margaret his arm and, a bottle of champagne in hand, closet the two of them in the summerhouse. Suddenly his heart began to leap like an exuberant if well-hooked trout, and pure joy pumped its opium through his veins. He took a deep breath: Another wonderful day was in the making, and he, *grâce à dieu*, was in it.

EARLIER THAT MORNING, when the streetcar stopped at the end of the extended spur line, ten people, four more than usual, had alighted and begun to walk up through the park, past the paddock, vegetable gardens, and greenhouse to the big three-storeyed stucco house, its portico of garlanded Ionic columns sharply profiled in the June sunshine.

Six days a week the Douglas servants made this journey back and forth from their homes in and around east Nashborough. The stop was almost a mile beyond the end of the commercial line, Hamilton Douglas having built the spur line at his own expense to get his servants to and from town. Every morning except Sunday the streetcar arrived promptly at eight o'clock on its extended journey, returning at five to collect its half-dozen passengers.

Only the cook, her husband, and Calvin Douglas did not commute, but lived in cottages on the place.

From his "office," a rather gloomy room accessible from the conservatory, Hamilton Douglas had watched the troupe arrive and, laying aside the morning paper, stroked his carefully trimmed white whiskers and thought suddenly, unexpectedly of his wife. Not of Jane who was at that moment already directing the day's momentous preparations, but of Flora, the impossible, headstrong Flora who had refused to see other than the comedy in life but who, laughing and teasing, had got hold of his heart and twined herself around the fibers of his being like a young vine putting out tendrils in every possible direction. Clear as day he saw her standing on the lawn under a yellow parasol, her collar unbuttoned in the heat and her head thrown back in laughter at the site he'd chosen for their new house, three miles west of Nashborough, in a green brook-fed valley.

"We'll call it Elysian Fields," he had said, instinctively turning to the classical world for reference, like all Southerners, believing himself to be the continuance of it.

"Elysian Fields, my eye." Her mirth bubbled forth unabated. "Out in the middle of nowhere, why, darling, it's Timbuctoo!" Poking fun—even though she had taken to it at once, seen exactly where the house should stand, the direction it ought to face, and where the gardens, cottages, and stables could be put—had drawn it up instantly as a finished mental vision. And forty years on, laid out as she had envisaged, but only one stop from the city streetcar line, wired for electricity and piped with town water, it remained "Timbuctoo," the name Flora had so spontaneously picked.

That so much life, such an intensity of spirit, could so suddenly be quenched had been the shock of his life. It made no sense at all, and the tiny life that triumphed over Flora's, defying all the accepted premises of battle, that curiously victorious infant, was now about to be married. He saw that there was much here for reflection but he felt only the dull blunt fact of it, leading nowhere.

Not a religious or a sentimental man, Hamilton's creed was that of self-reliance. He was a man who submitted himself, and others, to the power of his own will; outside that perimeter he had schooled himself to meet the whims of fortune with an unflinching composure. He believed, too, in the importance of routine, and since retirement from the bank—though he remained chairman—he had continued to follow a meticulous schedule. From seven-thirty until noon he read and worked in his office, then lunched *à deux* with his wife, after which he lay down on the bearskin rug in the library, resting his head on the stuffed head of the grizzly, his long, lean body stretching the length of its carcass, and napped for half an hour. At three he went out for a drive, not in a motor car but in a carriage; he preferred the pace of a horse and said he saw more, and besides he liked the rhythm. On the way home he always got out at the front gate and walked the half mile up the driveway to the house. The family dined at seven, including as many of his six children as were about. Afterward he and Jane always played a game of backgammon, but without ever creating any stakes. In never deviating from this routine Hamilton automatically reinforced the awesome respect in which he almost universally was held, and, like those countries whose trains have always run on time, he engendered strong feelings of security and dependability—attitudes he knew with certainty were valuable in both directions.

Consequently he had been more than a little surprised, even on a day dedicated to disruption, by an early knock on the office door and the appearance of his eldest son.

Questioningly Hamilton gazed into the pinpointed eyes that like his own slanted downward at the outer edges, the same bony patrician nose, though Bayard lacked his father's height and, at thirty-four, was already inclined to stoutness.

"Come in, come in." He underlined welcome with a motion of his hand. "The bridegroom hasn't done a bunk I trust?"

Bayard smiled and shut the door. "No, but that reminds me, he asked me yesterday, not very obliquely, about that job in Thebes."

Sitting down rather heavily on the leather sofa, Bayard crossed his legs with a casual elegance typical of the Douglases. "Jim's a dependable sort of fellow, too cautious to stray off the beaten path, just like all the Blounts. He ought to make a fairly decent banker."

"A good spare wheel"—Hamilton confirmed the assessment in his own style—"though Chloe needs it less than the others do. Well, if she's happy to move to Thebes, why not give it to him?" And placing his hands on his knees, he leaned forward, observing his son closely. "But Jim and Chloe's future isn't what brings you here I gather?"

Rapidly apologizing for intruding, Bayard removed a document from his coat, and, popping the gold-rimmed pince-nez dangling from a cord, firmly on his beak, he began to tell his father about the loan needed from the family bank in order to tide over the insurance company purchase. Buying that third company down in Mobile had left them temporarily short, until the stock rose, which would be very soon.

OUTSIDE HAMILTON'S OFFICE, the maximum chaos, from which order must in a few short hours be extracted, had been reached. The bridesmaids' dresses were being delivered by two seamstresses in black and hung up in the front guest room, where a maid with an iron awaited them. Nobody knew what had happened to the bridal flowers, and the cake van reportedly had suffered a puncture setting out. Wedding presents were still arriving; they had to be cataloged and space found for them in the dining room, where they were being displayed. This task belonged to Chloe but she was somewhere out in the garden. In addition there was the food to be seen to, the waiters to be instructed, the parking of cars arranged, and everybody on the place, thirty people at the very least, would have to be given some lunch.

Stuffing pins back into her gray hair and nodding assent at the positioning of a huge vase of flowers in the hall, Jane Douglas spoke into the telephone mounted on the wall, as to a deaf person. No, she told Alice Nash calmly if loudly, she didn't know why only two of Dartania's three children had been delivered, but the third was not with her. Yes, Dartania was dressing at Timbuctoo; she would mention it when her stepdaughter arrived; but meantime why not ask the other children where their baby sister was?

She hung up the receiver. "Alice has misplaced a grandchild," she said as Bayard kissed her good-bye. "She's having a fit. I hope your father didn't bite your head off, dear."

"Seemed almost glad of the interruption, said it fit right in. I've left some papers for Robin and Dan by the way. A messenger's coming round to pick them up."

Out on the front porch a small crowd had gathered to witness the tardy arrival of the huge, multilayered wedding cake slowly being carried up the steps by two men in white overalls.

Good God, it's a Balinese temple procession, Bayard thought, as, speeding down the front steps toward his waiting car, and getting in, he told the chauffeur through the speaking tube to take him to the State Insurance Building.

Bayard had been confident of his father's backing, but it was absolutely necessary to guarantee that support to the insurance company board. Prudently he had kept the details of that meeting to himself. His father was of the old school, where a good investment meant it was a safe one. But Bayard was interested in challenges of a broader sort, investments that in addition to collateral and sound research, required a blending of courage and intuition. Without question this approach had led to more profitable uses of money. Bored by fixed horizons Bayard was interested in the wider ramifications of creating wealth—both in terms of personal power and as it benefited the community at large. In six years he had turned his father's very substantial kingdom into an empire, the largest banking and investment business in the South. Now newspapers and insurance companies were being added, and though it was too soon to tell his father, Bayard was currently negotiating to buy a fourth insurance company. In such a conglomerate, with rivals easily eliminated, policies could be sold at lower premiums—a twofold joy to Bayard, who, attracted to an expensive lifestyle for himself, was also, as a man of liberal instincts, anxious to improve lives less felicitously endowed.

And with that pressing problem under control, Bayard switched his attention to another: his wife, Ellen, whom he suspected was unhappy. She never said so, being English, but it was obvious she found the town tedious and uninspiring. "Everyone knows everyone else too well." She had declared that to be the nub of Nashborough's cultural malaise. "They're all either kin or related in some way through marriage."

Bayard acknowledged its truth: When people were at their ease, it rarely followed they were at their best, and kinship had knitted local society into a sprawling family circle where, as in family life everywhere, gossip, chitchat, teasing, and repartee drove out more highly developed modes of thought and conversation.

Insufficient outside stimulus, he had privately diagnosed. Well, that was changing now. The town was growing: It was nearly seventy thousand. Moreover the South was waking up. She could clothe herself in the latest fashions and hold her head up in the world again. Bayard felt a rightful surge of pride, his own efforts having contributed so significantly to this mushrooming financial emancipation.

As they entered the downtown area the streets became more crowded. The old brownstone buildings, the town's original center near the river, were mostly office buildings now, the residential areas having spread to east and west, away from the river, and along surprisingly pecuniary lines. Nobody knew how it started, but the wealthier areas had consistently spread west; first to the "midtown" district, where big square houses, built at the turn of the century in eclectic styles and with surprisingly little ground, had recently been vacated by the richer section of the community, opting wholesale for the new and fashionable suburb of Blue Hills, now the town's westernmost boundary, and beyond which a number of big farms like Timbuctoo continued their traditional, plantation-style existence.

To the east however, across the old iron bridge, brick warehouses, now derelict, still lined the river bank. River traffic had long been unprofitable, but no one had bothered to pull them down, since there was plenty of land beyond. Here the poorer suburbs stretched, the housing consisting of shoddy, one-storeyed clapboard buildings sheltering in separate sections, like distinct but neighboring villages, the poorer whites and blacks. While a couple of miles beyond, on the horizon, Cottoncrop, home of the Nashes, the town's eponymous founders, reposed like a great beached whale, in the middle of a thousand acres—the founder having got the profitable direction of his city wrong.

Outside the brownstone law offices of Nash and Polk, Bayard had caught sight of his brother-in-law, Seneca Nash, in conversation with the Chicago railway's lawyer. That interested him; Seneca Nash interested him too, for the young man appeared to have some stuffing.

Bayard mistrusted the easygoing informality fashionable since the war. Lack of reserve meant quite literally lack of a reservoir, and so, in hard times, famine. A man ought to stand back a bit and play his cards close to his chest. His father, a master of this art, inspired a positively Pharaonic awe in people, but among Bayard's generation he could think of no one other than himself and possibly Seneca Nash who fathomed the utility and scope of this position. As Ellen had said, they all knew each other far too well.

But with Ellen the real problem wasn't Nashborough's cultural aridity, it was childlessness. That was the hole at the center of their domestic life, which neither a highly cultured environment nor their joint enthusiasm for collecting art could fill. The main focus of a woman's life must be her children; that was obvious, and the rest was by comparison hobbies. Yet there was his sister Dartania, the apple of every eye, with three of her own, and hardly aware of their existence.

How to remedy the ironies of fortune, he wondered, as the car arrived at the chrome and plate-glass entrance of Nashborough's newest and most modern office building, at ten storeys avowedly a skyscraper. By adoption perhaps. He did not like it himself but it might fill the gap for Ellen.

AT THE TOP of the house, in the studio (which had been Dartania's bedroom), Jasmine, the penultimate Douglas, her hair bobbed and shining like mahogany, streaks of paint on her pretty face, pointedly ignored the wedding fuss and continued painting. It was a view of the garden from above, capturing the light and shade and color of it in a dazzling impressionistic blur. Disregarding utterly the transformation going on below, she concentrated instead on the chiaroscuro effect that clouds were having on the grass.

"What a funny book."

In a corner of the studio, her brother Dan, crippled in infancy by polio, sat in a wheelchair reading, so quietly she had almost forgotten he was there.

"You'd really go for this I think. *Crome Yellow*, by a fellow named Aldous

Huxley." Pushing back a shock of brown hair, he looked up eagerly, conveying in an open boyish smile his own keen pleasure in the book.

"I always did like chrome yellow," she retorted smoothly.

"The English are so . . . dry," said Dan. "I can't help feeling there's something missing in their makeup though. But Ellen isn't like that is she?" And in the absence of any response he went on with his book.

"Speaking of the latest," said Jasmine after a few minutes, leaning back to scrutinize her canvas, "would you believe it—Bayard has bought a Klee!" She pronounced it to rhyme with "glee." "I'm crazy to see it. Everybody says he's out of his mind of course. 'So hideous, my dear' "—she mimicked the women at her stepmother's mah-jongg table—" 'doesn't look like *anything at all.*' They blame it on Ellen you know. Or would if they dared."

"Maybe it's that Ellen isn't what you'd call *postwar* English," Dan proposed, following his own line of thought. "Have you read *Decline and Fall*? They're all so sick of life."

"No," muttered Jasmine uneasily, aware that the cultural world might be getting ahead of her. "But then I bet you'd never heard of Klee." She lit a cigarette and, putting her brush in turpentine, went over to the window sill, and sat down, observing for the first time what in reality was taking place below.

Down both sides of the central aisle, fat garlands of daisies were being swagged, attached to upright metal rods in an enormous daisy chain. Jasmine preferred to see them as two giant fuzzy caterpillars. The altar, also garlanded, was further adorned with a pair of heavy silver candelabra. Hardly appropriate at a four o'clock wedding outdoors she thought.

"Too too pretty," she reported sniffily to Dan, "sickly and excruciatingly sentimental." She puffed on the cigarette, holding it between her thumb and first finger like a man. "And Jim Blount's lethally boring." But then Chloe, she secretly believed, was rather boring too. The youngest and least like the rest of them, lacking their wit and high spirits, Chloe appeared to her the lone pedestrian in an otherwise aerial family. The disability perfectly suited her to ordinary life, however, which was exactly what she was getting.

To Jasmine the prospect of an "ordinary" life terrified as much as it profoundly bored. How people survived it was to her the strangest of mysteries, and she strongly suspected Thoreau had got it right: that they were all of them at the end of their tether—quietly desperate.

Jasmine knew she must work hard, work and work, if she was going to be a successful painter, a truly first-class painter—for nothing less would serve her purposes. Caring not a whit for those advantages she already possessed in life, she yearned to launch herself upon a larger, more impressive audience, to live among interesting and famous people, and to be famous and interesting herself. So intense was her longing it was almost a secret life.

But what if I have no talent? she wondered for the hundredth time, consoling herself as ever in the thought that talent only meant a thing came easily. Any sufficiently dedicated person should be able to keep their end up through hard work.

At that moment, as the grandfather clock chimed in the downstairs hall, the gong was rung for lunch, and mashing her cigarette out in a tin lid, Jasmine called down to Chloe who was coming inside. "Those candelabra are all wrong. As maid of honor it's my duty to tell you."

Robin who was with Chloe called back, "They're there to distinguish the altar from the bar." Already he was feeling somewhat pulled between the two.

Chloe, her long legs lost in a loose flapping skirt, looked up and smiled, shading her eyes against the sun with her hand. "They were at Mother's wedding," she explained. "Aren't you coming down for lunch?"

2

....

On the other side of Nashborough, at Cottoncrop, Alice Nash, lying fully dressed on the huge canopied bed, in a white lace-trimmed frock that matched her white hair, opened wide her blue eyes and, using a pre-arranged signal, pressed a button attached to the bedpost. Then, picking up the telephone, she spoke to the kitchen, "Have the children had their lunch yet, Rosetta; did they eat it; did they eat any dessert? Then tell them to come upstairs right now. They must have a good long nap before the wedding." She hung up and a minute later the operation was repeated. "Is Ben down there, Rosetta? Tell him to bring the car round at a quarter to three, and ask Martha to hang the children's dresses in the *front* seat so they won't get crushed."

An hour earlier the missing two-year-old, about whose whereabouts Alice had so frantically telephoned Jane Douglas, had been discovered playing happily in the boxroom. Victorian clothes lay scattered about her like pastel tissue paper in the unwrapping of a china doll. The boxroom door had been locked from outside and Phoebe's sisters solemnly reported she had gone abroad (information denied to Jane Douglas by Alice Nash).

Now the boxroom was formally out of bounds, locked, and the key carefully deposited in the top drawer of Alice's bedside table. What if Phoebe had suffocated in a trunk! Alice could not remove this vision from her thoughts and shivered repeatedly at the imagined agony of suffocation, of not being found for days, years perhaps. It was too horrible, the thought could not be finished, for how she adored these little girls. The joy of being a grandmother was beyond all belief and expectation, and the fact that they were girls intensified the pleasure: She could dress, dandle, and wholeheartedly indulge them.

Like many elderly people, the Nashes had withdrawn into a corner of their house, occupying only two rooms in the historic old mansion, the earliest brick residence in the county. Alice Nash's bedroom, dominated by the huge canopied bed in which she read the days away, doubled as the couple's sitting room. Off it, down a short corridor lined with closets, a big old-fashioned bathroom, once a bedroom, with a cold, liver-colored linoleum floor served also as the doctor's dressing room. The doctor's bedroom adjoined his wife's and the door between the rooms was always open.

Downstairs, the elegant triple parlors, the long central hall, supported by a pair of columns and making a family picture gallery, the damp library with its collection of musty volumes, and the adjoining guest bedroom, displaying like a state bedroom its fine eighteenth-century bed, were under wraps—dust sheeted and shadowy, a macabre and ghostly setting, where the grandchildren roamed excitedly on visits, flitting through the dark high-ceilinged rooms, thrilled by the hot pursuit of phantoms and bogeymen.

Nowadays only at Christmas did the house come out of mothballs and, filled with family and friends, display once more the hospitality Cottoncrop was so famous for. The rest of the year the only other permanent area of activity was the annex, comprising the kitchen and laundry with lodging above. This was the original four-roomed house Edward Nash's forebears had built when, in 1780, they settled in the fertile bottom lands near the Chickasaw River. It was now the domain of two beautiful Negro sisters, Martha and Rosetta, whose high cheekbones told of Indian blood, and of Ben, Martha's husband, whom they so charitably and discreetly shared.

Having opened out the little gateleg table in front of the fireplace in Alice Nash's bedroom and brought in two trays, Martha went next door to tell the doctor lunch was ready. The doctor was sitting at his high, glass-topped desk writing in his diary. A mild stroke two years earlier had altered many of his habits: A tedious salt-free diet had been prescribed, he went only half a day to his practice, driven there and back by Ben, and he steered clear of fatiguing social events, which was why he wasn't going to the wedding.

Every day the doctor wrote in his diary and it did not occur to him what dull reading it would make for his descendants; that wasn't his purpose in writing. His purpose was to pin down the days and to mark in some tangible way the general course of his life, to make an orderly record of it. Thus, he noted the weather, touched upon world events, his medical practice, the farm, and happenings in his family. Of no one did he speak ill and only very rarely did he permit a personal observation about himself, such as noting very occasionally the onset of an unaccountable depression. It always surprised him and taxed his tolerance, for without any doubt he knew himself to be a happy man.

"The children are so excited," Alice told him, "and they look adorable in their dresses; we tried them on this morning."

Sally, the elder, was to be a flower girl but an identical dress had been made for five-year-old Emma, who, used to receiving hand-me-downs, had recently added the word "partial" to her vocabulary and used it in a continual harangue for privileges and status, claiming everyone was being partial to Sally.

The doctor ate his grapefruit salad and tuna fish sandwich, pleased to learn his wife was enjoying herself; even the boxroom drama had been good for her, he thought, and he would have liked to see little Sally trotting down the aisle at Timbuctoo, wearing the dress her grandmother had made with her own hands; but he was mainly thinking of something else.

That morning, walking in the grove, he had again encountered the Indian. The doctor had been walking near a group of trees that made a sort of island in the grove, when suddenly he had seen the Indian standing at the edge of it. The Indian stood very still, looking at the doctor as he came closer—looking him in the eye—and the doctor had returned his gaze. But then the Indian had half-turned, as though listening to something in the distance, and had suddenly vanished.

The doctor was tempted over lunch to tell Alice about this encounter— he wanted very much to talk about it—but he decided against it. Alice thought it was so much foolishness; the subject irritated her, as if some character defect were being forcibly brought to her attention.

Unlike his wife, Edward Nash had a religious side. He was not a churchgoer but he possessed a developed spiritual life and he knew that there were many things great and small that were—and might remain—outside human comprehension. But Alice was irritated by "nonsense about ghosts," so he kept quiet.

The doctor had first seen the Indian when he was about twelve years old. He was walking back from the creek with a tin full of crayfish he had caught and the little packet of salt pork he had caught them with. The crayfish would come out from beneath rock ledges in the creek, clutch the salt pork dangling from a string, and you could draw them up neatly out of the water, for getting a crayfish to let go of salt pork was like removing a tick. He was coming back through the woods when suddenly, not ten feet in front of him, the Indian had crossed his path, paid him no attention at all, and had vanished into the undergrowth. The Indian wore long buckskin trousers and he had dark-colored necklaces on his bare chest. He had long plaited hair that was going gray, with two turkey feathers in it. The straightness of his bearing and his silent rapid step contained a dignity the boy had never beheld in any human being.

Thrilled but astounded by this vision, he had told no one. Later on, when he did tell, they had laughed at him for seeing a ghost, and some people looked at him a little peculiarly. But one old fellow working the ferry boat down on the river had patted him reassuringly on the shoulder. "Could be you seen Escali," the man said, and he had told him Escali's story. How, being driven out of his homeland when the Cherokee were forced to take the Trail of Tears into Oklahoma, Escali had killed a soldier to protect his wife and had escaped together with his family into the woods. But later on, they were surrounded and the soldiers granted Escali's family asylum if Escali would give himself up for killing the soldier.

"So ole Escali stayed behind, watching over them huntin grounds and buryin grounds the Cherokee loved so much that leaving em like to broke their hearts. He was the only one left. And some folks say he's guardin it for em, and that one day they'll be coming back." The old fellow spit his tobacco juice into the black river and, hunched over the railing, stared at the ripples he made and nodded approvingly. "Ole Escali. If you seen *him* you're a lucky young feller."

After that the boy had respected the copse where the Indian graves were and had made no more attempts to collect arrowheads or to disturb the burial mounds. From time to time he would glimpse the Indian on the edge of the copse or in the woods down by the river, once right up near the house, and the dogs had made a terrible racket, their hackles had stood straight up, and the doctor was pleased if a little surprised by this canine affirmation of his vision.

Today it seemed the Indian had almost smiled. The doctor always smiled deep inside whenever he saw the Indian; it made him happy for days afterward. But if old Escali really had smiled after all these years, what could that mean?

Alice was talking about the dangers of open trunks and about keeping cupboards locked and, getting no response, raised her voice sharply, "That child might have suffocated! Edward, do you ever hear a thing I say?"

Since his attack the doctor had become harder of hearing and his mental responses were slower, and Alice, whose own mind had retained its remarkable acuity, was easily irritated. Now she sighed and changed the subject, sitting back in her chair with a glass of iced tea, rattling the ice. "Did you see Seneca this morning when he brought the children?"

"He drove by while I was out walking. Seemed very enthusiastic about that railroad case."

"Oh I hope he wins it!"

"He said Bayard Douglas was going to help him. He's planning to talk to him about it this afternoon."

"They say Ham Douglas is flying in caviar and smuggling champagne from France. Do you think anybody in Nashborough's ever seen real caviar?"

"Unlikely," replied the doctor, "and that means they won't eat it." For despite partial retirement his hand still felt with accuracy the local pulse. "Ham Douglas sure knows how to cut the mustard," he added with amusement, after a minute.

"Hmmmph," said Alice, rattling the ice with vigor. "Well I never could imagine him in bed with a woman." She had said this many times before and if you mentioned all the children, she always said, "I bet he pushed poor Flora across the bed and raped her every time. Ham hasn't a tender bone in his body. And those poor children, growing up over there like weeds, nobody paying them any heed or giving them any affection. It will tell.

"And now Chloe's marrying a Blount." Rapidly she reconnected her line of thought to the wedding. "It seems no time ago that that unfortunate child was born."

"Flora was a very courageous woman," replied the doctor, and in his mind, a picture passed fleetingly of Flora Douglas bleeding to death in childbirth, and there had been nothing he could do. "A very courageous woman," he repeated.

Alice glanced at her husband. She knew what he was thinking and she regretted having brought it to his mind. Hardly a family known to them had not at some time placed their lives in the doctor's kind and capable hands, and she was ashamed of having thought him slow and stupid five minutes before. Old age was such a terrible thing! And rising to change for Chloe's wedding, she stopped behind her husband's chair and grazed his bald head with her lips, tears welling in her still beautiful cornflower blue eyes.

*B*y three o'clock the white aisle cloth had been unrolled and a pair of rosewood prie-dieux with embroidered cushions stood in front of the altar. Inside the house the five bridesmaids, slipping into waistless *eau de nil* chiffon, the skirts floating in uneven lengths about their knees, crowded round the guest-room dressing table, inspecting their makeup and taking turns facing back and front before a tall pier glass in the corner. Cries of how nice, how attractive this and that was filled the room. The pale green cloche hats made of wired organdy met with only limited success. Margaret Elsworthy was privately declared least suited, since her hair bunched out under the brim, and *eau de nil* gave her skin a sallow, greenish hue.

Only one dress remained on its hanger, for Dartania. Chloe's matron of honor had not arrived.

"Oh she'll be here," Jasmine blandly asserted. "Dar can dress in five minutes. She's in and out."

There was a knock at the door and it immediately opened. "You look *lovely*, girls," exclaimed Jane Douglas, thinking too how dreadfully thin girls were these days. "Your bouquets are in the hall, ready for you when you come down." She peered at the diamond watch, pinned by a platinum bow to her shoulder. "And that should be in about ten minutes if you can manage it."

"What a racket." Robin's delighted voice could be heard outside the door. "What are all those women *doing* in there?"

"Come in and see," one of the girls taunted amid laughter and one or two earnest pleas for caution.

"I wouldn't risk it for the world." Robin cleared his throat in a superior way and went downstairs to get the elevator for Dan. Somebody had forgotten to shut the gate.

Having admired one another before and during dressing, the girls now repeated their exclamations with regard to the finished product and, trooping down the stairs, whoever passed by told them yet again how perfectly lovely they were.

Inside Timbuctoo's front gate, a gray Cadillac was parked on the grass with its four doors open: another changing room. The little Nash girls, Sally and Emma, having ridden across town in their petticoats, were being stuffed into their white organdy dresses at the last minute. The children were in a state of great excitement. Throughout the journey they had bounced restlessly about in the backseat, choking Ben, who was driving, with their embraces, pressing their noses against the windows, and resisting all their grandmother's efforts to hold on to them and keep them still. Now, standing outside the car, Alice buttoned up the backs of the dresses while Ben stood, holding on a hanger, two immaculately ironed green taffeta sashes. The children were thrilled with the dresses: square necklines and puffed sleeves trimmed with *broderie anglaise* and a row of decorative glass buttons down the front; but what delighted them above everything was that the dresses were long and seemed to them, despite the current fashion, very grown-up.

"Two little snowdrops!" declared their satisfied grandmother, tying the taffeta sashes in two big puffed bows. "Now children, get back in the car and sit up straight so you won't crush your bows. And remember, Sally, do exactly today as you did at the rehearsal yesterday: Walk slowly down the aisle when they tell you to and then stand on one side so you can see Aunt Chloe."

"Mama's in the wedding," Emma announced authoritatively.

Ben drove slowly up the winding drive (almost as slowly as the doctor, thought Alice impatiently) and stopped in front of the house.

"Now pick your skirts up, girls, going up the steps, way up, that's right." She took Ben's arm and they also ascended, the children running ahead toward the front door, which a maid was holding open.

"Welcome, Miz Nash. Hidy Ben. Oh my, don't they look *cute*!"

"Don't they, Eugenia!" and she tacked on a little whoop of laughter like a swirling sprinkler on a summer's day. The laugh was almost a trademark of Alice Nash's.

Soon a steady flow of cars was winding up the drive in a sedate and glossy caravan. Passing the house, each stopped at the far side—the house being off limits to guests before the wedding. Standing by, ready to park those cars without chauffeurs were several black youths in starched white jackets. This job was the most popular to be had, affording the chance, even for a few minutes, to drive an automobile, often a very big one—and the tips were good.

In the broad front hall, square shaped, carpeted, and furnished with sofas and chairs, the bridesmaids lolled or shifted uneasily, examining their bouquets and smoking a final cigarette, when suddenly the front door was flung open, and Dartania, wearing jodhpurs, her braids of red-gold hair falling down her back, flashed by them up the stairs.

"I told you," Jasmine coolly declared, looking at the clock; it was twenty to four. "*And* she'll have a bath."

But the others remained silent with disapproval.

OUT ON THE lawn the pianist massaged her hands and, given a signal from the window, attacked the familiar opening chords of the "Wedding March." A hundred and fifty guests rose and simultaneously turned, smiling and expectant, toward the aisle and beyond it to the side door of the house. Behind the guests the Douglas servants and several of the chauffeurs lined both sides of the aisle.

Pushed forward by several pairs of hands, little Sally Nash and a boy of about the same age wearing satin knee breeches came out first, Sally clutching a beribboned rosebud posy and the boy solemnly bearing the bridal rings teetering on a velvet cushion. They were followed, a little too closely, by the bridesmaids walking swiftly two together, their faces pasted with self-conscious smiles that on one or two could be called a smirk. A little behind the bridesmaids, and on her own, walked Dartania, her long braids twisted into a chignon at the nape of her neck, without any vestige of a smile, and without a hat.

"Look, darling," whispered Alice Nash to Emma standing on a chair beside her. "There's your mama." Dartania, she thought, was right about the hat.

"Here Comes the Bride," tum tum te tum. The pianist leaned into it fortissimo as Chloe emerged from the house supported on her father's arm. Two black-frocked seamstresses were bending down behind her like a pair of pecking ravens, arranging the long satin train and bridal veil. The veil was bound across her brow nunlike in the current fashion and secured on each side with white blossoms.

Everyone looked with pleasure and every woman smiled instinctively. They admired the dress and fine old *rose pointe* veil stretching the entire length of the train. They agreed as one mind that Chloe had never looked more handsome, her strong Douglas features strikingly impressive if not beautiful, her Junoesque figure almost sylphlike beside the lean and ducal frame of Hamilton Douglas. They approved the gentle seriousness of her demeanor and the special kindness of her smile directed toward the servants as she passed.

All this they did, and found much pleasure in it, but the aisle was long and the eye is notoriously quick. Chloe without doubt created a charming vision but the person on whom all eyes lingered and to which they reverted throughout the ceremony was as ever Dartania. That delicately wrought profile and perfect figure, which had been her mother's, those green, flecked eyes that when excited, showed the whites all around, and the tiny twist of humor that occasionally lit a face that in repose was faintly sad, even a little sullen, captured their gaze and worked mysteriously on their imaginations. In some the pleasure was marred by pricks of envy, even disapproval; in others, older people, it was tinged with the mournful knowledge of ephemerality. Dartania, they knew, took her beauty for granted, and so wore it lightly, which—even if owing to misapprehension—was highly creditable. But whatever their opinions, every eye feasted irresistibly—every eye except that of Dartania's daughter Emma, who, at the sight of Chloe on her father's arm—trailing draperies like a princess, her strong features faintly androgynous—was consumed with a sudden passionate adoration.

That chin, thought Alice Nash as Chloe went solemnly by, it'll meet her nose one day. But in her heart there was only kindness.

For the most part Chloe kept her eyes downcast in the approved manner and longed for it all to be over. Arriving at last in front of the prie-dieu, she looked up perfectly on cue into the eyes of her bridegroom and what struck her outstandingly was how absurd he looked: He was as red as a radish. But almost instantly this vision was replaced by one of the intelligent, manly individual whom she loved and wished to marry.

When asked who gave the bride away, Hamilton Douglas rapidly fulfilled his role and then sat down beside his wife, impressed by the circularity of life, not at all convinced it was a spiral. This daughter, whose life had cost his wife's, now took a husband, and though Hamilton's feelings were affectionate, he could not believe that the couple in any way improved upon their progenitors, or promised to contribute more in life.

Soon the pianist was beating out the fast-moving tempo of the recessional, and the bride and groom, followed by their retinue, sailed nodding and smiling down the path recently trod with such solemnity and pomp. Veering off behind the rows of chairs, they stopped under the huge magnolia tree where they were to receive their guests, the bridesmaids swarming forward with kisses and congratulations like pale green butterflies besieging a large white flower.

Only Jasmine and Dartania held back and, catching each other's eye, smiled a little sarcastically: "We deserve a drink." They trotted off toward the bar already obscured by a screen of morning coats, and at either end of which waiters issued forth bearing silver trays of champagne glittering with exceptional brightness in the afternoon sunlight.

Seneca Nash, arriving at the last minute, had stood among the servants at the back, and now he came forward to greet his mother. He was a tall young man, broad skulled like his father, with dark curly hair already beginning to thin, and dark eyes, like the bottom of a skillet, his nurse had said. He also possessed his father's slightly bulbous nose, but their expressions differed, though it would be hard to say how this was so.

"Wasn't Sally good!" exclaimed Alice in front of the excited child.

"You were swell, just swell," he told the little girl and, bending down, lifted her up in the air.

Sally gurgled with delight. "I'm going to marry Peter Samonela," she announced, but it was lost in the familiar forest of adult legs to which she had so swiftly been returned.

"Your father said you thought you might win that railroad case," said Alice gazing with proud pleasure at her darling boy.

"I *am* going to win it," Seneca confidently declared and, taking two glasses of champagne from a waiter, gave one of them to his mother. "Tom Buzby is about to feel a draft inside that crustacean armor of his. What's more it's a pincer movement: We're going after him on both the business and political fronts."

Tom "Boss" Buzby, owner of the Nashborough–New Orleans railroad, had for several years relentlessly ruled Nashborough politics, and consequently the state's. He never held office himself: Buzby was a fixer, whose candidates unfailingly led the Democratic ticket, the only ticket that counted for anything in the South.

"Good heavens, here it is!" cried Alice as the silver tray of jet beads sprinkled with hard-boiled egg and piled on tiny rounds of toast was offered her. "Real Beluga caviar. Well, this beats the Wali of Swat!" No one knew how Alice Nash came to know of this obscure Indian prince—or his lifestyle, if in fact she did. But lodged somehow in her imagination, he epitomized high luxury, and local endeavors were always set alongside this exotic standard— invariably triumphing over anything the mysterious prince might have produced.

"It's simply delicious," she affirmed half a minute later, her mouth still full.

The maid watched, laughing. "Nobody else wants any Miz Nash, they're all turning up their noses."

"Mildly overrated," was Seneca's verdict. "I bet you anything if country ham was as hard to get, or even bacon, people would prefer it to caviar." But he rapidly had another and Alice Nash did too.

"Will you just look at Ham Douglas," she continued, referring by metonymy to the entire event. "Would you believe he ever had holes in his shoes? Of course we all had them then. Reconstruction starved nearly everybody."

But Seneca was scanning the crowd in search of Bayard. He did not know his brother-in-law had missed the ceremony.

4

....

At the bottom of the garden, where the creek ran, Calvin Douglas sat in a faded canvas deck chair beside the springhouse. He had watched the long line of cars winding up the driveway to the house, the people getting out—colorful specks from where he sat—and the cars whisked away by boys who, like his grandson, were eager to sit behind a wheel, though his grandson wasn't among them.

A little breeze hummed about under the tree branches shading the cool gray stones of the springhouse. Calvin could see the wedding in his mind, their being all alike, and he had chosen to stick with his job, which was that of a sort of lifeguard.

Whenever children were on the place they gravitated to the springhouse pool, as they had done the minute the ceremony was over, and it was Calvin's task not so much to see that they didn't drown—it was a shallow pool and children were no fools—but to satisfy the grown-ups' fears by being there and keeping an eye on them.

Shoes and tiny white socks littered the bank. The girls, their skirts around their waists, waded hesitantly, testing each step with caution, while downstream the boys threw pebbles and taunted and splashed each other. There were occasional pleas for arbitration, for several children were engaged in panning for gold, a highly volatile game at any age.

Calvin kept the lid on but his mind was partly on his absent grandson

Rob, who had refused to help with the parking. Calvin couldn't make the boy understand. He couldn't himself understand his "bondage," as Rob kept calling it. But certainly he *was* bound; in that respect the boy was right. Yet it was ties that made a man's life what it was. Nobody was free, not like Rob thought anyhow. In a year the boy would be in a job himself, taking orders from "the man," from some man. Did his freedom depend on whether he loved this man or not? This was the question that vexed the old man's mind.

Calvin had been twelve years old when the Northern army had arrived near the Douglas plantation on the Yazoo River in Mississippi. Old Mrs. Douglas, Hamilton's mother, had hitched up the wagon, put her children in it, and told those slaves who were left that she was taking them to Nashborough, at gunpoint if necessary, because they were in it together and were obliged to protect each other.

The two-hundred-mile journey to Nashborough had been an exciting time: sleeping rough, crossing the Yankee lines in the night—a grand adventure for a boy. And their all being in it together had without question tightened the bonds.

Why did Calvin go with them, his grandson wanted to know; he didn't have to.

He supposed it was lack of an alternative. He was only a boy, his mother wanted him with her, and there was a war going on. Not that things were much easier in Nashborough. They were often hungry during the war, and afterward. There was plenty of fighting too. Why, not half a mile from where he sat that very minute, up on Peach Orchard Hill, he and Hamilton had seen hundreds of corpses frozen in the snow—fifteen hundred, the newspapers had said—killed at the Battle of Nashborough. In short, they had more reason to stick together than not. Yes, the war had tightened the bonds, it hadn't loosened them.

The elder by four years, Calvin had taught Hamilton how to hunt squirrels and opossum, and how to fish for catfish in the river, enabling the two boys willy-nilly to supply their families with some food. To this day nothing tasted better—he suspected this was so for Hamilton too—than catfish, unless it was a well-cooked squirrel.

Hamilton had looked up to him, though it never surprised Calvin when the pendulum had swung the other way. Both boys had started to work at fourteen, Calvin in a blacksmith shop and Hamilton running messages at the bank. Today everybody looked up to Hamilton; it seemed very natural; but in those days Hamilton had looked up to him, and that was a special thing—looked up to him and to old Mrs. Douglas, whom Hamilton had loved too much. A tough old bird. The day Hamilton tore his trousers on a barbed-wire fence his mother got so mad—he hadn't any others—that she had made him wear a burlap sack for a week, with a head and arm holes cut in it. To teach him. Her heart was all for the youngest one, who died.

"Hey, look at this." A little boy tugged at Calvin's sleeve. "I got a crawfish."

"Gonna eat em?" the old man asked, suddenly feeling rather tired.

"Naw. He's gonna be a pet."

Calvin looked down at the boy holding the crayfish. "Then you got to name him," he said.

Rapidly the child reviewed his small library of pet names. "Spot," he concluded, holding the crayfish between two fingers. "I'm gonna call him Spot."

"Spot. Well now, Spot is a fine name for a dog, but you want to name a crawfish by a crawfish name."

"I don't know any crawfish names," the little boy said crestfallen.

"Well lemme see now." The old man closed his eyes and pushed his mouth out in an air of deep reflection. He was feeling a bit short of breath. "Speedie," he said at last, opening his eyes wide to deliver his verdict. "That be a crawfish name."

"Speedie," the boy exclaimed, delighted. "Hi Speedie," and holding the crayfish so they were head on, grinned into its pointed face and beady eyes on stalks. "Hi there Speedie."

"Better go and put him in some water," Calvin admonished the boy. "He got to have water to live."

IN THE DINING room, the wedding presents were displayed on the table, which when fully let out, as now, sat twenty-four people in armchairs. More presents spilled onto card tables erected under the windows.

"Evidently marriage is a licensed form of looting," Dan cheerfully observed, wheeling into the empty dining room alongside his younger sister Jasmine. Normally it was women who inspected the accumulated booty, comparing presents against the donors' names; but cutting the wedding cake had drawn everyone outside, and, with typical clannishness, Jasmine and Dan had retreated from the crowd.

"Double rings *and* the presents on display. Where does Chloe pick up such practices?" demanded Jasmine, scanning the table with distaste.

"The midtown set," her brother amiably supplied. "But just imagine, if you can, a twentieth-century tomb discovered a thousand years from now, the husband and wife having been buried with all their possessions. This is what it would look like—plus the principals of course."

Silver trays and cutlery, silver candelabra, goblets and julep cups were ranged in phalanxes down the table; china for good and china for everyday, sets of glasses—everything by the dozen. There were even a few gadgets, among them a vacuum cleaner and a beaten biscuit maker.

"Behold." Leaning forward in his wheelchair Dan held up a pair of silver tongs with flat pincers.

"A candle snuffer," Jasmine declared. "How very genteel!"

"Ah, not for putting one's napkin untouched into one's lap as I had supposed."

"Look at *this*," said Jasmine in an altogether different tone. It was a small oil painting of a wood, in a very modern style. Jasmine had found it half hidden beneath a pile of damask table napkins. "This is really good! J. Dinson. I wonder who he is."

"I wonder who gave it to Chloe."

Jasmine picked up the white card that had fallen on the floor. "Good Lord, the Fentons."

Brother and sister ogled one another significantly. Bertha Fenton was Jane Douglas's sister, and recently widowed, she now lived at Timbuctoo.

"I'd have expected a tea cosy." Jasmine propped the picture up in front of a silver jug and suddenly saw Bertha Fenton's son, Stark, standing in the double doorway at the end of the room.

Though she did not think he could have heard her, she nonetheless tried hard to pulverize the grit of her remark. "Why Stark, Danny and I were just admiring the picture your family gave Chloe. Do tell us something about it."

Stark Fenton stood at a considerable distance. His lean frame and black hair would have made him handsome, except that he was too thin, raw boned in effect, and his face was too long. "Uriah Heep," the younger Douglases always said, although more congenial circles claimed a resemblance to the young Abe Lincoln. Stark, trained as a lawyer, worked for Buzby's railroad, but abhorring his employer's politics, he had leaked the incriminating papers on which much of Seneca's present case was based. Since his return from Harvard, it was said that Stark entertained radical ideas, and this had appealed to Seneca, himself opposed to what he called the cotton-wool conservatism of the town.

Having no alternative, Stark now marched uneasily into the room, shame and anger curdling within. He had not overheard Jasmine's remark, but, though pleased by her obvious appreciation of the picture, he felt humiliated by her facile patronage.

"It's painted by a friend named Jenny Dinson."

"You don't mean she's from around here, not painting like this?"

"She moved here two or three years ago from California," he answered laconically, stopping in front of Jasmine, his hands defiantly thrust into his trouser pockets.

"Well I am truly impressed. I'd love to meet her sometime."

"I'm sure she'd like to meet you," said Stark, who, not at all sure this was so, nonetheless found himself out of politeness vaguely promising to fix it.

"Our stylistic approaches have something in common," Jasmine graciously observed.

UNDER THE BIG magnolia tree, bride and groom now formed part of a circle of young people sitting in deck chairs. Approaching the circle Seneca saw his daughter Emma standing a short distance away and gazing with forlorn and puppylike adoration at the bride. Scooping the child up and joining the group he perched her on his knee. "I never saw such a hoard as you've collected in there," he said to Chloe. "Dartania and I were fools to have eloped."

Chloe leaned forward slightly in her lace-encrusted satin, one hand toying nervously with the edge of her veil. "Why on earth *did* you elope?" she earnestly inquired. "It seemed so pointless at the time."

"We thought we were being smart, avoiding the hullabaloo," he told her affably, but in his mind he could see Dartania in tears outside her father's study, having announced the news, and Hamilton Douglas demanding gruffly, "What's the matter, sorry you married him?"

"Then too, they wanted some identification at the hotel up in Red Springs where we were hunting," he added, "so it became expedient."

Chloe reddened visibly.

The truth was that Dartania had been pregnant, and their elopement had taken place later than officially announced. Seneca thought it naive of Chloe not to have suspected and gauche of her to ask about it now. Her embarrassment served her right.

"We got it wrong," he said lightly and, addressing the child on his knee, added, "Don't elope."

"Antelope," she repeated, and was reduced to a profound humiliation, since for some reason suddenly everyone was laughing at her.

5

....

Later, when the lanterns had been lit and were hanging like moons where night flyers orbited and crashed, the young people who had stayed on danced to a three-piece band on a platform erected at the bottom of the garden. The music wafted across the lawn, fox-trots alternating with the animated strains of Dixieland and, at least twice, that current rage, the Charleston. Champagne had given way to bootleg whiskey and gin, drinks they were considerably more at home with.

After a perfunctory fox-trot with Margaret Elsworthy, Robin moved into action, but finding the summerhouse occupied, he had to think again and quickly. The conservatory would, he decided, be approximate. There, under a potted palm and next to the noisy aviary nobody had thought to cover, he sat down with Margaret on a stone bench, champagne to hand and, filling their glasses, plunged in his usual matter-of-fact style directly toward the point. "What do you think about getting married, Margaret?"

The expression on Margaret's face made it necessary to add, "I mean to me." But the initially speculative aspect of the proposal admitted discussion, and Margaret softly replied that she *would* like to—said it in such a sweet and gentle fashion that the conditional tense appeared to be politely positive— but, becoming more specific, added that where Robin was concerned, she knew her parents would never give their consent. They didn't approve of him—as a husband that was; oh they liked him well enough as himself.

Robin was bowled over. That he might be thought unsuitable as a husband had never entered his head, and when it did, as a pronouncement
from someone else, a university professor who taught he couldn't remember what, Robin could not make head or tail of it.

"Not suitable? Do they think I'm some sort of monster?" He felt his chest
and cheeks. "Am I a monster? Come out Mr. Hyde, if you are in there," he
commanded.

Margaret smiled and looking at the floor hesitated. "It's because you
haven't got a job," she brought out finally.

"A job?" Robin grinned and shook his head. "But darling Margaret I don't
need a job. I've got enough money as it is, and I'm on the board of a bank."
To spend time making more money struck Robin as a sort of greed, and
most certainly as a thorough waste of time.

"A man ought to have a job," she added quietly. "That's what Daddy says.
Some sort of skill or profession. He must do something." The presentation
hid her own concurrence in the matter.

"I doubt they'd like it very much if I were a plumber would they? Would
they let you marry a plumber d'you think?"

"They think work is healthy," said Margaret quietly, sidestepping this
awkward truth.

"I think it's healthy being with you; it's healthy just living and enjoying
life, if one can. But what on earth is healthy about slogging away in an office
when one doesn't have to?" Privately Robin concluded that he was up
against Puritan values, Puritan Yankee values—the Elsworthys were from
Massachusetts.

"How *do* you see yourself then?" asked Margaret timidly. "What sort of
self-image have you got?"

Robin thought about this, largely for the first time. "I see myself as a fairly
pleasant sort of fellow. I bear no ill will. I behave honorably, I hope. I love
you and now I begin to see myself with a wife and family. We could elope,"
he concluded, "like Dar and Seneca—make it a family tradition and save all
the fuss."

Margaret shook her head, the responsible head of an only child.

But already Robin was rethinking, and with purpose, for he wanted to
marry Margaret more than ever.

"What if I were a farmer?" he suggested. He could easily buy a farm. More
self-images arose: walking over fields in the early morning, seeing the harvest
off to market and watching his cattle wending o'er the lea—whatever that
was. But he knew he had no more wish to run a farm than he did an office.
Adapting this image more usefully however he envisaged himself paying a
farm manager who would run things for him.

"What do you think?" he said, putting his arm around Margaret's warm bare shoulder. "Darby and Joan?"

"I love you," she said, "as you are."

"I'll speak to your father. I'll go and see him tomorrow and explain about the farm." It was he thought a splendid compromise, even a master stroke of diplomacy, since nothing substantially had changed yet all were satisfied, and, the impediments having been successfully removed, they arose engaged.

6

....

*T*oward the end of the evening something occurred that, with different interpretations put on it, would be long remembered. It started with a fight. In a society where personal and family honor must, like regimental banners, perennially be kept aloft, fights were fairly common, the upholders being highly vulnerable to insult—and among heavy drinkers insult is never hard to find.

The fight was between Jack Piper and Matt Collins, and no one knew exactly how it began. Collins, a hulking bearish fellow, and possessing the sweetest temperament when sober, generally lost his head when drunk, his presence often accompanied therefore by a debris of broken furniture and glass. Piper on the other hand was not a man to lose his head. Slightly built, with an elegant supercilious manner, and always nattily dressed—when drunk he exhibited a regrettable instinct for bear baiting, and he had not resisted an apparently golden opportunity. Standing David-like before an enraged Goliath, he slung his words evenly, couched in a cold, sarcastic smile; and the honor-wounded Collins, bellowing that Piper was a lying sonofabitch, lunged forward, friends hanging on to him like Lilliputians and, despite much laughter, having rather a difficult time of it.

Mike Murray, a practical joker and also Blount's best man, appointed himself to sort things out and, rushing up to the house, soon returned with a parcel under his arm. Merrily shoving into the fray, he snapped open the lid of what looked like a humidor full of cigars, but in fact contained a pair of dueling pistols, their silver mounts elegantly engraved.

As Mike had foreseen almost no one took the offer seriously. His idea was to use the pistols to *deflect* the row.

"Where in the name of God did you get those?" a male voice laughingly demanded.

"Dining room," said Mike proudly. "Eddy Duggan sent them from Mobile. 'Ideal way for a couple to settle their differences,' it says on the card.

"They aren't loaded," he whispered to those who were nearest.

Lumbering forward, Matt Collins grabbed one of the pistols by the barrel and shook it like a boomerang at his rival.

Disdainfully Piper also advanced and, totally ignoring Collins, removed the other pistol from the case.

Murray was deliriously happy. As they had no powder the young men would soon look very silly and the whole episode would be defused. "Appoint your seconds, gentlemen," he declared with mock officiousness, "the thing must be done correctly."

"This is absurd," a girl's voice echoed nervously from the back. "Somebody stop them."

Piper, smiling thinly, beckoned palm outward toward his old friend Andy Webb.

"Where's my lawyer?" brayed Collins. "Seneca, Seneca, you got to be my second."

From beside the improvised bar, Seneca had been watching the scene with bemused interest. "I'll be your second, Matt," he said, coming forward, "but I warn you, if this business goes forward you're going to find it very expensive when we go to court."

"How do you load the damn thing?" Collins pushed the pistol toward Seneca. "Hell, man, you know guns."

Coolly, Piper's second, Andy Webb, who also "knew guns," had reopened the box and, removing from their niches a metal flask and a small leather pouch, deftly inserted from the flask a measure of powder into the pistol's barrel. Picking up the steel ramrod he rammed the powder home.

"Hey, I didn't know there was bullets in there," Mike exclaimed, frantically looking around, a pleading expression on his inebriated face. "Hey, I meant it as a joke. C'mon fellows. Cut it out. Enough is enough!"

"Never play with guns," Seneca retorted, examining the other pistol. "As they say, you never know when they're loaded." He was peering down the barrel, for some reason, tipping it against the lantern light for a better view, and squinting into the finely polished cylinder. Then he checked the flint and, following Webb's lead, poured a measure of powder down the barrel and, using the ramrod after Webb, rammed it down. Next he removed a small round patch of gauze from the box, placed it across the barrel's tip, and, dropping a lead ball from a pouch into the center, rammed it home. Each action was performed with methodical precision, but behind it Seneca was thinking fast.

A rapt aura of disbelief had fallen on the party; the band no longer played and the young people stood about as if mesmerized. There were no more protests, only appalled fascination.

"Now hear me a minute." Seneca addressed the two opponents, half-cocking the pistol and speaking loudly so that others might hear as well. "You've got a score to settle and I say you should be allowed to settle it. But this way you're going to add injury to injury, because apart from what happens to you, you'll have ruined Jim and Chloe's wedding day, and possibly got the Douglases into an embarrassing position with the law—not to mention yourselves."

A murmured chorus of concurrence followed, as though the audience was waking up.

"Now, what if instead of shooting at each other you picked a more benign but a more difficult target—you're both good shots, we all know that—and the winner can choose either to shake hands or fight it out somewhere tomorrow, if he still feels like it."

Piper, who was no fool, saw a reasonable out. A bear baiter whose tiny stature perhaps demanded it, he had no wish to be mauled or killed by one. "Suits me," he coldly declared. "This way I get satisfaction twice."

Collins was looking a little confused. "Yeah, OK, sure." He wiped his hands on this jacket, "But I'm gonna kill that sonofabitch." In truth he was feeling far from well.

"Choose a target at ten paces," Seneca urged, trying hard to keep his plan in action.

Piper looked about for a fair-sized target. A dueling pistol was, he knew, far from precise at ten paces. "What about that lantern?" he said, indicating the translucent paper orb hanging from the branches of a tree.

"Hell," said Collins, sitting down heavily on one of the folding chairs; "I could spit that out at ten paces."

"The lantern's fine," Seneca interrupted, holding a coin. "Heads or tails?"

The first shot went to Piper.

"Almost as good as a turkey shoot," one young man declared. The remark was widely repeated, and bets beginning to be placed, the darker thrill of a duel rapidly disappeared.

"Blow the damn thing's head off, Jack," one of his supporters shouted. "I got ten bucks on you, boy."

Standing behind two wooden cocktail sticks that marked the firing line,

Piper made quick work of it. Instantly the lantern collapsed, and as the candle guttered and went out, an enthusiastic cheer went up.

"Thank heavens it wasn't a *duel*," a girl in a blue dress said, wispy pieces of paper having landed on her dress and hair.

Stark Fenton brought the collected remnants forward. "A good hit," he announced, "but the lantern's collapse snuffed the candle I'm afraid, not the marksman." He showed Piper where the bullet had hit the frame.

"At any rate he knocked the target out," Seneca admiringly interjected. "We'll have to find a new one for Matt. Now, where's my client?"

Laughter had arisen on the sidelines as people moved back to reveal Collins, his head lolling backward like a chicken with its neck wrung; his mouth was open and he was snoring loudly, hunched sacklike on the little folding chair.

"Hot damn, our boy's passed out," a red-haired young man laughed delightedly.

"Well wake him up," Piper insisted, pulling his waistcoat neatly down.

Someone shook Collins and he toppled sideways, where, after breaking his fall, they laid him out, a beached whale, on the crowded lawn.

"Hey, Collins, wake up, old fellow, wake up. We got our money on you."

"When Matt goes out he don't relight before the sun does," an old fraternity brother assured them with a grin.

At this, grumbling predictably arose among the punters, their dissatisfaction mixed with a growing sense of anticlimax.

"It seems my client is in no condition to appear," Seneca observed drily, turning to Piper. "Will his second do?"

Piper's eyes narrowed. "My fight's with him," he said.

"Oh, c'mon, don't wake up poor ole Matt," voices said; the whole thing was wearing a bit thin. "Just get on with the match. Let's get it over with."

Sullenly Piper nodded agreement.

"That's very sporting of you, Jack," said Seneca, ignoring the man's expression. "Now we need a target, perhaps something less malleable in the hoped-for event of a direct hit." He was looking about.

"A tree," someone loudly guffawed, but many were beginning to lose interest. "What happened to the music?"

Seneca turned to his wife. "Get a lemon off the table Dar," he told her and, turning to Piper, asked politely, "Is that agreeable to you?"

Piper, who, after all, knew something about the range of dueling pistols, readily agreed.

"Set it on a chair over on the dance floor," Seneca instructed his wife.

Dartania walked over to the platform with the lemon, and someone produced a chair.

"Right there in the middle," Seneca said evenly.

With the tiniest smile Dartania turned gracefully toward her husband. "I'll hold it myself," she said.

"Dar," cried Jasmine and Robin simultaneously, "don't be silly, put it on the chair."

Others shouted in agreement. Dartania and Seneca had had as much to drink as anyone; they all knew that.

"Somebody stop them!" Dan, unable to maneuver through the crowd, demanded in a fury of frustration. The whole business was idiotic.

Dartania continued to look at Seneca. "I'll hold it," she repeated, still smiling at him enigmatically.

Seneca stood stock still, sizing up the possible ramifications. Then, after a minute he said evenly, "Stand over there in the light," and added to Sam Davis. "Walk off ten paces will you Sam?"

"Oh don't," Jasmine cried out. "Please don't. This is crazy. We're all of us drunk as skunks."

"Don't do it man," whispered Sam. "The accuracy of a dueling pistol at ten paces is about the size of a plate, not a lemon; believe me, I know, you'll blow her hand off!"

"Is that the mark?" Seneca offered in reply, and taking up his position, standing sideways at the cocktail stick marker, he fully cocked the pistol.

With a deep and disgusted sigh Sam moved back.

The atmosphere was like a corrida as the matador, taking up his killing sword, prepares for the final encounter. There was absolute silence. In the lantern light faces shone open-mouthed with anxious and horrified expectation.

"Tell me when you're ready," Seneca said to his wife, his tone that of a quietly given order.

Dartania, sitting on the platform edge, stood up. Solemnly she made a fist with her right hand and set the lemon upright in the cup of it, between her thumb and first finger. Then she extended her arm out straight and to the side. "Shoot," she said coolly, looking her husband in the eye, then turning her attention toward the lemon.

Raising the pistol slowly to shoulder height, his arm fully outstretched, and as part of a single continuous action, Seneca took aim with both eyes open and with cool and methodical precision slowly squeezed the trigger.

Bang! The lemon popped upward splattering like a crushed egg.

With balletic grace Dartania lowered her hand and a great shout went up.

What a show! Men clapped Seneca on the back. They congratulated him on his marksmanship and on his brilliant management of the impending duel, nobody more enthusiastically than Mike Murray.

"I didn't know they were loaded," he kept on saying, "honest."

The party had taken on new life. The band, having reassembled, struck up with gusto "When the Saints Go Marching In." Couples flooded the dance floor in a sort of conga line, joining wholeheartedly in the chorus. "Oh Lord, I want to be in that number when the saints come marching in!" Few could remember ever having felt more exuberant or alive.

Beside the platform Dartania was deluged with exclamations and admiring looks, and yet instinctively people stood back, awed and incredulous. Few men would have done what she had done, and no one could think why any woman should. They were baffled by an act so deeply, blatantly unfeminine, so . . . "eccentric" as one or two carefully chose to put it.

Dartania, strangely pale, smiled and shrugged off the applause, but inside she experienced like a fever the rising of an extreme and intoxicating exaltation. It swept her above them all, up into a pure and rarefied apotheosis; she could have moved a mountain, and it was glorious.

"You were terrific," Seneca said proudly, his lips pursed in suppressed emotion.

Dartania gave him a dazzling smile. "You were too," she said. "Now can we please go home?"

It was the first time anyone had known Dartania to want to leave a party before the end.

7

....

Standing before the marble-topped dressing table at Longwood in a yellow silk dressing gown trimmed with minute embroidered roses, Dartania rapidly combed the cascading flame of hair that she could sit on. Her bandaged thumb made it an awkward business. Behind her, a breakfast tray lay on the unmade bed, and her two elder children were playing quietly on the floor nearby. Sunlight streamed through the open windows, and in a corner of the room, Theodora, a yellow cockatiel with bright red dabs like rouge on either cheek, gabbled from her cage at intervals her one phrase, "Happy days, happy days: What! What! What!" pecking nonchalantly at a piece of toast.

Of her set, only Dartania had not bobbed her hair, and as she pulled the brush repeatedly through the heavy tresses in long, evenly drawn-out strokes, she began to review, in the manner of her brother Robin, opportunities for happiness that day. The chestnut filly Bayard had given her, although weak in one hock, should with work be ready for the hunting field that autumn. Dartania decided she would take the filly out that morning, before it got too hot. They might even try a few jumps. Then after lunch, though no activity sprung immediately to mind, she firmly resolved that she would not go into town.

Braiding her hair into two thick plaits, her thumb held awkwardly at an angle, she coiled the plaits around her head in a sort of braided halo, securing them with half a dozen tortoiseshell hairpins.

Sitting on the floor Sally and Emma watched this familiar ritual with rapt attention. They thought their mother very beautiful and, as soon as the last hairpin was in place, crowded eagerly around the dressing table like devoted acolytes, fascinated as always by the glittering boxes and bottles, the cosmetic jars and silver-mounted brush set that had been Dartania's mother's—treasures they were not allowed to touch.

"Mama, can I have that bottle when you're dead?" Sally eagerly inquired.

"And me that butterfly box?" put in her sister, whose gaze as ever clung to a pink-and-green enameled box that reminded her palpably of ice cream.

"Will you put that in your will, Mama?"

"I'll think about it," said Dartania, hiding her bemused surprise. "It depends on how you behave." Where on earth did they pick up such things, she wondered. Seneca talking about Mrs. Eagleton's will, perhaps. No doubt they were now in for a protracted stretch of the children seeing everything in terms of future possession.

"You won't forget? You'll will me that bottle for my very own?"

"We'll see." Dartania's impatience flared perceptibly. "Now you children skedaddle. Go outside and play. I've got to dress and I'm in a hurry . . . Miss Allen," she called.

And Miss Allen, their diminutive nurse, an orphan, lamed from birth by a tubercular spine, called in turn to the children.

Five minutes later, as Dartania was buttoning with some difficulty her cotton blouse, the bedroom door opened without a knock and Robin entered, looking rather pleased with himself, she thought.

"Mornin," he casually saluted and, moving aside the breakfast tray, flopped backward in a diagonal across the bed, arranging the pillows beneath his head.

People often forgot these two were twins; they could see no close connection or resemblance; yet there existed between them a deep, instinctive rapport that, expressed chiefly through irreverent banter developed in childhood—and which they saw no reason to change—was very easy to miss.

"I hope you aren't going to go on about Chloe's wedding," Dartania told him brusquely, tucking her blouse into a pair of brown twill jodhpurs. "That shoot-out business I mean." She gave the impression it would be unwelcome trivia.

"The subject hasn't blipped across my mind since the dramatic event itself," Robin candidly declared. He'd had fish of his own to fry. "Hello!" He sat up suddenly like a marionette rudely jerked from its box, pointing in amazement at the bandaged thumb. "You got hit!"

"Grazed to be precise; it's just a scratch. But for God's sake don't tell

Papa or anyone. People are making enough fuss as it is." She knew they were saying Seneca had behaved irresponsibly and that the two of them had been extremely lucky. The news that she had been wounded, even slightly, could ignite what already appeared to her a bonfire of Salem proportions.

"Seneca wouldn't have done it if it wasn't safe," she said. "You know that. He always knows exactly what he's doing. It just looks dangerous to other people because they know less about it, that's all. The magician's art," she added proudly, shaking the tip of a cigarette out of its pack and extracting it of necessity with her teeth.

"Dar," said Robin, "the range of a dueling pistol—"

"I know I know," she mumbled, and briefly removed the cigarette. "But they were some special kind of pistols." She threw the box of matches at her brother. "You'll have to light it for me."

Dartania and Seneca's bedroom communicated with the library, making the latter, despite its books and guns, into a sort of boudoir. The layout, with master bedroom on the ground floor, was unusual in a two-storeyed house, but Longwood was a very unusual house—a log-built house. Built by some of Edward Nash's forebears when they settled the region, the original cabin had been considerably enlarged after the Civil War. The "dog trot," as the breezeway through the cabin's center was called, had been enclosed to make a central hall, its wide-planked chestnut floor now beautifully waxed. A second log storey had been added and a kitchen wing built on the back. The result was a sort of frontier manor house and, being fifteen miles from Nashborough, still very much in the country. There were fine views across the rolling pastures and, behind the house, lay the stretch of wood that, having supplied the building timbers, gave the house its name.

The library or gun room where the twins now sat drinking coffee had been furnished by Alice Nash, but most of the house's furniture was already there, left by the doctor's brother when he died. This might have displeased many women but it had greatly pleased Dartania, who took no interest in what, with mild derision, she called "compulsive nest building." Inclined to take her surroundings very much for granted, it would not have occurred to her to change or move things in the house any more than it would to move the rocks and trees about outside.

Curled up on the sagging chintz sofa, Dartania listened with surprise to her brother's sudden curiosity about the farm. How many acres were there? Were beef cattle easier than dairy cows to raise? What crops did they grow and how much help did they have? "I don't think I've ever been out back." Robin gestured vaguely, referring to the three hundred acres of farmland stretching beyond the woods. "Is it a lot of work?"

"Most of it's farmed in shares," Dartania told him. "Then there's the livestock and the garden and so forth. Robert and Frank do that, and sometimes James comes in."

"Ah," breathed Robin contentedly, "farming I think would suit me admirably."

"It distresses you even to pick a flower," she retorted, pouring more coffee and setting the tray at a level position on the magazine-strewn table. "Besides, what would you do with yourself all day out in the country?" Dartania did not add that although she herself insisted on living in the country, and despised the new and fashionable suburb of Blue Hills, she found little enough to do there and, without really noticing it, went into town most days.

"I'm afraid my news is standing on its head, so I'll upend." Robin cleared his throat, his eyes crinkling like tissue paper at the edges. "The fact is I've decided to assume, like you, dear sister, matrimonial responsibilities. Or in common parlance I am getting married."

Dartania looked at her brother with amused disbelief. "First farming, now marriage. A fantasist is what you're becoming, Robbie dear. I suppose you'll tell me next you're going to marry that humorless, butter-wouldn't-melt-in-her-mouth Margaret Elsworthy. Grave as the grave," she drawled lugubriously.

Feeling sharply the sting of this remark, Robin retained the outward equanimity of his usual style. "Bull's-eye," he replied. "If I may be permitted a metaphor from shooting."

Dartania set her cup down and stood up, her back to the empty grate. "You've asked her then?"

Sipping his coffee, Robin nodded into his cup.

"And she's accepted, of course."

Again Robin nodded. "There is, however, an insect floundering in the ointment," he went on. "It appears that I must have a job."

Dartania let out a snort of disbelief and sat down sidesaddle on the sofa arm. "Robbie, I'm sorry about what I said a minute ago. I hardly know Margaret Elsworthy and I'm sure she's really very nice, but it doesn't sound to me like she knows you very well."

"She would willingly take me as I am," he declared in a manner that implied penniless, unregenerate, and devoid of prospects, "but Daddy insists otherwise: Puritan Yankee values I'm afraid." He shrugged. "So employment is in the marriage contract, so to speak, which is why I have settled on farming. And from what you say it's about as I imagined—virtually looks after itself." He gave the empty fireplace a wistful smile. "After all, what is more natural than that things should grow and multiply? It hardly needs much assistance for plants and animals to perform tasks for which they are already fully programmed." He uncrossed his legs and, leaning forward very upright, in the manner of his father, rubbed both knees. "So there it is: My future is settled and I'm sure you'll like Margaret when you get to know her. Now what about nipping off to the golf club for some lunch?"

With difficulty Dartania resisted this temptation. She had no desire to exhibit her sausagelike thumb in town and to have old biddies staring and nodding meaningfully to each other. "I've a better idea," she said. "Seneca's on the back of the place exercising bird dogs and mulling over some new case. We could ride back to meet him with a picnic, and then you could see the farm."

That being agreed, Dartania rushed off to instruct Delphine.

"If you want a thermos of martinis," Robin called after her, "I'll willingly exert myself in their preparation." He had settled back on the sofa, a gentle, half-dreaming expression on his prominent features, his long thin hands, the fingers outspread resting listlessly on his thighs, as he gazed, smiling vaguely, into the empty grate.

"Happy days. What! What! What!" shrieked Theodora from next door.

8

....

I can't believe you did such a thing!" Alice Nash had exclaimed on the day after Chloe's wedding when Seneca came out to Cottoncrop to collect his daughters. "Using your own wife as a shooting target! I never *heard* of such a thing!" (She always pronounced it "hoeud.") "Why, the telephone hasn't stopped ringing."

As Nashborough's *première dame* Alice was kept informed of all that went on by a dedicated network of highly voluble women forming a vital linkage with the outside world. Surprise, sympathy, and little whoops of laughter greeted each item of news that she received; but only rarely did "Miss Alice," as everyone, including her son and husband, called her, sit in judgment. "That's the way they're doing it now," she would respond to a reported change in custom or social protocol that others tended to view as an infringement. Emotive and without stuffiness Alice Nash moved with the times.

They were sitting on the shady wrought-iron balcony outside the doctor's bedroom. Carved acanthus-leaf capitals curled familiarly overhead, topping the fluted wooden columns, and a stiff gin and tonic was doing much to alleviate Seneca's acute hangover.

"It *was* a bit of a stunt," he now admitted, wondering if he was giving up too much ground. "But at least a couple of fools were prevented from shooting each other."

His father, who sat nearest the iron balusters, leaned forward, one hand cupping an ear, a look of strong disapproval mixed with the more familiar irritation of poor hearing.

"It was nothing like it seemed," Seneca explained matter-of-factly, noting with unease the exaggerated pinkness of the older man's complexion in the sultry heat. "The fact is those were Mortimer pistols—first ones I've ever seen." And in response to his father's deepening frown, *"H. W. Mortimer. Made in England in George III's day,"* he almost shouted. "They're the only dueling pistols, so far as I know, with hidden rifling in the barrel."

He turned toward his mother. "Which makes them extremely accurate. A lemon at ten paces was a cinch."

"Oh heavens, a lemon!"

"It was a damn fool thing to do," the doctor roundly declared. "Too much whiskey and too cocksure of yourselves. You young people think you know everything."

Seneca accepted this generation-embracing rebuke with something like gratitude. At the best of times he was uncomfortable in his father's presence and since childhood he had found it difficult to talk to him. Their styles somehow did not align. But despite Seneca's fixed intention to outstrip his father professionally, and to make a greater name for himself in the world, he felt deep down a certainty that his father was the better man, and always would be. He supposed it was a fact of nature, but one his father too must be aware of, which added an obscure disquiet to Seneca's sorely felt inferiority.

But his mother as he knew adored him, and Seneca adored his mother. Quicker and cleverer than his father, to his young eyes, she was more perceptive into the bargain. And now he could rely on her to spread word of the pistols' exceptional accuracy, lauding at the same time his wide-ranging erudition. He felt grateful indeed for so loving and influential an ally.

"I doubt the fellow who sent those pistols to Jim and Chloe knew what collectors' pieces they are," he went on casually. "A damn nice present, despite the labored joke behind it."

"I never saw anything to equal Ellen Douglas's necklace." Alice rocked back in the white-painted metal rocker. "Cabochon emeralds that looked like polished pebbles. Now there's understated elegance for you. But do you know I think she's a lonely woman, and I *wish* there was something I could do for her. She's a fish out of water in Nashborough, and always will be I'm afraid. But the worst of it is she's childless."

The talk began to eddy around details of the wedding—how so much champagne could have been smuggled across the country in a time of nationwide prohibition (Alice had heard it was in the governor's private railroad car); Bertha Fenton's envy of her younger sister (Jane Douglas, having given her lodging at Timbuctoo, was hated for it), then moved on to news from the fashionable suburb of Blue Hills, once Alice's father's plantation (the house itself now belonged to Bayard Douglas). As always Alice relished a thoroughgoing postmortem, and Seneca, seeing that his father now made little effort to follow the talk, knew that, except for his own conscience, he was probably off the hook.

AT THE SOUND of two sharp, high-pitched blasts from a whistle, the white setter bitch reluctantly ceased her joyous nosing in all directions and circled back toward her master. The broad strip of sage grass where the dogs were being exercised was a worn-out, badly eroded piece of land lying beyond the cultivated fields and highly prized by Seneca for quail hunting in winter.

Despite the necessity of thinking through the railroad case, Seneca had that morning forced himself to examine the shooting incident in detail and to reach some conclusion about his own behavior.

At the time, success had produced a heady exuberance, and rightly it had seemed: He had brought off a double coup. More important, Dartania's show of perfect faith had struck a chord at the very mainspring of his nature, reaffirming his abundant pride and love for her.

The possibility of some sort of challenge on Dartania's part had certainly crossed his mind, and many believed she'd put him in a difficult, even an embarrassing, position. But both of these he rejected. At a word Dartania would have stepped aside. Nor did she need to challenge his courage, believing in him so utterly as she did. But why then had she done it? They were in the car before she had revealed the wound. She had wrapped one of the chiffon panels of her skirt around her thumb to staunch the blood and cleverly conceal the wound—instinctively protecting him. Seneca smiled at the visible pride with which, like a novice warrior, she had displayed her bleeding thumb. Dartania had more guts than any woman he knew, more beauty and more joie de vivre. He almost pitied men who were condemned to live with less, and at this reflection his spirits rose somewhat.

Had she not so astutely concealed her injury, hindsight told him the situation could have become seriously unpleasant. It was this that astonished and mortified him. Not once had he considered the result of failure—not for one instant had he believed he would fail. He was a first-class shot and he had known the capacity of those pistols. Yet even a small injury he now saw would, if discovered, have had unsavory repercussions, undermining people's confidence in a young and rising lawyer and seriously impairing the chances of one who planned to enter public life—one who already had a political battle on his hands. Clear as day, he envisaged the Buzby-controlled *Echo*'s front page: "Lawyer Shoots Wife at Society Wedding." A legitimate headline with sinister and, worse perhaps, ridiculous undertones.

But if word of the injury did not leak out, he now reasoned, the affair would rapidly blow over. It only remained for him to square things with himself.

Seneca had learned in the war, and before that at military school, the importance of full assessment of the facts as a prelude to any serious action. Therefore he was appalled by the magnitude of his error. Obviously drink created a more illusory state than he had been aware of, for as he now saw, he *had* acted foolishly, and he and Dartania had indeed been lucky.

To be in the wrong was for Seneca a form of moral disemboweling. He possessed no strategy for deflecting personal failure, and in such circumstances simply rejected himself. A soot-black gloom descended as he floundered in the wretched purgatory of his inferiority.

In response to another whistle blast, a liver-and-white pointer appeared on the edge of the sage grass, and a short command brought the animal skulking to its master. Seneca looked at his watch and, leaving the scrub land with his dogs to heel, made his way to the brown, gullied farm track that led eventually to the house. Already the humidity was rising. It was humidity that made the Southern sun a punitive and repugnant force, devoid of all pleasure, something systematically to be shunned.

As he continued along the track he forced his mind to address the railroad case. Should he call Buzby to the witness box or would Buzby's notoriety and outrageous showman's personality win the jury over no matter what was revealed? He began to build up an examination, but his usual aggressive pleasure in it did not catch fire. The chief accountant was probably the one to go for, he decided.

Largely oblivious to his surroundings as he walked along, Seneca's eye was nonetheless drawn unconsciously to a tin roof rising above the crops in front of him. Glistening like a sheet of beaten silver in the morning light, the effect offered some of the wonder of a mirage.

Drawing nearer he was vaguely aware of a commotion in the cabin yard; people were running about and shouting, and small children scurried in from the adjacent field. Yet as he approached, things suddenly became quiet and there was no sign of any life. Even the dogs underneath the cabin failed to set up their usual raucous barking.

Mildly curious, Seneca out of politeness kept his eyes fixed on the road. He was almost past the house when Mattie Tebbit burst out of the front door, halting abruptly on the porch as on the edge of a precipice.

"Mr. Nash," she whispered breathlessly after him, "Oh, Mr. Nash." She seemed incapable of continuing and there was a moment's pause while, as Seneca turned back, she collected herself. "I wonder kin you help us? A snake done bit my boy Sammy over at the creek; he say it's a rattlesnake for sure."

Putting the two dogs on leashes, Seneca gave them to one of the children now crowding onto the cabin porch. "Whatever bit him, Mattie, wasn't a rattlesnake," he reassured her. "You got to go a far piece up-country to get yourself bit by a rattlesnake. Now, where's your boy?"

"He in on the bed; he mighty scared, Mr. Nash." But the woman herself was gaining confidence, having committed herself to action and finding she was able to make things happen.

Entering the cabin Seneca saw a boy about twelve years old lying wide-eyed on one of three beds in the room.

"Let's have a look, Sammy," he said, sitting down on the rickety bed beside the boy.

The cabin, its walls lined with old newspapers for insulation inside the thin plank carapace, had the pungent smell of humanity living together at close quarters. Under the crude plank floor, the mongrel dogs had begun to bark uncertainly at the intruders. There was a pot-bellied stove in the fire-place, a couple of wooden chairs, and a table.

"Where'd he get you?" Seneca asked the boy.

The boy pointed to the outer side of his right foot just below the ankle.

Taking the foot in his lap Seneca could see no sign of fang marks in the dark of the cabin. "You say it was over at the creek. Did you get a good look at him?" he asked.

"Naw sir." Sammy, coughing hoarsely, wiped his running nose on the back of his hand. "Could be I stepped on him like; next thing I know, wham, and then he jump into the creek just like he was a fish."

"How along ago was it?" Testing the boy's foot for swelling, Seneca was surprised by its horny sole, which had developed into a sort of hoof, and he admired this example of the body's ability for adaptation, being reminded with some pleasure that shoes were not so necessary as people nowadays supposed.

"Must be bout a hour," Sammy reckoned, watching his foot in Seneca's hand, as though it were an object belonging to someone else.

The boy's mother was standing at a polite distance, near the open door, two small children clutching her stained calico skirt.

"Well, if it went into the water it could be a cottonmouth, so we can't afford to take any chances," he went on calmly. "And if the poison's there, we got to get it out." He patted the boy's foot. "Won't be more than a pin prick. Where's your husband, Mattie?" he asked.

"He gone into town on the mule to buy some feed."

Continuing to sit with the boy's foot in his lap, Seneca told Mattie to bring him a sharp knife and some matches and paper, some water, a clean cloth, and a tin pan.

Having washed the boy's foot he set the paper on fire in one of the pans and heated the tip of the knife.

"Now you're a brave fellow and this won't be more than a scratch," he said, and without waiting he made a small incision in the boy's foot below the ankle; then, as the blood welled up, he held the foot to his mouth and sucked hard, spitting the blood into the pan. He repeated the action a couple of times, then, taking the dipper from the water pail, rinsed his mouth, poured some water over the wound, and refilling the dipper, gave it to the boy. "Drink up," he said. "The operation is over and the patient has survived."

While Sammy drank, staring over the dipper's rim, Seneca bound the cut with a strip of white cloth that the boy's mother tore off a larger piece.

"Make sure you keep it clean," he told the boy.

Everybody smiled a little and Seneca stood up, his head lowered slightly under the cabin ceiling.

"Well, I got to get these dogs and myself home for some lunch," he said. "Tell Samuel I'm sorry I missed him, Mattie, and though I doubt you need worry about your boy, if there're any complications send up to the house and we'll get a real doctor to come and have a look at him."

Mattie turned to one of the children. "Go out back," she ordered the child, "and git Mr. Nash one of them skins."

And despite Seneca's protests he was awarded a few minutes later with a newly cured raccoon pelt, the bushy tail of which would have shamed any fox.

"Make a mighty fine huntin hat for winter," said Mattie. "Mr. Gregory over on Mr. Dillon's place, he know how to make it up, and he do a good job too."

"Why that's as fine a coonskin as ever I saw, Mattie, and really beautifully tanned." His admiration, which was genuine, registered clearly in his voice. "And come winter, you're gonna see him sittin on my head," he promised her.

Taking the dogs from the child who had been holding them, and saluting the family assembled on the cabin porch, Seneca set out in long strides down the track, jumping lightly across the gullies and the deeply furrowed ruts made by innumerable wagon wheels. As soon as the cabin was out of sight he unleashed the dogs but kept them whistled in.

The well-hoed fields looked set for an abundant crop; the cotton plants were just beginning to flower, signaling a period of deserved rest for its cultivators as the blue flower gradually turned to white and the cotton emerged from bolls like thousands of rabbits bursting out of hats. A fresh breeze had dissipated the humidity, and Seneca, breathing deeply, surveyed his land with a sudden burst of pleasure. The dark cloud had miraculously vanished and a renewing energy rose in his body as if absorbed from the iron red earth on which he trod, a regenerating force suffusing him with inner ease and restoring his readiness, his strong desire, to take life at full tilt, to make the best of it and in doing so to give the very best of himself.

Rounding the next bend, a pair of mating quail got up, to the intense excitement of the dogs, and fording the nearly dried-up creek that trickled haphazardly across the track, Seneca, looking up, caught sight in the distance of two figures cantering toward him along the gullied track. Grinning, he quickened his long stride, waving in an exuberant welcome the glossy coonskin high up in the air.

9

・・・・・・・・・・・・・・・・・・・・

*T*he minute the automobile had stopped in front of the square-
columned portico of Blue Hills House, Albert, the chauffeur, jumped
nimbly out and with considerable flourish opened the car's back door. It was
an exercise Bayard rarely countenanced. He was perfectly capable of opening doors himself, he always said—it was about the only exercise he got. But
when Albert instinctively performed this rite, as now, Bayard accepted it
gracefully as a special gesture, whether a mark of unusual sympathy or simply Albert's own private exhilaration at the time.

"Now take that basket straight to the kitchen," Bayard told him rather
sharply, "and see they put it in a safe place." He looked at his watch. The
Chicago train had been late; it was after eight o'clock. "And be sure to give
John and Clara my instructions *in full.*"

"It's all writ down in my head exactly like you done tole it," Albert
assured him, a smile of good-humored tolerance wreathing his affable face.

"Very good, excellent," said Bayard who envied as much as he admired
the mnemonic skills of the illiterate. "It's important to get the details right."

"Sho is," Albert rhetorically confirmed, for both men enjoyed having the
last word.

To Bayard's surprise Ellen wasn't in the library, their usual sitting room,
but in the parlor, or drawing room, as she called it, which was generally
reserved for guests. Her gray silk dress, broad white collar, and the pink silk

cabbage rose at her waist reflected the delicate pinks and beiges of the Aubusson-tapestried furniture. Over the fireplace, Picasso's harlequined acrobats gazed out from the isolation of a desert no-man's-land.

"This is the coolest place in the house," Ellen quickly explained, greeting him with a kiss. Her soft brown curls framed a gentle face that in its tenderness epitomized her entire demeanor. Pale translucent skin, such as only an English climate can produce, accentuated the dove gray eyes wherein sympathy was writ large for all who sought it. The combination of skin and eyes often brought into Bayard's mind two pearls, the one milk white, the other smoky gray.

"I've been sitting here very pleasantly the past hour, enjoying the cross draft," she told him serenely, "and having a little think."

Bayard dropped onto a gilded settee opposite his wife, whose hint of solitude stirred a familiar uneasiness.

"Did you have a good trip, darling?"

"*Comme si comme ça.* Lunched with the governor yesterday and talked politics and railroads till we were blue in the face. Then nipped out and bought an insurance company—at least I think I did."

"Goodness," Ellen breathed, happy in the knowledge he would never bore her with any of the details. "I'm afraid I've done very little myself." She smiled vaguely. "Oh yes, Alice Nash paid me a visit yesterday. She came to tea. I like her so much, Bayard. She can be brittle but she feels things strongly and doesn't hold back from it, even upsetting things. Not that I upset her, I hope," she laughed. "What I mean is, she's positively fearless about feeling. Does that make any sense?" She laughed again and, smoothing the gray silk of her dress, scrutinized her husband. "Would you like a drink, dear? You look a little on edge."

Bayard shook his head. "Miss Alice doesn't go about much these days," he said to show he had been listening. "I'd say she paid you a compliment."

"Oh, I hope so. And would you believe it, darling, she liked our Klee!" Ellen's eyes sparkled in amusement. "Yes, indeed. We were sitting in here, and suddenly she said, 'What a delightful picture, Ellen.' Then she said she loved children's pictures but it had never occurred to her to frame one. She thought it a brilliant idea." Gazing at the silvery fish on its purplish-blue platter, surrounded by orbiting nonsense, Ellen smiled with pleasure at this recollection.

"Cottoncrop will now become a gallery dedicated to the promotion of grandchildren's art," Bayard wryly predicted.

Ellen had paused, her eyes still resting on the Klee. "She's asked me to join the board of Saint Michael's orphanage," she said, her gaze suddenly reverting to her husband. "Don't you think that sounds interesting?"

Instantly he saw the kindness behind this gesture, together with a pragmatism that was typical of Alice Nash. "It could be, but once you get involved in a thing like that you know . . . Now who the devil is that?" The front door bell had interrupted him, ringing with an almost rude insistence.

Clara the cook rustled into the hall wearing her carpet slippers. "I got it, Mrs. Douglas," she called. "John, he out at his house right now."

Ellen frowned. "What can be upsetting her?" she whispered to her husband. "She looks likes she's been crying. Oh, I hope they haven't had a row."

"Mrs. Douglas," Clara called from just outside the parlor door, "it for you." She was evidently upset about something, sniffing and rubbing her hands nervously on her apron.

"Who is it, Clara?" Ellen gently inquired as she stood up.

"I ain't sure, Mrs. Douglas . . . but you better come. Come on now," she almost commanded her, retreating toward the door herself.

At this, Bayard also stood up.

"I wonder what *is* the matter," Ellen whispered, hurrying past him toward the front door.

There followed an eerie silence. Then, "Oh, Oh!" and "Oh, Bayard! Bayard, come quickly!" his wife called out. "It's . . ." Her voice, a mixture of amazement and alarm, was laced with yet another quality too. "Oh, Bayard," she cried. "Bayard you won't believe it but . . . It's a baby. A baby on our doorstep!"

Clara's tears now poured forth, and John, a little breathless, joined them from the kitchen, grinning rather foolishly, while Ellen, still standing in the doorway, gazed in rapt amazement at the tiny creature asleep in its ample, white-painted wicker basket.

"Hadn't we better bring it in?" her practical husband suggested. "Don't want to leave it there all night do you?"

"Let me git that basket for you, Mrs. Douglas," said John, rushing forward. "It ain't so light."

Ellen stood back, dazed; her gray eyes, luminous as a girl's, still riveted on the wicker basket. "There on the chest," she told John breathlessly.

Then almost on tiptoe she approached the basket.

The baby yawned, made two indignant little fists, and began to wake up. Its dark eyes, an unfathomable color, opened and rested on Ellen's face without surprise as, leaning down, she gingerly lifted the infant up and, straightening its long muslin gown, cradled the child comfortably in her arms.

"A baby! I can't get over it. And such a beautiful baby. Yes you are, *beautiful*," she addressed the child. "The most beautiful baby I believe I ever saw.

But . . ." She turned her gaze suddenly to Bayard. "Whose baby can it be?" The question, full of innocent wonder, contained too an ineffable sadness.

Removing his pince-nez, the very picture of solemnity, Bayard kissed her lightly on the cheek. "Happy birthday, darling," he said, preserving his dead-pan countenance. "Oh yes, it's legitimate. So to speak," he added to erase the disbelief lingering in her face.

Ellen's eyes were swimming. "Is it . . ."

"A boy," put in Clara. "I done changed his diaper in the kitchen."

"Bayard, I think I must sit down."

"Do you want Clara to take the baby?" he suggested. "It's well past dinner time, you know."

"Oh Clara, do you think you could hold dinner back another fifteen minutes? Would you mind awfully?" she begged. "I can't let him go quite yet."

"Ain't nothing out there won't keep, and that's a fact."

"There's so much to think about, too: a nursery, clothes . . ."

"He'll be fine in a basket for tonight," replied her sensible husband. "Or we could make up a drawer."

Kissing the baby gently on its forehead, Ellen smiled down at the child and, to her delight, elicited a similar response in the baby. "Has he . . . got a name?"

"Just Baby so far, I believe." Bayard's eyes roved searchingly about the ceiling. "Why don't we call him . . . Moses?" he suggested owlishly.

Ellen ignored his teasing. "I think we should name him after Papa."

"If you do he'll be Ham or Hambone at school," predicted Bayard. "He'll hate it."

"I meant after *my* papa darling, she said liltingly. "William," she addressed the baby. "My sweet sweet William. Yes, you are!"

"Wiyum is a mouthful for a baby," Clara interposed. "Now when you want your dinner, just let me have him and we can look after him in the kitchen. We been gettin on fine, ain't we Willie honey?"

Over dinner Ellen's eager questions exploded one after another like an erratic fireworks celebration, and Bayard, seeing her so animated, so suffused with happiness and purpose, saw, as in a palimpsest, the eighteen-year-old girl returning to England on the *Mauretania*, overly protected by reserved and formidable parents and waiting chrysalislike for her own life to begin.

He told her what he could—that he had got the child in Chicago. He knew nothing of its parentage: Orphanages never told one a thing; it was standard policy not to. "He's about two months old, male, Caucasian . . ."

"I can see all that," she stopped him indignantly.

With each course John brought the latest news from the kitchen: "He smilin, he eatin a bit, he kickin."

Before dinner was over the nanny question had been mooted, the nursery decided upon, and questions of vaccination, christening, and general announcements sorted out. Oxford had even been mentioned, but an open mind was kept regarding Harvard.

"Oh darling, you've made me so happy." Ellen beamed. "And then, too, we have so much to give; I'm so very glad of that."

"Whatever money can buy," Bayard cheerfully responded and, although he thought the baby rather boring, added, "and all the affection of two doting parents."

John's head appeared around the pantry door. "He yellin his head off now, Mrs. Douglas."

"Oh, I'm coming," she cried. "Excuse me, darling," and she raced eagerly toward the kitchen.

Bayard shook his head. Female responses were wonderful indeed. He had encountered several business difficulties in Chicago, some of them unresolved as yet; but now he finished his dessert satisfied that one at least of his more pressing problems had been sorted out. He reflected that he might have acted sooner, or perhaps, all things considered, a little later. Ellen's brother Tom Ferris was arriving in two weeks, escorting on a private visit none other than His Royal Highness the Prince of Wales, to whom Tom Ferris was an equerry. In all this nursery fuss the great man might get insufficient attention.

10

....

*B*ayard has bought a baby," Jasmine announced, slipping into Stark Fenton's little two-seater and smiling up at him in a friendly fashion as he closed the door.

"So everybody says." Stark rounded to the other side, adjusting en route the car's canvas top, which had been folded down.

"Well, not *everybody*. That baby's origins are much speculated on, believe me; but the truth is Bayard got it in Chicago."

"Have you seen the sales slip then?"

"Why Stark, that's very witty." She turned toward him appreciatively, adding, "This is going to be fascinating. I've been looking forward to it so, and you were a darling to set it up."

Despite his reservations, Stark had succumbed to Jasmine's wish to meet the painter Jenny Dinson and with some difficulty had persuaded the busy, socially disinterested woman to let him bring her to lunch. "I haven't seen any of her work," he'd felt it necessary to say, in response to Jenny's even, questioning gaze, "but her family—her brother and sister-in-law that is— collect modern art. So, who knows, something might come of it." And that presumably had done the trick.

Stark believed that his doggedness to abide by promises had motivated him; he was not simply doing as he was bid, even though grudgingly he acknowledged Jasmine's inordinate hold on him. There was, however, no question of love he had decided, attractive though she was; it was simply that quite mysteriously she'd managed to get the drop on him, and once that demeaning position was overcome, free will would automatically be restored. Meantime he sought (cravenly) her good opinion, while resenting it deeply. "Very witty," she had said in that unconsciously patronizing way she had, utterly blind to the fact that in no way was he an ordinary fellow. And there as he saw it lay the crux of his problem: getting her full attention so she might see him as he really was. Yet for all his ableness, he had, he knew, never been much of a showman.

Holding her narrow-brimmed hat with both hands, her pretty nose tilted into the wind, Jasmine was full of agreeable anticipation. She had been overjoyed to learn that a serious modern painter existed in provincial Nashborough and she was looking forward eagerly to enjoying a painterly conversation—perhaps one with a kindred spirit—over a pleasant and hopefully drawn-out studio lunch.

Climbing the rickety outside stair of the warehouse loft that was Jenny Dinson's studio and home, Jasmine turned and unexpectedly smiled conspiratorially at Stark, enveloping him in a bonfire of sudden pleasure. She looked incredibly fresh and delicate in a slim yellow dress and little cloche hat, her tiny hands encased in pristine gloves resting lightly on the stair rail. There was, he had to admit, something unbeatable about a lady—though what that might be he couldn't guess—but surely it ran deeper than matters of style. Suddenly it occurred to him that Jenny Dinson's social ineptness, her lack of *ton*, might in Jasmine's eyes augment, by mere association, the inferiority with which he was already stamped. The thought's shabbiness appalled him, and knocking on the loft door, its black paint festered and peeling, Stark forcibly reminded himself that Jenny Dinson and her colleagues were creative, highly able people; they were professionals. It was maddening that the gazelle-like, overly sheltered Jasmine might nonetheless queen it over them, as on some obscure hereditary principle.

No one answered the door, so Stark pushed it open, revealing a long bare room with a rough unvarnished plank floor, the cathedral-like ceiling lit by a pair of huge skylights. Some canvases were stacked against the dingy graying walls, and at the rear, two faded calico screens cordoned off Jenny Dinson's bedroom. A long, scrubbed-pine kitchen table stood in front of the screens and parallel to them, covered with a jumble of rubbish and painting materials, while the screens themselves were draped with clothing in the manner of changing booths in ladies shops. Jasmine's overall impression was of dust, gloom, and profound untidiness: Empty bottles lay in a corner on the floor and jar lids full of stubbed-out cigarettes were littered about, causing something inside her to cringe and withdraw despite her eagerness.

Standing at an easel under one of the skylights, Jenny Dinson beckoned to them with a sweep of her paint brush in the air. She was, Jasmine guessed, about thirty. She was dressed in a pair of baggy men's trousers and a loose shirt, both of which blended into the dingy color of the walls. A sturdiness of build, together with the clothes, gave her a faintly manlike quality. She had straight brown hair and bangs. Her face was long and plain with pale brown eyes that though sharp as pins failed to give it any particular character.

"Stark tells me you're a painter," she said tonelessly. Laying down her brush, she wiped her hands on a badly soiled towel, as dubiously she examined her beautifully turned-out guest. "I think I've seen your picture in the newspaper, haven't I?"

Jasmine blushed. "Oh, possibly." Her photograph often appeared in the social columns, but it had never occurred to her that it might be noted by people she had never met, possibly even caught in some corner of their imaginations. A momentary thrill of unknown worlds stirred in her mind.

"I so admired the landscape Stark's family gave my sister," she confided enthusiastically. "And I wanted so much to meet you and to see your work that I press-ganged poor Stark into bringing me, I'm afraid. I hope you don't mind."

"That picture was painted a few years ago," said Jenny. "You'll find I'm working very differently now." Jasmine's openness and sincerity had caused a small thaw that sharing the same profession evidently did not.

Though she had not asked them to sit down, Jenny herself perched unthinking on the table edge, explaining to Jasmine that she was part of a group of painters attached informally to the university, or more specifically to Dudley Spears, the art professor there. She and others had come to Nashborough especially to study with him.

"I'm surprised you haven't heard of us," she said. "I don't mean locally, but there was an article in the *Dial* a couple of months ago. We call ourselves the River School since we work and live in these old river warehouses . . . Oh, excuse me!" She jumped self-consciously off the table, blushing. "Please, do sit down!" Hurriedly she pulled out the only chair at the table, and Stark collected two others, placing them at the end of the table, where they were gathered.

"It'll only take me a few minutes to get lunch together," Jenny said, almost apologetically. "It's really a sort of picnic—and afterwards I can show you round the studio."

"May I look at what's on your easel?" Jasmine called as Jenny disappeared behind the screens.

"If you like," came the laconic reply.

Mention of the group's inclusion in the *Dial* had made a great impression on Jasmine, who, in any case, being in a new environment, was unusually alive to everything around her.

"She's nice," she whispered confidentially to Stark. "Do you know that professor she was talking about?"

Stark nodded, a little surprised at Jasmine's ready awe. Jenny might reign in her own kingdom after all, he decided.

Approaching the easel, Jasmine found to her surprise a canvas covered with myriad tiny blocks painted in tones of aqua, yellow, and rose. The effect was curiously three-dimensional, but it was the choice of color and the subtle development of its tonalities that to her mind made the picture so appealing.

"Jen," a male voice suddenly called out from behind the screens. "Is there any booze left?" There was a crash. "Oh, for God's sake!"

Jasmine widened her eyes at Stark, who she could see looked instantly annoyed. At that moment a young man wearing a short Japanese kimono emerged from behind the screens. Stocky, ginger haired, and unshaven, there was a faintly simian quality about his solid stance and overmuscular arms, which swelled almost grotesquely between the wrist and elbow. The Japanese kimono had seen better days.

It was startlingly obvious he must be sharing Jenny's bed, and Jasmine, despite herself, was horrified at the blatancy of it and, given the dreary surroundings, general sordidness.

The pendulum, Stark suspected, had begun to swing.

Rummaging in a cupboard against the wall, the young man removed a paper bag, then disappeared behind the screen again, nodding in a desultory way at Stark.

"Who's the butterfly?" they heard him demand, his tone unmistakably derisive, though the reply could not be heard.

"This is a wonderful picture," Jasmine exclaimed, blotting out the intrusion. "Have you seen it, Stark? Do you keep up with this sort of thing?" She sounded almost affectionate.

But before he could answer, the young man had returned carrying a bottle and a clutch of streaked glasses in his pudgy fingers.

"Ah," he breathed, pulling up the remaining chair, which was missing a couple of slats, and sprawling on it. "How goes it, Stark? Drink old man? Drink?" he indicated Jasmine.

"No thank you." She had removed her hat and gloves and, sitting down again, was waiting elegantly for the next event, as planned.

"This is Frank Noland," Stark announced deadpan. "Jasmine Douglas."

"How do you do?" said Jasmine coolly, sliding instinctively into fine if patronizing manners.

Noland, pouring out the drinks, ignored her. "Bootleg rye from a source in whom I have very little faith," he announced to Stark, giving him a glass.

Jenny reappeared having changed into a white blouse and dark skirt. She looked thinner and Jasmine noted for the first time a handsome regularity in her profile. "You've met," she observed offhanded, beginning to clear a space at the end of the table where they were sitting, shoving the residue to the other end.

"Your picture is wonderful," Jasmine told her. "The colors are practically alive."

Leaning back in his chair, Frank Noland took a deep swig. "Here to buy a picture, Butterfly?" he inquired, not looking at her.

"I'm here to see some pictures," she coldly answered him. "I'm a painter myself."

"Ah, a very decorative painter, no doubt," he observed ambiguously.

"Are you going to get dressed, Frank?" said Jenny shortly.

Noland looked at her with interest but did not move. One leg was crossed so that the ankle rested on his thigh and, to Jasmine's astonishment, she could see as he leaned back in the chair his reddish hairy balls under the kimono—a mesmeric if disturbing sight, riveting but disgusting too.

Jenny began to put knives and forks about haphazardly on the table and this was soon followed by bread, tomatoes, ham, and hard-boiled eggs. The men drank whiskey throughout.

"I hear you're running for the legislature, Stark old man," said Noland.

"That's right, as a sort of stalking horse to unseat big Boss Buzby."

"Think you can do it?"

"Well, the odds are strongly against us, I'm afraid."

"You're a romantic ass, you know that?" Noland rubbed the ginger stubble on his chin. His nose was rather small for the broad freckled face and high receding brow. "A goddamn fuzzy wuzzy liberal."

"I am indeed a liberal," Stark acknowledged genially with a little bow.

"Yes and like all liberals you can't face facts; you're too busy pretending life's going to be rosy for everyone, if you can just get your paws on the reins."

Suddenly Noland looked grim, and wrinkling up his insignificant nose, he glared indignantly at the table top. "The truth is human life isn't worth a nickel. Nothing's cheaper or easier to replace. You liberals can't face that fact, but believe me it's something any political leader worth his salt sooner or later has to face. Then and only then can he build his program on reality, and not some vapid fantasy."

Demolishing a hard-boiled egg in one bite, Noland raised his hand to mark a pragmatic pause before continuing. "A real leader needs draconian qualities. He must if necessary send men to their death and do it without a qualm. Knowing the worthlessness of human life is part of his strength, you see. And knowing comes from an awareness that since everyone's going to die it doesn't really matter when. The logic's very simple: *Dead men don't suffer loss.* They can't miss *themselves* can they? Ergo it doesn't, after the fact, make a damn bit of difference when they die."

Hunched forward in his chair, Stark listened with a patient smile, as to an opposing lawyer arguing his brief in court.

"You'd see all that if you could clear those liberal cobwebs from your head. Then and only then, you might be worthy of office, possibly high office."

"But people must be kind to each other . . ." put in Jasmine.

Noland ignored this. "You're hiding behind a veil, old man, and you think it's a solid wall." Again he wrinkled his tiny bulblike nose. "I've lost all my illusions but you're afraid to take the initial fence."

"But illusion is absolutely necessary to an artist," Jasmine persisted. "After all, it's by creating illusions we're able to show truth." The man was detestable but she was determined to hold her own and to get the conversation off politics and around to painting, which was why she had come.

For the first time, Noland looked directly at her, and confronted with his ice blue stare, Jasmine was genuinely startled. The penetration was alarming. Few people, she suddenly realized, ever looked you straight in the eye; they focused more generally, around the mouth, which was less embarrassing, and for some reason demanded much less in return.

"There's a famous photo of Walt Whitman with a butterfly on his knee," Noland said, his thin lips twisted like a zest of lemon. "It took a long time to make an exposure back then, so people often asked Whitman why the butterfly had stayed put so long. And Whitman used to say, 'Well, I guess it shows how much the critter liked me.' "

There was a pause. Jasmine's face had turned pink with anger and embarrassment. Was he suggesting that she was staying there because of him? The man was clearly insane.

"When Whitman died, they found among his belongings a butterfly made of Bakelite," Noland added.

The point seemed clumsy and obscure, if indeed there was a point, and conceivably it was insulting.

"Painting isn't about illusion," he continued, as if to clarify. "And it isn't about expressing truth either, whatever that is. It doesn't have to imitate the world or anything in it. A painting exists in its own right; that's what makes it a work of art. It's simply there. Created."

"Frank has broken away from our group," Jenny languidly explained, leaning forward on the table, her chin cupped in her hands. "The rest of us are still exploring cubism but we use color to enrich it, as you saw." She nodded toward the easel.

"Cubism is a dead duck in America," Noland said to no one in particular. "Ever since the Armory show Americans have imitated cubism, because we lack the confidence to try something of our own, something out of our own experience and roots. Cubism grew out of a European background, which is something we can never really know or understand."

Having eyed the whiskey bottle for several minutes, he reached across the table and, without offering it to anyone, helped himself to a substantial dollop, evidently reflecting the while on what preoccupied him. Most of the whiskey went down in one gulp. "My advice to any serious painter is this"— his tone contained a sudden ironic gentleness—"Make it new and make it you." He smiled a little. "Succinct and on the nail, eh, Fenton? Slogans for living." He raised his glass.

Jasmine, who had no means of judging, even of investigating such theoretical truths, thought nevertheless that what he had said about painting sounded convincing. Like all good ideas, once uttered, it had seemed obvious and "on the nail." If what he said was true, however, then her own preoccupation with landscape's light and shade was thoroughly outmoded.

But Jenny, who had heard it all before, stood up. "Come and see some phony American cubism," she said unperturbed.

Jasmine found instant reassurance in her tone. Why, after all, shouldn't several different styles coexist, if individually expressed?

Among the paintings against the wall was one in a completely different mode: It was built on a series of wild superimposed swirls, some of them impasto and intersected by carefully drawn lines in vivid primary colors.

"One of Frank's," said Jenny, with evident pride, holding the canvas up to the light for Jasmine.

"I've never seen anything like it," Jasmine softly exclaimed, repelled and yet aware of its extraordinary power.

"Frank's going to be a famous man one day," Jenny blandly confided, putting the canvas back. "You see, unlike most people"—she glanced momentarily in his direction—"he's always, if boringly, himself."

The young men, continuing their political philosophizing, did not immediately acknowledge the girls' return. "But it's the *quality* of life I want to improve," Stark was saying. "I grant you, quantity is less important." He pushed his fingers through his hair in mild exasperation. "You know you ought to read Turgenev, or Lermontov. All that nihilistic gloom—it's right up your street."

"If you think that then you've entirely missed the point," Noland bluntly retorted. "I'm not *disenchanted* with life; that's not it at all." He poured the remainder of the whiskey into his glass, giving the bottle a shake. "It's exploitation of the inevitable that interests me."

Jasmine had collected her hat and gloves from among the debris on the table, and noting the cue, Stark, visibly relieved, stood up.

"My brother and his wife collect art," she breezily announced, glancing from Frank to Jenny. "Perhaps you'd like to come and see their pictures sometime?"

Stark's face registered strong surprise.

"A moneybags, is he?" Noland said. He, too, had stood up. "Got Duveen scouring Europe for him then?"

"They collect modern pictures," Jasmine went on pleasantly. "They've a Braque that I'm sure would interest you, Jenny."

"Anything brand new?" Noland asked.

"Yes, they recently bought a Klee."

Frank cast Stark a faintly sarcastic smile, but whether it was aimed at Jasmine's pronunciation, her misunderstanding of the question, or her evident wealth wasn't clear.

"I'd love to come," said Jenny, glancing rather uncertainly at Frank.

For the second time that day, Frank Noland's ice blue eyes looked directly at Jasmine, and again she felt their strange annihilating power. He looked right through her and gave no sign of seeing anything.

"OK, we'll come," he said. "You telephone Jenny and fix it." His tone appeared to confer a special license.

"BOHEMIAN ENOUGH FOR you?" Stark dryly inquired on the way home, irritated by Jasmine's unexpected silence.

"It's all so depressing, isn't it?" she exclaimed, evidently very puzzled. "Not that I didn't enjoy it, oh I did! And thank you for arranging it Stark." Giving him a half-smile she tucked a disobedient strand of hair under her hat and began searching for cigarettes in her bag. She found them on the seat. "She's living with that man, isn't she?"

"Oh, sort of, I suppose. Vice versa if anything I should think."

"But isn't she a lot older?"

Stark shrugged and, lighting with one hand Jasmine's cigarette, added ruefully, "I'm sorry about all that, by the way. It was crude of them to drag you into it."

"He *is* crude isn't he—and so boorish." Never had she been treated in so peremptory a fashion. Suddenly she realized that Frank Noland had made her feel exactly as he had chosen to see her: frivolous, empty-headed, and inadequate.

"Then why on earth ask them out to Blue Hills?" Stark demanded. He didn't like it at all. Oil and water. It had been uncomfortably obvious all afternoon that people in other people's environments lost their own strong definition.

"I had to return their hospitality somehow, didn't I?"

The clatter of a streetcar crossing Fourth Avenue in front of them halted conversation. Jasmine puffed her cigarette. "She thinks he's a genius," she got out at last.

Stark guffawed. "Right now he's simply obsessed by death, scared stiff of it I shouldn't wonder. You know what artists are like."

Jasmine, who in fact didn't know, looked across at Stark with something like admiration. "You have a broad acquaintance," she said sweetly. "I'd no idea there were such interesting people tucked up in Nashborough. What else have you been keeping secret I wonder?" she added flirtatiously.

And noting this small and unexpected crack in the steely armor of her inattention, Stark experienced a sudden, even vengeful surging up of personal ambition.

11

....

I want to see that baby!" Alice Nash had declared the moment the news was out. And the new parents, desirous of every advantage for their child, and touched by the warmth of Alice's interest, drove over to Cotton-crop that same afternoon.

"A fine healthy baby," the doctor readily pronounced, holding the infant in his arms, his guileless smile and bald head mirroring wondrously the baby's own.

Ellen showed him a curious birthmark on the infant's spine, a large bluish bruise, the sole blemish on otherwise silky white skin, and the doctor thought he recognized a Mongolian spot, so called because it only appeared on those of Asian descent. Inwardly pleased by this telltale and perhaps unique link with the infant's past (if it was true), he saw no reason to speculate on genealogical matters with the Douglases, though the baby's pediatrician might do so.

"Look at those eyelashes!" Alice enthused. She kissed the child and rocked him in her arms, the infant showing the while a well-behaved tolerance and convincing Alice its forebears must have been "somebody," by which she meant people of consequence.

"I expect he's got a canteen full of silver spoons," she said, handing Bayard a silver julep cup for the child. If they would kindly see to its engraving, the jeweler would bill her for it. In this way she left the birth date to be sorted out without an awkward discussion. And Bayard and Ellen departed aware that news of their prodigious infant would that day be spread far and wide: Young William was launched indeed.

But Timbuctoo was a different kettle of fish. Introduced to his relations at the family's customary Sunday luncheon, enthusiasm proved muted and transports of delirium virtually nonexistent. This was not due to attributes or lack of them on the baby's part. The Douglases were a notoriously clannish and unsentimental lot, with a preference for horses and dogs over babies if it came to that.

Ellen had arrived at Timbuctoo with the child in her arms, Bayard and a young black nurse following with mountainous accoutrements.

"Is that the young heir's scepter you are bearing?" Robin inquired of the orange plastic rattle in Bayard's hand.

For a split second, having no response, Bayard looked a trifle abashed; then he shook the raucous object violently in his brother's face, declaring gleefully, "Who's rattled now!"

They were gathered in the hall, where drinks were being served, and Ellen was rapidly ensconced madonnalike on one of a pair of damask-covered sofas. The baby's dress—elaborately embroidered batiste, trimmed with lace, and twice the infant's length—fanned out over her knees, drawing at least as much attention as the baby, being in Douglas eyes the rarer item.

Everyone in the house, black and white, satisfied their curiosity. Cook Anna briefly deserted her kitchen, and Calvin, out of politeness, offered that it "looked like folks," while Hamilton, having extended a forefinger, approved the infant's firm and steady grip and, so far, equable temper.

"If anybody ever tells him he's adopted I shall strangle them with my bare hands," Ellen repeatedly declared, her tigresslike vehemence, though gently delivered, surprising everyone.

"I hear it's got a Mongolian spot," Jasmine, standing nearby, whispered to Bayard.

"If so, then I'm a Chinaman," quipped the new father with a little shrug, and went outside to help Albert bring in the baby's bassinet.

They had just got the wooden wheels safely up onto the front porch, and Albert was fluffing the organdy skirting, when Dartania sailed up the front steps followed by her three goslings.

"Women!" Bayard cried out in mock horror as the identically dressed little girls approached. He was looking through his pince-nez as through a microscope. *"I hate women!"*

The little girls giggled with delight. Enormously flattered at being labeled "women," whatever the circumstances, they knew in their hearts that it was women men adored above all else, and that one day their own glorious reigns would begin, as so obviously their mother's had. Uncle Bayard really was a card.

"How's fatherhood?" Dartania asked dryly, giving him a peck.

"I'm a natural. As a matter of fact, Miss Alice has already awarded me with a silver cup."

"Do come and see the baby!" Robin's new wife, Margaret, called from the doorway. Three weeks married, in a quiet ceremony befitting her father's university income, babies were much in her mind.

"Babies are as common as pig tracks, Margaret," murmured Dartania coolly, quoting with conviction a saying of her old nurse and opting without any hesitation for a group of men. But the children sped forward to inspect their "new-bought" cousin (as everyone was saying) and Sally was so captivated by the lace-encrusted infant that she was permitted to hold him in her arms for several ecstatic seconds. Emma, adopting her mother's line, however, affected disinterest. Her own recent passion for Aunt Chloe had been replaced by one for a colt her Shetland pony had so mysteriously produced.

When the dinner gong sounded—a four-note xylophone affair raucously played by some enthusiastic child—the party rapidly fell in behind its sire and, gossiping and making jokes, proceeded in ragged formation into the dining room next door.

"Saved by the bell, Dar," Jasmine whispered as the baby was wheeled away.

LIKE ALL ESTABLISHED rituals, Timbuctoo's Sunday luncheon never varied. Hamilton and Jane Douglas sat at opposite ends of the table, laid that day for fourteen. Jane's sister Bertha, whom few heeded, sat on Hamilton's right and Ellen Douglas on his left. Bayard, eldest of his generation and far and away its most successful member, sat on Jane Douglas's right, and Dan opposite him, the chair at that place always absent, to leave room for Dan's wheelchair. The others ranged themselves willy-nilly down the sides, while Dartania's children, too young to come to the table, sat with their nurse, Miss Allen, at a card table under the window.

Oyster soup was always followed by roast lamb, which Hamilton carved himself, standing at the end of the table. This was his duty and prerogative as host, as well as emblematic of his role as progenitor.

Standing at Hamilton's elbow, Calvin delivered each plate to its destination, having first given the carver explicit instructions. "That's enough for Miss Jasmine; Mr. Seneca like it underdone; you can give Miss Dar some of the outside."

The carving ceremony always produced a hush of polite anticipation, after which talk wafted forth again in scattered gusts, with occasional jests or witticisms studding the many silences that at family dinners pass unnoticed and without self-consciousness.

After carving, Hamilton customarily asked Bertha Fenton politely about her arthritis, before turning for the rest of the meal to his own thoughts and dinner.

Seneca had begun to find these luncheons tedious. Sitting between the newlyweds, Margaret and Chloe, he could find little to say to either. They were incredibly nice, he thought, but lacked either sufficient wit or beauty to cause him automatically to fluff his plumage or begin to strut his stuff.

"Thebes is way ahead of us in one respect," he told Chloe, who had just moved there, her husband having got the much-wished-for job in the Douglas bank. "It's a lot more democratic, being a river town, which we no longer are, and it's not so insular as here." Seneca sometimes tried law cases there. Two hundred miles away, on the banks of the Mississippi, still shipping their cotton and timber on it, Thebes had outstripped Nashborough, becoming the largest city in the state.

"People say Thebans put their money on their backs and we put ours into our houses," Dartania offered from across the table, though she herself did neither. Purchases of any sort absolutely failed to interest her.

"I hope you'll stay with us next time," Chloe warmly suggested to Seneca. "The house we've bought is in midtown, so it's very central and we've plenty of room."

Thanking her, Seneca decided to eschew this invitation. The couple were altogether too conventional for his taste, and he determined to stick, if need be clandestinely, to his usual room in the Palace Hotel.

Jasmine, who normally sat beside Dan, had parked herself on this occasion next to Bayard, telling him at length, despite his evident disinterest or preoccupation, about the River School. "Do you think a picture can exist without saying anything at all, I mean can exist purely as a work of art?" she wanted to know.

"My guess is it would have to say something. Art *is* expression after all," he said.

"But if there isn't an agreed vocabulary then surely it's going to be misread."

"Some critic will announce the correct interpretation, and the aspiring artist would be an idiot to dispute him."

"You're very cynical."

"Am I? I thought I was being business minded, as I'm trained to be."

Taking the plunge at last, Jasmine asked if she might bring two River School painters to see her brother's collection.

"Certainly, so long as I don't have to be there." Pouring gravy from the silver sauceboat with one hand, he held the redundant ladle showily in the other. "Does Ellen? You'd better fix it up with her in any case."

Ellen, Jasmine knew, was so suffused with happiness she would agree to anything. In fact she was at that very moment reflecting with wonder on the miracle of her flawlessly happy life, and had a beggar come by and asked her for a nickel, she would eagerly have bestowed the contents of her pocketbook on him.

"Shall I tell them to bring their portfolios?" Jasmine's query had all the vagueness of an afterthought. "They could leave them for you."

Bayard's beady eye over his beaky nose fixed on Jasmine briefly. "Definitely not."

After the main course had been eaten, numerous gaps appeared at the table as people wandered in and out in a sort of tidal undertow, though no one took any notice. Cigarette smoking was not allowed, and all of Hamilton's children smoked, could not in fact get through a meal without one. Moreover, though drinks could be brought to the table there was no provision made for the refills many felt to be a necessity. Only Cook Anna's famous chocolate roll—a chocolate sponge coated with whipped cream and rolled into a cylinder—successfully refilled the table.

Robin had just begun to tell Dartania about the new farm, "five hundred acres of cotton, popping like popcorn, or very nearly," when suddenly Hamilton stood up, something so unusual that few noticed it at first.

"And what are *you* going to do, Bro," Jasmine was calling to her brother. "Your famous job, I mean."

"I shall endeavor to manage the manager," he replied benignly. "As gentlemen farmers are required to do."

At which Margaret demurely examined the bouquet of flowers painted on her dessert plate. But everyone else looked toward Hamilton, having recalled (for Jane had warned them) that his memoirs, privately printed for members of the family, were ready for circulation.

"Pray silence for Papa," someone called unnecessarily.

Hamilton stood very erect, the embodiment of composure, his fingertips resting lightly on the immaculate cloth as he looked down the table at his progeny, and from another angle, his accumulated responsibilities.

"I am nearly seventy years old," he began, his gaze flickering for a moment inward, toward the past, "and during that time I have witnessed momentous changes in this country." His voice, calm though strong, easily filled the room. "I can well remember plantation life before the Civil War—a life of many pleasures for those who were among a privileged few. And I remember too the terrible ravages of that war and the stark deprivations after it—

deprivations that taxed *to the extreme* the courage and resources of all who had survived.

"Yet on top of this truly unimaginable devastation has been built a standard of living better than any ever seen before in the South, and it has happened in a very short time. Our whole history has. My grandfather knew George Washington well, and I myself vividly remember him. That's three lifespans compassing this nation's whole existence. Think of it." And he paused that they might do so. He then said that he was proud to have endured the struggles preceding such unrivaled prosperity and pleased to have experienced its eventual rewards. Pleased, too, like Abraham to have reared a tribe.

They all knew that he had set down his recollections of events, "as they affected and helped to shape my life; for those struggles have, like wind and rain and sun on a young tree, substantially made me what I am." He said there was a copy for each of them on the hall table and he sincerely hoped that they would read it with interest and with some enjoyment and would keep it safe for their own children, "so that they may know something of their forebears and the world they came from and also helped to make."

Hamilton sat down amid warm applause and roundly murmured approval. But his children's faces for the most part showed entertainment rather than any deeper responsiveness to what had been said. Only Seneca, sensing the courage and ambitious application of his father-in-law's life, was moved. He alone had heard echoed in Hamilton's words a lion's roar in the face of challenging and chaotic events, something that, though not an introspective man, Seneca understood perfectly in his bones.

Dan was frowning, as though wrestling with some philosophical or personal complication. In fact, an idea was blossoming in his head. I myself could write a history, he was thinking, a family history. It could be done from a wheelchair. For wasn't the bardic calling perhaps a natural sphere of the disabled? People said that Homer was blind. Yet Homer's inner vision had raised the Greek and Trojan dead, and, in recounting their history, he had made them walk and talk again.

The others however had blocked the speech's valedictory tone with their ebullient good humor. After all, life lay at their feet, full of promise and, almost certainly, happiness. They were deaf to mortal intimations. Their father's life, by contrast, was substantially over, a closed book, by his own admission, while for them the glorious chapters of action had yet to be inscribed, and any grand retrospective lay unwritten volumes away. Or so they believed anyhow.

"Darling, that was eloquent," Jane would tell her husband afterward, knowing intuitively what he felt, that it had been so much chaff in the wind, that not one of them, not even Bayard, had any feeling for the force and wonder of history—cared not a whit. But in this he may have underestimated Dan.

Hamilton had known much hardship and it comforted him to see things in the larger context. To his eyes the present formed only the thin single stratum of a multilayered tissue that, viewed as a whole, gave the present richness and focus, weaving as it did all life into a developing pattern. His children's lives, however, protected from birth and replete with material advantages, had engendered a different attitude. For most of them the future appeared to be some sort of an extravagant, genie-led cornucopia designed to satisfy whatever inclinations and ambitions they developed.

It had seemed right to give them all the protection he was capable of, but later on he had had his doubts. No grit no pearls, as he was fond of saying. He had hoped that they would build on their advantages, going further perhaps than he had done, feeling the high moral obligation of it. And certainly Bayard had distinguished himself, albeit in a highly favorable climate, while Jasmine, with her half-baked schemes about art, showed at any rate a desire to make her mark. Perhaps he was being unfair, but observing the pleased, and for the most part, self-assured young faces round the table, a profound irascibility had seized hold of him. His children took so very much for granted. Well, why shouldn't they, of course?

For very different reasons Seneca too was out of sorts. He had wanted a word with Bayard, who was not easy to contact during the week. The anti-Buzby campaign needed Bayard's advice—it also needed his money. But even after lunch Seneca had failed to get a single political ball into the air, Dartania's steady flow of anecdote and repartee so beguiled her brother and all who listened. Dartania was a storyteller par excellence, and, rare among women, she was also funny, ready even to make fun of herself. Her mother's comic flair they said. But entertaining and diverting though it was, Seneca told himself that it was not conversation but a performance at which Dartania excelled, and it was inimical to conversation. Seneca had wanted to discuss the fledgling trade union movement emerging in the South, to weigh it against deep-rooted traditions of self-reliance, and examine its need of political support. Such questions interested him, and he believed the issue was a potentially important one in the South.

Seneca and Dartania had occasionally argued about their discrepancy of styles. Dartania, brought up to believe that well-bred conversation should be light and amusing, claimed that politics, like religion, was a boring subject, that what people wanted socially was fun—they wanted to laugh, or engage in a little flirtatious repartee. If it wasn't so, then the topics that interested Seneca would be easier to introduce.

Seneca strongly disagreed, but observing his wife's repeated triumphs, he privately suspected he lacked true social gifts. At the parties and country club dances they frequented, he fell victim increasingly to patches of isolation, felt himself to be a fish out of water, or was just plain bored. Moreover, he had made a number of enemies through politics and legal battles and he doubted that he was widely liked—one of the reasons he was so grateful for the warm and sympathetic welcome women sometimes gave him. Socially wary, Seneca needed to be warmly welcomed and, where possible, made much of.

With no one to talk to now, he removed a book from the stack on the pedestal table in the hall. Bound in brown calf, the title, *An American Life*, was engraved in gold. Hamilton's signature, also in gold, was on the front.

Seneca thumbed the pages. There were a few plates showing photographs of Hamilton's children and some poorly painted portraits of his forebears. A picture of Hamilton's mother, whom Seneca had never known, received a whole page. She looked a regular martinet. Miss Alice had said she was, that she had "suffered chronically from high principles."

"The gifted man is always generous," he read at random. "But I was not gifted, merely able, and the able man must cut his cloth efficiently for he has not the gifted man's unlimited resources, and so must practice that frugality which, together with tenacity, defines the able man." The sentence, though revealing, Seneca likened to a serpent biting its tail. Two hundred and ninety pages, roughly calculated, came to about four pages per year. But words, like Japanese paper flowers put in water, bloomed and expanded in the mind—a strange and wonderful phenomenon—so that a whole life might conceivably be captured in a single poem. One day he too would write his memoirs—or it might be someone else would write them; he might conceivably become that famous. It was a thought that gave keen pleasure.

Others had begun to crowd around the table, collecting their copies before leaving.

"Yummy binding," someone said.

"This photograph is awful. Did I really look like an armadillo at twelve?"

Taking a copy, Dan rested it on his knees unopened, in silent contemplation. The possibility of a worthwhile future was tentatively emerging. If he was ever going to make his mark, he would, given his disability, almost certainly have to make it on a piece of paper. But could he do it? Would he be up to it? He looked at his siblings gathered around the table, his sharpened attention mixed with deep affection. Could he, with pen and paper, make them walk and talk? The task seemed overwhelming.

Dartania, however, collecting her copy, weighed the volume showily in her hand. "Papa has become a lightweight," she announced airily to her twin. "He's reduced his whole life to about a pound."

"Oh for God's sake, Dartania!" her exasperated husband cried. "Get the children together and let's go home."

Seneca was getting so stuffy, the younger Douglases unanimously agreed. The problem was of course he took himself too seriously.

SEIZING AN OPPORTUNITY, as the others examined Hamilton's book, Stark had ushered Jasmine into the red damask-hung Victorian parlor. He had decided to exploit her newfound taste for the bohemian and invite her to the university Beaux Arts ball. To their surprise the new baby's bassinet stood in a corner, its organdy drapery crowned with a blue satin bow, strangely out of place in the opulent vermilion room, on whose heavily carved rosewood furniture no one ever sat. The infant was sleeping soundly, his nurse having slipped off to join the servants in the kitchen.

Jasmine approached the bassinet on tiptoe and, leaning over the sleeping child, eyed him carefully, then made a face. "*Pro*creativity," she whispered derisively to Stark, wrinkling up her nose.

"Stop being a dismissive, superficial little fool, and grow up!" Stark hissed furiously and, seeing the utter astonishment on her face, surprised them both by kissing her outright.

The phrase "stark-raving mad" tripped amiably through her head but she said nothing. She quite liked him, had come to like him rather more the past few days, but not as a suitor, had she wanted one. He was too dull. She now saw she must make the situation clear and resolved at once to do so, though for reasons of her own, presumably artistic ones, she did accept, while displaying an impeccable reserve, his invitation to the Beaux Arts ball.

12

The Prince of Wales's visit, which occurred early in October, excited local imaginations as had no previous event, for it pierced to the very heart of Southern mythology and culture. Luminaries had not been scarce in the town: Thomas Edison had visited Edward and Alice Nash; and Scott Fitzgerald, followed by Prince Yusupov, Rasputin's murderer, had been guests of Bayard; while Pavlova, Nijinsky, even the "divine" Bernhardt, performing on tour, were at the time much feted. But the patrician Southern mind, rooted in manorial tradition, yet lacking confidence outside its own provincial borders, saw English royalty at the top of a tall aristocratic totem pole on whose lower reaches they themselves were lodged precariously, like poor relations. Added to which the Prince of Wales was single and famously a prince charming. He might as easily have emerged from childhood fairy tales as from the ancient halls of Windsor Castle, and so imaginations ran riot with gilded if unspecified expectations.

The weekend visit, strictly private, was a carefully kept secret. It was not even known that the prince was in America, as, calling himself Mr. Eastman, a favorite pseudonym, he had sailed up the Carolina coast in a rented yacht, together with his equerry Tom Ferris. Ferris was behind the prince's visit, of course. He had set it up months before, as an excuse to see his sister Ellen, while the prince for his part could see, and perhaps buy, some fine horse-flesh at Bayard's famous stud farm. He could flirt with beautiful and flirtatious Southern belles and savor without formality the hospitality the South was famous for. It was just the sort of jaunt the prince enjoyed, and Nashborough's newspapers could be easily muzzled.

But only a month before the trip was to begin, the prince, without prior notice, suddenly gave up his stud farm and sold his horses at auction, in preparation it was widely believed for a more serious role, the king, as all the world knew, being dangerously ill. But the crisis passed, the king recovered, and the visit had gone ahead.

Though the prince did not buy any horses, with this single exception, he easily lived up to every expectation. His manners, charm, and good humor, the twinkle in his fine blue eyes, his handsome face—easily compensating for a slightness of stature—enchanted all, while his self-deprecating informality put them instantly at ease. Enough for some to wonder if in fact royalty was so very much grander than they were after all, or perhaps they were themselves grander than had previously been supposed. The prince's delight in all things American helped to encourage this view. He positively reveled in its easygoing style, lack of reserve, and open-handed friendliness—even if on occasion it transgressed, lèse-majesté, into familiarity. In short, America was a much needed breath of fresh air.

"Just call him 'sir' and treat him like everyone else," Tom Ferris roundly advised, and the intimate foursome at dinner on Friday night was an immediate success. Ellen, though attentive to the prince, whom she had met as a girl, was overjoyed to see her brother and introduce him to his miraculous nephew. She admired her brother's new nut brown mustache and thought him handsomer, less insouciant, and altogether more substantial than before.

Tom's good spirits bubbled contagiously, since, like the prince, he too found much in American society amusing, even overtly risible, with its transplanted English customs that often bloomed so curiously in new soil. "Your butler calls His Royal Highness, 'Your Royal Harness,' " he whispered gleefully, referring to John, as Ellen handed him a cup of coffee in the drawing room after dinner.

"It's the most appropriate title I've ever had," insisted the delighted prince. "The fellow has summed my position up precisely." He took a sip from the tiny Sevres cup, then still smiling shook his head appreciatively. "America is simply marvelous."

On Saturday morning the Nashborough hunt was to provide some sport and exercise for the two illustrious young men, and on Saturday night a party at the country club was planned—for the mercifully gregarious prince must be seen and shared. There was talk of a breakfast on Sunday.

The hunt met, as it so often did, at Herbert Mason's plantation out on

Auntie Nell Pike, an 800-acre property bordering the back of Timbuctoo. Robin accompanied the prince and Tom Ferris, as neither Ellen nor Bayard hunted—Bayard's equestrian interests being solely devoted to developing a first-rate stud.

It was still the cubbing season, when new hounds are trained prior to the opening of the season proper in November. By tradition an informal affair, members of the hunt were nonetheless scrupulously turned out, not a turtleneck to be seen. Most of the women, the prince at once noticed, rode astride. "So sensible and go-ahead; awfully dashing really," he assured his hosts, for he found it rather exciting, and he thought the women extraordinarily pretty.

By English standards the hunt was small, the field no more than twenty riders and dominated, as small hunts often are, by one family. Herbert Mason and his sons comprised the entire hunt staff: master, huntsman, and whippers-in, while Georgia Mason, a large no-nonsense woman, outspoken, well upholstered and renownedly good-hearted, sailed like a billowing galleon in the field.

Georgia had a tremendous liking for Dartania who, like herself, crossed male-female borders as it suited her, creaming the best of the two worlds. "Mind, if I looked like you, Dar-chile, I would just set myself down in a lot of ruffles and let the men coming running," she had often declared. "Yes indeedy, I'd queen bee it and never move a muscle, I wouldn't go out of my way for a one of em. I damn well mean it too." But no one could imagine Georgia Mason inactive for more than half a second, or sartorially within a mile of a ruffle.

Now, as Dartania with the help of a groom led her little filly out of the horse trailer, Georgia's strong voice boomed unselfconsciously across the lawn. "Dar-chile, come over here and meet the prince. You too, Jassy," she added, seeing the younger woman sitting in the car.

Dartania, giving her chestnut filly to the groom, and her gaze fixed steadily on the prince, made on arrival a little nod, offering him her hand. To curtsy in riding breeches would have looked absurd she felt, and she made up for it with an exceedingly brilliant smile—one that the prince was easily able to match.

But Jasmine, gazing absently on the scene, or through it, did not come forward.

"Well, Prince," Georgia Mason declared, as though at the beginning of *War and Peace*. "We'll call you 'Sir' if that's what you want, but around here every white man over twenty-one gets that distinction. It's yessir, no sir right, left, and center. Sure you don't want to run it up a notch or two?"

"Oh I'd much rather fall in with the rest," insisted the beaming prince, whose main idea at thirty-five was to have a bit of sport and at the same time meet some pretty women, which he found he was beginning to do. Ceremony was the last thing he desired, and he felt wonderfully free of it among these good-natured but well-mannered and considerate people.

"I'm told we're near the Nashborough battlefield," he said to Georgia between introductions, for like many Englishmen he was fascinated by and highly knowledgeable about the American Civil War.

"You can say that again! Why a dozen Confederate officers were laid out wounded on the front porch over yonder after the Battle of Nashborough." She pointed to the broad wooden veranda running the length of the house and shaded by the dark shiny leaves of twin magnolia trees.

The prince, who had longed to see action in France but had been molly-coddled at his father's insistence, looked almost enviously at the veranda, picturing this appalling scene. Having passed that war feeling like a ship preserved in a bottle, he almost envied the heroic opportunities of these wounded officers.

Instead of drinks served on a silver salver to the mounted riders, as in England, hip flasks of bootleg brandy were pulled out and passed around with impunity, and the prince, offered swigs from every side—before the flask touched its owner's lips—soon felt very jolly indeed. He was mounted, despite Bayard's strong objections, on a big gray stallion called Hannibal—fast and surefooted over jumps, but like all stallions headstrong and temper-amental. Bayard had wanted his distinguished guest to ride Old Hickory, a more dependable horse all around, for the thought of pulling the Prince of Wales from a mud bath or reassembling parts of the royal anatomy was most unsettling. But Hannibal had caught the prince's fancy, so Tom Ferris took Old Hickory, assuring his brother-in-law that when it came to horses the prince could easily take care of himself. Also that he was particularly sensitive to feeling mollycoddled.

"How many foxes do you usually kill?" the prince asked Robin by way of conversation, but Robin's reply was so vague, his guest wondered if in fact he hunted much.

The truth was they almost never killed a fox and scarcely ever found one. Members blamed it on farmers' shotguns and the lack of good covert, but whatever the reason the result was that when they did find a fox, hoping it would give them sport throughout the season, they were particularly loath to kill it. Today however all were prepared to sacrifice the forthcoming sea-son with a kill, being nothing if not hospitable Southerners and wishing pas-sionately to please their royal guest.

At the sound of the huntsman's horn the riders pocketed their flasks and took their mounts fully in hand. The hounds, yapping and straining at their leashes, were being led out of the stable yard toward the muddy cart track behind it and, reaching the big cotton field opposite the stables, were turned loose. Swarming forward, noses to the ground, even they seemed aware that today an extra effort must be made.

At the master's signal the field moved forward in unison behind him like a tiny if ingenuous cavalry exuberantly advancing into battle.

A low mist lay across the cotton fields as they trotted along the edges, the prince politely given a place behind the master, with Tom Ferris, Robin, and Georgia Mason close behind—Georgia's chestnut gelding wearing at the base of its tail the narrow red ribbon denoting a kicker.

In the first hour or so, three coverts were drawn, each of them small second-growth woods with thick underbrush through which the pack crashed helter-skelter, sniffing furiously but without result. One of the young hounds went after a rabbit and had to be disciplined by Eddy Mason as whipper-in, but at the next covert it unfortunately happened again.

As each of the coverts was drawn, the field waited patiently nearby, chatting and passing their brandy flasks, then trotted forward to the next one single file, as the crops, not yet harvested, had to be circumnavigated.

By eleven o'clock an aura of mild uneasiness had set in, with many sideways glances to find out how the prince was taking it. In fact, did they but know it, he was loving every minute. He thought he'd never seen so many pretty women, and astride, and he found the tiny hunt, with its paucity of foxes and endless supply of booze, hilarious. He particularly liked the look of that standoffish young woman whose dark bobbed hair and fashionable thinness looked so familiarly English, and he hoped they might before long find themselves in closer proximity. But just then, other equally strong instincts prevented following the inclination through. Drawing a narrow strip of bottom land beyond Ed Jeeter's farm, the eager hounds had suddenly found scent, and rushing vociferously through the tall sage grass, they charged furiously across the open countryside beyond, after the elusive prey.

"Tallyho!" cried Maybelle Spencer, standing up in her stirrups and glancing sideways merrily at the prince. She was sure she'd viewed the fox leaving the tall grass, saw the grass parting in a wave behind him.

"*Ta, ta ta ta, ta taa ta,*" the horn sounded, "Gone Away."

Instantly, and as a single gathering wave, the riders broke into an exuberant gallop. Now they were in for it. Crossing a pasture of alfalfa they fanned out broadly in a line and, jumping the rail fence at the far side, struck out diagonally across a fallow field studded with skeletal cotton stalks, the heavy, wet soil slowing them down like a movie grinding forward in slow motion. A cornfield reduced them to galloping single file again, and to queuing to jump the sagging gate no one could pause to open.

Beyond the corn, a large pasture fenced with barbed wire loomed, and grinning competitively as Tom Ferris galloped up beside him, the prince spurred Hannibal ahead, making for the strip of cloth that bound the barbed wire to make it safe for jumping. He cleared it by six inches.

Beyond the open pasture a deep gully, like an open wound, divided the scrubland from the arable farms. Descending into it pell-mell the horses splashed through the muddy water at the bottom and scampered up the slippery far bank, finding little footing. Robin's horse slid back again more or less on its knees, with Robin, like a boy on a rocking horse, smiling and rocking in bemused surprise.

"Shift into first," shouted Dartania as she passed.

The hounds were running frantically up and down the bank, but despite encouraging noises from the Mason boys they sadly failed to pick up the fox's scent on the far side.

So Johnny Mason, after a hasty consultation with his father, decided to draw the woods lying in a thin line along the horizon—in desperation as the morning was nearly over.

Approaching the woods, the riders listened anxiously to the hunt staff's cries and to the less frequent voices of the hounds combing the undergrowth. A mild depression had descended on the hunt, once so hopeful of producing a dead fox for the prince. A few flasks were quietly passed about as they waited outside the wood, and Georgia Mason produced compensatory cookies from her bulging saddlebags.

Blind to any anxiety, the prince enjoyed a healthy swig of Tom Ferris's brandy and, munching one of Georgia's homemade cookies, covertly ran his eye across the group in search of Jasmine. She was still at the rear, a little apart, lazily allowing her horse to nibble tufts of grass beside the track. She looked sad, he thought, yet it added to the attraction of her fragility. Should he ride back and speak to her? They had not been introduced but this seemed to be unnecessary in America, where everyone always spoke to everyone else. He could of course request an introduction. He fancied Georgia Mason would relish such an appeal.

As he sat debating, Hannibal, sensing the mood of relaxation, thrust his neck forward to munch the hedge beside the track. The prince pulled him up sharply, turning Hannibal's head toward the master in the proper fashion—something few others, he noticed, bothered doing. But the action unsettled Hannibal, who, shifting his hindquarters, backed squarely into Dartania's little filly and, getting a hysterical response from the animal, kicked out. With a shrill squeal the filly, began to hop about, her rear leg raised delicately off the ground.

"Watch your goddamn horse!" Dartania lashed out, leaping off to examine her mount's already vulnerable hock.

An embarrassed hush fell. The outburst had stunned them all. It was an accident, and besides he *was* the Prince of Wales! Dartania had taken unpardonable leave of her senses.

"And you better watch your mouth, Dartania." Georgia Mason was the first to speak, pronouncing her name in full.

But Dartania, whose one thought had been that the entire hunting season might be over for her, was intently examining the little filly's hock.

And suddenly, so was the prince, and being very apologetic and solicitous into the bargain. "You're quite right," he told her, "I ought to have been more careful, especially on an unfamiliar horse. But I think she's not lamed, you know."

The filly was standing quite still now, and, reaching forward, the prince ran his hand gingerly down the animal's leg. There was no reaction. "Just move her forward a bit."

Dartania did as she was told. The rudeness of her outburst had begun to dawn, but for the moment, silent cooperation was the most conciliatory gesture she could muster.

"I'm sorry if I overreacted," she managed a few minutes later, glancing sideways at the prince and frowning slightly. The sun glimmered through the haze behind him and she shielded her eyes with her hand. "She already has a weak hock, so when Hannibal kicked her, I thought that would be it for the season. I'm sure she's all right," she added sweetly, "but to be on the safe side I think I'll take her in now anyhow." As the prince was standing quite close, she whispered conspiratorially with a smile, "Besides it's the last covert, and though we never find many foxes in this hunt, we never ever find one here."

To the hunt's acute dismay, the prince insisted on accompanying her, leaving the members grudgingly respectful of his gallantry but waiting helplessly before the notoriously empty covert. Probably the single "find" had been the result of a drag, the scent having been artificially laid down by the Mason boys that morning. No one said so of course: They fully accepted the necessity of this reliable back-pocket plan. Besides they were used to it. But the day, all were forced to admit, had been a flop.

The prince however, had they but known it, couldn't have been in better humor. It was the first time in months that he had ridden to hounds, having formally given it up, and he had experienced something of a schoolboy's glee in getting away with the prohibited. Then his attentions had suddenly been riveted by a beautiful high-spirited young woman who, astonishingly, treated him like flesh and blood, had spoken to *him* and not to some awesome or deferential-making image. That she had spoken sharply—or was it something in her demeanor—struck a chord whose intensity caught him unawares, revealing he knew not what about his nature, only that like the doting Mark Antony he'd readily slipped off after her.

"I'm awfully keen on America you know," he told her as they rode side by side along the muddy track. The sun still came and went veiled by a heavy haze. "Tom tells me I'm developing an American accent, what?"

"I can't say I've noticed it," she laughed softly. "But if so you'll need an American vocabulary to go with it. We aren't 'awfully keen' on things over here, we're 'wild' or 'crazy' about them." The prince's use of the word "what" had brought to mind Theodora's incessant "What! What! What!" Perhaps the bird had been to England.

"Ah, but I know a bit of the lingo," he assured her, looking quite pleased with himself. " 'Here's mud in your eye.' " His own, like two aquamarines, sparkled opulently. "And 'Okey dokey put em up, you guys.' "

"You must have been taught by a Yankee," she said, smiling rather slyly. "Down here we'd say, 'Would you-all put your hands up, please?' "

"In that case I'd prefer to be robbed by a Southerner," he flirtatiously insisted. (And who knows, perhaps the gods overheard him.)

"But you're quite right, you know, my teacher is, or was, a Yankee," he admitted of Lady Furness, who at that moment might easily have occupied another planet. Her bright diamond-hard glitter seemed harsh when compared with the freshwater charms of the South.

Dartania's thoughts kept reverting with much wonder to the fact that she was riding through Ed Jeeter's cotton patch with His Royal Highness the Prince of Wales. On the one hand it seemed perfectly natural, despite the underlying thrill; on the other, the experience was too epoch-making to take in. She could tell her grandchildren about it, but that was a hazy far-off world.

As they turned along the Jeeter farm's west border, a startling high-pitched whinny suddenly issued from the pasture on their right, and galloping hell-for-leather across it, her tail raised high in the air, a bay mare was barreling headlong in their direction.

Instantly the stallion was transformed. Jerking up his head, nostrils flaring, neck magnificently arched, he pranced sideways toward the fence; then tossing up his head again, he neighed robustly in return.

The mare was evidently in heat, and Hannibal, as Dartania knew, had in similar circumstances bolted, jumped a fence, and, pursuing a mare inside a low-lying barn, scraped the rider off at the entrance, causing a bad concussion.

Now, despite the prince's efforts to keep the animal on the path, the stallion, in the even stronger grip of his genes, inched greedily toward the barbed-wire fence and, pawing the ground grandly like a menacing and angry bull, suddenly reared up slightly, coming down stiff-legged with a jolt. A second later the act was repeated spectacularly as a perfect vertical.

To Dartania's amazement, the prince quick as a flash got off, simply slid down Hannibal's back as he reared up. To have abandoned ship so quickly struck her, despite his august and respectful position, as a display of jitters bordering on chickenhearted. Besides, he now had very little control. Hannibal could easily rip the reins away or, worse, trample the prince should he not let go. Impending disaster descended like an icy mist, together with the enormous gravity of her responsibility. She'd been turned loose with a celebrated treasure: What if she wantonly lost it?

"Let go of the reins!" she cried out, her voice clearly registering exasperation as she maneuvered the little filly round to face him. *"Just let him go!"*

But incredibly, the prince was now preoccupied with slipping out of his coat, as though it had suddenly become too hot and, in order to do so, was holding the reins dangerously with one hand at a time. Dartania was in complete despair.

Having reached the fence, the mare strained over it. High-pitched whinnying blared shrilly from both sides in archaic trumpet blasts, when suddenly and without warning Hannibal plunged wholeheartedly toward the mare, throwing all his considerable weight in the direction of the fence. The prince was practically lifted off his feet, Dartania shouting at him again for God's sakes to let go, or he would be murderously wedged against the fence. But to her utter astonishment, with his free hand, he suddenly tossed his coat in a great arc up in the air and over Hannibal's head, blinding the intoxicated stallion. It produced an instant if intensely frantic standstill. Dartania was as dumbfounded as the horse.

"I'll lead him till we're definitely clear," the prince declared. His voice, calm and matter-of-fact, showed no sign either of fear or excitement; in fact it showed nothing at all: He was a model of self-possession.

Dartania's judgment underwent quick revision. The man was obviously a first-class horseman and fully familiar with the tight situations they could put one in. Moreover, she had imbibed a sobering double dose of English manners. Evidently the prince faced all encounters with a show of outward equanimity and politeness; his self-command was awesome. She by comparison was a barbarian. But the need for self-command had simply never occurred to her. The South, so like provincial Russia with its serfs and country estates, its lack of urban polish, displayed among its privileged the same ungoverned spontaneity, the same excesses of anger and affection. Suddenly Dartania yearned, as people will for what is farthest from their reach, for the cool-headed composure and equanimity of the English. But natures develop early, and hers was already firmly rooted and well watered in the South.

They walked in silence for several minutes single file and leading the horses, Dartania in front, the prince half dragging the reluctant stallion until the pasture was well behind them and the mare, who ran eagerly along the fence line to the end, shouting her favors, was out of sight. Then the prince removed his jacket from the horse's head and at Dartania's suggestion they led the animals through a gate on the left and down a shallow slope to a small muddy pond. Weeping willows edged the pond's far end, and as they approached, a pair of wild ducks skimmed low across the water like torpedoes. There was a fallen tree half in, half out of the water, and they sat down on it, giving the horses a full rein to drink. The flanks of the stallion still breathed nervously in and out.

The prince offered her a cigarette and, having lit one for himself, their mutual and deeply inhaled puffs sounded unmistakably of relief.

"That was a pretty quick-witted response," she humbly admitted. "I've never seen anyone do that before. When you dismounted I thought you . . ." The heat rose perceptibly in her face: "I thought you might get trampled or something. I'm sorry if I sounded rude." From the corner of her eye she saw he was looking directly at her. "I suppose deep down I thought you were some sort of city slicker, and I was wrong."

"A city slicker!" Reverently, he repeated the expression. "What a splendid phrase. No, no, scratch an Englishman and you nearly always uncover a mild, country-loving sort of chap.

"I've always been fond of horses," he told her a moment later. He was hunched forward, his arms resting on his thighs, his hands clasped, holding the cigarette as he gazed vaguely across the little pond. He said he had been forced to give them up: first point-to-pointing, then foxhunting. And recently, he said, he had sold his entire stud.

But why? she wanted to know. Who could make him? After all he was, well, practically the King of England.

"And what is King of England? A suit of magical clothes that so long as it stays clean creates awe and therefore I suppose respect. I can't tell you how suffocating it is to be inside it; how ill fitting for me at any rate, and how deeply I envy you your wonderful freedom here. I've had a hellish year," he added quietly, "and the nearer I get to becoming 'King of England,' the more straitjacketed life is—and will be."

Deeply astonished, Dartania was also moved. Vulnerability always touched her, though it was the last thing she would have expected from a royal prince. That so admired and glamorous a figure—surely the most envied man on earth—should live anything short of a life perfectly designed, amazed her. Yet he described it as a kind of slavery, and apparently gave not a snip for its rewards, which must be myriad.

"Your Royal Highness makes it sound pretty bad," she said simply.

"Do call me David, won't you? All my real friends do."

Dartania smiled in acquiescence, wondering nonetheless if she should do it.

"Freedom's a great thing, isn't it?" he said. "Like you Americans I too equate it with happiness. Funny thing, but you know it used to be that only kings possessed it—by fighting, by getting and then holding on to power. And it was worth the fight. You might even say freedom was the supreme trophy of a king; it was that rare." He narrowed his thin lips. "But life is full of ironies, isn't it? Today freedom is more common to the many than the few." He turned toward her. "You won't believe this, but to be sitting comfortably on a log without bodyguards, protocol, or forced pleasantries, and talking to a beautiful woman—for me that's paradise! I truly mean that."

A bird in a golden cage, she thought, entranced. But though touched, she found his vulnerability confusing. A Southerner would have covered it up, as something shameful, hinting at failure and loss of face. Yet he was undiminished. She looked at him with some tenderness, then remembering of a sudden the outside world, glanced quickly at her watch.

"I know," he said gloomily. "We'd better be off before they send search parties out."

They stood up, Dartania mashing her cigarette out with her boot, when suddenly quite easily he kissed her, sealing in the simplest, seemingly most appropriate way, their serendipitous encounter. Then, remounting, they rode the last half mile back to the Masons' in an unselfconscious, wholly pleasant silence.

The hunt had been back for half an hour, and as the prince predicted, talk of a rescue party was underway, the percipient Tom Ferris stolidly urging patience, insisting all would eventually be well. He knew his man.

Though the pair's return was greeted with immense relief, its tardiness provoked some penetrating looks and, in one or two unusually fertile minds, downright suspicion. Dartania was radiant. Riding gracefully through the gauntlet of piercing stares, she felt mildly uncomfortable—her conscience was not immaculate—but a sweet and heady triumph prevailed unscathed. And in such circumstances what young woman would have felt otherwise?

13

....

*B*lue Hills Country Club, a two-storeyed building with odd angular wings jutting backward at each end, was fronted by four columns set on a low concrete wall. Creating a porte cochère, the columns added that touch of elegance necessary to the high temple of Nashborough social life.

In the gray-painted foyer a portrait of Robert E. Lee, sitting in an armchair, hung above the fireplace and, opposite it, a kiosk for checking coats was occupied by the plump and smiling form of Earline Battle. A regular custodian of mink, sable, and vicuña, Earline's disappointment was acute when the Prince of Wales produced a silk top hat instead of a dazzling crown studded with precious stones and fringed in snowy ermine. And probably she was not the only one.

Off the foyer a broad hall with groups of sofas and chairs created several intimate circles. Two rooms for private dinner parties opened off the hall, and at the far end lay the ballroom, also painted gray, and lit by four huge chandeliers dripping heavy crystals. The bar, called the Chickasaw Room, was off the ballroom's other end, each bottle behind the broad expanse of mahogany labeled haphazardly with a member's name, in the event one day of a police raid. The noisier, younger faction gathered here, around the low tables circled by leather chairs, and at the bar, over which a maple-framed painting of the eponymous racehorse Chickasaw reposed. The club bought the painting when Blue Hills House was auctioned in 1910, both horse and painting having belonged to Alice Nash's father.

At one end of the bar, Jasmine was leaning on one elbow, dressed in a white above-the-knee chiffon dress edged in pearly sequins; she was flanked by Johnny and Eddy Mason. Avidly reviewing the day's hunting, the young men were even more avidly speculating on Dartania and the Prince of Wales's flirtation.

"She sure gave him hell for kicking her horse," Eddy, who was busy fighting Dartania's corner, quickly reminded his brother. "Practically knocked Ma off her perch. Now that really was a hoot."

"The two of them went trotting off together big as you please," Johnny Mason maintained. He'd never have drawn that dud covert had he known the prince was going to hightail it for home. "Maybelle Spencer swore the fellow had lipstick on his face when they got back."

"Maybelle Spencer swore she viewed the fox," retorted Eddy, grinning triumphantly at his brother.

Jasmine picked up snatches but she was really wondering whether she ought to see a doctor. Only a week ago she'd been a sane and happy woman, her future perfectly cast and, except for repeatedly faltering confidence in her talent, hadn't a care in the world. Now she was as sick as a dog, as miserable as it was possible to be.

It had started at the Beaux Arts ball. The theme had been characters from the arts, and, given her short dark bob, she had narrowed the choice to Hamlet or Madame Butterfly. Madame Butterfly she had every reason to eschew, so she chose Hamlet. The bottle green hose, setting off her long legs, made a becoming outfit. She could tell by the looks she got.

Stark had arrived to collect her in a baggy black suit with an open collar, a red cotton bandanna tied around his neck. He had on a flat-topped black hat with a wide brim, the sort Spanish flamenco dancers wore.

"The mayor of Casterbridge," he announced with a deep bow.

"Oh," she said, in that flippant tone she for some reason always used with him. "I took you for one of Carmen's boyfriends."

The ball was held in the depressingly austere venue of the university gymnasium, where she soon found herself engaged in animated talk with Jenny Dinson dressed as a Toulouse-Lautrec barmaid. An even more extended talk had followed with Frank Noland. Noland's costume consisted of a black Scaramouch mask with a pointed cardboard nose he must have pasted on himself. Jasmine couldn't help wondering whether he was compensating defensively for his own nasal shortcomings, but the mask, for the most part pushed up on his forehead, unicorn-like, made comparisons if anything more pronounced. She saw he was a little drunk. Most people were.

Only later did she accept that, despite his disagreeable shortcomings, she had made a beeline for him. In fact, if she was honest with herself, he was the reason she'd come. Yet how could such a foolish thing have happened? A man so vulgar and abrasive—no, not vulgar—there was nothing common about Frank Noland. Something off-putting rather, a rudeness of manner, an irascibility. Nor was he conventionally attractive. What he possessed was magnetism. It flowed around him like a lake of molten lava—Jenny obviously felt it too. And when Jasmine had danced with him, she knew herself in his grip in more ways than one. Not only was he the most forceful personality she had ever met, he was the most talented individual—his every act one of total self-expression.

Well, whose wasn't? Stark had pointed out. But Frank's actions were uniquely Frank: Everything he said or did had his own special stamp on it, an original style evolved out of the courage to be himself.

During the evening she found herself renewing the invitation to see her brother's pictures. But to her surprise this time Noland demurred. In that instant she had perceived with a kind of horror the absoluteness of his power over her: Their not meeting again would be unbearable. The poisoned dart had struck home, and in desperation she repeated the invitation, shamefully mentioning Bayard's influence in the art world as a lure. Had she given away how mired down and drowning in lava she was? And was her life to stop here, fossilized like those unfortunates who had not the wit to flee Pompeii? Was this then to be the end of her?

Noland promised to telephone, and protected by this commitment, she had left the ball in high spirits, thanking Stark profusely, and magnanimously allowing him to kiss her cheek. Jenny was not a problem, she reasoned, being so very obviously a convenience.

But as each day passed and there was no word, a feeling of loss, worse, of rejection swept tidally in, until she wished almost that death would come and release her. She couldn't paint, she couldn't think of anything but him. Her life had turned upside down, and for what? She hardly knew this man, this dreadful man with whom she had suddenly, inexplicably, surely insanely, fallen in love. Her state was ridiculous, desperate, unredeemable.

"I saw the Big Fish eyeing you this morning, Jassy," Johnny Mason punned. "But you were playing hard to get, too hard it looks like."

The prince had just entered the Chickasaw Room with Bayard and Dartania, who was introducing her husband. The two men shook hands. Seneca, easily a head taller than the prince, said something that made the great man laugh, turning to share his pleasure with Dartania. Then Seneca laughed in turn at a remark of the prince's.

"Come and dance, Jassy," Eddy Mason insisted, closing his eyes like an embarrassed child. He did it with everyone.

"I'm cooling my heels, not kicking them up tonight," she told him. "Why don't we all sit down?" And glasses in hand they followed her to one of the tables where Tom Ferris sat chatting with Maybelle Spencer, her silver lamé gown shining like an automobile headlamp, in Jasmine's jaundiced view.

The prince had performed his social duties with professional rigor, standing in a reception line for half an hour being bowed and curtsied to and producing genial remarks to match those he received. But it was soon obvious that, in spite of many attractions, he had eyes only for Dartania, dancing with her at every possible moment. Even Seneca noticed, finding them tête-á-tête inside the open door of a private dining room. Mildly irritated, involuntarily he was flattered too.

"I danced with a man who danced with a girl who danced with the Prince of Wales," Jasmine sang teasingly to Dartania when Eddy Mason finally lured her onto the dance floor. It was nearly 1:00 A.M. and most of the older people had gone. Those who remained were in high spirits however and in the Chickasaw Room, Matt Collins, who to everyone's relief had retained his good humor, started to juggle bread rolls, showing, given the hour, a most remarkable dexterity. The prince watched the performance with undisguised admiration, evidently finding it highly entertaining.

"Catch, Your Royal Highness," Collins suddenly called out, throwing a bread roll to the prince, who caught it agilely and threw it back again, putting a slight spin on the ball. Collins missed and the crust hit Herbert Mason on the back of the neck, causing much laughter, some of it embarrassed, because of the origin of the blow.

"Good God, I've been dubbed," said Mason, who, as master of hounds, was adept at handling shenanigans of all sorts.

Soon an improvised ball game was underway, the prince bowling bread rolls like a cricketer and Mat Collins batting them baseball style with Bayard's silver-knobbed cane. Eddy Mason moved behind Collins diplomatically as catcher.

"Tom Ferris told me that in Africa last year the prince threw all the phonograph records belonging to some club out the window as a lark, that he really knows how to party," Johnny Mason said. "I'm beginning to see what he meant."

Stark, standing with Seneca, watched the performance, smiling thinly, until Maybelle Spencer, her short blond hair drooping seductively over one eye, came over, and, making further conversation impossible in Stark's view—though Seneca didn't seem to mind—he joined Jasmine's table, pulling up a chair beside her.

"Having fun?" Her eyes, he noted, were glazed by drink.

"The mayor of Casterbridge." She introduced him with a sweep of the hand to Ferris, sitting opposite.

"Always wanted to meet you," Ferris retorted smoothly, putting out his hand.

Almost everyone's attention was on the ball game, however, and Stark, watching it too, said after a bit, "By the bye, I ran into Frank and Jenny yesterday, and they asked me to tell you they'd like to come and see the pictures on Tuesday at five o'clock if that's OK. If not, call Jenny, will you? They suggested we have dinner together afterwards. It'll be some dive. They're on their uppers you know." Then, downing the remainder of his drink, "I've seen enough of this nonsense. Want to dance?"

"Like anything!"

But the exuberant Dixieland tempo, as they reached the dance floor, trailed suddenly into "Auld Lang Syne." The band had already stayed an extra hour and rumblings were underway among the young to go somewhere else and let Ellen and Bayard go home to bed. The prince wanted to see a speakeasy, it was reported, and a party of rearing-to-go stalwarts had begun to assemble. But Seneca, like his hosts, wanted to go home, causing widespread exasperation.

Why was he so stuffy! they wondered. Dartania was longing to come, she simply must come.

Eventually a compromise was reached. Seneca would be released if Dartania could stay on and join the party. Ellen and Bayard would give her a bed for the night—there was one left—and Albert would drive her home in the morning.

"In time for supper I should imagine," Bayard observed, looking at his watch.

And that was what happened, and might have been the end of it had not Sally Nash knocked herself unconscious on Sunday morning, jumping off the barn roof in an effort to impress the cook's daughter, Little Delphine.

It was about ten o'clock when Seneca telephoned Dartania to say he was taking the child to hospital but didn't think it was serious, as she had immediately regained consciousness. Ellen was up, drinking her coffee in the nursery with William on her lap, and answered the phone. "Oh dear, how dreadful!" she cried, and kissing her own child on its downy head, rushed upstairs to wake Dartania.

When she saw that the bed had not been slept in, visions of a hideous car crash flooded her imagination, and fumbling with the pearls at her throat, she crossed the hall on tiptoe and cautiously opened her brother's bedroom door. He was sound asleep, even gently snoring.

"I believe she went to her father's with Robin," Ellen told Seneca, her tone conveying an immense relief. "There hasn't been an accident or anything: Tom's here sound asleep."

What Ellen thought ultimately about the whole affair no one ever knew, for she never mentioned it to a soul, not even to Bayard. Evidently confused when Dartania suddenly appeared, wearing the dressing gown her hostess had laid out for her, Ellen, with true English aplomb, quickly collected herself. "I'm afraid your daughter has had a fall," she told her gently. "Seneca telephoned a couple of hours ago but I got mixed up and thought you were at your father's. I believe the child, it was Sally, is all right though."

"I'll go home at once," was all Dartania said, though she continued to examine Ellen intently as the woman studiously busied herself with her little boy.

It was almost one o'clock when the Douglas Rolls, driven by Albert, bumped slowly up the graveled Longwood drive, and Dartania, wearing one of Ellen's dresses, got out looking rather fatigued.

Seneca met her in the doorway.

"How is Sally?" she asked, looking him manfully in the eye.

"Goddamn you to hell!" he hissed ferociously through clenched teeth.

Casually she stooped to deposit her things, but Seneca, not to be out-maneuvered, grabbed her roughly by the arm and, dragging her into the library, banged the door shut.

Dartania's own anger flared defensively. "Let me go," she ordered him indignantly.

"A stupid little twerp whose only *other* idea of amusement is throwing bread rolls about like a five-year-old!" He shook her fiercely. "You bitch. *How could you!*" And he threw her from him with all his might.

As she reeled, hitting her side hard against the gun-case corner, she suddenly perceived, buried protectively in his anger, how profoundly hurt he was, a deep and primal anguish she would never have suspected. She wanted to say it had nothing to do with them, that she loved him and had not meant to hurt him; it was a thing apart, the sort of adventure he would easily have accepted in a man. But as she found her balance and turned toward him, brimming with contrition, a pain shot knifelike through her side, knocking her to the floor.

"You goddamn little fool! *Don't you understand anything at all!*" he shouted out in exasperation, as to a deaf-mute.

14

....

"The Prince wrote Ellen a perfectly splendid letter," Alice Nash informed her husband with that triumphant satisfaction only a vested interest can produce. They were sitting in her bedroom in front of the first fire of the autumn, the coal piled so high they had been forced to move their rockers back, and now it was a little chilly behind. Coal fires were impossible to get right.

"He said Southern hospitality more than lived up to its name and that he'd never been better entertained or met so many nice people. Ellen didn't mention it but Bertha Fenton, who saw the letter, said he asked especially to be remembered to Dartania; she had been such good company and he hoped her little filly's leg had completely recovered." She let this sink in. "Well, he made quite a set at Dartania, you know, couldn't take his eyes off her, everyone says. He made no bones about it." Again the vested satisfaction was evident.

"Dartania is a beautiful woman," the doctor concurred, sipping his toddy from a silver julep cup kept in the bathroom for this purpose and staring transfixedly at the fire. The doctor meant what he said, but the sentiment underneath his words was dead, clouded by a mild depression. His eye went to the carriage clock on the mantel. In half an hour Martha would appear with their luncheon on two trays, but without any salt, eating was merely another effort. And yet he had so much to be thankful for; there was such ease and happiness in his life. Why on earth could he not feel it? It was as if a master circuit had been snipped.

"She *is* a beautiful woman and what's more she's a woman I can get on with: She doesn't make a lot of fuss," said Alice, who nevertheless followed the remark with a disquieting sigh. "Those two have everything in this world going for them, but do they value it, I wonder? Have they any idea how fortunate they are?"

The doctor, who knew only too well that you could see a thing and still not feel it, felt unable to comfort his wife on this point. Her own feelings always precisely dovetailed what she was thinking or doing; they never got lost or misplaced or became shriveled up in obscure emotional drafts. For Alice every moment had a felt intensity. It was an enviable, possibly even a rare condition.

"It worries me that Dartania has no interests, only diversions. That's no sort of life. There isn't a grain of pettiness or smallness in her nature. I know that. But what does she do with herself? If only she were a little more family minded and could enjoy her home and those little children more. I simply don't understand it. The Douglases are a fine people: attractive, brave, the best sort of people, but there's a wild card there somewhere and it turns up every time."

A red coal, splintered by the flames, flew sizzling onto the carpet, and leaning forward, Alice kicked it irritably back with her shoe. "Of course the poor thing never really had a mother, none of them did. They just racketed around over there after Flora died, and no one paid them the slightest attention. I've the greatest respect for Jane, but she was all for Ham; she was never much of a mother to those children."

News of Dartania's broken rib had reached Cottoncrop earlier in the week, the result of a riding accident, they were told. The rib had been taped up, Dartania had no pain so long as she moved carefully, and little Sally was as right as rain. They were still coming to dinner the following night, Seneca's thirtieth birthday.

"When I go down to give the dogs their biscuits," the doctor said, "I'll get a couple of bottles out of the cellar. There's still some of that Beaune left if I'm not mistaken."

"Oh, and a bottle of champagne if there is one. There must be one bottle left. Damn this prohibition!" She got up and went over to the canopied bed. Sitting down rather heavily on the edge, she picked up the telephone receiver, ringing at the same time the buzzer tied to the mahogany bedpost. "Rosetta? Rosetta! Don't forget to put plenty of sherry in Mr. Seneca's cake; spruce it up. What? *Has he?*"

"Ben's got some brandy!" she announced sotto voce to her husband, her hand covering the receiver. "Tell him to be sure and let me know what it costs. He does? Well how very kind. Mr. Seneca will certainly be delighted. We all will.

"Ben is giving us some brandy for the birthday cake," she said, returning a trifle stiffly to the rocker opposite her husband's. "Our bootlegger evidently isn't a patch on his!" She gave a little whoop of laughter. "Now I must remember to tell Seneca so that he can thank him."

Standing beside the icebox on the back porch, the latticed balustrade making a balcony above the kitchen yard, the doctor called the two black Labradors and gave them each four biscuits, leaning down afterward to pat them on the head. "Good boy, good boy." The dogs, named Nip and Tuck by Alice, accompanied the doctor on his daily walks, and their affection toward him was returned in full. The innate fidelity of dogs was curious, and strangely feminine, he thought, with its extraordinary capacity for a selfless devotion. It must be inherited, as so much of character seemed to be, good and bad. Yet every trait had its uses, he reflected, descending the back stairs—and misuses, which could be what created "bad."

From the kitchen at ground level on his left, the soft drone of voices, one male and two female, issued like blurred music notes through the screen door. How civilized that shared domestic arrangement was, and how affectionate. He couldn't begin to understand it, but it showed a superior form of courtesy that gave hope generally to the human race. He could smell fried ham and corn bread through the door. If only he could eat fried country ham! He envied them that, imagining against his will its salty sweet savor and the accompaniment of delicious red-eye gravy. Wouldn't it be better to kick over the traces and indulge oneself than to live without any savor—simply exist—he wondered.

The wine cellar, a half-basement under the back porch, was fronted by a nail-studded door, and, removing the key from his pocket, the doctor turned it in the lock. As he pushed the door open, cobwebs pulled apart like gossamer veils. It had been several months since he had visited the cellar. There was little enough in it nowadays, and what was there was treasured. The bootleg spirits they normally drank were locked in a closet upstairs. It struck him as odd that whiskey and guns were the only things people in the South locked up. They never locked their front doors. It was believed that whiskey and guns were the only things Negroes wanted to steal, and both of them led to overwrought behavior. White people were afraid of that.

Feeling along the wall inside the door, he located the coal-oil lamp on its shelf and, having lit it, turned it up as high as it would go. Then holding the lamp in one hand and the guard rail made of iron piping with the other, he descended the half-dozen stone steps.

On the left side of the low-ceilinged, narrow brick room a row of shoulder-high racks stretched like a giant honeycomb, largely empty. The doctor thought he had some decent claret left, some of that Lynch-Bages laid down before the war, but perhaps it was all gone. He knew for a fact that there were several bottles of Châteauneuf du Pape left over from the case that old Mrs. Wiggins gave him when she recovered from pneumonia. He moved slowly along the rack, experiencing for no reason an obscure anxiety. The blackened neck of a bottle lying alone was barely visible, and frowning slightly, the doctor pulled it out. Setting the lamp down on the top of the rack he dusted off the label. Château Haut-Brion 1914. He stared at it blankly, then it came to him. Seneca had brought the bottle back from France when the war was over. That had been quite a celebration, but how differently he had felt then. He'd been in his prime—and now paradoxically it was the bottle's turn, which seemed ridiculous.

"We have saved the best wine till the last." The biblical phrase crossed his mind together with the thought that, like Christ, people would soon have to figure out ways of turning water into wine if they were to get any in America, and he smiled thinking of Alice's determined attempt to make her own. Each year she made two or three cases, and about a month later the corks started popping. A merciful release in his view—the wine was far too sweet. Church wine, Seneca rightly called it. But Alice liked to keep standards up, and drinking wine represented such a standard. She was right, of course. He knew that women's seemingly small preoccupations with trimming frocks and fooling over flowers had built up civilization, that without their initiative men would probably have remained in caves, much like this one, which Alice had upgraded from a root cellar after they were married.

He decided to drink the Haut Brion. If they served some white wine to begin with, then had champagne with dessert, there would be enough for four. He scanned the racks and, holding the Haut Brion, moved slowly toward the end of the room. It was only a few steps and yet he felt utterly winded, as if some unseen enemy had suddenly hit him a ferocious body blow. Stunned, he leaned against the wine rack for support, and as he fell he was already mentally checking his symptoms, rightly predicting the searing pain that followed.

The precious bottle lay broken and the wine was flowing toward him in a dark red pool. He knew he must get up. His chief instinct seemed to be to avoid getting wine on his clothes, but a deeper knowledge told him the truth of his predicament. And yet he felt curiously light-headed, almost happy to stay there. Another symptom. He must get up, get help, and quickly.

He half sat up, leaning back against the wall, his knees drawn up to avoid the wine. Suddenly he recalled having hidden in the root cellar as a child, to avoid a whipping, crouching like this behind a mound of potato sacks. He could even smell the cool earth-moist odor of the potatoes, as though his nose were again pressed hard against them. He could almost feel the rough burlap against his cheek and smell, too, the cloying sweetness of stored cooking apples, barrels and barrels of them. It came back so vividly, and then his predicament.

He tried to call out, tried several times, and perhaps he did call out, or else Alice, with her acute sense of timing, raised the alarm, for someone appeared silhouetted in the open door. It was Ben, thank God.

The doctor made a feeble attempt to rise. Ben would have trouble getting him up the stairs, he thought, but instead he sunk back so that he was virtually lying down. The pain was now intense, it had moved into his left arm and upward to his neck. For a second he saw himself as from the doorway, like a man in a painting he had seen somewhere, raising his hand for help in a poorly lit dungeon. He couldn't remember what painting it was.

"Ben," he tried to say cheerily, looking up, and then, despite the intensity of his pain, an exhilarating thrill enveloped the doctor. It wasn't Ben at all. It was the Indian. The Indian had actually entered the premises, a thing he had never done before, in order to help him, and the doctor was flooded with gratitude.

Silently the Indian stooped down beside the doctor on one knee. His bare hairless chest shone like copper in the lamplight and the doctor noticed for the first time that his necklaces were made, not of bone, but of teeth—surely bears' teeth. But were there bears . . . ? The thought dissolved as quickly as it had arisen, for looking up into the Indian's deeply lined face, the doctor saw that he was smiling. This time there was no doubt about it, a wise and welcoming smile, infinitely gentle, as carefully the Indian slipped one hand behind the doctor's neck and another under his knees and, though the doctor was a big man, lifted him up like a babe. It was marvelous.

The doctor could hear his dogs barking excitedly in the distance. Ben must have put them in the kennel.

Escali, he wanted to say, such a fine name, he had often repeated to himself. Are you Escali? But that question too faded away, for as he was carried slowly up the stairs into the soft afternoon sunlight, a profound understanding came upon the doctor. It was something that had always been with him, but now, as the distractions of ordinary life dropped, useless, evanescently, away, he could see for the first time clearly, with his whole being. Everything was of a piece, it was part of him and he of it, an indivisible unity of infinite and indescribable beauty. He had always known it was so, but now he felt it utterly; it became in the fullest sense a revelation, marvelous beyond anything. A single all-encompassing truth. And thus, his heart bursting quite literally with grace, the doctor was gathered to his forefathers.

*W*inters of *D*iscontent

✛✛✛

*M*uch as the doctor's death marked the beginning of a refocus of Nashborough's generations, the party for the Prince of Wales provided the last great show of Nashborough and of Douglas prosperity, making a fitting high-water mark in the flamboyant upswing of the post–World War decade. Two weeks later, the New York stock market collapsed, scything in one great apocalyptic sweep America's apparently inexhaustible wealth. The tallest heads fell first, crushing or laying bare those more vulnerable beneath, mown down piteously in their turn. Like all disasters, it was sudden, and no one was remotely prepared, even though with hindsight, inevitability glares like undipped headlights in a fog.

Ironically, the first crack in Bayard's sprawling empire had appeared some four months earlier, at Chloe's wedding. Having missed the ceremony, Bayard had on arrival closeted himself with Papa in an effort to increase the already substantial loan secured that very morning. He was, we later learned, bidding on some big insurance company in Chicago and, expanding rapidly, found himself hard-pressed to lay hands on sufficient capital.

Of course a crack is a revealing hieroglyphic in any material and it must be made note of, but the first hint I had of anything being amiss wasn't till later, when an unprecedented event occurred at home: Papa went out to dinner. Papa never went out to dinner, and suddenly there he was, Jane with him, standing in the front hall in a dinner jacket and being driven over to dine at Bayard's. It was unheard of, like a river running backward; Papa really was that dependable, and even during the Prince of Wales's visit, everybody wild to meet him, Papa hadn't gone to the party simply because he did not go out at night. So we knew it was serious. But it was not something you could ask about. No one ever asked Papa for explanations of his behavior, though soon enough the whole world had the news and a massive number of questions were being asked too late.

A crack is, as I said, an important hieroglyphic. Their study and treatment would make a highly illuminating and informative treatise. You have to examine the damage, study the stress that caused the crack and the stress caused by the crack and then undertake the necessary repairs. And that's what Papa and Bayard were attempting to do.

Bayard had borrowed heavily from his investment company to finance the newspaper and insurance company takeovers, and he had borrowed heavily from Papa's bank to plug up the investment company's deficit. Temporary maneuvers: A sort of jugglers' golf game where, instead of filling a hole, you moved it from one place to the next till the money appeared to fill it once and for all. It was not uncommon practice and Bayard was an exceedingly accomplished juggler, while Papa, when it came to financial probity, was the Rock of Gibraltar.

A bitter feud broke out between those directors who felt the hole could be filled given a little time and the crack plastered seamlessly over (the family and most of the directors), and a few like Jim Jarvis who insisted on calling attention to it. Jarvis said it was his public duty to do so, and perhaps it was; the upshot, however, was instant panic. Within six months Douglas House had collapsed like a house of cards—it was that overextended. And unfortunately, its biggest creditor was Papa's bank.

I ought to have known that. I was a director of the bank, and when it closed its doors, 120 smaller banks throughout the South closed theirs. That's how tentacled the Douglas banking and investment interests had become. One hundred and twenty banks represented the savings of a lot of already poor people, who were now destitute.

Who would have thought a fellow like me, a polio victim confined to a wheelchair, could contribute to so much havoc! One hundred and twenty banks, thousands of families penniless, and many of them people who had also lost their jobs. I, Dan Douglas, was an accessory. I had lived on the bank's profits and I'd never asked any questions. Now everybody asked them.

It took some three or four years to properly assess the damages and point out the guilty. Bayard was criminally indicted in six states, Papa in two. But Tom Buzby fixed it, or helped to fix it—and this political favor knocked Bayard, as an *éminence grise*, out of politics for good. But in the end there were no trials: The cases were all thrown out of court, since by that time the affair had lurched back from a moral to a business thing that could have happened to anyone, that had happened by this time to a very great number, so that in the end, the disaster only served, like some medieval corpse hanging at the crossroads, as a warning to future investors. Meantime across America people went hungry, farms became worthless, thirteen million were unemployed, and everyone who'd had any money was flat broke.

And yet, strange as it may sound, life at Timbuctoo went on much as before. The trolley line at the foot of the garden was stopped and the number of servants reduced, but the clan still gathered—all that went on as usual. We still had family luncheons every Sunday and we still had the same things to eat. Papa still sat at the head of the table, and with the exception of Bayard, the rest of us were young enough, at least at first, to still enjoy ourselves and being together. But the great heyday was over, and from that moment, looking backward, I can see that the family, as a family, began its slow and sometimes poorly anesthetized dismemberment. Not that this was due so much to the Crash. Family life was everywhere in decay; it was symptomatic of the times, because other priorities were suddenly on the rise.

One reason why so much appeared to be unchanged was that nearly everyone we knew still had a few assets. When Papa had sold his Southern Electric shares back in 1926, and left the board, he'd asked for and got a thousand dollars a month for the rest of his life. He knew from experience that life resembled nothing so much as the weather, minus a weathercock, and a thousand dollars a month was a lot of money in the 1930s. Then too, like ourselves, many people grew their own food. And of course labor was dirt cheap.

It was chiefly cash people we knew were short of. But Southerners were used to that, or the older ones, who remembered Reconstruction. They trotted out their pedigrees and, mesmerizing others with these often imaginatively concocted shibboleths, kept the upper hand.

Bayard fought on. He must have been under a tremendous strain, but he was curiously able to abstract himself, to somehow stand apart, to a degree that confounded, indeed was misinterpreted, by many. He sold his racehorses and he would have sold his pictures, only nobody wanted to buy them, nobody was thinking about pictures. But Bayard refused absolutely to sell Blue Hills House, or in any obvious way to reduce his standard of living. Losing Blue Hills House became emblematic of defeat, and Bayard was, as it transpired, a most determined survivor.

But Papa surprised me most of all. It was inconceivable that being in a boat with him, that boat could sink; he conveyed such perfect security. When it finally did sink, however, Papa appeared miraculously to walk on water. He didn't moan or groan or change his ways or talk obsessively about his affairs or the past. And of course people put most of the blame on Bayard. But Papa, who must have been profoundly wounded, showed the same confident indelibility as before—though I think he suddenly was looking older, that was all that showed. The most interesting thing, however, was that both these men, who had been so interested in power, in making solid top-of-the-mark successes, when things collapsed about them, they were not remotely destroyed. Their centers were clearly somewhere else.

Paradoxically I was better off than most. A cripple is never told to go out and fend for himself, as the others had to do. Robin, having recently married Margaret, and despite never having had a job, managed to get one clerking part-time at the Cotton Exchange. There was no money to be made in farming and hadn't been since the war. In fact, it was a well-known liability, indulged in for traditional reasons by the rich, and clung to for other, often desperate reasons, by the very poor.

Jasmine's situation, on the other hand, was becoming hazardous for another reason.

My own uselessness, I suspect, gave me the courage to undertake this memoir. So much happened so suddenly it seemed to me our lives, and the times we lived in, would alter very quickly, as, in fact, they began to do. But everywhere, family life, as I've said, was changing, its traditions beginning to crack in that push for personal freedom so soon to accelerate across America.

Of course, Nashborough, like most towns, is a microcosm, comprised of myriad smaller microcosms, of the families that make it what it is. In focusing on the one I know best, perhaps I shall catch, if fleetingly—as the stroke of a watercolor brush catches the flight of a bird—some of those changes, themselves so microscopic, that will probably alter forever family life as I have known it.

I shall include myself in this memoir only peripherally, and apart from an occasional sally into essay, as now, appear, like everyone else, in the third person. But chiefly I shall endeavor to be a fly on the wall, seeing but largely unseen—not difficult in a life lived chiefly through reading and observing others.

1
....

*B*y June 1930, the Depression had only begun to bite. A few fat fish and some thin were already swallowed whole, but the majority of lives as yet lay clear of it, and despite the colossus crumbling Ozymandias-like about her, Jasmine was one. She was wildly in love with Frank Noland and after much overt encouragement had found her feelings more or less returned. Nothing else greatly mattered. Moreover, having long envisaged herself part of the vanguard in a radically altered world, she vaguely perceived that it was in the making.

Frank, for whom love had cost him rent-free lodgings, was taken in by his former professor, which was a compliment, Noland's work having so radically diverged from that of his cubist mentor. The room had a gas ring in it and Jasmine would appear with a hamper of food from Timbuctoo and make coffee or heat soup on their "aureole" of a stove. For her it represented the first staging post in their joint destination, a naive vision of which—two painters sharing every aspect of their lives—was etched as sharply in her mind as any piece of experienced reality.

Then too, a recent perception had mixed her obsessive attachment with a melting, quasi-maternal love. She had discovered behind Frank's freezing stare, his flinty shell and vaunting boastful egotism, the acute shyness and festering sensitivity he was laboring so boisterously to hide. With no protection other than this home-forged mental armor and a basilisk eye, and no self-assurance beyond those crumbs his hungry ego managed now and then to scrape together, Frank Noland was single-handedly taking on the world.

Jasmine's intuition told her rightly that for her support to be effective it must be absolute—and she had given it, with the exception that, unlike Jenny Dinson, she remained a virgin. Oddly enough Noland accepted this, perhaps was even in a corner of his mind respectful of it. But marriage must there therefore be, and that having been agreed, Jasmine boldly set out to face down family snobbery, inviting Frank to Sunday lunch at Timbuctoo.

It was not a success, but such occasions, essentially confrontational, rarely are. Noland's strategy was simply to refuse to speak. Dug into this unassailable foxhole, he reckoned to hold his ground, and up to a point, it worked. But after refilling his glass several times, his carefully planned campaign toppled before an overpowering instinct for center stage.

Pulling poor Stark along with him, Noland launched into a rumbustious monologue. "Of course there are people going hungry," he exclaimed, interrupting Stark's own commentary and speaking very loudly down the table. "Nothing new about that; nothing to moan about either. Hunger makes people struggle, and it's struggle that gives life its edge. What's more it's a spur. In fact you could call hunger the *primal* spur. You could even say that that is its evolutionary purpose.

"Those with a spur in their flanks, from whatever source, to my mind are the lucky ones. Sure, some people are going to pull ahead of the others; there are always going to be those who are out in front, whether you call them innovators or exploiters, creators or despots, depending on your point of view."

It fell to Stark out of politeness to reply. The remarks, mainly addressed to him, could not simply be left hanging, even though no one else appeared to have paid much attention, unless those eyes focused so intently on their plates counted for something. "If more people have a chance, more people will be able to get ahead," he said, mildly embarrassed. He felt obscurely responsible for Noland's presence. "As much as possible there should be equality of opportunity."

"Listen, old man," said Frank, brandishing his dessert spoon like a large paint brush. "Inequality is a by-product of progress, no more no less; you don't get one without the other. It was inequality that produced the pyramids, the Renaissance, and, if I may say so, our sitting here this very minute. But wherever you get equality, in some of those African tribes or out in New Guinea, for instance, it exists for one reason only, and that's because no progress is permitted."

Too astute to risk a major collision, Stark said that nonetheless providing an underpinning for those on the bottom was bound to produce a greater number of able men. Besides, not everyone was blessed with Frank's get-up-and-go.

"Wishy-washy liberalism." Noland gestured dismissively, though his tone was affectionate. " 'Underpinnings' as you call them end up as a breeding ground for dependency; they're the reverse of a spur. I'll eat my hat if they've produced a single giant—just you name me one."

"There hasn't been any underpinning yet," Stark calmly pointed out. "But this country is going to need a lot, and soon."

"May the best man win," Dartania mischievously injected.

"Hear, hear, Mrs. Nash," Frank called out, the bit still firmly between his teeth. "This Depression is a healthy shake-up, whatever else it is. And those without any get-up-and-go will simply have to accept their inferiority."

At which several heads rose round-eyed from the elaborate study of their plates.

Seneca was enjoying it hugely. For once Timbuctoo's tedious Sunday lunches were livening up. Noland's was an up-by-the-bootstrap philosophy but the man had a head on his shoulders. His rugged backwoods individualism, plus the fact that he at least had views, even if half-baked ones, strongly appealed to Seneca. "You'll admit the need for equality before the law I trust?" he said, entering the fray with a tolerant half-smile, "if not in social reform?"

Rubbing his tiny nose Noland returned the challenging smile, which on both men seemed to be saying: Show me how good you are, if you're worth tangling with.

"As a matter of fact I don't," said Frank, having quickly assessed his not unfriendly opponent. "I think the law ought to make a special allowance for exceptional people, ones who, through their achievements, rise above those who in the end will feed off them. Such men almost by definition are abnormal, and ought to be treated as such. If they've achieved more than the average man, and he benefits, why not reward them with a special license? Look at Socrates, Galileo, Oscar Wilde—all great men persecuted by the courts for nonconformity, when they should have been set above it in payment for services rendered to the world's improvement."

"You're as radical a conservative as ever I came across," Seneca affably remarked as they were leaving the table. "You've certainly worked out quite a philosophy for yourself."

"I have," Noland boastfully agreed. "But my personal philosophy is simple. Partly it comes from the motto over the entrance to the oracle at Delphi."

" 'Know thyself,' " quoted Seneca, determined if unconsciously to keep the upper hand.

But Noland confidently held his own. "I've improved on it," he said with a tiny smile. " 'Know thyself, be thyself, express thyself.' That's a motto for the whole conduct of a life, and as far as I can see, it works well only in that order."

Seneca, who would always function profitably in the latter aspects of this dictum, was impressed. There was something likable about Noland almost in spite of himself, though on longer acquaintance his didacticism could well become a bore.

"At least he's not a Communist!" Jane whispered with considerable relief to Dan. "Is he?"

Clannishly hostile to newcomers, the Douglases instinctively stonewalled strangers, and the value of anything Noland said or did could not possibly receive its due among them. The men chose to peg their dislike on his immodest and haranguing mode of speech, while the women noted with dismay, and later on with loquacity, the peculiar way he held his knife and fork. When asked about his people, all approved the ready admission that his father was an electrician in Detroit, but it made little headway against their disappointment at the fact of it. Looks were exchanged that Jasmine could sense without having to see them. She knew what they were think-ing, because in their shoes her thoughts would have been the same. She reminded herself that nowadays origins didn't matter, that being an "old family" didn't mean much anymore. And her reason muting this deep-set prejudice, her devotion brazenly unshaken, she privately declared a victory in the initial heat.

But Frank's appearance at a family luncheon had declared the attachment to be serious, and no one who knew her wanted Jasmine to marry him. In no respect was it a suitable match; she must be sat on quickly and effectively. Behind a curtain of nodding heads, therefore, a campaign of dissuasion was rapidly assembled.

Jane Douglas discussed the matter at length over the telephone with Alice Nash, but soft on love matches, Alice staunchly resisted membership in the ladies' ad hoc committee of ostracism.

"What a shame Bayard isn't able to buy the boy's pictures," she declared. It would be equivalent, given the situation, to placing a prospective in-law in the family firm. "It's hopeless now, I know, but surely Bayard could intro-duce him to the right people up in New York? Get him started."

Jane explained that Bayard's New York dealers had no more interest in an unknown painter than banks did in a pauper.

Who were his people, Alice wanted to know, and on being told, there was a pause. But Detroit wasn't exactly on the doorstep, she obliquely observed, hinting that his relations might conceivably be mothballed. Was he a nice young man?

Jane was at a loss. It was so hard to tell, she said. He was from such a different background, and then he was "artistic," which always made people odd. "Stark Fenton likes him," she recalled, "but even he can't see him married to Jasmine."

Alice wondered whether Noland couldn't do something less artistic, but this it seemed was simply out of the question.

"But they love each other?"

"Well, I think so: Certainly she's wild about him. She says there's no question of them living in Nashborough though."

To marry a nobody and live in a place without connections would be miserable indeed, said Alice. But more important, what of their poor children? What chance might they receive in such a world? Clearly there was no decent future in it, and with great reluctance, therefore, she cast her black stone, crowning the ladies' united campaign of dissuasion.

Dartania, direct as always, came right out with it. "I didn't like him much Jassy," she said, "and I didn't like him at all for you. But how you could think for a minute of leaving where you come from is beyond me. It would be like taking leave of yourself. It's inconceivable."

But Jasmine was dead set against Nashborough: Such backwaters were not for her, and she and Frank had more than once discussed New York. Though how to make ends meet there remained an unsolved conundrum. So Jasmine secretly plumped for Paris. The financial slump had not affected Europe, she argued, and it was well known that people could live abroad on practically nothing. But Frank was loath to leave his own country, even proved quite superstitious on the subject.

Meanwhile Jasmine countered the collective effort to sit on her by pointing out how much she and Frank had in common. They both lived for painting, she said, something others couldn't begin to understand. They both wanted to be out in the world, free and unencumbered, and not part of an established or conventional society. They loved each other, and being young and strong, could face anything together: The world was indeed their oyster.

But as she struggled to convince the opposition, Jasmine longed, too, for at least one sympathetic ear, someone if possible from her own milieu, and at length she sought out Ellen.

Poor Ellen had woes enough of her own. The Crash had devastated her existence, and sitting like Hecuba forlornly among the blackened ruins of Troy, she, unlike Hecuba, could not blame this calamity on the gods. Human culpability was involved—her own husband's—which made her anguish all the more acute. For the collapse of Douglas House, although fortuitous, was not entirely so: There had been mismanagement—that fact could not be sidestepped now.

Yet over tea Ellen brought her mind and heart to focus on the younger woman's unresolved dilemma. "I was impressed by his knowledge of pictures when you brought him here," she generously began, trying hard to recall the young man in more detail. He had been oddly dressed and she had thought him standoffish—defensive or shy perhaps. "He understands modern pictures so well, and perhaps he sees very deeply." In truth Ellen had not known what to make of the portfolio Jasmine had insisted Frank bring with him, but she had found it original, preferring however his companion's brilliantly colored cubism.

"Oh yes," cried Jasmine earnestly. "He does see very deeply. How right you are Ellen. But unlike everyone else around here you understand artistic life. The others don't at all—and they don't understand him either: He's too new-fangled for them, as Jane keeps on saying ad nauseam."

Ellen could see the young man was a fish out of water. He would be so in any polite society, and she feared Jasmine had failed to grasp what life outside it might be like.

But Jasmine had no idea of being outside it. "When he's famous, and he will be famous, I'm absolutely sure of it," she insisted, reading Ellen's thoughts, "he'll be accepted everywhere, no matter how eccentric he may appear to others—whose opinion we don't give a damn for anyhow."

A faint shadow crossed Ellen's composed and gentle features. "It may be unwise, perhaps even impossible, to sever one's roots," she said. "I find the older I get the more important they become; I believe we begin to grow backwards in a way."

Jasmine however declared herself to be a highly adaptable species, young enough to undergo transplantation with complete success. Nor was she one bit afraid of the unknown: In fact she saw her future so clearly it wasn't in the least unknown. Everything was imagined in detail. Visual images gave one something to work toward, she insisted. They created a mold into which you poured your life, giving it a desirable shape and definition.

"But adapting life to fit the imagination can be so arid," Ellen shrewdly observed. Dreams and real life were and should be worlds apart, and trying to unite them was a dangerous trick, symptomatic of an overly romantic mind. It could so easily bring delusion. "Mightn't it be better to let reality develop on its own?" she timidly suggested, lacking either the courage or confidence to actively dissuade. Moreover, she knew a woman in love would be unreachable, sealed in a hermetic capsule that could prove to be her chrysalis or a coffin.

Skipping easily over such diffidently presented caution, Jasmine, leaning forward, put her hand on Ellen's. "You're the first to know, but the truth is Frank and I are engaged. Look!" Pulling from her bag a tiny circular painting on wood she propped it up gingerly against the teapot. "My engagement ring."

Some two inches in diameter it was edged with an intricately painted gold band suggesting a frame. In the cerulean center tiny showers of something that resembled blossoms fell in an opulent cascade. "Isn't it unique! And Frank is going to see Papa tomorrow, beard him in his den," she giggled nervously. "Whatever that actually means."

"Oh Jasmine," cried Ellen, sincerely moved. "Then I do hope you'll be happy. You're such a strong young woman, far stronger than I, so if you set your mind to it . . . but so many things can happen in a marriage that are totally unforeseen, even in the most secure . . ." She stopped herself. "I wish you every happiness, my dear, oh I do!" And she embraced her warmly.

"I knew you'd understand, dear Ellen," cried Jasmine, having successfully concluded the rendezvous in accordance with her prefigured needs.

After she had gone, Ellen sat in front of the silver teapot wondering how anyone could possibly judge another's chances of domestic happiness. She had herself fallen in love with a most eligible young man: bright, witty, rich, and affectionate. Her parents had approved, despite their sorrow at her being obliged to live abroad. Then slowly the awful specter of childlessness had arisen and had seemed to threaten the very core and point of marriage, only to be exquisitely erased by the joyous arrival of her precious William. All had seemed perfect, the marriage in every way whole and complete, and now once again she found herself suddenly, gloomily, confronting a bottomless abyss. Her conscience gave her no rest. Perhaps she deserved what had happened. She had been so unreservedly blessed, she'd received so much above her due in life that now, inevitably, the gods had chosen to exact their price. Moreover she was guilty of negligence. Her clear wish to remain apart from Bayard's business affairs, basking in its sun without even the tiniest interest in its constituents, had been unpardonable.

Oh, she blamed herself, but worse, much worse, she could not refrain from secretly blaming her husband. She no longer understood him; perhaps she had never understood him, for he was not much changed, indeed he was not, and that too unnerved her. He had kept his dry and mordant humor through it all, and though she knew he must be suffering, struggling with all his might in the dark waters of unaided shipwreck, he gave no sign of it. Nor did he allow her in any way to share his difficulties. The pattern of their marriage had long been set, and to her great dismay she found herself unable to change it. At home Bayard expected the same inconsequential discussions as before, as if nothing had happened. Her isolation therefore was complete.

Yet how could they possibly continue to live in the same high style when others who had trusted Bayard were homeless because of him? Whenever she entered a shop, or as that very morning gone to the hairdresser, she felt sure people were staring at her, wondering that she could continue so, when, because of her husband, they were themselves shorn of a lifetime's savings. She had urged Bayard to sell the house at once: furniture, pictures, everything. It was only right. But he had refused, and in this he would not budge. He had even suggested putting the house in her name, to make it safe from his creditors. But she in her turn had refused, weeping and obstructing his wishes for the first time in a dozen years of marriage. The next day she had gathered up her jewelry and delivered it herself to the receivers. Bayard had been furious, but he admitted the jewelry was hers to do with as she pleased, and so the matter was dropped; he was never an unreasonable man.

But to go on as before, to behave as though nothing had happened, was dreadful. It smacked of Marie Antoinette's appalling insouciance. And yet surprisingly their friends seemed not to mind and had remained uncritical, even though many of them had lost a lot of money in Douglas House. Her dilemma weighed heavily upon her: what to do and where her moral duty lay, wretchedly divided between two interests as it was.

"Mrs. Douglas," said the young nurse standing shyly in the doorway, "do you still want to take him outdoors? Look like it might rain."

"Oh yes," she cried, rising and willing away the anxiety in her face. Here, after all, was her one joy, setting the balance against all the rest. "Will you bring me his hat and coat please, Annie? I'll put them on him myself."

2
....

*O*n receiving Frank Noland's note, Hamilton had replied at once, asking the young man to come to the bank (where Hamilton was spending a great deal of time with the receivers). He credited Noland favorably in his request. It was not a nicety Hamilton had expected from that quarter, though Jasmine perhaps had pushed him into it. She was mulishly obstinate and would, he suspected, strenuously resist the reluctant exercise of his duty to protect her, should that be necessary. As for Noland, Hamilton had not much heeded him at lunch. He was aware, of course, of a united female front of disapproval, but he had decided to reserve judgment till he had formed a legitimate view himself.

Noland arrived punctually. He was wearing a suit that belonged either to a smaller and impoverished friend or else represented a collective investment. The shiny blue serge was pitifully stretched across the young man's doughty form. The trouser cuffs, though turned down, still failed miserably to meet their destination. Hamilton's heart softened at the sight, recalling that he himself, at that age, would have been similarly dressed. Amused, too, by the stiffness typical of any youth on this particular errand, he shook hands warmly before installing Noland opposite him at the vast and unusually cluttered desk. Normally meetings of this sort were formalities, with reassurances noised on both sides and, once minor financial details were reviewed, finished with peace-pipe puffs on large Havana cigars. Noland however was a stranger about whom little was known, except that he was a penniless painter with no substantial connections, whom Jasmine, foolishly perhaps, had lost her pretty head over. Hamilton's sense of responsibility was therefore keen. He did not think for an instant that his daughter, who knew nothing of hardship or the world and little enough of herself—whose judgment, such as it was, was now blinded by love—could be trusted in the making of any decision involving a lifelong contract.

"As I think you know," said Noland, rearing back in what proved an untiltable chair, "I want to marry your daughter and she wants to marry me. We would both be pleased to have your blessing, sir."

Hamilton's own approach was somewhat less direct. He too leaned back, but his chair, mounted on a swivel, readily accommodated his intention. "You're a painter, Mr. Noland, a very modern painter, I believe? New styles in painting must, like new anything, be pretty difficult to sell. And we are living in hard times."

Guardedly Noland agreed that this was so and, on being delicately pressed, admitted to having sold "one or two" pictures. But the mocking incredulity he had expected to greet this minuscule figure was not forthcoming.

"Everyone must begin," Hamilton genially observed. "And given time and a bit of luck, it may be you will become a successful, highly sought after artist. A modern . . . Raphael," he added generously. "I know my daughter thinks so." But to this was added that love being indigestible how was Noland in the meantime going to support his daughter? What small income Jasmine had previously enjoyed no longer existed, as he surely knew. "My own financial position is very greatly reduced," said Hamilton, "but that does not mean I can allow my daughter to leave the safety of her home with no prospect of finding acceptable shelter elsewhere."

"She has some jewelry and stuff she wants to sell," said Noland, looking menacingly at his interlocutor, "and she's going to learn shorthand and typing as something to tide us over."

"Could you live off a woman's earnings, then?" asked Hamilton, suddenly severe. A basic canon was being transgressed. How many more might there be? A man's code of personal conduct was of prime importance.

"Yes, before I would give up painting," Noland replied with an impressive firmness. "Jasmine understands that and she's ready to make the necessary sacrifices. I believe she sees me as what's called a 'long-term investment,' " he added in a thin appeal to the business-oriented mind.

"Mr. Noland, I've known my daughter for some years and while not wishing to abuse her in any way, for she has many merits, I nonetheless believe her to be a highly romantic creature who will not stick at any chore that doesn't interest her, and that most certainly will include shorthand and typing. She has never worked in the ordinary sense, isn't qualified to do so, and in that capacity has no discipline. At her age, a year or two is a very long time and if I am not mistaken even great artists often only make their reputations well into middle age. What then, if after several years, your own situation is unchanged?"

"Then I must persevere," said Noland flatly. "But I will be successful. I am a first-rate painter, I can promise you that. If a man has talent, he knows it right here in his gut." He pointed to the appropriate organ. "I do know it and I'm prepared to do the work needed to develop that talent."

"I admire your confidence and ambition, Mr. Noland, but you cannot expect me to share spontaneously your perfect faith. Let me put my position to you in a manner I hope will help you to comprehend it.

"What if you were the sole trustee of a friend's estate and the opportunity arose to purchase a certain racehorse with the capital in your possession. Would that not be a very foolhardy investment, especially when you learned that the horse, though showing stamina and health, had never won a race? I'm afraid you're asking me to do just that," he said, regarding the young man solemnly but with some kindness in his eye. "I have absolutely nothing against you personally, believe me, and you may well become a famous and highly successful man. But for the present it is glaringly obvious that you are not in a position to marry, being totally unable to support a wife and children, and strongly disinclined to do so by your own admission. I don't wish to stand in the way of true affection were I able to, but as I see no prospect in the foreseeable future of any change in your financial position, and since Jasmine is at an age when her affections should be free to form an acceptable attachment, I regret I have no alternative but to withold absolutely my permission."

"We don't need it, you know!" was Noland's spit-fire return, but checking himself, added, "Though we'd very much like to have it, sir. Believe me, we feel sure that we can manage. Enough people are doing so who're in worse shape than us." (He might have laid this brutally at Hamilton's door.) "As to children, they needn't arrive before they're wanted."

Noland was going as softly as was possible when opposed, but then he had strong reasons for doing so. He and Jasmine had concocted a harebrained scheme whereby they planned to have a big wedding, sell all the wedding presents, then move to New York and live comfortably on the proceeds. But a big wedding needed Hamilton's consent.

"You'll appreciate," said Hamilton evenly, "that my duty to my daughter is considerable. I have lived in this world longer than your two lives combined and I cannot, despite what romantic novels claim, regard love as a be-all and end-all. Human relationships are as fluctuating as anything can be, and as circumstances change, believe me so do attitudes and affections. That is why character is ultimately so important in both partners. My daughter's character I know to a degree, and I do not think that, despite her sincere feelings for you, she would sustain them unaltered in a deprived and alien background. Her fidelity is not of that order. Your own character is of course unknown to me, except that I perceive on short acquaintance a fortitude and a professional dedication I admire. But Jasmine has no money, you have no money, and your priorities do not include going out and earning any. Therefore you must both be sensible."

"Jasmine's of age," Noland said shortly, hating to be crossed. "We can elope if need be."

"You can, but let me assure you, sir, that in those circumstances Jasmine will not receive one penny. She will be without the benefit of a substantial marriage gift and she will be deprived of those presents that, frivolous though they often seem, serve so usefully to set young couples up in married life." He stood up. "I hope I have convinced you, for I must insist my daughter break off all further communication with you while she is under my roof. And hard as it may sound, I would greatly welcome your cooperation in the matter. Indeed, if you care for her, I do not think you can refuse it." Hamilton paused, then said with some gentleness, "The best thing for you both would be for you to remove yourself from her environment. This must sound very harsh, it is harsh—"

"It's plain crazy," shouted Noland, who also had stood up. "And you won't get away with it." He was glaring furiously, his pale eyes almost murderous in their freezing hatred.

Hamilton didn't like the fellow's look one bit and, reminded of unanimous female disapproval, reflected that ladies were generally pretty perceptive beings. "It is harsh, as I said," he continued evenly, choosing to ignore Noland's perhaps understandable outburst. "And no doubt leaving Nashborough would inconvenience you in many ways, and, in the circumstances, be a most unsettling experience. But if you will assist me in putting Jasmine's welfare first, I will willingly assist you insofar as I can." And rapidly writing out a check for five hundred dollars, he handed it to the young man who without the slightest hesitation took it.

"FRANKLY, I SHOULD have had more confidence in Jasmine's future were he a *house* painter," Hamilton confided to Jane over backgammon that evening.

"Oh, he would never do," she warmly concurred. "Jasmine should never have met such a person. It's too unfortunate. You were absolutely right to send him packing." She paused for a minute. "Surely Jasmine won't do anything foolish—I mean run off with him. Oh dear . . ." and she moved the backgammon piece disadvantageously along the board.

"I'll talk to her in the morning," said Hamilton gravely. "Her young man will have told her the news. I expect she's with him this very minute. But no, I don't believe she'll do anything really foolish. Jasmine's head is well screwed on and it's my bet that in the last resort common sense will prevail."

Brokenhearted and defiant, Jasmine wept stormily and threatened her father hysterically, claiming she would leave the house, she would follow Frank Noland anywhere, and she would certainly see him despite her father's wishes. They would elope like Seneca and Dartania.

"These are not only my wishes, they are my orders," said Hamilton with formidable severity, standing before the library mantelpiece. "And so long as you remain in this house you will obey them. If you haven't the sense to value what all who care about you have with detachment unanimously agreed, it shows your inability to follow any line of action on your own right now. The fellow has no money and no intention of earning any. Any decent young man, if he truly cared for you, would stop seeing you for your own good—as I believe he will. But if you defy my orders and leave this house, remember you will not receive one cent."

In a deluge of tears, Jasmine rushed upstairs to her studio, where Dan, reading in his usual corner, regarded her with mildly skeptical surprise.

"Oh Danny, Danny," she cried, flinging herself down beside him and laying her head upon his inert knees. "I can't lose him. I'll die if I do. Oh, what am I to do? If we elope, how will we live? I expect I could find a job . . . I'd do anything for him, anything."

"They say even experienced workers can't get jobs these days. Things are that bad," cautioned her brother. He regarded her solemnly for a moment. "Jassy, you really do surprise me, you know."

"I do? I can't think why."

"Because I thought you wanted with all your heart to be a painter, and now you tell me you want with all your heart to be a painter's moll. Is that right?"

Through her tears the Douglas sense of humor bubbled up in response. In adversity it was always their joker in the pack. Irreverence, humor, laughter—mainsprings of survival, but mainsprings more usually associated with the oppressed. "You're getting so goddamned English; it's all those novels you read." She laughed a little, wiping her face with her sleeve. "I'll be both, just you wait and see. They won't defeat me. I won't let them!" But this splurge of confident defiance was soon blotted by a renewed outburst of broken-hearted sobs.

Half-distanced from the event, Dan sat stroking like a cat her glossy mahogany head, until finally the anguish of deprivation gave way to exhausted repose. Jasmine, in his view, had definitely lost round one, and it looked like a knockout blow.

3

·····················

$\mathcal{M}$iss Allen's day off on Thursdays usually came and went without her taking it. She had almost nowhere to go. But the annual Methodist Ladies Bazaar was an exception. Each year Miss Allen knitted a pair of maroon and green argyle socks for it and, on attending, bought two jars of Miss Ada Pearl Dunn's crab apple jelly, giving one jar to the cook, Delphine, and the other to the Nash family generally.

Unacquainted with the Methodists' social calendar however Dartania was incommoded. Having assumed Miss Allen would stay put, she had engaged to lunch that day at Robin and Margaret's. The older children would be in school, of course, but someone must be found to look after Phoebe. Cottoncrop was too far to deposit the child, so Dartania appealed at short notice to her stepmother.

Ladies were coming to play mah-jongg, as on every Thursday, Jane pointed out, but someone could surely be found to keep an eye on the child, and she could play with Cook Anna's grandchild who was visiting her.

When Dartania arrived, the ladies were already at their game, fingering slivers of embossed ivory with an air of high concentration, for quite a bit of money could change hands. Dartania was therefore able to exit quickly, and little Phoebe, taking Calvin's hand, was led off toward the kitchen. But not before the old man had reprovingly quizzed her mother on the front doorstep.

"How come you always rearin to go, like you gon miss somp'n big?" he demanded. "You ought to set still some."

"Oh I don't know, Cal, I'm just impatient by nature, I guess. I always like to get a move on."

He cocked his head to one side. "Act jes like you was a gypsy."

Dartania smiled. "Maybe that's it, maybe I'm part gypsy," she said, blocking his objections with agreement. "I certainly don't like sitting around."

"You out in the pasture too much," he said. "Stable door wide open but you don't pay no nevermind."

"I'm sure you're right, Cal," she agreed again, adding to her daughter, "Now be a good girl, Sugar, and do as Cook Anna tells you."

Calvin looked down at the four-year-old, patiently holding two fingers of his callused hand. "Well, come on now, little Phoebe. Theys a young'un waiting for you in the kitchen, and fore long Cook Anna gon give us all some lunch."

ROBIN AND MARGARET'S two-storeyed clapboard house, set back from the road, stood in the middle of a shady oasislike grove, surrounded by cotton fields. Driving up the avenue of poplars, Dartania could make out even from a distance Robin sitting in a two-seater swing on the front porch.

"Margaret's in the kitchen making a syllabub," he announced, his tone suggesting behind a faint smile that the work might be reckoned on a par with the casting of Cellini's *Perseus*. "She's a magnificent cook, you know. They teach girls that sort of thing up north." He handed his sister a freshly mixed martini and topped up his own.

"But what does the cook do?" Dartania flippantly inquired. In her mind cooking was the equivalent of housecleaning, clothes washing, and mucking out stables, and being in her small experience the work of an underclass, was tarred with the inferiority of servitude.

"As a matter of fact we've let her go," said Robin chirpily. "The slump . . . and too many cooks, you know." What was more, he told her, crossing his legs and rearing back rather grandly in the swing, cotton prices were so low it wasn't worth bending over to pick it anymore. He said they feared for their sharecroppers, who hardly made ends meet as it was. How was it over at Longwood?

Dartania, for whom well-bred conversation should be light and amusing, shied instinctively from so drear a topic. Evidently Margaret's earnestness was rubbing off on her brother, taking the dust off his brilliant butterfly wings. Nor had she any idea what "it" was like at Longwood and said so.

Margaret, her pregnancy much in evidence, picked up this thread again when she came outside. "We're thinking of giving up our share of the crop income this year," she announced with quiet seriousness, sitting down rather heavily in a black-painted rocking chair Robin had pulled up beside the table for her. A woven straw fan lay in her lap. "Our sharecroppers will go hungry otherwise. And it isn't just the Depression," she added, declining a drink with a wave of the otherwise dormant fan. "There's so much cotton being grown in South America these days, it's driving the price down here. We simply cannot compete."

"And then there's *rayon*," said Robin in a tone Dartania recognized with relief. "It seems I have omitted a prime ingredient from my initial agricultural equation," he added, rising nonchalantly to mix another shaker of martinis. "Even though plants are programmed to grow and multiply, the market as it turns out requires that people must grow and multiply at similar rates. It's called supply and demand."

"Darling," said Margaret gently, "that bottle of gin has got to last all week."

"We have recently drawn up a budget," Robin lightly explained, "and are submitting to its rigors with the zeal of novice flagellants. Ten gallons of gasoline, two cartons of cigarettes, and one bottle of spirits per week."

Dismayed by so much talk of money, Dartania was further disheartened when Margaret turned to the subject of cooking, telling her with earnest enthusiasm what a large number of things could be successfully pickled. She said she was showing their tenants how to do it, and in turn she'd learned one or two tricks from them, especially about salting meat. They'd also taught her to pickle pigs' feet.

"As a result, we're no longer living quite so high on the hog," put in Robin, his eyes crinkling in ironic amusement.

When Margaret went back inside to lay out lunch, there being no one present to serve it, Dartania chided her brother outright. "Robbie, you really surprise me, you know. Being short of money doesn't make much difference. We're all of us just the same and we always will be."

"It may look the same, but it isn't at all." It was the first completely serious thought he had ever been heard to utter.

"Well I hope you won't tell us all about clerking, over lunch," she retorted sharply.

Ignoring this tiny dart directed at his wife, Robin smiled sadly. "The subject doesn't bear thinking, let alone talking about, believe me. It's gray gray gray." And rising at Margaret's call, as he waved his sister before him with an open sweep of the hand, he stumbled suddenly against the rocking chair, quickly righting himself in a highly comical gesture of readjustment.

"Why Robbie, I believe you're tipsy," laughed his mildly incredulous sister.

"Gravitas and gravity are, it seems, inextricably connected," he observed with mock solemnity.

Over lunch Margaret's presence created a barrier between the twins, making their usual prattle and private jokes impossible. Conversation was forced, but Dartania admitted the food was excellent. "Papa's always said that if a man took his cook out to dinner instead of his wife, home cooking would be a lot better than it is," she interjected, hoping to leaven the conversational loaf. "And you two have proved him right." Then she gave a short and wry account of the mah-jongg table at Timbuctoo, and in particular of Mrs. James, sitting with a Pekingese on her lap "like a Chinese dowager growing her fingernails." She said Cal had "set her down," and had called her a gypsy. To which Robin replied that Cal had missed the true pattern: "Longwood, the country club, Timbuctoo, and Longwood again. You're running in circles," he languidly declared.

"Like all good thoroughbreds," she countered, watching distastefully as Margaret collected and *stacked* their luncheon plates.

AT TIMBUCTOO, SMOKED trout, grapefruit salad, and tall glasses of iced tea crammed with mint were being served to the ladies at a small table in the dining room window alcove. This ritual break in their mah-jongg game enabled the tom-toms of the local bush telegraph to beat out the latest news, and several topics were gingerly touched upon. Laments about the need for cutting back were freely and frequently uttered, but never once was any allusion made to the collapse of Douglas House or the Douglas bank—even in subtexts. Good manners reigned, which in the South meant keeping always to the sunny side and wherever possible using superlatives.

How was Jasmine getting on? the ladies wanted to know, now that her young man, oh so unsuitable, had been sent packing.

"He's in Detroit, thank God," said Jane, her own relief being instantly mirrored around the luncheon table. "Poor Jasmine's taking it very hard, as you'd expect. It is hard. I remember I was sat on once . . ." She paused ruminatively but gave no further enlightenment. "To tell the truth, we're a bit worried about her health. She just sits there, and if some diversion isn't found pretty soon, it's my view she could make herself really ill."

"Oh, a Nashborough boy this time, let's hope!" said Mrs. James, speaking with confidence of the tried and true.

"The trouble is she thinks she's above them all," sighed Jane. "Though I can't see why. She's got all these romantic notions: wants to live in a garret and paint and so forth. Still something must be done, and soon." A significant pause followed, and the ladies all leaned forward in eager anticipation.

"As a matter of fact we're thinking of sending her abroad. She's bound to get him out of her system over there, and hopefully this 'artistic' business too. Well, ladies?" she signaled, rising; and looking out through the open windows, added cheerfully, "How nice to get this fine weather; it's such a blessing so late in the year.

"Oh my. . . ." she was peering with narrowed eyes across the lawn, "has one of you lost a yellow scarf? Look, it's blown right over there into the fountain."

But even as the ladies were busily confirming they had not, Jane, calling in a strangely high-pitched voice for Calvin, had excused herself and was hurrying, running almost, toward the dining-room's double doors.

In the alcove the ladies, having sat down again, were peeking out, casually at first in mild bewilderment, then with swiftly mounting apprehension, as Calvin, followed by Jane, one hand against her breast, rushed across the lawn, their gait faster than elderly people safely ought to move. Mrs. Ellis was busy saying as much, more in wonder than dismay, when suddenly a chilling shriek, its anguish unmistakable, escaped from Jane and sent the ladies rushing terrified to the alcove window.

Jane was leaning precariously over the low rim of the fountain, holding out her hands, as Calvin, rapidly but with such evident caution, gingerly lifted out the scarf that was not a scarf and, from the alcove, appeared at first to be a bundle of clothes.

In that second, utter silence descended in a clap, for the ladies had recalled there was a grandchild on the place.

Gazing in growing horror as the tragedy relentlessly unfolded, no longer able to meet each other's gaze, the ladies nonetheless clutched one another tightly and held on. For it was clear from the way the little leg dangled from the cradle of Calvin's arms that the child was almost certainly dead.

An incessant whimpering had sprung up from Mrs. James's little Pekingese.

Jane, out of breath, her gray hair coming unpinned, held open the front door for Calvin. "Lay her down on the sofa there," she whispered huskily, reaching forward as he passed to touch the little face lightly, helplessly, with her free hand.

"Nome, be better to put her upstairs on the bed," said Calvin, whose rheumy eyes expressed a grief that Jane, under the impact of despairing fear and horror, had yet to fully feel herself.

"Oh yes, that is better . . ." She turned around aimlessly in the hall, first toward the dining room, then back to the old man going slowly up the stairs, the little inert body in his arms, then with a look of terror toward the telephone on the wall, its mouthpiece protruding like that of an evil mask. "I must call my husband," she murmured aloud, shock still performing, if imperfectly, its biological shield.

The three ladies, horrified and deeply embarrassed by being spectators at so terrible and deeply personal an event, released themselves from confinement in the dining room and, creeping forward, clustered wordlessly around Jane, embracing her where she sat, for she had not looked up.

"Is she . . . ?" Mrs. James began, and when Jane nodded into her handkerchief, they moaned softly in the fateful, futile unison of Greek choruses.

"I must call my husband," Jane repeated vaguely, and the ladies understood at once the full extent of notification weighing on her.

"Is there anything . . . can we . . . ?"

She assured them with a rapid motion of her hand that there was nothing. "You must let me see you out," she volunteered gently, the instinct producing a fleeting shred of normality.

Of course the ladies wouldn't hear of it. They would telephone first thing tomorrow. "Now, you just sit right there," they told her, and as Calvin came downstairs, they departed hurriedly in a despairing huddle.

"All these years we done worried bout that creek," Calvin said sorrowfully from the stairs, "and heah come this . . ."

Word had reached the kitchen, and Cook Anna appeared in the hall, her apron to her face. "I done told Annie Lou to stay with her," she spluttered helplessly, hopelessly. "Oh Mrs. Douglas, I can't tell you how awful I feel. Oh I pray the good Lord to come and take me, and give that po child back her life!"

"It's all right, Anna," Jane comforted. "It wasn't your fault and you mustn't think so, ever. You go on now and see to Annie Lou. She must be dreadfully upset."

Gravely, Hamilton asked the necessary questions. It seemed the girl, who was supposed to keep an eye on Phoebe, had left her for five minutes; she was only a child herself and had gone to the kitchen to fetch a skipping rope. Jane begged her husband to call Dartania at Robin's. "Oh God, try and catch her before she leaves! Try and prepare her. Oh I feel so *responsible!*"

AN HOUR LATER Dartania and Seneca were sitting side by side on Timbuctoo's library sofa, and Hamilton, standing before the fireplace, was reminded how very young they were, untouched till now by disaster or by sorrow of any kind. And yet they took it in their stride, he thought, pleased by their show of inner fortitude.

Dartania had said almost nothing, and Seneca, finding little he could do there that was practical, prepared to go to Cottoncrop and break the dire news to Miss Alice. All agreed this was imperative, before his mother should hear of it from others.

"Would you like to go up and sit with her?" inquired Jane softly, sitting down beside Dartania, who resolutely shook her head.

"I think you'd feel so much better if you did," the elder woman urged, partly restored to a functioning being, since no one appeared to hold the tragedy against her. It was seen by all as an accident pure and simple. And yet she could not refrain from blurting out her apologies. "If only I'd looked out the window sooner . . . if only I hadn't let . . ." she kept on repeating to no one in particular.

Dartania continued to sit on the sofa, enfolded in the fragile security of deep bewilderment. The sight of that vacated little body had been horrible, for it was not at all like sleep. Yet despite the horror of it, she had felt no devastating anguish, no wrench of heartbreak or abysmal chasm of loss, and so did not pretend to it. She was aware chiefly that something very momentous, but also strangely unreal, strangely remote, had happened. She'd heard women say a mother never got over the loss of her child, but people in the past had lost too many for it to be always true. Her own mother had lost two.

And at the thought of her mother, whom she could just remember, laughing at her and tying a red silk ribbon around her disheveled hair, calling her a hoyden, a sudden almost overwhelming and unnerving sadness, cousinage to grief, crept stealthily over her. It was broken by the thought of her old nurse saying so often and with such now comforting acquiescence, "Lord knows, you can't expect to raise em all." The remembrance of this oft-repeated maxim, and the old black woman's cheerful resignation, lifted Dartania's spirits slightly, and she clung to it as sailors cling tenaciously to a ship's mast in heavy storm.

Seneca, still distanced from the actual tragedy, was dreading the harrowing distress the news would cause his mother. His keenest dismay just then was that he should give her pain. She imagined so many disasters as it was, and worried incessantly—it had got much worse with age and since his father's death. How could she sustain the heavy blow of real calamity?

To his great surprise however Alice took the terrible announcement in her stride; her reserves of fortitude, her philosophical acceptance of fate's invincible power, proved to be far greater than her son supposed was possible. Later that evening Alice even telephoned to reassure poor Jane, who was convinced that Alice Nash would never speak to her again, would blame her unreservedly for what happened. The call gave infinite balm.

But wisely, Alice, in the midst of things that must be done, did not contact Dartania. The Douglases always buried or rejected difficult feelings. Time and again she had seen it happen. The trait, not unusual in men, was, in Alice's view, unfortunate in women; and again she lamented the lack of affectionate female counsel in Dartania's youth. But as the young woman's feelings could not be reached or soothed, Alice knew her commiseration would be unwelcome. It would force Dartania into empty words of response, putting her thereby in a painfully false position.

As the news spread, becoming the talk of the town, local ponds were rapidly fenced in and several mothers lowered the level of their offsprings' bath water. The country club swimming pool, only recently opened, was closed suddenly for "repairs."

There followed too the inevitable avalanche of condolences, but mercifully much of it went to Cottoncrop and Timbuctoo. Expressed in often banal outpourings and the usual clichés, Jane Douglas and Alice Nash perceived the letters' heartfelt gist and were grateful for the kindnesses of friends. It eased their grief as it was meant to do.

But Dartania loathed receiving such letters, and jibbing instinctively at their sugary content, answered none. It was none of their business; it was entirely a family matter and, among the Douglases, such things, being private, were therefore never discussed. Which was how it ought to be.

THE CHIEF MOURNER at Longwood was of course Miss Allen, who wept long and piteously for her innocent lamb. The warm plump arms no longer around her neck were as an amputation; the tender focus of her care-worn days, sharply and forever erased, left her bereft and sad.

"Your little sister has gone to heaven," she told Sally and Emma who, though envious of such a desirable-sounding trip, were quite pleased nonetheless to be rid of her.

"I have just as many stars in my heavenly crown as Phoebe, haven't I, Miss Allie?" Emma asked, mulling some possible injustice.

Of necessity Miss Allen now found it necessary to consider her future, and she was badly frightened. Sally and Emma would soon have little need of her, and where at her age would she find another post? Without one, how would she live? Gazing out the nursery window into the dark, as rain pelted upon the panes and the long wood rose gloomily in the distance, Miss Allen visibly trembled. All she loved and had so lovingly nurtured threatened of a sudden to disappear. It had happened before, repeatedly, but this time would be final. And as her uneasiness grew, her sweet nunlike smile took on a pleading nervousness in the presence of her employers. Lame, orphaned, and now old, the world made little provision for Miss Allen and her kind once their usefulness was gone.

4

....

As the months went by and the trauma of Phoebe's death began to recede, Jasmine's plight willy-nilly returned of necessity to center stage at Timbuctoo. Finally the much discussed restorative was agreed upon. Jasmine was to go to Paris for a year. She would study at a reputable art school, unearthed through Bayard's connections, and she would receive, in addition to its fees, a monthly allowance, modest but sufficient for her needs. Nashborough friends who "traveled" were appealed to for introductions and a few secured, though Jasmine, convinced that they would be foreign versions of what she had grown up with, had no intention of looking any of them up. Her departure having been fixed for February, a tutor was hired to advance her rudimentary knowledge of the language.

As to Jasmine's aching heart in the midst of so much bustle and absorbing preparation, all was not quite as it seemed. It still ached, ached horribly at times, for she longed passionately to be with Frank again; but the festering open wound of frustrated love was much alleviated. Secretly the couple were keeping up an intimate correspondence via a private postal box.

In accepting Hamilton's five hundred dollars, Frank had engineered his own piece of pragmatic reasoning. He felt himself duty bound to seize on any straw that helped his work progress, which naturally the acquisition of money did. Moreover, as an artist, he held himself outside the tight-laced corset of bourgeois morality. If Hamilton wanted to bend him to his will by exploiting his need of money, he in turn was free to adapt Hamilton's unacceptable desires to his own needs and wishes.

But if Frank's ready misuse of Hamilton's check was in its way morally suspect, what of Jasmine's considerably larger deception? It was she who in their letters had erected the scaffolding and, later on, the completed construction, of a scheme perfectly in keeping with her needs, a scheme that in its fine simplicity seemed highly unlikely to fail. The idea was that Frank should join her clandestinely in Paris. Hamilton's severance check would more than provide the fare and meantime Frank was saving money living at home. Once in Paris they would marry and could live and paint in comfort, thanks to Jasmine's allowance. Eventually of course they would come clean and show they had been right to follow so apparently nefarious a course. After all, Seneca and Dartania had married secretly, and no one had ever called that devious. And when Jasmine and Frank finally announced the news they would have more to show for it than just a baby.

JASMINE ARRIVED IN Paris three weeks in advance of Frank, her prayers answered, her hopes fulfilled, and every impediment successfully overcome. She had achieved it entirely by the application of her wits and fortitude, and she deserved the booty of Paris—to which was added the profoundly female joy of building a nest in its bosom.

Within twenty-four hours she had rented a studio in a tumbledown neighborhood north of Montparnasse. A bedroom, bath, and tiny kitchen were clustered at one end like apsidal chapels. Eagerly Jasmine began at once to paint, but not on canvas; she was too busy painting walls, and under her brush the studio emerged looking larger and pristinely white. She even sanded the old floorboards splotched here and there with the oily droppings of numerous predecessors. In the flea market she bought a secondhand bed and a badly sprung sofa covered in brown rep, an easy chair and a small drop leaf table that could be pushed against the studio wall. Nor could she resist at least one decorative bauble—a gaudy orange-red candelabrum, its branches festooned with brightly painted birds from Mexico. Never in her life had she felt so creative, for having conceived a vision of her future existence, she was successfully bringing it to life.

For a few hours each day she gave herself up to the allures of Paris, walking along the broad boulevards and leafless tree-lined streets lit by an opalescent winter light. Paris was the first great city she had ever seen. Its grandiose architecture, set so unselfconsciously alongside homely side streets and cafés where people seemed to sit all day, enthralled her utterly. She marveled at the overpowering hulk of Notre Dame and the vast, seeming-unending expanses of the Louvre (whose doors she had yet to enter; she would wait for Frank). But the museum's magnificently carved architectural relief made it seem fit for gods, not men, or even kings (artists very rightly Frank would say). She was fascinated, too, by the old *hotels particuliers* with their courtyards and concierges, their magnificent high-rising slate roofs pierced with elegant dormers, and the huge double entry doors through which, until recently, horse-drawn carriages would have clattered. Some of these buildings, she learned, still belonged to grand and ancient families, each generation occupying quarters of its own, as in a well-appointed if not very industrious hive.

Then one afternoon, window shopping in the elegant Faubourg St. Honoré, she saw something totally unprecedented and extraordinary. A tall, svelte magnificently dressed woman came out of Mainbocher. Her hair was combed severely back in a bun and the tiny cone of a most elegant hat was perched miraculously on one side of her head. Walking idly in front of the woman, there strode a leopard on a leash, its head moving sinuously to left and right, its collar glittering with brilliant stones. But most astonishing of all, the woman was black. Jasmine stared in disbelief. Others stared, too, and as this remarkable vision passed, a quiet applause sounded in accolade on both sides of the street.

"*Qui est-ce?*" whispered Jasmine to an elderly woman standing beside her, holding a glossy hatbox.

"Good heavens," replied the admiring English voice. "Why, my dear, that's Josephine Baker. She's the toast of Paris!"

For the rest of her life, and the many changes that would accompany it, that image always epitomized for Jasmine the wonder and exotica that was Paris in the early thirties, when in one grand euphoric blaze her world had turned upon its axis giddily upside down.

ON THE APPOINTED day, Frank's ship arrived and on the virtually empty deck stood Frank, gazing stiffly about him with measured wariness, sizing everything up carefully, as a man might do finding himself suddenly on the borders of a dark and hostile forest.

But the studio, or *atelier* as Jasmine called it, produced in Frank raised eyebrows and a soft admiring whistle of approbation. He began to set out his things. Yes, he told her after another kiss, he was going to paint; he had been unable to do so for the past ten days. What was more, Paris could easily wait a day, since, unlike him, it wasn't going anywhere.

Jasmine sat down on the brown rep sofa, gazing at Frank as on the globe itself, and in whose orbit she was now so firmly set. Then after a bit, humming lightly, she went out to the nearby market to buy their food for dinner. It would be the first meal she had ever cooked and wisely she kept to paté, charcuterie, and pastry, attempting with some success to dress and toss a salad.

A few days later they were married in a registry office exactly as planned; their witnesses were the concierge (anxious that her house preserve its respectability) and a waiter met that morning in the local café. Ostensibly it was a humdrum affair, but to the principals it was grander than the very grandest wedding, a unique event in keeping with their newfound freedom and rare soon-to-be-applauded originality.

*N*ot many weeks after Jasmine's departure, Dartania, to her acute dismay, discovered she was pregnant. The thought of another life mysteriously asserting itself, blowing her body out like a sideshow monstrosity, was as bewildering and incomprehensible as it was undesired, and with Phoebe dead barely six months there was obscure embarrassment in the timing. Women in the past, Dartania read, sometimes claimed to be possessed by alien forces, devils, and the like, and she could guess at some of the origins: her own body now housed uninvited a voracious parasite.

"Ugh," she blurted in disgust to Robin, combining in one girlish outcry all her feelings on the subject. But as Margaret had just given birth to a baby girl, Robin was loyally noncommittal, even though Dartania sensed he shared her own sharp-edged bewilderment.

"Raising the population raises in multiples the demand for cotton," he smilingly observed, "and other staples. We must all do our part."

UNCHARACTERISTICALLY DARTANIA KEPT her true feelings about the baby from Seneca. A minute change in the microclimate of their relations, exacerbated in part by her brief dalliance with the Prince of Wales, now hung like an impenetrable film between them—a film whose fabrication had been slow, subtle, and unperceived. But the Prince of Wales episode was not its origin. At the time, Dartania had longed to say how meaningless that adventure was, that it had nothing to do with them, and that in a man would be forgotten as an inconsequent peccadillo. It was no different with her. But instinct urged her not to transform into adamantine fact what, despite some evidence, must otherwise retain the fluidity of conjecture— and so more easily flow away. And it had. She loved Seneca and had made it up to him. Phoebe's death had thrown the incident further into the past, and the impenetrable film was simply a buildup of the detritus all marriages collected, though few married couples would admit to it. Yet Dartania failed to see why Seneca welcomed so eagerly another child. Of course, he wanted a son. Well, so did she if in fact they must have something.

Only recently and for the first time had Seneca begun to consider at any length his role as a family man. The thing had crept up on him, or his aware-ness of it had; for like so many others, he had marched willing but unthinking into nature's best-laid trap. The role of paterfamilias was now a facet of his being. He had never expected otherwise, but he had not planned for it either; and doing so now, his thoughts dwelled increasingly on his imagined relationship with a son. This surprised him greatly but nonethe-less it was so. He saw in the boy an eager and felicitous companion, sharing his recreations and learning to hunt and fish under his tutelage—eventually perhaps following in his own footsteps professionally. He saw the boy too as the recipient of things Seneca himself had learned through trial and error and which, being imparted, would not then be wasted experience. What father has not perhaps had similar imaginings? Yet what Seneca in fact envisaged contained as its appealing core a largely self-refractive element, having created in essence an all-admiring lieutenant, with himself magnifi-cently reflected in the enlarging mirror of the youngster's eyes. Never once did he imagine the boy trying to outstrip him (which as a son he himself had done) or remotely slipping in his estimation, or for that matter not falling in with his plans. And the more this fantasy caught in his imagina-tion, the greater he felt would be the loss to family life if unfulfilled. Girls were fine but they married and that was that. They did not merit a serious investment of his time in either training or enlightenment. And in this Seneca was fairly typical, for it had always been so.

Dartania took pregnancy in her stride, paying it little heed. She was rarely ill and never suffered complications. What she disliked were encounters with women who for some reason linked this baby with the dead one, say-ing what a blessing it was after her "great loss" and so forth. Nor did she always respond politely, provocatively trotting out her stock phrase about babies being as common as pig tracks, and leaving many a well-wishing matron openmouthed and not a little put out.

Why on earth were women such fools, she wondered.

But the months of pregnancy fell heavily. Robin was now working full-time at the Cotton Exchange and Dartania eschewed the country club because of the old biddies. Nor did riding give much pleasure. Though still the best horsewoman in the county, she had noticed since the birth of her children subtle changes in her balance and in her aptitude for rapid response, all of which increased with pregnancy. Used to doing something better than others, she got no pleasure from a second-rate performance.

Like most of her friends Dartania filled her days entirely as she pleased, but in the evenings she sat beside her husband reading, and, except for Saturdays, they generally refused all invitations. Dartania, who flourished in the gaiety of social life, never once complained of its infrequency. Seneca did not like to go out; he was her husband and his word was law. If the days were hers to dispose of, the evenings belonged to him. Moreover the pace of social life was such that, among the younger set at any rate, a Sunday was normally needed for recuperation, making midweek entertaining rare.

Dartania took little interest in Seneca's work—few wives did—and she loathed everything to do with politics. Willingly she left that side of things to Alice Nash, though not without some sporadic teasing, suggesting masculine weakness and a closet mama's boy. For Seneca's every endeavor was trawled over and listened to attentively by his mother, and sound and sensible counsel usually followed, tied to the stabilizing weft of maternal encouragement. It bucked him up—it always had—and kept the needy fires of ambitious achievement stoked.

"You can depend on Stark Fenton," his mother had observed that very morning on the telephone. "He's as sound a shoe as ever has been made."

Stark's failure to make much impact in the 1930 primary suggested from the political angle, however, that a more dynamic candidate might do better this time around. The decision was important because Seneca and Stark, together with Jim Dillon, editor of the *Herald*, and Harry Sayle, a cotton broker with political ambitions, had forged the nucleus of a new and increasingly well-organized political party: the Reformed Democrats, and they planned to run their own candidates on this ticket. Aimed at unseating Boss Buzby, the state's Democratic voters would for the first time in years have a choice before them in the state primary: honest, well-intentioned candidates who represented the public's real interests as against the corrupt yes-men regularly installed by Buzby.

Seneca's reservations dutifully set aside, it was agreed that Stark would stand again for Congress, while hopes for Harry Sayle as governor ran high. But the senate seat was another matter. To oppose the incumbent Senator Judd would be about as foolhardy as opposing the Christian religion. They would have to let that prize go. No matter: In 1938, when Judd voluntarily retired, Seneca at thirty-nine would be of respectable if not yet venerable senatorial age. In the meantime he relished participation in a fight where high ideals were allied to his pugnacious instincts. It lifted his soul in a way that practicing law, even winning difficult cases, could not do.

But political tickets need money. The loss of Bayard's backing probably didn't matter, however, as a replacement was fast emerging in Mr. Ebenezer Catty, the Chicago Railroad's new president (and Seneca's biggest client). If not the most reformed of Democrats, Catty was a willing competitor on any front against his opposite number, Buzby, and a political dinner party was planned at Longwood to secure his formal commitment. Georgia and Herbert Mason, liberal-minded Democrats, as well as stalwarts in the hunting field, were also invited. And to Dartania's surprise, Stark asked to bring a young woman who was going to help in the campaign, Miss Mary Ann Webster.

Predictably, talk fixed limpetlike on the new party's hopes, which during dinner rose to greater and greater heights, helped along by bottles of Châteauneuf du Pape sent over from Cottoncrop for the occasion. With a laudable brevity, the party's platform was outlined for Mr. Catty, together with the briefest glimpse of costs, and followed closely by a fulsome reminder of the benefits awarded with victory's laurel crown.

"I can't imagine anything worse than living in Washington," Dartania confided to Herbert Mason, sitting on her left, as they sat smoking comfortably after the dessert. "Unless it's moving to New York. All the hoo ha and the la de da. They say everybody lives in identical houses all joined together, row after row of them. It's like living in a Pullman, isn't it, Mr. Catty?" She turned, smiling, to bring him into the smaller circle.

"You'd like it if you saw it, Dartania," put in Stark who, sitting two down, had overheard this mildly disobliging remark with some alarm.

Mary Ann Webster gazed reverentially, her clipped brown hair and the few freckles on her pencil-thin nose making her pale brown eyes into two larger but equally opaque spots. "Georgetown has some beautiful houses," she declared in a surprisingly firm low voice. It was almost the first time she had spoken.

"Well, to me a house is a place with grass all around it," Dartania pointedly declared. "And it's not a copy of the one next door."

"I agree with you about big cities, Mrs. Nash," Mr. Catty conceded heartily, "but aren't you interested in the coming race?" He was a large man, bald, popeyed and potbellied, with an easy manner that comes with general good humor and the continued assurance of power.

"I prefer horse racing, myself," she said, her large eyes fixed playfully on

Mr. Catty's startlingly protruding ones. "They're so much better at it, and being bred to do it, look more dignified in the process." Which was as close as she dared come to saying politics was a vulgar and ugly business. "Maybe the Reformed Democrats should buy a racehorse," she went on frivolously. "I don't mean to replace any of the current runners, but to advertise your ticket. You could name the horse after the party. It's Reformed Democrat coming up on the left, Reformed Democrat nosing ahead in the home stretch, Reformed Democrat wins by a length, and *what* a magnificent race! I'd be glad to train him for you," she added sweetly, for Mr. Catty actually seemed quite fascinated by this whimsical suggestion.

"Unfortunately the party needs every cent it can raise to support the human runners," interposed Stark, folding his napkin neatly beside his plate, as though expecting to use it again in the future, Dartania thought.

"Dar-chile had a sweet little racehorse a couple of years ago," Georgia Mason said, mildly apposite, "a pretty three-year-old. I remember she rode it right up the front steps and onto the veranda one day out at Timbuctoo, just to show it to Herbert."

"I was hoping he'd buy it," said Dartania smiling broadly.

Mr. Catty smiled too. He admired spirited women, and the beautiful, slightly pregnant young woman sitting beside him, her eyes asparkle, put him in a high good humor.

At the opposite end of the table, however, Seneca's mood was steadily in decline. Petty annoyances had been biting him like fleas throughout the meal. First, he had discovered his pepper shaker was empty, so presumably were the others'. The soup had been lukewarm and the silver dessert bowl visibly bronzed by tarnish (Delphine having made a last-minute substitution). His table napkin had a hole in it. Coming from a superbly run house, inattention to such domestic details annoyed him on principle. He had said so to Dartania many times and yet she never bothered, couldn't see the point of it, not even on so important an occasion as this one. In his view she was simply not doing her job. Her obvious success with Mr. Catty had been pleasing but it had also nettled, deflecting as she had the evening's serious purpose. Seneca glowered morosely down the table at his wife, who, following Stark's request for news of Jasmine, was busy explaining to Mr. Catty: "My sister's a remittance woman in Paris and is recovering there from a recent heart attack."

But before the railroad magnate could respond to this droll and confusing picture, a huge shadow fell ominously along the dining room wall, the candles on the table guttered crazily, and the startled guests looked around in some alarm. Swooping perilously overhead, Theodora circled like a golden missile around the room, before alighting on the lip of a silver ewer standing on the oak sideboard. "Happy days. What! What! What!" she shrieked, cocking her crested head and brilliantly red-rouged face.

Mr. Catty, laughing uproariously, raised his wine glass and called back merrily, "Happy days to you, too, gorgeous!"

For Seneca, talk was now quite literally at bird-brain level, and he suspected that Dartania, who could never be made to close a door when she left a room, might purposely have left Theodora's open.

"Drat, I wish I'd brought my gun," lamented Georgia Mason mischievously to her host.

"So do I," came the blunt rejoinder.

Later on, the evening's travesties, as Seneca saw them, were the subject of an animated dispute, its contents sadly familiar. "You've not got a damn thing to do but run this house, and there are plenty of people on the place to help you," Seneca furiously insisted. Such inefficiencies never occurred at either Cottoncrop or Timbuctoo, besides which there was no excuse for sloppiness and inattention to detail. He sat down on the bed to remove his socks. "Goddamn it, Dartania, that bird's shat on the bedspread!" Seneca held his hand up distastefully, looking down indignantly at his shorts.

Dartania, who found the whole thing highly comic, tossed one of her husband's lines of bravado in his face, "Well, it won't hurt you," she said airily, "a man of the woods and fields."

Seneca, who would never have lost control in a courtroom, felt increasingly disposed to indulge himself in this respect at home, and ripping the bedspread off, he tossed it to the floor like a gigantic gauntlet. Then, striding across the room, he reached inside the open birdcage and, grabbing Theodora roughly from her perch, opened the bedroom window and threw the squawking creature out.

"For God's sake, Seneca!" Dartania in her nightgown, her long hair streaming about her, rushed to the window and, leaning out, called frantically to the bird, but without success.

"What an idiotic thing to do!" she cried. "Goddamn you, Seneca. The dogs will get her for sure."

"Well then, she's gone to the dogs," he firmly declared, unrepentant, and what's more, fully determined not to be.

AN EMOTIONAL FROST still hovered the following evening, when, as previously arranged with Miss Allen, Dartania and Seneca appeared outside the nursery door—their purpose: to make room for the next incumbent. But mood and inexperience produced an inept and unfortunate mishandling. Sally and Emma were just climbing into bed; a night-light was on in the room; and the children's parents, lit in the doorway from behind, gave the impression of colossal silhouettes. They did not come in. They never had. The nursery was Miss Allen's exclusive kingdom, and patriarchal tradition decreed that children should visit their parents, not vice versa.

"You girls are getting too big for a nursery," Seneca told them, putting a flattering edge on the coming announcement. "You're both of you old enough to look after yourselves and take some of the burden off Miss Allen."

"We look after ourselves already. Don't we, Miss Allie?" Sally asserted self-importantly.

"We already look after ourselves," Emma repeated in refrain. "And we look after Miss Allie. I cut your hair, don't I, Miss Allie?"

"And I make all Miss Allie's handkerchiefs."

"Well, from tomorrow, you're going to have your own room," Seneca continued undeterred, "the one at the end of the hall."

Immersed in their own repetitive discord, the couple were utterly unprepared for the response. But the prospect of being torn from their beloved Miss Allen's bosom was devastating to the little girls, and leaping out of bed, they clung weeping and protesting to the diminutive, heavily corseted nurse, as to a barrel in a flood. They loved their Miss Allie and would not be parted from her.

"We don't want to leave Miss Allie," wailed Emma piteously.

"We want to stay here." Sally fervently took up the cry.

Seneca, who had no notion of how to comfort a child, chose to regard the matter as one of insubordination, which was something he *could* deal with effectively.

"You'll do as you're told," he fiercely ordered them. "Now let that be an end to it. Get back in that bed and if I hear one more peep out of you I'm going to lay about me. Is that clear?" His tone, a relic of the tough military-school discipline he himself had undergone, provoked more hysterical despair.

"You heard your father," said Dartania shortly. Where the children were concerned, she and Seneca habitually stood as a united front, and at this moment, unification from whatever quarter visited great relief. "Miss Allen will see you off to school every morning as before," she added in a more conciliatory voice, sensing with her unwavering honesty some remote unfairness.

Who can tell which childhood traumas will persist engraved on tiny personalities and which ones evanesce, floating away as bad dreams do, forgotten the next day? That night the little girls cried themselves piteously to sleep, but within a few days they seemed thoroughly adjusted to the new regime and, delighted with its comparative freedom, had invented some raucous bedtime games they could indulge in undeterred. But imperceptibly, a seam had opened up between them and their adored Miss Allen, one that with time would deepen to an impassable gulf.

When the girls were settled, Dartania came to see them and, sitting on one of the beds, told them they were going to have a little brother or sister. She said it as if announcing a special treat, but the recipients were far from pleased; they could see no possible advantages for themselves—indeed quite the reverse.

Only Miss Allen was jubilant. The gathering clouds of insecurity had rolled miraculously back, even if they had failed to disappear, hovering instead on the remote horizon. For the present the sun shone again immediately overhead. A reprieve had been granted and Miss Allen thanked the good Lord with all her heart; but her sweetest smile went to Seneca, her more proximate savior. That she had at least as much to thank Dartania for did not occur to the poor woman.

6

....

*G*ood God, Dar's having a baby—in December." Jasmine and Frank were
sitting at a street café, La Framboise, a few doors from their studio, and
a favorite haunt. The letter was the first Jasmine had received from her elder
sister during the six months she had been in Paris, for Dartania rarely put
pen to paper. "I bet she's furious," Jasmine chortled with sibling glee. "She
always claims there's nothing to it, though: like falling off a log."

"Indecently soon, isn't it?" Frank's offhand delivery made it difficult to
tell if he was joking. But Jasmine, who could tell, smiled with affection and
read on.

"Would you believe it? Stark Fenton's gone and got engaged."

"Poor old Stark," said Frank. "With those ideals of his, she's a
schoolteacher for sure."

"As as matter of fact, he used to be sweet on me," said Jasmine with a
superior little smile. "Didn't you notice? I, not some schoolteacher, was his
beau ideal."

"Sure you didn't imagine it? You're not at all his type."

"Well," continued Jasmine after a minute, "it transpires she *is* a
schoolteacher. Third grade—teaches it I mean. The 'sincere' type, Dar says,
wild about politics and thinks Stark could be president of the United States
one day. That shows how naive she is, Dar says."

Doodling on a pad, Frank lifted it with a flourish, as the waiter, Maurice, their best man, appeared, a metal tray adroitly balanced on a pedestal of fingertips. *"Attention, attention: dormez pas."* With quick efficiency he set out plates of paté, bread, and bottled water on the table.

Jasmine and Frank had got into the habit of taking all their meals at La Framboise. The discovery that eating out in Paris cost about the same as eating in had resulted in the rapid atrophy of Jasmine's budding culinary skills. Each day began therefore with coffee and a cigarette at La Framboise, after which Frank, and often Jasmine, painted in the studio all day. Three mornings a week Jasmine went, not to the art school where she supposedly was enrolled, but to study with Monsieur Boireau, a tutor secured through the art school syllabus. In this way most of her fees, being saved, were pocketed, which, added to her allowance, gave them a decent monthly stipend.

"I wish you knew Dar better," Jasmine told him, folding the letter and putting it away. She had skipped the bit about her hoped-for recovery from "that dubious dauber."

"She's such an unusual person. She has tremendous courage, you know."

"A dated flapper," Frank solemnly opined, shoveling up his paté. "Pretty one though."

"Oh I admit she loves parties and she plays cards and rides horses, like everybody does at home, but Dar is different from the rest. There's a sort of greatness about her, just waiting for its hour, existing for it perhaps. Everyone feels it. And men are wild about her of course. Why the Prince of Wales, a tiny man, jumped right into the palm of her hand! She's our star, just you wait and see." Jasmine signaled to Maurice for coffee, then looking at her watch, took a deep breath. "Oh Lord, six more hours to go."

"Her husband's OK," said Frank, ignoring this last.

It was a day on which great hopes were pinned, a day on which, in extending the realm of their artistic and social acquaintance, they might, among other exhilarating things, conceivably find buyers for their pictures. Suddenly, full of promises, the future was rushing forth to meet them: Paris in one great single sweep was about to throw open her cultural doors in welcome—doors that to Jasmine's innocent eyes at any rate were veritable gates of Paradise.

A few days earlier she had come across in a suitcase the list of introductions dutifully collected by her family, and glancing at it with smug superiority, one name had stuck out as curiously familiar. "Toklas," she had called to Frank working next door, "Miss Alice Toklas. Haven't we met her somewhere?"

"I wish we had," he called back. "That woman lives with Gertrude Stein."

Now *tout* Paris and a steadily growing slice of America had heard much of Gertrude Stein. Not because of her writing—at which she prided herself, believing herself to be a genius—but because, early on, whether visited by luck or inspired choice, she had been among the very first to collect the works of artists who would become as famous as any the world had yet produced: Picasso, Cézanne, Matisse, Derain, Rousseau, Gris, and many others. Miss Stein was inclined to collect the artist, too. Her flourishing talent for self-promotion and her now famous Saturday evenings, when people came to see her pictures, and each other, had helped no end to extend her reputation, spreading it like a fine oil slick across western Europe and America.

Jasmine had written at once, and a polite note had arrived by return of post, inviting them to Miss Stein's atelier on the Saturday. But as the day approached, Frank's eager anticipation had given way to surliness and apprehension, resulting in some abusive remarks about the famous lesbian pair.

"Picasso may be there," Jasmine kept saying, "Bucher or Kahnweiler might be there. Or Monet."

"Monet is dead," said Frank.

The famous atelier was approached through a courtyard opening off a staid and dignified-looking street near the Luxembourg Gardens. Miss Toklas opened the door herself, a somewhat plain, long-faced woman with prominent aquiline features, middle-aged and wearing baggy draperylike clothes that fell rather than flowed about her bony figure.

"We are so glad you were able to come," she said pleasantly, wafting in front of them down a narrow corridor and through a small dining room to the atelier. "Miss Stein is so looking forward to meeting you. There are not many Americans here now, you know, as we are all so very depressed. She has heard of your brother's collection, Mrs. Noland. I believe he had to pay top prices, didn't he?"

Jasmine made goggle-eyes at Frank behind Miss Toklas's slightly curved thin back.

Few guests had arrived as yet and the ringent spaces of the big high-ceilinged room served up with greater emphasis its offerings. From top to bottom the walls were filled with pictures.

The room's other point of focus was at the far end. Sitting beside the fireplace in a low chintz armchair, their hostess was stolidly enthroned, dressed in a gray skirt, print blouse, silk stockings, and brown leather sandals. Her strong face and short haircut, her voice, too, as they would soon discover, were those of a man. Jasmine went forward with Miss Toklas to be presented, but to her dismay Frank chose instead to tour the room, turning his back with casual disregard upon his august hostess.

In 1931 there were few opportunities to study the development of modern painters' work, for museums rarely contained their pictures. Three or four times a year, salon exhibitions showed modern artists, but usually recent work, so that a painter's individual progress remained obscure, a feat of imperfect and often confabulated recollection. Frank therefore was thunderstruck. Like the hungry peasant whose slender harvest, though he would like to fall upon it greedily, must be made to last the year, Frank took up his feast methodically, forcing inner control in the face of such enticing and overwhelming plenty. Very slowly he began to make his way around the high-ceilinged atelier, going back and forth to review and look again, to feed, to gloat, to devour and to revel in the munificence that lay so unexpectedly before him.

Miss Stein eyed him coldly as he went, his back always to her; and fully comprehending her *froideur,* Jasmine's embarrassment was keen. Brought up in society she acutely perceived its special pressures and priorities. The pictures should have come after the *politesse.*

The atelier was beginning to fill. English, Russian, and American expats predominated, and wealth and poverty rubbed easily and unselfconsciously together. Couture-clothed women from the Faubourg St. Honoré were chatting matter-of-factly with contemporaries draped in imaginative exotica from the flea markets of Montparnasse, stitched together with varying degrees of success.

Jasmine's heart beat with high anticipation. Everyone seemed either connected to or interested in the arts: Some were famous, others might be soon. The vivid scene, ornamented by so staggering a display of brilliant cultural plumage, capped all expectation. Miraculously, in one balletic leap she had been translated from one of the audience on to the proscenium stage. But wishing to preserve both points of view, she half-consciously alternated between the two perspectives, getting for her effort a greater pleasure.

Miss Stein continued to sit in the low chair accepting the salutations of visitors who, given her physically inferior position, were obliged to bend down to her. She welcomed them coolly, even somewhat vaguely, Jasmine thought, noticing too that from time to time Miss Stein's gaze still fell stonily on Frank.

Eventually she managed to drag him in her formidable hostess's direction, Frank looking stony-faced too.

"I ought not to mind my wonderful pictures taking precedence over me," Miss Stein told him good-naturedly, "but my tolerance is finite." She waited for the young man's apologetic response but he said nothing at all. Frank always seemed to talk a great deal when nothing much was required, becoming awkwardly mute on occasions when it was.

"Mrs. Noland tells me both of you are painters, and Miss Toklas tells me Mrs. Noland's brother is a collector I should know," Miss Stein continued evenly. "Unlike me, a very rich collector, or was before this empty trough began to starve us all. Why do young Americans continue to come to Paris? What do they want? The great days are over here. It's too late; you ought to go back home."

"I can paint anywhere," Frank said shortly in reply. "But why are all the Americans in Paris writers and never painters?"

"That observation hasn't occurred to me, so I am unable to tell you," said Miss Stein. "But writing is the most sublime form of artistic expression. I am a veritable Parnassus myself. Maybe other Americans tend to share this view. Do you know Monsieur Picabia?"

The painter was standing alongside, his head bent more than slightly forward.

"Not personally," said Frank flatly and without any nod of recognition.

A faint smile flitted across the mannish countenance of Gertrude Stein. Abruptly she turned to Jasmine. "Miss Toklas and I would very much like to see some of your work—yours and your husband's, Mrs. Noland. We would be happy to come to tea tomorrow at four o'clock if that is convenient for you. We have grown rather fond of tea," she added by way of courteous dismissal.

Throughout the evening, Jasmine strove to keep in mind the fact that Frank was someone special, and so above ordinary expectations of behavior. Miss Stein and Miss Toklas, moving in artistic circles, would surely understand this; indeed they must be very used to it. Meanwhile, despite Frank's unnerving austerity, her own social poise, instilled from infancy, bounced resiliently back, and she soon found herself well-assimilated into the gathering's gregarious crucible. She talked to an eccentric Spanish painter, quite literally the cat's whiskers—or rather he talked to her, about the contamination of being physically touched. She talked to an American composer who claimed to be collaborating with Miss Stein on a musical composition of great originality. An American interior decorator, sporting the English title of Lady Mendl, expressed real interest in her work, and a Russian prince dressed as a woman, who earned his living driving a taxicab, offered her a lift home—for a reasonable fee. But she met no art dealers.

"Did you see that woman in the mauve suit?" she asked Frank, as they were walking home. "She writes a column about Paris in the *New Yorker*, and who knows, maybe she'll put us in it one day: two talented Americans lighting up the artistic scene abroad."

But Frank hadn't met anyone, it seemed, and instead of coming to bed he went into the studio and, pulling out a picture or two, sat down on a stool and stared gloomily at them for several hours.

His silent depression was unabated when punctually at four o'clock the next day Miss Toklas and Miss Stein arrived, as promised, bearing a jar of cookies made by Miss Toklas from her own recipe, they were told.

A bright July sky filled the huge atelier window, but the room for the most part was depressingly bare. Having tidied it as much as Frank would allow—cleanliness had low priority in his life—Jasmine had succeeded in stacking their paintings, faces to the wall, so as to make a greater impact individually when shown.

"We will look at the pictures first and have tea afterwards," Miss Stein declared, marching heavily into the center of the denuded room and searching about with an imperial frown.

"If you and Miss Toklas would kindly sit on the sofa, where you'll be comfortable, I can show them to you there," Jasmine softly urged.

"Very well," said Miss Stein, retreating on her big, brown-sandaled feet. "Let's start with yours, my dear."

"Oh, I think we should start with Frank's," Jasmine modestly insisted.

"Ladies first," declared Miss Stein, and she and Miss Toklas smiled in lofty oneness.

Jasmine produced her canvases one at a time: a couple of landscapes, a corner of the Luxembourg gardens under snow, and two studies of the street below. "We haven't been here very long," she offered into the silence, "so there isn't a great deal to show."

"There is enough," Miss Stein dryly rejoined.

"Such charming colors," suggested Miss Toklas, whose job, as Jasmine had begun to see, was effectively to soothe and placate.

"Frank's pictures are over there." Jasmine pointed toward a corner. "I'll bring them over."

But Frank said he would do that himself. Confronted with a potentially demeaning experience, that of abjectly spreading his wares before others and exposing himself to a broadside of unpredictable response, he told himself an artist must have the courage or the indifference to submit his work, even to fools and philistines.

Striding purposefully across the room, he brought back a large canvas and propped it up on an easel in the center of the room. Vividly colored lines went in all directions, many of them dribbled onto the canvas straight from the tube. The background by contrast was a carefully textured blue, Frank's idiosyncratic little circles pimpling the paint-encrusted canvas overall.

Miss Stein's eyes widened slightly; there was no other visible response.

Grimly Frank showed two smaller, very similar pictures, holding them up, not bothering to put them on the easel.

"They are very abstract," Miss Stein observed in a noncommittal tone.

Frank said nothing. Replacing the two pictures, he brought another larger one forward and placed it on the easel. A composition denser than the previous ones, it was also very much darker: Olive greens and black contrasted with bright chartreuse, the lines and circles being laid on in black or pink and yellow. The effect was of a deep forest, thick and sunless, seen from overhead. Or so Miss Toklas thought out loud.

"Your line has a certain vibrancy, Mr. Noland," Miss Stein solemnly intoned. "Now let us have some tea."

Jasmine, serving tea for the first time, was unaware that Europeans put milk in it and had none to offer her guests. She regretted not having watched Ellen's elaborate tea-making more carefully, for Miss Stein did not hesitate to ask for milk outright, not finding any on the table. But Miss Toklas said that like the Russians she preferred hers with lemon.

Then, following Jasmine into the kitchen with the empty teapot, Miss Toklas whispered confidentially as they refilled it, "A vibrant line is what Miss Stein is always searching for. That is what speaks to her you know. I can tell she likes your husband's pictures a great deal—and your own are charming my dear: The postimpressionists are always tops with me."

Jasmine yearned to tell her volcanic-looking husband of his unsuspected success. As it was, the atmosphere was brittle: Frank smarting silently, Miss Stein's talk steaming along as if she were hurrying at top speed to catch her bus. She asked about Bayard's collection, rather competitively, Jasmine thought, and lamented the Depression, at last beginning to be felt in Paris. But even her sally into the supremacy of writing as an art form failed to prick Frank's charred and smoldering crust. And since Miss Toklas wouldn't have dreamt of interrupting her companion, she could not anoint this awkward lack of exchange with her usual balm.

As the pair arose to go, however, Miss Stein, standing foursquare like a ready pugilist, said offhand in her deep contralto, "We are always at home on Saturday evenings."

Miss Toklas smiled warmly at Jasmine, confirming that a definite conquest had been made.

Breathlessly Jasmine informed her husband, when the pair had gone, what had been imparted in the kitchen. But Frank resisted too quick a demolition of his carefully constructed barricade. "The truth is she didn't know *what* to make of them," he retorted fiercely, beginning to put the pictures back in place. "In my view there's something ridiculous about that woman. They call her the Mother Goose of Montparnasse behind her back. Did you know that?"

But Jasmine's own delight was unassailable. They were a success. It was all coming true as planned. Frank's work had been seriously admired and they were to frequent, as intimates, the epicenter of the artistic world— even though Jasmine in future would be compelled to sit with Miss Toklas and the wives, talking of hats and pets and omnibuses, while Miss Stein grandly presided among the geniuses, which now included Frank.

7
....

*I*n mid-October Dartania, punctual as always, was taken to hospital in labor. Alice Nash, present at the birth of all her grandchildren, arrived simultaneously from Cottoncrop. It was an easy birth but its result was utterly unforeseen: another girl. No one had thought it possible, and at the news, Seneca felt some part of himself break off and float mysteriously away. Only Alice Nash seemed delighted by the new arrival. Dartania, mightily glad it was over, showed little interest in the red and wrinkly bundle, hastily named Flora after her long-dead mother. But later, watching the tiny creature nursing at her breast, its fine brown hair standing on end like the curlicue of a Kewpie doll, its minute hand resting with such comfortable assurance on her breast as the little mouth worked away, Dartania felt a sudden welling of affectionate pleasure, a soft, blooming surge of tenderness. But almost at once the baby was whisked away, and, except for brief feedings before it began a bottle, she saw very little of it. Responsibility fell to the capable, loving hands of Miss Allen, who more than anyone had reason to welcome the new arrival. With ardent intensity she pressed the baby to her heart, for as she rightly guessed, Dartania and Seneca had agreed this was the last; so it would be Miss Allen's, too.

Visiting his wife in hospital, Seneca encountered Ellen Douglas, a designated godmother, in overt raptures about the baby girl. Alive to Ellen's own inability to conceive, he listened patiently, feeling an obscure sympathy connected with life's perverse tendency to supply needs indiscriminately and with such profligacy where they were not required.

They left the hospital together, and Seneca scanned the horseshoe driveway for the Douglas Rolls.

"I'm afraid I came on the bus," Ellen shyly confessed. But noting her brother-in-law's surprise, and fearing some adverse reflection upon her husband, she managed a white lie to the effect that Albert had taken the car to be serviced. "Besides, I like going about like other people," she innocently proclaimed.

Seneca insisted on driving her home, and Ellen, glad of the opportunity to discuss aspects of her husband's affairs with his attorney, had, by the time they reached Blue Hills, screwed up the courage to ask whether the failure to put Blue Hills House in her name had in his view been a mistake.

Seneca said that certainly it was, that in rejecting a perfectly legal safeguard, Bayard was exposing himself to the very real chance of forfeiting his home. He himself was doing what he could to protect his client's interests, but he might not be 100 percent successful.

"But if the law decides the house should go to the creditors, then surely it should do so," Ellen bravely suggested. "And we must wait and see."

"If Bayard's responsibility to his shareholders is eventually decided in court, then we must act according to that decision. But meantime it's my job to supply what tools the law permits to help him hold on to everything he can—and he'd be a damn fool not to use them all."

Ellen looked down uneasily at her white-gloved hands. "There is, in addition to the law, a moral responsibility too."

"You know it can be a lot harder to resist the pull of conventional morality than to take the cosier option of falling in with it," Seneca declared with marked conviction, his eyes brightening as he spoke. "Sometimes a man has to block out moral niceties, put his head down, and push forward just as hard as he can. That's the warrior instinct, if you like, but in my view it's the basis of manhood—*the ability to do what becomes necessary*. Bayard understands that. He's doing the best he can and he has my very real admiration."

"But for us to live as we do—so, well, grandly—when others who put their faith in . . . the company . . . are now destitute. . . ."

Glancing at her, Seneca noted the real anguish on what was normally so serene a countenance. "Investors take a chance," he said, leaning forward to light a cigarette. "Even if they forget it at the time. When things go wrong naturally they want to claw back what they can, and their opposite numbers want to hang on to what they can." He opened the window slightly so that the cigarette smoke rose toward it. "Whether Bayard is legally culpable is for the law to say; it's out of his hands now. What remains in his hands however is a primal responsibility to his family—not just you and the boy but to the Douglases generally. And he has a position in the community to uphold. All that has a monetary side, as Bayard knows only too well." Pausing at a crossroads he looked over at Ellen. "But above all that, he has in my opinion a duty to himself to survive intact."

"But how can he when he's had to sacrifice so many of the values that he's cherished?" There was a swift intake of breath, almost an inner sigh. "Getting help from that Buzby for example!"

Seneca smiled. "Well I guess that's one reason why wives are usually so much nicer than their husbands," he said kindly. "In extremis it's wives who generally preserve the finer values and keep them safe. But without a man's larger protection that wouldn't be possible, would it, because the so-called finer values are ultimately preserved on battlefields." He had begun to see Ellen as a sort of hothouse flower, a rare foreign species that could only exist in a consistent, well-regulated climate—a greenhouse. It had its appealing side.

"Bayard's in the fight of his life," he said. "He's under a tremendous strain, carefully hidden though it is, and he needs all the support that he can get, believe me."

"But he won't even talk to me about his business!" she cried out bitterly. "He never has." The gloved hands fluttered and fell. "It's just as well really. I seem unable to help him, unable to be of any use at all. How I wish I had Dartania's mettle. She'd stand by you in any trouble, no matter what it was. Yet I can't do even the one thing that's been asked of me."

Seneca felt it was true about his wife. Dartania would stand by him against all comers, if necessary to the death. And yet he envied the tender anguished concern of Bayard's wife, who clearly loved her husband very much.

They had entered the gates of Blue Hills House. "You know, my grandfather lost this house because of debt. He lost it in a poker game. That sounds foolhardy in the extreme, but he was in many ways a very superior individual, a brilliant man, and at one time quite rich. But he could never keep his nose to any grindstone—he was too impatient. And before long he'd turned from raising horses to betting too much money on them."

Seneca had stopped the car in front of the square-columned portico. He sat reflectively for a moment, gazing across the newly clipped lawn. "You know we're mostly border folk here. Our forebears came from the Scottish-English border, and there never was a more turbulent place on earth. Fighting is in our blood. And it's a funny thing, but some men, lions in battle, just go to pieces in peacetime. That was Grandpa's trouble. He was one helluva fellow in the Civil War, but he never could settle down afterwards. He needed excitement, he needed to live on the edge; and cards and horse racing were the nearest postwar things he could find. That and women.

"Bayard's different. He's a cultivated man with many civilized interests that give excitement and pleasure and, in hard times, can pretty successfully divert the mind. It should help to see him through—that and his inborn toughness. And after the fight it will make excellent ballast."

The tough self-assertive Douglas nature had always alarmed Ellen, who secretly disapproved of it. It seemed so primitive, a throwback to the rough-and-ready pioneer society that was over. But seduced by Seneca's words, she now briefly fathomed the utilitarian advantage of combativeness, its worthiness in hard times. And for the first time in months, her heart went out unreservedly to her husband and was filled to overflowing by a tender precious joy. But was society really, as Seneca had suggested, supported Atlas-like on the shoulders of ruthless warring men, putting their heads down and pushing on, regardless? England she felt sure was ruled by gentlemen.

On the hall table lay a letter. The uneven writing scrawled in pencil caused Ellen instinctively to sit down. The paper was of the type shopkeepers used to tot bills. Ellen's hand went to her throat, where the pearls she twisted habitually when agitated no longer hung.

"Dear Mrs. Douglas," she read.

"I done took a liberty in writing and I hope you don't mind so much. You see my husband Billy he was the janitor down at Mr. Douglas's office and I know Mr. Douglas thought mighty highly of him. He even gave him a tip on some stock he had one time. Well Billy he's been out of work now since summer and not from want of trying neither. There just don't seem to be no work around. I do some sewing myself and I try real hard to keep Billy bucked up some. But right now things just go from bad to worse. There's five little ones and my Sally has took sick and we can't afford to call no doctor. Then yestiddy Mr. Callan the landlord done told Billy that if we can't get the rent together what we owe him then we got to go. Well Mrs. Douglas I just didn't know where to turn. Billy done told me what a fine lady you was, a real lady from over yonder across the waters he said. He don't know I'm writing you, mind. He don't hold with humbling none. But it seem to me I ain't got no choice. I got to think about my children and Billy too. Mr. Callan done said we owe one hundred dollars for rent but I speck he would take less so long as we was able to give him something. I know you got your troubles too Mrs. Douglas. And Mr. Douglas he's had a right bad time of it for a man like him. But if you could see your way to helping us out some right now, why soon as Billy gets back on his feet we'd pay you back quick as we could. You got my word on that. Excuse me for being so forward like and if you cant help us dont you go feeling bad about it none. We all got our troubles and that's the gospel truth. But I know the good Lord sees it all and we are safe in his hands. Your friend Carrie Pritchard."

The address was somewhere in East Nashborough.

Ellen sat with the letter open on her lap. A heavy sadness for this woman's troubles, for all women who could do so little to help themselves, but who, being dependent on others, were at the same time the protectors of their children, filled her with aching sympathy.

How much better a wife was Carrie Pritchard than herself, how much more she seemed to understand and to accept in life. Ellen was especially struck by the woman's efforts to protect her husband's pride. She had been taught that pride, to be acceptable, flowed from doing the right thing. The fact of a false pride lovingly promoted now earned her strong admiration.

But where was she going to find a hundred dollars? Bayard rightly would be incensed by such a request, representing as it did a drop in the bucket of other equally needful outlays.

After a bit she went into the pantry and told John to pack up the candelabra on the dining room table and that she wanted Albert to drive her into town. The candelabra had been a wedding present from her aunt and therefore, she believed, belonged to her.

She had Albert park the car at a corner near Main Street and insisted on carrying the bulky parcel herself. "Go over to Richmond Brothers," she told him, "and buy the best leg of lamb for dinner you can get. I'm just going to drop these off. I'll only be five minutes."

Entering the pawnbroker's shop Ellen was aware of a massive collection of stock filling the grimy shelves along the walls. But though covered in dust, everything was carefully labeled and in categorical order. Cameras, clocks, and watches predominated. Two automobile tires leaned against one wall beside what looked like an antique weather vane. The pawnbroker, a thin bald man in braces and shirtsleeves with garters on the arms, removed the jeweler's glass from his eye and, regarding Ellen with polite incuriosity, nodded but did not speak. He knew his role to perfection.

Ellen set the parcel down heavily on the counter. "Silver candelabra," she reported breathlessly, giving him a familiar pleading look.

The pawnbroker unwrapped the parcel. He removed the branches of one of the pair, then its trunk, and set the branches in place.

"They're English," Ellen said, "and really quite old, I think."

The pawnbroker, who had found the hallmark, knew his silver. He had never seen such a pair before but it was roughly as he had supposed, perhaps a little better. Paul Storr 1810. They were certainly valuable or would be once people were in the money again. He could send them up to New York and fetch a pretty good price. The pawnbroker revered fine silver: He thrilled to its soft glow and beautiful craftsmanship, and now a kind of aesthetic covetousness possessed him. Removing the mate, he examined its condition and at the same time shrewdly assessed his client. Well-to-do ladies who pawned things were usually in some kind of trouble that they couldn't confide to their husbands. Chances of redemption were therefore poor.

"I need one hundred dollars," Ellen announced imploringly.

The pawnbroker regarded her solemnly. Would this lady, with her foreign accent and quiet elegance, be able to redeem her property more readily than others, he was wondering. Instinctively he narrowed that chance. "One hundred dollars," he said evenly. "For three weeks." It was half the normal retrieval time.

Ellen almost held out her hand.

If Bayard missed the candelabra she had decided she would tell a lie. She would say they were being repaired. And who knew, by the end of three weeks she might have found a means of redemption. Meantime she replaced the pawned pair with two Regency candlesticks whose graceful simplicity she privately preferred to the ornate design that pleased her husband best.

"I CAN'T SEE what you're serving me or, for that matter, what it is I'm eating," Bayard declared to John that night.

The latter moved the plate of carved lamb nearer, raising it toward Bayard's chin.

Frowning, Bayard continued to pick exaggeratedly, as in the dark. "Where the devil are those candelabra, John?"

John scrutinized the platter, frowning as Bayard had done. "I can't rightly say," he loyally declared. "I reckon they be somewheres about."

Extending the inquiry, Bayard peered down the table at his wife.

She waited till John had left the room. "I'm afraid I pawned them darling," she confessed outright, looking down at her plate.

"Good God! Are you that short of money? Why the devil didn't you say so?" But as he spoke, another possibility was rightly gathering force in Bayard's mind.

On hearing Ellen's story, an angry frustration boiled over into the vacuum of ensuing silence, painfully cauterizing an already gaping wound. He was doing everything he could to hold their home together and to secure a decent level of living for his family. Yet on any provocation, Ellen readily, even eagerly, gave all she could away. Worse, the very alacrity of her largesse plainly declared her disapproval of him. It was his culpability for which her charity sought so avidly to compensate. He had been judged and found guilty. He could not make her see.

Always he had kept the vulgar aspects of moneymaking from their hearth. For him Blue Hills House was an inviolate sanctuary, a place where he might enjoy so many of those things he cherished most, and for which he had so long and ardently labored, a sanctuary where he could find treasured civility and repose. And Ellen was its adored high priestess, his dream girl.

But fathoming her sadness, her dismay and wretchedness at the coarseness that had crept into her life, crossing in muddy boots the threshold of their tranquillity, besmirching and sullying, the effect was so acute, the contamination so complete that plainly they could not continue as they were. Nor could he ask outright for her support; he would not plead; and he knew she would have offered it were she able. He loved her still and he knew that she loved him. But at some moral level, they were enemies.

"Give me the pawn ticket, Ellen," was all that he said then. "We'll get those candelabra back tomorrow."

And miserable at having let him down again, at having so abjectly shamed them both, she meekly obeyed. But the hundred dollars was gone.

SOME WEEKS LATER, standing before the library hearth after dinner, his weariness and approaching defeat well hidden, Bayard presented a carefully thought-out plan.

"My dear I think it would be a good idea if you took the boy to England for a bit. Gave his grandparents a chance to get to know him," he said pleasantly, raising his hand against her own instantly launched protest. "No, hear me out. There's no hope of their coming here in the foreseeable future, and as things are going to be pretty difficult, possibly pretty acrimonious for a while, I'd prefer to think of you enjoying your parents' company and not sitting at home with your hands tied, worrying about everything."

Ellen said she wouldn't dream of leaving at such a moment, let alone waste their money frivolously on travel. But she quickly saw that this was what he wanted. This was what he had decided was for the best, and that for his sake she must obligingly give her consent. After all, she was a hindrance not a helpmeet, and Bayard would be burdened with one less worry if she went.

Without further protest or discussion, therefore, the proposition was agreed on, and the die having been cast, they dutifully addressed themselves to its accomplishment. So that by early June, William was toddling along the chair-festooned deck of the *Berengaria* like a drunken sailor, as Bayard solemnly kissed his wife on the forehead before going ashore.

"I'll send money over regularly," he told her.

"But we don't want any money."

"Everyone wants money, my dear, and there are William's expenses as well as your own to see to. Besides I've no intention of sending you home a pauper." And he almost smiled.

The thought of Carrie Pritchard underpinning so faithfully her husband's pride flitted across Ellen's mind, and she kept silent. The steamship tickets were for first class, but their being one-way tickets poignantly bespoke his lack of ready funds. In an obscure way, it also left their marriage open-ended.

A wild urge to cling to her husband, to throw her arms around him and beg him to take her home seized Ellen's terrified heart. If only he would make some sign, give her the smallest encouragement. But Bayard remained his impenetrable, apparently unperturbable self, and she could not do less, or more, than match the solemn affectionate dignity that so belied their bleakly wretched interiors.

Her sad gaze followed him down the ship's gangplank. Then, waving to him on the shore, holding the excited William by the hand, and forcing a radiant smile, she reluctantly bid her husband good-bye after fourteen largely happy years of marriage.

8

The honey-colored stone manor house where Ellen had been born, tucked comfortably into the fold of an Oxfordshire river valley, was colder and the weather far less pleasant than she had remembered. But the open fires, the old oak furniture polished into glistening opaque mirrors, the threadbare Turkey carpets and peeling, badly painted family portraits, produced a benign and reassuring contentment. She was home.

From the moment of her arrival, the Ferrises had instinctively cosseted their daughter and, after the warmth of an earnest welcome, had left her largely undisturbed by plans outside the household's own indelibly set routines. A well-bred reticence prevented the couple from quizzing their child about the corners or even the supposed reception rooms of her private life, or of ferreting out some hint regarding the length of her visit. But with typical English pragmatism, they did not hesitate to ask after Bayard's financial affairs—of which they had read much but heard surprisingly little—and whether Ellen might still be reckoned to be comfortably off. It produced little ready coinage in return, however, for in truth Ellen knew next to nothing about it.

Before their daughter's arrival, Lord and Lady Ferris had been full of another kind of fear, a mutually felt alarm, long repressed but finally uncaged in the face of the impending visit. Their putative grandson's existence had from the beginning nourished in them a remote distaste. He was, albeit innocently, an imposter, a cuckoo hatched gratuitously into their venerable and well-feathered nest, but nothing really to do with them. Blood was blood, lineage, lineage; it was not something you could pretend about.

But the little boy's good looks, his black eyes with their intense and eager curiosity, the way in which he looked so penetratingly at things, his little hands clasped thoughtfully behind his back, rapidly worked their charm. For William at three years old was already a seductive child, charismatically attracting attention and exciting generous affections, without his needing to give much in return. Before a week was out, Lord and Lady Ferris were wrapped around the childish fingers as thoroughly as doting grandparents will permit themselves to be, their enchantment veering unreservedly toward undisciplined indulgence.

Two quiet months went by. Each week a letter arrived from Bayard expressing with customary formality his affection, but rarely conveying any news about himself or his affairs. Occasionally a bank draft was enclosed. Then in one sharp pen stroke came the dreaded news that Blue Hills House was lost. Reported matter-of-factly, Ellen divined with a sure instinct its fierce and heartbreaking disappointment for her husband. The house's emotional and symbolic value had been of such enormous importance to him; and she was miserable. The calamity was ultimately her fault; she could have prevented it; and she did not now hold back from rigorous and repeated self-examination, for it was in her nature to demand much from herself.

She knew that she had judged her husband. She had judged him and had found some of his actions wanting and irresponsible. Was sitting in judgment on a husband wrong? Did for better or worse mean she must renounce her own values and take up unreservedly her husband's, whatever they might be? If so, it was not within her character to do it. But Carrie Pritchard, she felt sure, would never have sat on such a bench or been part of such a jury.

Still, Ellen could not bury the knowledge that Bayard had done wrong. She could not turn away from the fact that willfully he had mismanaged money entrusted to him by others. Yet he had sought no forgiveness, he had expressed neither guilt nor any conscientious wish to make amends to those who had been injured. That was the truly terrible thing. For at one word of genuinely felt remorse, she could, she believed, so easily forgive all. If only it would come, how she would cherish that!

But the fact remained that it could not be right to abet, on her husband's behalf, wrongs against others, which saving Blue Hills House from creditors would, as the court had now confirmed, be doing. And yet this very action, this stubborn inaction on her part, had undone him. Never might he be able truly to forgive her, or to trust again so inherently critical a presence.

He had, he wrote, moved at short notice into a small apartment, and most of their belongings were in storage. She could not then, as she saw, go home, taking William with her, in the conceivable future—had Bayard even asked her—for the present there being no home for her to go home to.

Alive to her daughter's despondence, which fed so readily on a nature predisposed to introspection, Lady Ferris began to come up with schemes of social diversion, but always Ellen demurred, saying she was unprepared as yet to take up social life. She did not say, however, as she believed, that this was properly a time for mourning and, not wishing or able to spare herself, of sad and regretful reflection.

Daily she went for ruminative walks along the riverbank, occasionally climbing the pretty pastured hill above the house. She read, she played with her son, she began to teach him the alphabet and to name his colors, finding in all these activities unexpected shards of sweetness and comfort. Perhaps melancholy suited her, filled her out and enlarged her otherwise weak and diffident character; or so she sometimes felt.

Then one day an unavoidable diversion was suddenly offered her. Improbably it was the result of drains. Serious waterlogging on the Ferris estate, hazardous to spring sowing, prevented in the eleventh hour Lord Ferris from accompanying his wife to Paris. And Lady Ferris, instead of forfeiting the trip, compounded its potential blessings by seconding Ellen. The tickets were paid for and they could share a room; there would be no additional expense.

To Ellen's surprise, a coiled spring of eager anticipation released itself in her bosom, matching in equal measure her dismay at parting for the first time from her son.

For his part, young William did not go for it one bit and said so emphatically with his whole body, his little fists beating out his pronounced displeasure on the nursery carpet.

"Is he becoming spoiled do you think?" Lady Ferris nervously wondered. "Perhaps he is only strong willed. Usually a good thing in a man."

"Don't be unhappy, darling," cried Ellen, holding the sobbing child in her arms. "It's only for a few days, and I'll bring you a wonderful present back from Paris. Oh yes, a great surprise. Well, wait and see," she whispered, having successfully lured the child's attention into speculations of what in fact this wonderful present might be.

Eager to notify Jasmine, Ellen discovered her sister-in-law had no telephone, and they were to leave that very night on the wagon-lit; everything had happened so fast. She might still send a telegram, of course. A servant could run down to the village with it, but the seductive appeal of producing a surprise, with its capacities for giving and receiving pleasure—recently so very successful with young William—snared her imagination, so that she held off, intrigued at the prospect of offering unexpected pleasure of her own making.

A joyful presentiment enveloped her therefore, when, on the morning of her arrival, having overseen their unpacking, she took a taxi to a *quartier* that was utterly new to her, and, carrying in one hand a prettily wrapped English cashmere scarf, eagerly rang the rusty doorbell of Jasmine's atelier.

March had left its promises imprinted on the budding trees and, madcapping the dome of sky with purest blue, set the birds to twittering for mates. Beside the front door, a tub of daffodils trumpeted their golden silences in the wind.

The door was flung open by Frank Noland, looking none too pleased at the interruption.

At first both parties failed to recognize each other.

"Je me trompe," Ellen began apologetically. *"J'ai pensé que ma belle-soeur Mademoiselle Douglas habite ici."*

The puzzle for Frank fell rapidly into place. A shrewd smile lit his highly intelligent face. "Mrs. Douglas, isn't it?" he said pleasantly. "Frank Noland. We met in Nashborough, if you'll remember. I came to see your pictures." He offered his hand, which Ellen, thoroughly drilled in good manners, automatically accepted and would have done so in any event as the only apparent rock in heavy fog.

"Mr. Noland!" she exclaimed, flushing in bewilderment. "Why yes, I do remember you."

"Jasmine's at an art class," he explained, looking quickly at his watch. "She won't be long so why don't you come in and wait? I can make you a cup of coffee if you like."

Her thoughts swirling in startled confusion, Ellen moved forward uncertainly in response. What on earth was Frank Noland doing in Paris—and in Jasmine's studio?

"I've come to Paris on the spur of the moment, with my mother," she hurriedly explained. "Unfortunately there wasn't time to write." Despite everything some sort of an apology seemed necessary. "I was hoping to take my sister-in-law to luncheon," she continued, stopping abruptly just inside the door. Over Frank's shoulder a man's shirt was hanging on a line to dry.

"Come in," he repeated, standing aside for her to enter. But as one turned into a pillar of salt, Ellen stayed firmly put.

"On second thought, I believe I won't wait," she said lightly. "There's an errand I'd like to run this morning and I've just enough time to do it." A chilly politeness had slipped into her gentle well-bred voice. "Perhaps you'd be good enough to tell my sister-in-law"—she could not manage the intimacy of "Jasmine"—"that I'll be back at my hotel by noon and would so like it if she can join me there for luncheon."

"I'm sure she'll jump at it," said Noland cheerfully, raising an impertinent eyebrow on learning it was the Ritz. He had been enjoying the minute transitions of light and shade that came and went over Ellen's serene features as their exchange developed.

"Don't worry, she'll be there with skates on," he called after her.

In the taxi Ellen forced herself to admit as a possibility the impossible—that Jasmine and Frank Noland conceivably might be living together—and she was deeply shocked. If things were as they seemed, and what else could they be, she had stumbled into a massive piece of deception, something too brazen to be fully taken in. What ought she to do? Suddenly she dreaded an interview with Jasmine, who, in the circumstances, were they true, must be equally reluctant to meet her. If only she could have written first. But perhaps now Jasmine wouldn't come.

"IT MUST HAVE been quite a shock!" laughed Jasmine, sitting opposite Ellen in the Ritz's grill and readily taking her into her confidence. "But we're married." She was smiling merrily, as though marriage, as was plain to see, made everything all right.

"Oh Jasmine, Jasmine, what have you done!"

"But we're married," the girl repeated. Ellen seemed unable to take the fact of it onboard. "And we're happy!"

This, at least, was perfectly evident to the older woman, who had instantly perceived the glowing animated bloom as, bursting with her news, Jasmine had volunteered her secret with eager intimacy. Of course she had little choice.

"And we're crazy about Paris. We're getting to know some fascinating people here—artistic people, some of them famous, too. We go regularly to Gertrude Stein's Saturdays. I suppose I've you to thank for that," she added, grinning broadly. She was eating quenelles with gusto and talking enthusiastically, nonstop. "Miss Stein is *very* impressed by Frank. Thinks he's a genius no less."

Ellen, however, refused to be diverted. "This secrecy, Jasmine. . . ." she began.

"Heavens to Betsy. Dar was secretly married and nobody thought a thing about it."

"Oh dear, you're not . . . ?"

"Pregnant?" Jasmine readily supplied. "Lord no, we're too smart for that." She skidded to a halt. "I mean, that can wait for a bit. Till we're settled and selling our pictures," she tacked on diplomatically. "As a matter of fact, I sold two last week to Lady Mendl. She's an interior decorator: Elsie de Wolfe. I expect you've heard of her. She says she's going to buy some more." Jasmine made a face. "She says they go so well with her new all-white decors. That's the fashion now, you know: floors, walls, ceilings, furniture—everything white." She ogled the elegantly appointed grill. "Could do with a facelift."

Stunned by such gushing insouciance, Ellen gloomily set her guns in place, ready for an inevitable assault. "But Jasmine, don't you see you're doing the very thing that you were forbidden to do, that you were sent to Paris in compensation for? And you're using your father's money to do it with! My dear, you must tell your parents at once. Living a hugger-mugger, hole-and-corner life, and deceiving the very people who care most about you—who are trying as hard as they know how to help you—it's terribly wrong."

"Did you know Papa tried to bribe Frank to give me up? Actually offered him money never to see me again!" She omitted Frank's own handling of the affair. Ellen was too conventional to understand it. "I'd no choice but to look out for myself. We both did. We were driven to it."

"But one's family is *part of oneself*," Ellen insisted. "You can't just turn your back on their wishes or ignore their greater experience of life. They have your welfare uppermost in mind, believe me."

"I grant you, they mean well," Jasmine offhandedly concurred. "But the world has changed so much since the war, and all their ideas are so outdated." She tried without success to sound more politic. "Their sort of life isn't for me, Ellen; it isn't what I want. I'd be bored to death living in Nashborough, playing bridge and seeing the same old people. You of all people can I'm sure understand that. Frank and I want more from life. We want to make our mark in the world, and if possible leave something behind for posterity." She laid her knife and fork down neatly together. "What it comes to, Ellen, is we've chosen a way of life that suits us, and I promise you, we're willing to take the consequences of that choice."

"But Jasmine, *you're using your father's money without his knowledge.*"

"I have to right now, till we're on our feet."

"Does . . . does your husband . . . agree to this?"

"Oh absolutely. An artist has to use whatever means he can to support his work. That's a basic tenet of Frank's philosophy. And I agree with him," she added proudly.

Inwardly Ellen shivered at this amoral reiteration of Douglas self-assertiveness, and in such an improbable context. "But my dear, you can't go on like this. You must tell your family the truth. It will be a shock to them at first, but now you're married, they'll accept it and make the best of it."

"I can't tell them yet, Ellen. Papa would cut off my allowance and then how would we live? You don't know him. He's fierce when crossed. He's an old-fashioned patriarch at heart who wants to be obeyed in everything, call all the shots. And where would we go? We couldn't afford to stay in Paris, and we couldn't go back home: Frank would never fit in, thank God."

Ellen seemed to accept this last, but as they ate their crème de menthe sorbets in silence, she was resolutely marshaling her courage for what was now inevitable.

Fixing the younger woman with as severe a look as she could muster, she began with an impressive firmness. "Jasmine, I implore you to inform your father of your marriage at once. Because if you do not, I myself shall be obliged to do so. And it will be far better, I assure you, if it comes from you."

Jasmine's look of utter astonishment showed how immature, how genuinely innocent she remained. Or did it show a contemptuous dismissal of honorable behavior? Out for oneself and that was that.

"But why?" Jasmine demanded incredulously. "It's not *hurting* them not to know. And it's certainly helping us."

"I'm deeply sorry to be privy to all this, believe me, but being so, as surely you must see, it would be deeply disloyal of me to keep it secret. It would be tantamount to taking an active part in a conspiracy."

"But they needn't know that you know; they don't have to know that you were even here. You don't have to say anything. And frankly, Ellen, what possible good could come out of telling them?"

Ellen's sharp intake of breath exposed a faint impatience. "It's a question of honor, Jasmine, and of loyalty."

"But what about loyalty to *me*? Don't I count?" She was getting close to tears. "It's my life that's being ruined after all, mine and Frank's."

Grimly Ellen stuck tenaciously to her guns. "I'm terribly terribly sorry. I would have given anything for none of this to have happened. But it has happened and it can't be swept under some conveniently introduced carpet."

Raising her hand she summoned the waiter. "You'll agree, I'm sure," she said with finality, "that it will be far easier if the announcement comes from you."

Jasmine stared at her appalled. "They don't need to know," she repeated lamely. "And if they don't, then no one will get hurt."

"But I would know, Jasmine." Ellen gazed in wonder, confounded by her lack of comprehension. "How could I live with myself, with my conscience, and be a willing partner to such . . ."—she was going to say dishonesty—"deception. I'm dreadfully sorry, truly I am, but I promise you, my dear, once you've made a clean breast of it, everything will fall into place. You'll see."

With a discreet flourish the waiter laid the bill before her.

Sitting gloomily in La Framboise that night, Jasmine and Frank confronted their future over several glasses of *pastis*, supplied free of charge by Maurice, as a tonic.

Frank was black with anger. "Silly old cow, nosing around over here; why can't she mind her own business? Threatening to blab and ruin other people's lives, just so she can live happily ever after with her precious conscience. Selfish bitch. That's all it amounts to really: bloody-minded selfishness."

Jasmine gazed morosely at the cloudy liquid in her glass and sighed briefly in exasperation. Having got this far she was not about to be undone by Ellen. "We'll think of something," she said. "And besides, we've got a bit of money saved."

"What's she doing over in England, anyway, silly old cow?"

"We never got round to that," Jasmine absently responded, her mind already turning toward the future. What was going to happen now? How would they cope? There wasn't very much money saved, and the fear of confessing to her father was only marginally less unnerving than his almost certain withdrawal of financial credit. But Ellen had left her little choice.

9

*A*s the Democratic primary approached in March, a nervous optimism swept through the tiny band of Reform Democrats. Its chances had grown, like flowers sprouting on a dunghill, out of the dire plight of others. In only three years, a hundred thousand American businesses had failed, the nation's productivity was cut in half, and two-thirds of the money supply had been wiped out. For farmers, fate held a particularly bitter cup. A bumper cotton crop that year would result in most of it plowed under by government order, so as to stabilize prices—a loss of ten million acres. The South, always so conservative, so independent, so mistrustful of legislative restraints, was, like the rest of America, finally ready to consider change, even radical change. The Reform Democrats felt their hour had come.

On the day of the primary, the two candidates, Stark and Harry Sayle, together with Seneca, their campaign manager, went early to their local polling stations and waved their ballots triumphantly for any reporters who happened to be about. In the evening, tense and excited, they gathered at party headquarters—two cheaply furnished rooms rented short-term over a downtown laundry—to await the emerging news. A couple of reporters had camped outside and Seneca declared this to be an excellent omen. "A good reporter can smell out news quick as a hound can scent a fox. Those boys have got real noses," he insisted.

Dartania sat smoking her cigarette with short impatient puffs, restlessly swinging one foot and tapping it at intervals against the corner of a desk. Despite her loathing of publicity, she had dutifully appeared alongside Seneca throughout the day. But a few words to reporters, or even a public smile, thoroughly exceeded her capacities. Not that it mattered, as the plethora of photographs in next day's papers would reveal. Dartania, even looking glum, had plenty of charismatic appeal.

Mary Ann Fenton, three months married, smiled and waved at the reporters, her delight in the occasion and her husband's role in it being wonderfully evident to all.

Why anyone should want to please people they didn't even know lay well outside Dartania's comprehension. But watching Mary Ann, Dartania admitted she had presence and contrived—no mean feat—to hold on to her dignity, while obviously enjoying the attentions lavished on herself and Stark.

By nine o'clock results began to come in and the little group clustered eagerly around the oval-shaped radio standing on a table against the wall. Yelps of glee or groans of disappointment greeted each result. As the contest increasingly took on the character of a horse race, even Dartania joined in, flushed and cheering with excitement. The gubernatorial vote, hair-raisingly close, lurched from one candidate to the other, but they had expected that; it was easier than confessing to a probable long shot.

Then suddenly Stark's East Nashborough district was announced. The result burst in staccato syllables from the radio: The Reformed Democrats had won the poverty-stricken district with a big majority. Stark was elected their next congressman.

A fizzing fountain of triumph erupted over the shabby room. The two reporters rushed in, cameras flashing, and scribbled sardonically on notepads. Everyone talked at once. Everyone agreed it was a landmark victory, a near historic event; and suddenly they felt awed by the remarkable size of their achievement. After twenty-five years, a well-aimed sabot had been skillfully tossed into Ed Buzby's creaking political machine, maybe bringing it to a juddering halt.

Champagne, poured for appearance's sake into paper cups, was produced mysteriously from storage inside the watercooler. But triumph overpowering caution, the two reporters soon received some too.

Mary Ann Fenton threw her arms around her husband and then stood smiling, holding his hand with unalloyed pleasure and gazing proudly up at him as he told reporters for the umpteenth time about the party's programs for reform.

But the central event, the race for governor, remained unresolved, and again the radio's disembodied voice took center stage. East Nashborough voted overwhelmingly for Sayle (loud cheers), but Blue Hills firmly declared itself looked after well enough by the incumbent. Representing the established order, Blue Hills had much to lose by change.

Finally, at 2:00 A.M. Harry Sayle narrowly nosed ahead and, holding his lead, crossed the finishing post an hour later.

Tired but exuberant, the Reformed Democrats saluted with cups of bootleg the emergence of a new epoch (the champagne having long since disappeared). Come January a stiff new broom would clean the capitol's marble halls, sweeping Buzby hangers-on into the proverbial gutter where they so obviously belonged.

It was nearly dawn when, heady with victory, Seneca and Dartania drove home to Longwood. Seneca's exhilaration had moved into a high and satisfied tranquillity. Like a surfer who has ridden a mammoth wave agilely and with well-managed success, he felt an exhausted pleasure coursing through his body like a drug. But above everything lay the grand assurance of having accomplished something to improve the life of those whose need was greatest. Such fights were the best. But such perfectly attuned triumphs did not come often, as he knew: This was the first, but with so many active years ahead of him, it almost certainly would not be the last. And possibly next time, the arena would be larger. He thought of Washington and all that might be done if Roosevelt got in, and for a second, he almost envied Stark. But that instinct was rapidly replaced by his awareness of Stark's amenity to guidance, while he himself could easily wait for a bigger reward.

They were approaching the Longwood drive when Dartania suddenly turned to him smiling, though it was too dark to see. "If I had a garland, I'd put it round your neck," she said. "That was a great race and it made me proud."

Knowing how much she hated politics, though she dearly loved a good race, Seneca smiled back at her with heartfelt pleasure in the dark.

BUZBY'S TROUNCING HOWEVER was not prime news in every household next morning. At Timbuctoo it was overshadowed by tidings of a more startling nature. A letter from Jasmine had arrived.

Hamilton, sitting in his office, eager to read the election results in the morning paper, had opened it hurriedly. "Dear Papa, I am married to Frank Noland." Hamilton sat up straight. "I know you'll be very taken aback, Papa, but remember Dar and Seneca eloped, and this honestly isn't much different. It's only because Frank's from such a different background that everyone was against him, that and the fact that our family doesn't understand the artistic temperament.

"I know you meant to do what was best for me, and I tried so hard to do everything you asked—agreeing to a separation and then going (willingly) to France. But the attachment proved, despite all this, too strong for us to break; and when Frank came to Paris, we found we could not honorably do otherwise than what we've done." There was no mention of the marriage date, but Jasmine appeared to be writing immediately with the news.

Hands resting open fingered on this knees, Hamilton rubbed them, looking out over the sloping lawn toward the old springhouse. "Flora," he said inwardly, "I did the best I could, but as in much else, I have failed." His jaw clenched at the waste of it. His daughter had willfully, stupidly, in her untutored innocence, destroyed forever her chances for the sort of life she so unknowingly needed.

The letter was two pages long, Jasmine's neat handwriting filling both sides of the paper. She begged her father to allow her to finish art school. She had made such enormous progress and had recently sold some pictures to a famous interior decorator there. Nowhere did she say why or how Frank Noland happened to be in Paris, or how he was managing to live there. But Hamilton's earlier perception of the young man led him to the instant conclusion that Hamilton was himself financing this perverse setup. The whole business smacked of conspiracy, with himself in the role of unsuspecting dupe. Hamilton's anger bristled. He had been crossed, and double-crossed. The pair of them must have been in collusion all along.

Stuffing the letter into his pocket, he hesitated, then with an audible snort, picked up the newspaper and resumed his normal routine. "Buzby Machine Breaks Down," the *Herald* triumphantly declared. Hamilton began to read the details with much interest.

Jane Douglas learned of the marriage before they went in to lunch. "Oh how very dreadful! She's ruined her whole life, in spite of everything we've tried so hard to do!" she cried. But her underlying sympathy for Jasmine remained firm.

"Poor little thing. Over there all alone and with no one to turn to for advice or help. And along comes that . . . cad! Oh it makes my blood boil. Falling into the clutches of such a horrid calculating creature."

The gong sounded for lunch, and as they went arm in arm into the diningroom, Jane lowered her voice perceptibly. "But what will they do? How are they going to live?" she whispered, incredulous.

"That, I'm afraid, is their affair," said Hamilton coldly. "She wanted it all her way and now by God she's got it."

"But what about money, dear?"

"She's got a husband, hasn't she?"

"Yes, who refuses to work. Who won't so much as lift a finger. You know that."

"Necessity is a great motivator," he calmly observed, pulling out his wife's chair, which was at a right angle to his own. Then he sat down, unfolded his napkin, shook it, and tucked it into his collar, as he liked to do. "Jasmine is badly spoiled. All my children are. They've had it too easy, and now hard times are going to try them—test their stamina." He began to eat the Eggs Benedict Calvin set down in front of him.

"Jasmine's marriage will bring maturity fast," he said when Calvin had gone. "Though frankly, I don't see how she's going to manage, confronted with life's uninsulated demands. So far, it's all just been play acting."

His sense of having been shamelessly used continued to rankle, though he said nothing to Jane. The very fact of it impugned his dignity. Jasmine had behaved dishonorably, but how much was she in fact to blame? Hamilton knew that a woman in love could be ruled heart and soul, becoming a puppet or an abject slave. And in such circumstances women were not, in his view, much responsible for their behavior. In this respect they were weaker vessels, and the strength of their devotion, so marvelous, so deeply admirable, could so easily lead to their undoing. The thought caused him momentarily to reconsider. Perhaps Jasmine, too, had been a dupe. But no, he knew his daughter pretty well. Her mule-headed and self-serving instincts lay behind it all. She had gone after Noland and it had been she, not Noland, who, he rightly guessed, had hatched their underhanded plot. Well, she had made her bed and she would have to lie in it. She was a grown woman. He washed his hands there and then of the whole affair.

JASMINE AND FRANK managed to hang on precariously in Paris for another year. Jane had persuaded Hamilton to send the young couple a wedding check, in keeping with decent behavior toward a daughter, and Jasmine sold two more pictures through her connection with the fashionable Elsie de Wolfe. But Frank, despite assiduous and glowing patronage from Gertrude Stein, sold nothing at all. He continued, however, to work with a ferocious dedication, his mood becoming increasingly bitter and taciturn, but his intentions doggedly undeterred, and his canvases accumulating in a corner of the atelier.

Then, like so many others before him, he quarreled terminally with his famous patron, further unsticking the couple's tenuous hold on Paris.

In March 1933, therefore, as Roosevelt moved into the White House for his first term, promising great changes in America's economic and social fabric, Jasmine and Frank came home, using their last few dollars for the passage. There was no question of going to Nashborough. Jasmine had little contact with her family, and fierce pride, plus Frank's "eccentricities" as they were politely referred to in the town, stiffened even further the case against it.

So they went to Detroit, staying out of necessity with Frank's parents until they were on their feet.

Poor Jasmine, her dream of a glamorous life at the pinnacle of the creative world having been burnt to a cinder, now found herself lodged in a small cheaply furnished apartment above an electrical shop. Sitting on the bed, she stared at the row of ramshackle houses opposite, their peeling facades and cheap net curtains summarizing poverty and defeat, and her heart sank into her shoes. But the bleakness that enveloped her in its ashen cocoonlike crust shielded for the moment, together with the shock of her descent, the full reality of what in fact she faced, having cast off so gratuitously the world she knew and having failed so pointedly in the one to which she so vehemently had aspired.

They had been given Frank's old bedroom, covered in school football pennants and with a single cupboard for their possessions. Their pictures remained crated, stored with Mr. Noland's electrical spare parts in the basement of the shop, patent redundancies in a rapidly evaporating past.

Frank's parents had been cautiously welcoming, his mother hesitant and intimidated, even a little alarmed by Jasmine's elegant appearance in a long fur coat. Times were hard, they said, and what were the young people's plans?

Jasmine was reluctant to leave the tawdry little bedroom except for meals, eaten rapidly by the family in an uneasy silence. It did not occur to her to help her mother-in-law prepare them. She read nothing and did no work, existing in a shadow world of depression, a miasmic limbo—vague, boundless and ghostlike—yet preferable to the banality of her surroundings and its collection of melancholy implications.

"Oh Frank," she cried out mournfully, *"we must think of a plan."* But no thought emerged to supply her gaping need, no pragmatic or inspired vision or any remedial scheme that would lift her with phoenix wings upon an airy current of hope.

Frank let her be; she would come out of it, he said, she would adjust. While for his part, he before long and with increasing acceleration, began to thrive. Roosevelt's great scheme to create employment using federal funds galloped Samaritan-like to his side and gave him a firm leg up. Soon he was painting huge vividly colored murals on tenement walls and on the outside of public buildings—sometimes on the inside, too—with little interference as to what they should look like or even be about. Detroit unfurled like an enormous canvas awaiting the application of his vision of it or, given his nonfigurative style, almost anything else.

But studying his new environment, uncovering its surfaces, and considering his available materials, physically and in the abstract, a most remarkable change occurred in Frank. Not in his style but in his philosophical view of things. This never showed in his painting in any recognizable way, but its manifestation was writ large in other areas of his life. Immersion in the expanding Detroit slums had sharpened unavoidably his awareness of poverty and its attendant helplessness. It had revealed, as he could never have imagined, the sad plight of the downtrodden and unlucky, who, often weighed down by their dependents, could not, even when given a slender foothold, claw their way upward and on to terra firma. This realization caused a grain of compassion to enter and to flower in Frank's egocentric young soul, altering his outlook and giving his fondness for speculative talk a new and passionate direction.

Stark Fenton had made sense after all, and he wrote to tell the Nashborough congressman so, pointing out that, being perennially wishy-washy, Stark hadn't gone nearly far enough. He'd been right about the need for a net, though, to underpin society. Only it wasn't enough. Not many men could achieve even moderate success, let alone flourish, in a position of unassisted freedom, especially if they had other mouths to feed. Therefore money must of necessity, and in all reasonable fairness, be shared out. Ditto the means of production; and artists like everyone else should be salaried by the state. In short Frank had become a Communist.

10

....

ow turn on the lights!" cried Alice Nash, standing in the doorway of Cottoncrop's big front parlor. The Christmas tree, stretching from floor to ceiling, as every year, and dripping heavy silver tinsel, had for the first time been electrified. As at last had Cottoncrop, the wiring threaded neatly through the old gaslight conduits. "Now doesn't that beat the Wali of Swat! It's perfectly splendid," Alice glowingly proclaimed.

The excited grandchildren agreed, though Ben, who had decorated Cottoncrop's Christmas tree for thirty years, looked glum. He preferred the softer glow of myriad white candles shining against the silvery cascades of tinsel to this garish string of multicolored gumdrops. Sometimes Miss Alice went too far in keeping up with the times, as now.

At the parlor's opposite end, on a table covered with a white cloth, and overcovered by a lace one, reposed the other significant totem of the day: a great crystal punch bowl containing eggnog and surrounded by innumerable cut glass cups, like dinghies floating beside a noble galleon. Cottoncrop's eggnog was famous: It looked like nothing but heavily whipped double cream, and tasted of nothing but whiskey.

The entire downstairs had been decorated for the occasion. Silver sleigh bells tied on with a satin bow jingled from an enormous wreath on the front door. Sprigs of holly crowned the family portraits and parlor mantelpieces, and in the broad hall, running the length of the house, a branch dripping mistletoe hung on a wide red ribbon between the two centrally supporting columns. The only religious note was a small crèche: The Holy Family, carved in what looked like coagulated salt, reposed below a framed flower-bordered sampler that read, "All for one and one for all," painstakingly stitched by Alice Nash during the Great War.

The Christmas party went back as far as anyone could recall. Once invited always invited, and this applied to whole families, so that by twelve o'clock, *tout* Nashborough, swelling to some 250 souls, was making its way across the city from Blue Hills, crossing the muddy Chickasaw River via the new steel bridge and passing through east Nashborough's slums, winding up the half-mile driveway to the historic old mansion with its gleaming Corinthian portico.

Children wearing hand-me-down velvet suits and dresses, and shod in shiny patent-leather shoes, tumbled out of the cars clutching that morning's favorite toy, as grown-ups, also in party finery, gathered up presents to be delivered on the spot. The next two hours would be spent consuming eggnog and other spirits, devouring Cottoncrop's excellent country ham, served between brittle beaten biscuits that left crumbs all over the floor, and exchanging news and gossip with friends and relations they'd known all their lives.

As in small societies everywhere, wit and humor formed the prized ingredients of talk, news or novel opinions being a rare commodity when people saw so much of one another. This Christmas however was a rare exception. A ready-made topic of conversation had miraculously presented itself, one so engaging that people everywhere talked of little else.

Two weeks earlier the Prince of Wales, for six months Edward VIII, had abandoned his throne to marry a commoner, what's more a divorced commoner, and even more to the point, in Nashborough anyhow, a Southerner. Feeling a special connection, everyone was merrily engaged in making the most of it. A direct link was instantly established between the prince's visit seven years earlier and this extraordinary, possibly even inevitable, upshot. The prince had been bowled over by the charms of Southern women, he had openly confessed as much, and plainly he had never got over it—this unprecedented marriage being the proof of the pudding.

Conflicting responses to the abdication had kept the topic on the boil. Some (mostly women) thought it admirable to put love first; others (mostly men) thought the prince an irresponsible fool. Time, all agreed, would tell.

"She *does* look a bit like you, Dar," Robin had mischievously observed, holding up the newspaper where a large photograph occupied most of the front page. "It's the hairdo. Perhaps it's some sort of fetish for braids—or rope—being a naval man."

"Oh hush, Robbie, I want to forget that silly business," Dar had said, nonetheless examining the formal studio portrait, as irresistibly it flashed across her mind with a fizz of innocent pleasure that the woman in the photo might conceivably have been herself.

Ellen Douglas's brother, it was widely if mistakenly reported, had, as equerry, accompanied the prince to France, and suddenly all Blue Hills thought about "dear Ellen," and for the first time decided that they missed her. The couple's estrangement, subtly established over so long a period, had, as a result, never been pinpointed or fully taken in. But when Bayard had moved into his little house in Blue Hills—a perfectly exquisite house, it was agreed—and still Ellen did not return, separation had become a solid fact, though still almost no one spoke of it, and Bayard never said one word. It was entirely a matter of divination.

Some opined that Bayard was too proud to ask his wife back to reduced circumstances, but others recalled that Ellen had found fault with Bayard's business affairs, and therefore might have refused to return, if asked. A few suggested that each had been waiting vainly for some signal from the other, producing an unfortunate standoff based upon a mutual misapprehension.

But in any case it was generally agreed that Ellen had never really fitted in. Her refinement obscurely intimidated and her sincerity mildly bored. They had let her slip from their minds as easily as from their company. But now many who had not thought of her for ages wrote warm letters, enjoying vicariously their connection with world events and hoping vainly for some intimate news about the newly married pair.

Dartania and Seneca uniquely never discussed or even mentioned the event.

SHORTLY BEFORE NOON, as the Nash family gathered in Cottoncrop's middle parlor to await their guests, cups of eggnog in hand, Alice was unexpectedly called to the telephone. "It's Mrs. Douglas over at Timbuctoo," said Martha apologetically from the doorway.

Alice looked rather put out. Ham Douglas refused to attend her Christmas parties, which was bad enough, but why should Jane call her now when, as she knew, there was so very much to do.

She returned to the parlor looking pensive. "Children, I think I hear a car coming," she announced, and they rushed toward the front door, betting each other a dime on who it was.

"There's some slightly worrying news," she went on, still in the doorway, looking toward Dartania and then at her son. "It seems they can't find Robin."

"Oh God." Dartania stubbed her cigarette out in exasperation. "He's on another toot!" Robin's drinking had in the past year, perhaps earlier if it was seriously thought about, become an distressing problem. He was never unpleasant or inarticulate; he was never unkind; but sometimes he could not stand up and at others he appeared to sink into cloudy, even sad, reveries of inattention.

Alice sat down in the blue upholstered chair beside the fire. "Jane said he didn't go home to dinner last night. Margaret wasn't too worried at first, its being Christmas, but later on, she called his secretary at home, and the secretary said he'd left the Cotton Exchange at five o'clock. She said there'd been a Christmas party and she admitted Robin had had a bit to drink. But he'd told her he was going straight home. Poor Margaret waited till this morning before she called the police. Thank God, no accidents have been reported."

Then tactfully she lowered concern another notch. "Jane wasn't really worried; she just wanted to let me know that Margaret and the children won't be coming. Margaret's staying put, waiting for news."

"Robbie could easily turn up here," Dartania murmured, looking ruefully at Seneca. "Under the weather, but then it is Christmas." Her brother's drinking both disturbed and mystified her. It made him a ghostlike version of himself—and ultimately unreachable. But loyally she excused him in front of others.

Cries of "Christmas gift!" and "My, what a beautiful tree!" sounded suddenly from the front hall, where Ben stood ready to take people's coats. The sleigh bells decorating the front door began to jingle incessantly, and the Nashes, rising to meet their guests and half-expecting Robin Douglas to be among them, banished the mystery from further appeal to their imaginations or even consciousness.

The house was quickly filling. After greeting their hostess, who remained in her chair beside the fireplace, everyone made a beeline for the eggnog bowl. Martha and Rosetta, in white uniforms and aprons and little white caps decorated with black silk ribbon, passed among the throng with platters of country ham and spice round, made from larded beef. They too exchanged greetings with the guests. At a lower level, children and dogs scampered wildly among a growing forest of legs.

"You never come to see us, Seneca." Chloe, up from Thebes for the week, looked tired, her thin face longer; her voice, tending to monotone, was strained. Taking care of three young children without help evidently took its toll.

Seneca said there weren't enough railroad accidents in Thebes. His services weren't in demand. But in truth when he did go there, he went straight to the Palace Hotel and never once contacted the Blounts. Working for a cattle feed company, as Bob now did, had not made him a more interesting person, while Chloe, although intelligent, was too earnest and lacking in wit for Seneca's taste. Then too, she always seemed to be searching somewhat desperately for topics. Her siblings sometimes called her "Cloy" behind her back, he now recalled.

"Hi, Aunt Chloe, thanks for the bracelet." Emma greeted her aunt, at the same time wrapping her arms around Seneca, who patted her absently on the head.

"I hear Robbie's gone missing," Chloe murmured, when Emma, after eyeing her suspiciously, finally bounded off.

"A little too much Christmas spirit is suspected," said Seneca, smiling. "I shouldn't worry if I were you."

"Oh, I never do worry about Robbie. He's a survivor in his own way, he'll be all right." She looked up at Seneca with an ingratiating smile. "But isn't it wonderful Mr. Roosevelt's got in again!"

Seneca, whose eye had begun to rove, heartily agreed. "He wants to move us from a do-or-die frontier society into an enlightened community," he said. "Let's hope he can do it."

"Oh look," cried Chloe, suddenly waving and beckoning over heads. "There's Red Mason." Rapidly she lowered her voice. "That's another drink problem." Her tone was far from uncharitable however. "Oh dear, why is everybody suddenly falling apart?"

"Not *everybody* is," Seneca said shortly.

Mildred Mason, Red to everyone, having as a child docked the "mild" from her name, came forward grinning and pushing a strand of honey hair back into the French roll on the back of her head. She wore a bright green dress covered in green spangles, low cut and clinging to her plump attractively curving form, which edged easily toward the voluptuous. She was married to Philip Mason, the master of foxhounds' younger brother, and the couple had for several years been living in Detroit. Philip Mason worked for the Ford Motor Company and as a result the pair hadn't suffered too much during the Depression. People bought motor cars no matter what, or enough of them did.

"What a sensational dress," cried Chloe, admiringly.

"Isn't it fun?" Laughing huskily, Red gave a little shake, so that the spangles shimmered.

"Very festive." Seneca grinned approvingly. "I heard you and Philip were back home. Welcome." He raised his eggnog cup in a salute.

"I can't tell you what a relief it is! Detroit is awful beyond belief. It's the tackiest place I ever hope to see." She turned toward Seneca with a smile. "I'd love some of that eggnog, if you please."

Seneca went to fetch it. He thought Red looked stunning. He'd had a crush on her in college and had tried without success to take her out. She was a couple of years older than him and had looked on him, rightly, as a boy. Like everyone else, he'd heard that she was a bit of a lush and that that was one of the reasons they'd come home—that and Philip Mason's plan to build an automobile plant in East Nashborough. There was something warm and natural about Red Mason that he liked a lot, something ripe but not yet overblown. A wonderful woman, he thought.

As the two women stood waiting, Chloe asked anxiously after Jasmine. "She never writes. Dar says she's working in a dress shop and that they live in an attic with no central heating. Isn't it awful! I expect you know she was ill for a long time after they moved there."

Red's face clouded in sympathy. "I only saw her a couple of times, I'm afraid. She didn't really want to be seen. You know how proud she used to be, and how ambitious. She was going to outdo everybody, and rub our noses in it too." Red suddenly looked sad. "Life is never what one expects, is it? Anyhow, I had her to lunch," she continued, "but she never returned the invitation, and that was over a year ago. She said she'd given up painting, that she wasn't talented enough, and that she'd never really wanted to be a painter, that she'd been mistaken about that. All of which was very strange. You know her husband's become a Communist, don't you?"

Seneca had returned with the eggnog. "I like the guy," he said, handing Red a cup and a little silver spoon. "He was a backwoods conservative in those days: survival-of-the-fittest, best man wins—all the good old frontier values. I'm surprised to hear he wants to even the odds."

"Well, he's making quite a name for himself, I can tell you, and not as a boondoggle painter, either, which is what I believe he does for a living. There was some trouble at Philip's factory. The men wanted to start a union, and of course Mr. Ford wasn't having it. He's dead set against the unions. They brought in private investigators to find out who the instigators were and the report said Frank Noland and the Communists were behind it."

Seneca lit Red's cigarette. "If I were at the bottom of the barrel," he said, "Mr. Roosevelt might not be moving quick enough for me either."

"Well I say thank God for Mr. Roosevelt," repeated Chloe with some fervor. "He's the only man who can hold this country together and give poor people hope."

"Try telling Philip that," laughed Red gaily. "He loathes the man."

"That's because Philip, unlike the rest of us, is in the money," Seneca affably supplied.

They were standing in the hall, and at the mention of Roosevelt, Miss Allen had leaned forward attentively in her chair just inside the open dining room door.

"Mr. Roosevelt is a fine man," she told four-year-old Flora, sitting at her feet, wearing the cowboy outfit she'd got for Christmas. They had the room to themselves. The table having been laid for Christmas dinner, with a red damask cloth and the Nashes' best china and glass, was off limits to guests.

By craning forward slightly, Miss Allen was able to see and hear much that went on in the hall, and she related tidbits to the child, much as she might to a companion sitting beside her on a bus. Flora, round-eyed and silent under her mop of curls, was either listening or dreaming. It was hard to tell. A toy six-shooter lay in her lap and a horse coloring book was open beside her on the floor.

As the servants passed through the room en route to the pantry, Miss Allen would engage them briefly with a remark, before they hurried on. No one among the guests came in to say hello.

"It was sex," Georgia Mason authoritatively declared, hands on her ample hips, to a group standing in front of the Christmas tree. "That's how she bagged him! But something *real peculiar*—well out of the ordinary anyhow." Georgia's head bobbed in emphatic confirmation. Though no one seemed to wonder where such interesting news might have originated, Georgia implied it had originated in Virginia, where Mrs. Simpson grew up.

"He told me he never wanted to be king," Dartania could not resist putting in before moving purposefully away.

"Well that's even crazier than a crazy sex life," cried Georgia. "It's the craziest damn thing I've ever heard."

Her carrying voice was matched by shouts of glee from Sally and Emma, bounding toward the front door. "Christmas gift, Uncle Bayard! Christmas gift!"

Bayard, more than usually owlish in his morning coat and pince-nez, had entered the hall with colorfully wrapped parcels bulging in his arms. The two girls, linking arms, made a circular prison around their favorite uncle.

"Women!" declared Bayard with some force. "I positively hate women!" This greeting was by now established tradition, and the two girls giggled and beamed, still keeping their uncle within their circle.

"What did Santa Claus bring you?" he asked them. "Ashes and switches?"

"Poker chips," said Emma.

"Yeah, we're gonna open a casino."

"Yeah?" Bayard repeated the word with disapproval. "Why not a speakeasy; they're much more lucrative these days."

"Yeah, a speakeasy would be great. Could you get us a still from somewhere, Uncle Bayard? We could make a lot of money in the bootlegging business."

"I cannot and you are not to ask your grandmother for one, as I fear the consequences." He handed each of the girls a slender parcel. "Handker-chiefs, not silk stockings."

They made a face and, dropping their linked arms for this more interest-ing purpose, went off to unwrap their presents.

"Your children are little reprobates," Bayard told Dartania, accepting a peck on the cheek. "Too flighty and impertinent ever to make fine ladies."

Dar laughed, not at all displeased, then rapidly changed the subject. "Have you heard anything about Robbie, Bayard? He didn't come home last night."

Bayard looked even more solemn, if that were possible. "I don't want to alarm you, Dar, but the fact is I hear they're planning to drag Ed Jeeter's pond this morning. Somebody thought they saw Robin's car parked out there yesterday."

"People are always seeing things," she replied dismissively, "and there's no stopping them. Dr. Nash used to see red Indians and Cal is always seeing Mama standing down at the springhouse. Some folks are plain suggestible. Robbie was in his office yesterday till five o'clock. His secretary told Mar-garet. But they'd had a Christmas party, and you know what that means. He'll turn up. You wait and see." Dartania was determined not to ruin her Christmas by useless worrying. "Doesn't Red look great?"

Across the room Seneca and Red Mason were perched side by side on a large ormolu table pushed against the wall. Red's long legs were crossed and a high-heeled sandal dangled perilously from one foot. Her dress shimmered and shone like fish scales as the spangles caught the light from Cottoncrop's newly electrified sconces. Both of them were laughing and Red, cigarette in hand, was pushing her strand of wayward hair back into place again. The scene, radiating so much warmth and color, would come back later on, a vivid and sharply edged engraving in the minds of those for whom, at the time, it epitomized Cottoncrop's hospitable Christmas parties.

From her chair beside the marble fireplace, Alice Nash watched sporadi-cally but with an impresario's attentive eye, the goings-on about her. At the same time, successive guests, taking the seat of honor next to her, paid their tributes and brought her up to date on this and that.

Bertha Fenton, sitting down, pulled the chair up as close as possible. "They say Robin may have got into some trouble with bootleggers," she whispered, craning forward in her eagerness to report a scoop. "He was seen by his servants talking to two men outside the house on Wednesday night, and there was an argument. Raised voices and all. About money." She paused significantly so Alice could absorb the full import. "Bootleggers are nothing but gangsters, and not to be fooled with either."

"I heard they were dragging Jeeter's pond," Sally pertly injected, warming her bottom in front of the fire.

"Go away," said Alice, not unkindly, "and stop listening to other people's conversations." She turned back to Bertha Fenton. "The whole thing doesn't make any sense, does it? It just doesn't jell somehow."

"If you remember . . ." But whatever she intended to say was interrupted by the arrival of East Nashborough's congressman and his wife and child.

"Just who I want to see!" cried Alice, who was getting tired of dramatic female speculation. "Washington must be humming like a teakettle on the boil, and I want to hear all about it. Nobody can beat that Mr. Roosevelt, to my mind."

"Not even the Wali of Swat!" asked Sally, who, having wandered back to the fireplace, was again hiking up her skirt in front of it.

Alice ignored the child's impertinence. "Mr. Roosevelt is a gentleman and a politician. At last we've got a statesman in the White House."

"I wish they shared your view in Blue Hills, Miss Alice," said Stark, looking about with bemused skepticism.

"Damn fools, the lot of them. Always have been," Alice declared, casting a suspicious glance in Sally's direction.

Bertha Fenton had relinquished the seat of honor to her daughter-in-law, who now sat, holding her baby on her lap. "Miss Alice, I can't thank you enough for sending me *Gone With the Wind*. It arrived two days ago and I can't put it down."

"Oh, that Scarlett," cried Alice Nash, "*such* an unfortunate woman."

"But she has such spirit," said Mary Ann with feeling. "You can forgive her anything."

"Hmpph," said Alice Nash with some impatience. "Well, I can't." She looked toward the door. "Now what on earth is all that!"

A loud commotion had arisen in the hall, a dog was barking and growling furiously amid excited voices. Stark, leaving his wife and Miss Alice to discuss the new best-seller, went to see. A crowd was gathered near the back door, which for some reason was open behind the closed screen one. A few feet in front of it, the Nash's old Labrador, his hackles raised and teeth aggressively bared, rigidly challenged an invisible foe.

"Who's out there?" called Matt Collins, urged into a manly challenge by his wife. The excited voices dropped as if expecting some reply.

"Is it Robbie?" Dartania, having moved forward, whispered to Dan, who, in his wheelchair, was nearest to the door. "Did you see him?" She knew her twin might well slip unobtrusively in by the back way. It would be like him to do that, and perhaps she should disperse the crowd to make it easier.

Skirting the obsessed animal, Dan pushed the screen door open with his stick and rolled briefly around the back porch, which, except for a big old-fashioned icebox, appeared to be empty. "I couldn't see anything," he reported with a shrug.

Instantly the Labrador, as if reassured, relaxed its stance, tucked its tail, and, whimpering, skulked sheepishly off among the crowd.

"He's an old dog," said Matt. "They get their wiring crossed sometimes. Remember Ann Marie's Doberman?"

Matt's wife, the former Maybelle Spencer, shivered conspicuously. "One day he up and went for their son, out of the blue, just like that," she told the others. "It can happen, you know, even with family pets."

But attentions were rapidly turning elsewhere, so that Dartania was soon able to slip quietly out onto the back porch. "Robbie," she called out softly, "is that you?" She looked over the latticed balustrade into the yard below. "Robbie? Robbie, it's me. Are you down there? Are you under the porch? It's OK to come out, everybody's gone. Robbie?"

Only little Flora, attracted by so much clamor, had seen her mother go outside and had heard her whispered calling.

"What was it, honey?" Miss Allen asked eagerly as the child sat down again on the floor. "Did the dogs get in a fight?"

Resuming the coloring in her book, Flora did not look up, but began to draw a sticklike figure on the paper. "Indian," she solemnly declared, adding two turkey feathers to the drawing, and a beaded necklace.

In the front parlor, unperturbed by canine hysteria, Seneca and Red still sat on the ormolu table chatting.

"I've heard an awful lot about you since I got home," she said, looking out of the corners of her eyes at him. "Everybody says you're the best trial lawyer in the state and that you're headed like a rocket for the Senate next time round." She looked at him admiringly but in a friendly way—a little mocking too. Her eyes, a trifle glazed, had taken on a luminous honey color that made them to Seneca's mind more dazzling.

"I must have a publicity team that I don't know about," he said, pleased at hearing praise from once disdainful lips. "And I can't think where it is. Blue Hills thinks I'm a dangerous renegade and a traitor to my class. But you look swell, Red, life must be treating you pretty well."

She shrugged. "I've three adorable children, a boy and two girls. And I'm damned glad to be back, that's all."

"I'm damned glad, too," he said enthusiastically. Suddenly he was feeling as pleased as if he'd won a big lawsuit against the legal odds. Suddenly life was humming with an extra if as yet undefinable buzz, and Seneca, casting his eye vaguely over the crowded room, felt like a man on a springboard, ready to jump up high into the air, to soar and take hold of all life had to offer him. Suddenly he felt himself to be a supremely happy man.

11

....

*M*r. Robin upstairs. I got to take his breakfast up to him." Calvin was sitting in the kitchen at Timbuctoo, muttering to himself, as so often now, obsessively, his hands interlacing and unlacing helplessly. During the past year he had grown frail and forgetful. Phoebe's death, and now Robin's strange and unaccountable disappearance, had snagged some corner of his mind that no dissenting voices could pull free. He was the family's lifeguard and somehow he was to blame.

"All them years we done worried bout that creek. . . ." The gnarled old hands restlessly joined together again and parted. "Miss Flora, she done warn me, I believe," he muttered to himself. For that death, too, had never left Calvin's mind. Only he'd been able to deal with it differently, maybe even advantageously, the human mind being such a remarkable abode. A high temperature at the beginning of February brought the doctor to the little cottage behind the house, and pneumonia was diagnosed. Pneumonia, the old man's friend, the Douglases agreed among themselves, thinking with distress of Calvin's growing infirmities.

Accepting that death was near, Hamilton paid his old servant a bedside visit. It was the first time he had entered the cottage since just after it was built. The bedroom was small but clean and snug. A big hooked rug covered the floor and a coal fire was burning at full blast in the iron grate, with an easy chair pulled up beside it. Calvin's granddaughter was nursing him. She stood up, giving Hamilton the upright chair beside the bed.

"It's Mr. Douglas come to see you, Granpappy," she told him, leaning over and speaking more loudly and distinctly.

The old man opened his eyes, turned his head toward Hamilton, and smiled a childlike smile.

"You're doing fine, Cal," said Hamilton warmly, and sat down, "just fine."

Still smiling, Calvin said something inaudible.

Hamilton leaned forward. "How's that, Cal?"

"Clover Bottom . . . when we got them squirrels."

"We got ourselves a lot of squirrels back then."

"That ole slingshot . . . member?"

But though nodding encouragingly, Hamilton could not. So much had happened since those long-past days. They were almost another age. His life had moved forward at such a hectic challenging pace, and always with so much in front of him, that thinking backward toward events of the past had got outside his way of going at things. Vaguely he could recall Cal having given him a slingshot, perhaps even making it for him. Certainly he had owned a slingshot, a perfectly formed Y of smoothed hazel wood. Hazel wood was supposed to be lucky and he remembered now that the wood had felt like silk. But so much had been blocked out for so long, it was now inaccessible. Time and the rush of events had cut off his conscious connection to childhood, like a disused path covered up and lost from lack of use. He had forgotten too that Cal had once been like an elder brother to him. Hamilton had thought of him for so long as a faithful servant. And in truth the former relationship had needed to be erased for the latter to become effective. So that looking at the old man now, Hamilton merely saw his aged servant, an employee on whom affectionate duty insisted that he pay a call.

" 'Pechard,' " Calvin smiled again, rather vacantly, the words slightly slurred.

Again Hamilton leaned forward to hear. The room was suffocatingly hot.

"Brought you down," Calvin asserted with gentle pride. " 'Pechardill.' "

Hamilton shook his head in polite incomprehension. That Calvin's thoughts should roam familiarly and at random in his boyhood was a good thing, he felt sure. It was one of the blessings of old age.

"Pechardhill," he repeated skeptically to himself. Then suddenly he understood. "Peach Orchard Hill!" He remembered Peach Orchard Hill all right. The horror and yet the eerie marvel of that battlefield of frozen corpses under snow. It was like coming upon Pompeii after Vesuvius had erupted, or discovering some antique ruin, the surroundings littered with oddly contorted stone sculptures.

A trench had been cut along the hilltop and looking down into it Hamilton had seen, lying beside an open leather purse, a most extraordinary and appealing sight. It was a brightly colored marble glittering in the morning sun. A great treasure for a little boy. But starting to climb down into the trench, he'd stumbled and fallen—fallen into the outstretched arms of a soldier hard as rock. And the body he had stumbled over fell on top of him. Caught in that freezing double embrace, unable to free himself, unable to move, he had panicked, screamed out in blind terror.

Cal had climbed down into the trench and pulled the frozen corpse off, then pulled Hamilton out. Hamilton was shaking uncontrollably and trying hard to pretend it was the cold. But he had got that marble, was holding on to it tight, experiencing for the first time the spreading satisfaction of a powerfully willed success. Then, having got his breath back, he proudly opened his fist.

Instead of the glorious marble, a frozen eyeball, beginning to melt, lay in his hand. Even now, Hamilton shivered slightly in the overheated room. The experience was so vivid, being so unexpectedly unearthed after all these years.

Calvin had taken it and thrown it away, then patted him gently on the shoulder. "Let's go home," he'd said. "We the only ones in this whole place what can."

How profoundly comforting that had been. Suddenly, almost as a revelation, Hamilton had sensed, as never again, the wonder and the gift of life, its reality as desirable as it would ever be—and in the face of so much carnage, its ephemerality.

Now, for no reason that he could put his finger on, something like homesickness enveloped Hamilton. He tightened his lips, manfully pulling himself together. "I sure do remember Peach Orchard Hill, Cal," he said most tenderly. "Why, I believe you saved my life that day."

Calvin chuckled softly, as if awaiting that inevitable conclusion. Then he began to cough and his granddaughter hurried over.

Hamilton stood up. "I'll come back tomorrow, Cal," he said. "Tell him I'll come back tomorrow," he repeated to the girl, when the coughing didn't stop.

"Yes, sir." She'd begun to mop the old man's mouth with a fresh handkerchief. "I'll tell him, Mr. Douglas."

Hamilton was greatly relieved to get outside again. The heat in the cottage had been overwhelming. He wiped his brow, ducking his head under the low porch and descending the two plank steps. On the path another figure was coming up, a young black man, evidently a preacher, carrying a worn Bible.

Hamilton nodded, "Afternoon."

The preacher, taken aback, looked up coldly and frowned, then he too nodded and answered in a formal-sounding voice, "Afternoon."

Calvin died during the night.

The funeral, held two days later at the Baptist church, was a long affair lasting several hours, with much singing and an extended peroration. Seneca said later that the oratory was of a better quality than you could expect to hear in court these days, and the singing, all agreed, homed in like a magnet pulling on the heart. When the choir sang "Swing Low Sweet Chariot" lumps had ballooned choking every throat.

"Oh Lord, deliver thy children from bondage and give them their longed-for freedom," declared the young preacher, the same one Hamilton had seen coming up the path to Calvin's cottage.

"Yes, Lord," said the congregation, and "Amen."

"Give us a sign, Lord, like you gave to Noah imprisoned in his ark, that our freedom, like his, is on the way."

"Yes, Lord," said the congregation, and again "Amen."

"Let the soul of Calvin Douglas rest in peace until that great day of rising up and coming into his true kingdom, the great day of celestial freedom, Lord, beyond all he knew or ever expected on this earth."

"Yes, Lord," and "Amen," said the congregation.

Then the choir sang "Let My People Go."

Bayard said that the Episcopal church needed to take some lessons from the Baptists if it wanted to hold on to its dwindling members. He was interested too in the strong political tone expressed throughout the service. Who was the young preacher?

Calvin's grandson, he was told. The young man's name, as the family discovered much to their astonishment, was Robin Douglas. Had they known that and forgotten it? No one was sure, but wasn't it so very extraordinary!

Alice Nash, who'd come over from Cottoncrop, pleasing by this gesture white and black alike, shook hands warmly with the young man when the service was over, and Seneca went over to talk to him, and drawing him aside, they talked for some time and seemed, the others thought, even to know each other.

Standing beside the open grave in the Douglas plot, where it was agreed Cal would be buried, Dartania mourned him, but repeatedly her thoughts ricocheted to her missing brother. He had loved Cal, and would so poignantly have felt his death, probably more than any of the others. Did he know, she wondered, that Cal had named a grandson after him? Robin would have liked that. And his being a preacher would have entertained him greatly.

Then she told herself, as she did every day, that she must learn to accept that Robin almost certainly was dead, even though, evaporating so mysteriously, he could not properly be mourned, as Calvin was now.

The possibility that Robin had been violently murdered was horrible to think about, and yet that possibility must be faced, though suicide was, she believed, more plausible. Something had broken in Robin, something as beautiful and as fragile as a crystal cup whose shattered refractions had altered his charmed perception of life, mirrored it differently, and made life for that sensitive and gentle soul intolerable. It had pulled against his natural gaiety like a stone tied to the leg of a drowning man. Dartania put much of the blame for it on Margaret, whose humorless, no-nonsense ways had dusted like a piece of parlor furniture Robin's beautiful butterfly wings, leaving him grounded and bare, doomed to a careworn and pedestrian life.

"Oh Robbie," she silently prayed, as Cal's coffin was slowly lowered by two ropes into the grave, "please don't be dead, please please Robbie don't be dead." But of course he must be. She repressed her tears, so unseemly in proud Douglas eyes.

When the burial was over, the Douglases, white and black, shook hands with each other and made polite if mutually self-conscious noises; then with a final word for Calvin on their lips, went their separate ways.

There was luncheon at Timbuctoo after the burial, and Hamilton, who had spoken in eulogy at the church, stood up again to propose with dessert a valedictory toast. The wine, an unheard of rarity at the Douglas's table, was served by a shy young man, Cook Anna's nephew Ned, who, taking Calvin's place, was also doubling as houseman.

The family stood, drank solemnly, and saluted "Calvin, an honorary and much loved member of this family," then regretfully turned their empty glasses upside down.

Seneca alone of the family party did not come in to lunch. He had an important political meeting and couldn't get out of it.

In fact he was lunching at a restaurant outside Nashborough with Red Mason.

12

....

$\mathcal{A}$s happens in a small society, the affair that blazed up so rapidly between Seneca and Red Mason soon became common knowledge. People recalled the pair sitting in Cottoncrop's front parlor on the ormolu table, engaged in cosy, animated talk. They remembered the shimmer of Red's brightly spangled green dress, her hair so charmingly disheveled, and Seneca's intent and beaming look. Christmas cheer writ large, they had thought then. Now they saw something else.

Of course, Dartania was among the last to hear, and as often happens, too, she learned of it by chance, only finding out because Lulu Piper had to leave the Tuesday bridge game: She was having a baby. Innocently Dartania had suggested Red as a replacement, and a sudden hush had fallen round the county club card table, but only for one second.

"Dar-chile," said Georgia Mason brightly, "Red is a wonderful person but she's no great brain. She can hold the cards in her hand all right, but I doubt she could hold them for long enough in her head."

Unanimous agreement followed and Maybelle Collins became the chosen replacement.

Afterward Dartania had gone to the cloakroom kiosk to collect a box of shotgun shells bought for Seneca, but Earline Battle wasn't to be seen. Impatient, she entered the kiosk from behind, where the storage shelves were ranged. A curtain of coats hanging across the middle of the kiosk shielded her from view, as the other women, waiting in front of the counter for Earline, talked together in whispers.

"I didn't know *what* to say."

"Honey, you handled it brilliantly."

Dartania's interest mildly stirred.

"His car's outside her house at lunchtime every day," Lulu Piper whispered with breathless excitement. "It's such a beat-up old rattletrap, everybody notices it." Her eyes widened into oracular circles. "I haven't told anyone this, not a single soul, I promise you, but when Philip was in Detroit the other day on business, the two of them went to Haverford Lake together. Jack saw them there, out in a boat. He and Eddy Mason were up there duck hunting. Oh I could bite my tongue for saying all that. You-all have squeezed it out of me like I was an orange."

"I hear she hasn't had a drink in over a month. That's something, anyway."

"Poor Dar, that's what I feel."

"And poor old Philip."

"Don't over worry yourselves about 'poor old Philip,'" said Georgia, whose sister-in-law he was. "He has his own lookout up in Detroit. It's one of the reasons she wanted to move back here."

Dartania narrowly avoided meeting Earline as she slipped out of the cloakroom door. Climbing into her car, she sat there dumbly, the blood rushing into her unhappy face. She might so easily have been discovered lurking in that kiosk. That was her first thought: the mortification of it. But that danger having been removed, the deep humiliation of being pitied, of being patronized by pity, was terrible to bear. She looked quickly about, making sure her car wasn't near any of the others. Then, safe from discovery, the reality of what she'd overheard began to emerge like the blooming of a strange and poisonous flower. Was it possible? Could Seneca really be having an affair with Red Mason? Could she have heard aright? A mental picture of Red in that shimmering fish-scale dress rose up before her. She had looked luscious. But no, it was ridiculous. Red was a very attractive woman, but she wasn't a patch on Dartania herself, and everybody, including Seneca, knew it.

As she drove down Blue Hills Boulevard toward the Longwood road, her mind continued to spin out its as yet unwoven threads. It would be silly to confront Seneca on hearsay; it might be silly to confront him at all. In fact, the more she thought about it the more improbable the whole thing seemed. She should know better than to listen to chattering biddies at the country club. Red Mason was practically a drunk and, according to Georgia, half-witted into the bargain. If there *was* something to it, then it would be a peccadillo, like her rendezvous with the Prince of Wales—light and unimportant—and she could readily forgive him that. In fact she was obliged to do so. Small sexual adventures were nothing to get excited about. Most men had them, and in her milieu, which was a tolerant one, it was covertly accepted, wives wisely turning a blind eye. Even if it wasn't easy, they sat it out. But that others should know of it rubbed and degraded, biting deep into Dartania's pride—and for her, pride was the staff of life.

Seneca's extreme good humor went far that evening to stemming her disquiet, but the following day, still mildly curious, she could not resist driving slowly past Red Mason's house at lunchtime. The house, of imposing size, red tiled and stuccoed in the Spanish style, was decorously set back from the road. But the driveway was clearly visible, and under the porte cochère, Dartania could see a new black Ford convertible. That was the only car. A bit ashamed of herself, she turned her car around in the neighboring drive. But backing out, suddenly in the rear-view mirror, she caught sight of Seneca's model T, parked against the far curb and in front of a little van.

Dartania drove straight home. Saddling her horse she rode the chestnut mare at a fast pace, galloping through the long wood, past the cotton and cornfields to the back of the property, and coming home at a leisurely walk, the reins resting loosely on the animal's neck. Never for an instant had her mind left its preoccupying topic. She thought and thought about it. What to do?

Lulu had said the car was parked there every day, which sounded like more than just a peccadillo. Yet it was impossible to entertain seriously the likelihood of an affair between Red Mason and her husband. Red was a scatty woman—emotive, glandular, a well-known lush. Not at all what Seneca admired in women. Of course it was a peccadillo.

At first Seneca denied the affair outright; then, later on, he declared it to be meaningless, a minor diversion, and finally, under extreme pressure, he agreed to give Red Mason up. He had not the faintest intention of doing so however. Red's warmth and spontaneity of feeling, her sexual abandon and her limitless admiration of him—even his power to keep her from the bottle—worked its many-tentacled charms. Seneca was in love, and Red Mason, he told himself, was there to stay. She filled an aching void.

Dartania had no intimate female friends, and unlike the majority of women who found themselves in her position, she did not make any now. Never would she have discussed or criticized her husband with outsiders. Such disloyalty was beyond her comprehension. Her misery therefore found no outlet, except for the incessant harangues she now launched against Seneca in the evenings. For the rows had begun in earnest: suspicions, accusations, resentful brooding sulks, and a mutual rancor that for Seneca was overlaid by nagging guilt.

Whenever of an evening he was late, Dartania, angry and suspicious, greeted him icily, demanding to know where he had been. No offered explanation, however, could effectively pluck out the painful thorn of doubt.

On a business trip to Thebes, Seneca had even called on Bob and Chloe to prove that he was there. In truth, so was Red Mason, booked into an adjoining room at the Palace Hotel.

Having precious little to occupy her mind, Dartania now fell headlong into the seething pitch-black cauldron of obsession. And there she stewed. Repeatedly she drove past the Masons' house on Chickering Road, alert as a hunting dog, fearing at the same time that she might be seen, not so much by Seneca and Red as by others in their set. Caught snooping. On one occasion she had to pull over fast and duck down to avoid Lulu Piper, and another time she narrowly missed colliding with Philip Mason's car outside his drive. Such behavior was, she knew, futile and ridiculous, it was powerfully shaming, but nothing whatever could successfully extract the all-consuming subject from her mind. Over and over it she went, round and round, examining every aspect, like the beads of a diabolical rosary she could not put down.

But of the myriad emotions possible in such a situation, outrage and bitter social humiliation remained her greatest woes. Sure of personal superiority over her rival—everything in her history solidly underwrote this view—she contrived without great difficulty to preserve her sense of worth, and so was spared the abject misery of having her self-confidence broken by a rival. She was a proud queen cast into the dust, but that massive laceration to heart and soul, so devastating and so full of heavy mourning—the death in life of the rejected woman—she was preserved from that.

Mercifully the two couples were kept apart socially by tactful friends. Though early on in the affair Dartania, unable to refrain from action, had brazenly called on Red one afternoon, as if innocent of any goings-on. She was anxious to size up her rival at close range and to let her know that she herself wasn't in the least perturbed—was sure she had no serious reason to be. It was a peccadillo.

Overt good manners saw both women through, but later that night the Masons' sofa, where Dartania had been sitting, mysteriously caught on fire. A smoldering cigarette burn was discovered to have been the cause.

Imprisoned by outrage, vehement grievances, and wounded pride, Dartania no longer knew whether she loved her husband or not. Certainly at times she hated him with all her heart. How could he humiliate and betray her so! How could he lie to her! Her wrath was justified. Seneca was grievously at fault.

For his part, cornered and made miserable at home—and kept by "home" from what he now desired with all his heart—Seneca saw threads of self-justification woven into their growing bundle of dirty linen. Dartania was a poor mother, an incompetent housekeeper, unsympathetic as a wife, and totally self-indulgent. She willingly took but she gave nothing in return. Her life consisted entirely of amusements. In short, she had never properly assumed the role of wife or mother—and now she was making his life unmitigated hell. Like an animal caught in a trap, he snarled and raged at any provocation.

And so did she.

The children were thrilled at first; there were possibilities for divide and rule. Turning a glass upside down on the floor above their parents' bedroom and putting an ear against it, they took turns listening to the altercations below.

"What's she saying?"

"She says she wants a divorce."

"What does he say?"

"He won't say. He says it's up to her."

"Well, are they going to or not?"

"They can't decide."

Then the girls got caught in the crossfire, even becoming a desirable target. For having no experience of misery or any expectation of it, and precious little self-knowledge, Seneca and Dartania's growing animosity spilled over into a growing irritation with their children. When Dartania, whose job it was to get the girls up for school, called to them in the morning, she shouted rudely and threatened punishments if they didn't move. Seneca, for his part, knowing how effective the rule of fear could be, now raged whenever it suited him, and at the slightest infringement of house rules, the older girls, now approaching their teens, received the sort of dressing-down raw privates enjoy under the correcting tutelage of a master sergeant.

Every night Emma and Sally filed through their parents' bedroom to kiss them good night as they sat reading in bed, glumly, like two effigies on a tomb. Privately both parents were convinced their children did them little credit and in some obscure way even marred, to a degree, their relationship. But when Alice Nash insisted Sally be sent off to school, as was proper at her age, Seneca refused point-blank to spend the money. There was a Depression going on, and Dartania fully agreed: Too much education did girls more harm than good. Only the dullest men wanted to marry a bluestocking.

So Sally and Emma remained at the local school into their teens, catching the school bus every morning from the front gate, their friends, the children of village shopkeepers and tenant farmers.

Through all these ructions little Flora occupied another world with other difficulties. Now almost eighty, Miss Allen's fears for the future had understandably revived, and she had grown increasingly uneasy and afraid. As the rows between her employers continued she would sometimes say to Flora, gripping her in her arms like two survivors of shipwreck, "Your mother and father don't care about you children at all. They don't love you like your Miss Allie does. What's going to become of you when I'm gone?"

Whatever the truth of this, Flora's grave young eyes swallowed it whole. Miss Allen was all she had. Evidently unloved by her parents, and with no children her own age to play with, black or white, she was always alone, riding her pony across the fields with an intense and curious zeal, living in some imaginary world populated by no one knew quite what.

One morning, when Flora was found weeping uncontrollably for Miss Allen on her day off, Seneca in a temper picked the distressed child up and shut her in a downstairs closet. "Let her stay there till she learns some self-control," he had fiercely ordered. "Her tantrums are plaguing the whole house."

The terrified and exhausted child was eventually rescued by Delphine, who wiped her face and gave her a cookie to eat. "Now don't you worry, honey, your Miss Allie's coming back. You know she's not going to leave you."

An inscrutable aloofness settled on the little girl's face under her mop of brown curls. She spoke little but what she said when she did speak was thought to be exceedingly droll and pithy, and her delivery, because she never smiled, remaining always deadpan, made for much amusement. Without having any idea of it, she was becoming the family pet.

It was Alice Nash who finally perceived Miss Allen's hidden fears. She one day overhead the poor woman lamenting to Ben in the upstairs hall. "You don't know how lucky you are, Ben, owning a house of your own. I've got nothing but the poorhouse when they don't need me here."

Alice Nash put down her novel, got up off her bed, and marched straight out into the hall. "Why, Miss Allen, what on earth are you saying? You'll always have a place in this family. There's never been any question about it. Surely you know that."

Unfortunately Miss Allen had not known, no one having previously undertaken to tell her so.

"Overnight she became a different person," Alice Nash claimed repeatedly afterward. "She simply glowed, and that sweet smile of hers bounced right back into place."

But in some respects the reprieve had come too late, for already Miss Allen's insecurities had been transmitted wholesale to her charge, something else no one had taken any notice of.

SENECA AND RED'S affair generated, of course, a supply of ready gossip. Alice Nash, who out of loyalty to Dartania, never spoke of Red Mason, did remark obliquely on the situation to those special friends who supplied her with information.

"They had everything in this world going for them," she would invariably lament. "And without a second thought, they've gone and thrown it all away. It's the saddest thing I ever heard, and frankly one of the silliest."

Alice was fond of Dartania, she admired her brave and loyal character and got on well with her; but she had always known in her bones that Dartania, despite her many fine qualities, was not the ideal wife for Seneca, and she greatly doubted Red Mason would have been. Her son's unhappiness made her wretched but her hands were tied; she could do nothing for him. Failure of any kind always devastated Seneca. And being substantially its author, as now, having wilfully turned his domestic life into a quagmire of angry recrimination, and having succumbed exactly at the point where he was strongest, in willpower, he was, she knew, being driven from himself as one fleeing from overt contamination, pursued as by the Furies.

Nor was Seneca's defeat to be confined to the domestic front.

One morning, not long after a much-publicized political dinner, an article appeared in Buzby's newspaper, the *Echo*. It made reference to Seneca's "radically left-wing" sympathies and ended by saying that not only was he a known promoter of Negroes, but, as the paper had discovered, he was also "in close communication with a Red." It was election year.

Unlike Oscar Wilde, Seneca was too astute to sue, but he could not avoid taking the article's insidious double meaning to heart. The piece had plainly declared that he could not now run for the United States Senate. If he did, the newspaper would expose his private life, he would lose the election and at the same time bring public mortification on his family. His political hopes, so deep seated and potentially so promising, were overnight stillborn.

He didn't blame Buzby, for he had brought it on himself: Politics, as he knew well, was a rough game. Yet suddenly his upwardly spiraling life, always so full of success and interesting challenges, was running wildly out of control, even threatening to collapse in failure.

THREE YEARS LATER there was finally a divorce, but it was not the one Nashborough had expected. Surprisingly Red Mason divorced her husband, Philip, who returned immediately to Detroit, taking in his pocket a multitude of potential jobs in East Nashborough. There would be no Ford factory now.

Gossip held that it had finally come to a divorce because Philip, confronting Seneca at the country club one night, had accused him face-to-face of seeing his wife, and Seneca had readily admitted it was so, and what was more, he intended to go on seeing her as long as Red allowed it. That had brought matters to a head.

The Masons' was the first divorce in Nashborough society since James Best, dead drunk, had attacked his wife with a poker, and it caused an uneasy if excited stir. Extramarital affairs were nothing new and in most minds hardly signified as a cause for legal redress. Divorce was a desperate strategy; it was also a trifle vulgar. But more important, it threatened the solid bedrock of respectable family life. Older people were shocked, but almost without exception everyone eagerly awaited news of ensuing developments. With Red now free to marry, Blue Hills seethed with speculation. Bets were even placed.

But to the delight of some, and the keenly felt disappointment of others, nothing further developed. Dartania held on. Having repeatedly threatened divorce, she now, in altered circumstances, took no action. Was it brave or cowardly, wise or foolish, Blue Hills wondered among themselves. But then, did Seneca even want a divorce? Dartania's stance might be a means of protecting him, for he could never have imagined that Red would leave her husband and land him in such an awkward and undiplomatic pickle. No one could decide, though the question, all admitted, was a fascinating one, and surely things could not stay as they were.

They had to wait another five years, however for the solution, during which time World War II changed everybody's lives and expectations—or all those who survived it, anyhow.

The Old Order

╬┼┼┼┼┼┼┼┼┼┼┼┼┼┼┼┼┼┼┼┼┼┼┼┼┼┼┼┼┼┼┼┼┼┼┼┼┼┼╬

*W*ars happen chiefly because we want to have things our own way. Equally, or next best, we want to make others as nearly like ourselves as possible. Is that the reproductive urge gone haywire, is it egotism, is it a vain attempt at war prevention? I don't know, but finally a deep-rooted need for change, or looked at another way, an innate incapacity for boredom, also underpins the instinct for war. Maybe it all turns on that.

But whether family rows, neighborly feuds, or outbursts of civil insurrection, each evaporates in the fixating scope of a larger battleground. I call that Dan Douglas's Benign Principle of Escalating Conflicts. While peace I define simply as the gap between wars, and frankly too much of it isn't only boring but dangerous; for without external threats, societies tend to fall apart, and on a smaller scale families do too. To claim wars are as good as they are bad therefore isn't cynical. I am in fact an optimist, which is how I came to note the felicitous or improving side of war. And of course I am not the first. War is the greatest tool for change there is. Marx made a lot of that.

But the war that reached out steely arms to embrace America in 1941, appalling in its carnage and hellish in the waging, profoundly changed our country and generally for the better I suspect. It changed the way we lived and how we thought about a lot of things, quite literally even how we actually saw them. It cracked a multitude of molds and it dumped a barrel full of pickled traditions down the drain, making a need for new ones in their place. Meantime it plastered over the cracks of domestic misery and brought fractious, unhappy families back together. But most important it brought prosperity: Conquering the Depression was, in America anyhow, World War II's most salient victory.

In the South the biggest change, though it took some time to come out, was probably white and black relations. A Negro exodus of biblical scale began during the war. It was a diaspora that involved upward of two million and would flow for years in a slow and steady current, as blacks set bravely out, a new generation of American pioneers, as impoverished, badly informed, and ill equipped as the previous, to make their way in the, for them, uncharted reaches of the North—like all frontiers a kind of promised land. They were lured by the promise of work—in factories making wartime goods and, later, all manner of things. Presumably they were lured by freedom too. But cheap labor was what they had to offer and it served them well. They made a lot more money than they had back home. Yet in that tangled urban wilderness they encountered too the myriad and unexpected problems pioneers must perforce encounter and must strive so desperately to overcome. Though legally at least they had their freedom.

Moreover, those who stayed behind could now ask for higher wages—well, slightly higher—for whites suddenly found themselves able to cut back on Negro help. They'd discovered the cheaper efficiency of machines—not just tractors and cotton-picking machines, which, supplanting tenant farmers, rapidly grew in use; but more transforming, perhaps, the industrial revolution entered the kitchen. As women undertook their own cooking and washing, luckily those who were displaced, unlike a century earlier in Britain, had somewhere to go: Chicago, New York, Detroit. The big cities boomed, their populations mushrooming alongside wildly spiraling productivity.

But so did the towns, and Nashborough was no exception. Suddenly farmland started to produce a brand new crop, if it was near the town, as naturally most of the old places were. That crop was suburbs. By 1947 a drugstore had opened its plate-glass doors a quarter of a mile from Cottoncrop's front gate, and beyond it rows and rows of tiny tidy redbrick houses with green asbestos roofs, treeless well-mown lawns and a car parked in the drive, sprang up, replacing cotton rows in fields once sowed by Negro labor now gone North. At Timbuctoo the steeple of a new-built Presbyterian church rose above the screen of trees across the creek. Town boundaries stretched like rubber bands, holding the increase; and taxes on land, even farmland, inside or near the new town limits, rocketed. But so did selling prices. Papa and Alice Nash both sold land. Complaining vociferously about high taxes they were certainly pleased with the remuneration they received.

I think war saved liberal reform in America too. Regrettably the New Deal failed in its main aims, though it had made a lot of people happier and feeling better off. And they were better off, only the country wasn't. The New Deal might have got tossed out the window in the next election, but war kept Mr. Roosevelt in the White House and he kept New Deal policies in place. Social security, farm subsidies, bank guarantees, and unemployment benefits continued to underpin American society. The country had ceased to be a free-for-all, winner-take-all, rip-roaring nation of individualism—assuming of course it ever had been one.

But as the state pegged its gossamer safety net in place, by which I mean extended its obligation to look after people, something new and totally unforeseen occurred; or rather human nature showed its natural cunning and self-interest, its sense of economy, in a new and unexpected way. With less reason to stay together, families started to splinter and fall apart. The Southern tradition of extended families—two or three generations plus the odd hard-up relation living under the same roof—already on the wane, evaporated almost overnight, though at the top and bottom of the social spectrum changes came more slowly, or did so as long as the older generation held its place.

To most people, however, the world was no longer such a threatening place. There was a big umbrella opening up across the country, and its bearer, disembodied and mechanical, made no personal demands: Forelocks didn't need pulling or caps to be politely doffed.

No fealty, gratitude, or patriarchal subjection was required—only regular social security payments—and there was now plenty of work about to help with those. It struck people as a pretty fine ticket operating without any strings on their behalf. It was, but then, change can collect its price in unforeseen ways.

MY GENERATION, THE younger generation, as we thought, found ourselves after the war suddenly middle-aged, by which time the die is usually cast; and among us, predictably, I suppose, only Seneca, now forty-six, had made a significant mark, Bayard's great star having been eclipsed in a warming penumbra of refined and civilizing pleasures.

The war made Seneca a famous man, a major-general cited for heroism as much as for battle tactics brilliantly executed and contrived. In willpower, drive, and intelligence he was indisputably of Papa's caliber, but though the two had much in common, their temperaments and, significantly, the times were different.

Both men were natural leaders but they were also formidable potentates—a role becoming unfashionable in the postwar world. Both kept a foothold in society, but society was, in their view, largely the creation of women, and so the running of and most of the living in it could be left to them. What Seneca and Papa needed was a fief. They were of that ancient caste. And of course the initial fief is a family. It's hard to understand how basic that need in some men is, even in those who go on to build great empires. In other words, Papa and Seneca were committed patriarchs, and unlike feudal lords demanding soldiering and rents, patriarchs want in return for their protection psychological payoffs: They want unswerving loyalty. That's the only difference I can see. Papa succeeded, of course, but Seneca's position was a whole lot trickier. Patriarchal protection, where on offer, was not by then much in demand. Moreover, as Bayard shrewdly observed, every successful ruler needs to have a committed and efficient chancellor behind him. He was thinking of Jane, and perhaps inversely of Dartania, too.

Papa was by nature a conservative. He supported the established order and his power, as I've said, lay in the rocklike security he gave out by being always the same—unmoved, unmovable. It was a question of style, and of self-discipline imposed to the point of being able to take things as they came, without personal hopes or any preferences—something few men will do.

Seneca was more emotional and, as often with warriors, sentimental into the bargain. He would have risked his life to save a member of his clan— that had been a great strength with his troops in war—but he wanted even more than loyalty and obedience in return. He wanted complete devotion. A tall order but that's how he was made. Papa operated altogether at a cooler level, never raising his voice or showing unreason, but Seneca, more volatile by nature, if warmer because of it, readily did so. Emotionally less self-governing, Seneca's was in fact a maverick style. At heart he was a reformer, butting instinctively against the established grain.

An early supporter of the Negro cause, in 1940 Seneca had attended the first integrated civil rights meeting ever held in the South, at Knoxville, Tennessee. (The Reverend Robin Douglas, a graduate of Howard University, also went.) That sat badly with Blue Hills, it sat badly with white East Nashborough too. But Seneca, despite political ambitions, didn't care much about popularity; he had stiff personal standards to live up to.

During the war Seneca and Red Mason had drifted apart. In truth they'd had little in common, so that even before the war, relations had begun to wane in the dullness of everyday out-of-bed encounters. The war finished it off. But Seneca's political ambitions having been wrecked by the affair, friends thought it was just as well; he was way ahead of his time, often embarrassingly so.

Now however, like so much else blotted out in larger conflict, public memory dimmed in the heady glare of Seneca's war success. Buzby was dead, and the *Echo* was in more liberal hands, so that the Senate once again stood conceivably within his grasp. But for the present, no seat being vacant, he willingly returned to law.

Dartania I think needed family ties the most. She was the most clannish of us all, and even though she wasn't interested in her home (the kitchen was left to Delphine and order within the rest of the house devolved on James), she profoundly needed a home.

Her daughters had grown up around her like mysterious plants sporadically viewed through misty greenhouse windows, bewilderingly remote, though a special affection for the youngest, Flora, had arisen almost without Dartania noticing, at a distance. But if motherhood confounded her, so did all familial attachment. Its ties she reckoned to be primordial, woven into a dense invisible connection, like thick vines growing in impenetrable jungle. But she couldn't fit her experience of these ties into any known description of them, for they were capable of binding without affection or tenderness or particular feelings of any kind. Though nobody ever said so.

Dartania had never paid much attention to her appearance, and now she paid even less. She showed no interest at all in the great female excitement for postwar Parisian fashions, or for fashions of any sort. The long red-gold braids, though faintly tinged with gray, remained unchanged. She was still beautiful, but her costume, developed during the war, slacks and a man's shirt, had become habitual Longwood dress.

Even when Seneca came home and she loved him again and wanted to make a go of it, it didn't occur to her to dress up modishly or take her household under control. It didn't occur to her to try to please her husband by artifice of any sort, or in any manner whatsoever to modify her ways. She was so much herself that change apparently wasn't possible.

Bayard on the other hand showed in trumps a most astounding resilience. Settled in his pretty *bijou* house, white clapboard with a lacy fretwork veranda (it had been the Blue Hills plantation manager's house), surrounded by pictures, fine furniture, and books, he had been transformed with apparent ease from bombarded, ultimately failed financier into an amiable gentleman of leisure and high cultivation. He and Ellen had remained separated but many thought that but for the war things might have gone otherwise, and might now, for they had loved each other, and as far as anyone could see, no irreparable breach or obvious incompatibility separated them, only the ocean itself, harboring lethal shoals of German submarines.

Of the rest of us, Jasmine had the most significant war. After Frank was called up, she stayed on in Detroit, living in a tiny attic apartment and working in an airplane factory organizing office production and translating documents in and out of French. Almost no one heard from her. Probably she could not face the picture of reality as set down for others on a piece of paper. So she had trudged on, tersely silent, enduring, and unreflective, as indeed so many other women were doing, taking it a day at a time.

Then just before the war ended, in one swift and cataclysmic stroke, her life, already long out of her control, foundered once again. Frank, leading a marine attack in the Ryukyu Islands, was killed during an amphibious beach attack.

So in October 1946, with no other options at her disposal, having held out as long as she could, and pointlessly, as she had come to realize, Jasmine at last came home.

1

....

$\mathcal{S}$tanding before Timbuctoo's imposing white-paneled front door, her car, an old Ford coupé, parked in front of the house, Jasmine's fingers slipped with gentle firmness around the familiar brass doorknob. It was not that she hesitated exactly, but certainly she paused. A dozen years had passed since, with so much certainty and determination, she had closed that great white door behind her. The very fact of which gave pause. And in that minute temporal gap her hand moved from the highly polished doorknob to the equally pristine bell. With a swift intake of breath she gave it a short, firm press.

Footsteps, light, rapid and unfamiliar, sounded in the hall. The door was opened by a young black man, polite but questioning. "Yes, ma'am?"

Again she paused. "It's Miss Jasmine . . . I mean Mrs. Noland," she corrected herself. She had not expected to confront a stranger, though of course it must be so.

"Mrs. Noland!" he exclaimed with pleasure, opening the door wide, and standing back in welcome. "We wasn't expecting you till bout supper time. You got some bags?" He looked toward the car.

Indicating the suitcase at her feet, Jasmine picked it up, but he took it from her as she stepped inside. "I drove partway last night," she offered, then added politely, "Excuse me, but who are you?"

"Ned, I'm Ned." They shook hands. "You won't remember me, Mrs. Noland, but I remember you from before you went away. Cook Anna was my aunt and we come over sometimes to stay with her. You once give me a slingshot I found in the pantry, told me I could keep it. I still got it somewhere back at the house. A real good slingshot, made out of hazel wood."

"Perhaps I'll remember you, too, Ned," she smiled warmly, "when things have fallen a bit more into place. It's been a long time. And Cook Anna?"

"She done passed away. New cook now, Cook Melia." He did not sound any too pleased.

But already Jasmine was busy searching the spaces beyond, her gaze traversing the big square hall with its familiar sofas and mural wallpaper depicting in neoclassical style the labors of Hercules.

"Mrs. Douglas gone to the grocery store," said Ned. "Mr. Douglas he in his office." The announcement was geographical and without suggestion.

"Is anybody else home?"

"Yes'm, Mrs. Fenton up in her room. And Mr. Dan he here."

"I won't disturb my father then. Thank you, Ned. And there aren't anymore bags in the car. This is all I've got."

Upstairs she noiselessly pushed open the studio door. Dan was sitting in a wheelchair at the far end of the narrow room, his back to her, writing at an old card table. Near the window the skeletal tripod of her easel still stood, giving an unpleasant shock.

"Danny," she almost whispered, huskiness taking sudden possession of her throat.

He turned around, turned the whole wheelchair around. "Jassy! Is that really you?"

"I suppose so," she parried, coming forward. "It's the name I answer to, at any rate." Quickly she pulled up a chair beside her brother and took his hands. They did not embrace or kiss. "How are you, Danny?" She smiled brightly into his eyes, a smile that said, I only want right now to hear the good things, please.

"Oh, I'm about the same. As you see I'm exactly where you left me, still scribbling away. I live a sheltered, you could even say a cloistered, life. Mostly lived upstairs." He pointed to his head. "But I've published a book, a history of the early settlers here." He was busy scrutinizing the smiling, querying face before him, noting the wispy crow's-feet emerging at the corners of her eyes, the tension round her pretty pouting mouth. Some of the old verve still seemed to be in place, but not a lot. "You'll find much else besides me still the same," he told her. "We're like flies in amber here. The world turns upside down and we stay put. Nothing is dislodged. Papa still goes like clockwork and Jane caters, devoted as always, to his every need."

"Does he?" Hurriedly she lit a cigarette. The fact of so much having been preserved had a profoundly soothing appeal. "Oh, give me all the news, Danny. I know nothing at all."

"You haven't seen Papa yet?"

She shook her head. "I didn't want to break into his routine. Or maybe I was just plain scared. Jane's at the grocery store."

Dan nodded his understanding. "Well now, newsreels: Let's see. Seneca's famous, thanks to the war, but you know that, everybody does. And Dar's not much changed, at least I don't think she is. During the war she sort of ran the farm and made a pretty good job of it, I hear. But I think she was getting fed up. She said she did it because it had to be done, but she couldn't see any point afterwards, when there were others there to do it."

"I heard from her once or twice," said Jasmine. "She sounded exactly the same; she always does."

Dan was tapping his fountain pen against the card-table edge. "By the bye, did you ever see anything of the Masons in Detroit?"

"The Masons?" Jasmine blinked. "Frank had some run-ins with Philip Mason out at Ford." She shrugged dismissively. "And I had lunch with her once. Why? Anyhow I heard they'd got divorced and that she'd moved back here."

"Well, so you won't put your foot in it, the *on dit* is Red and Seneca had a big affair before the war. Everybody knew about it, and the affair was what caused the Masons' divorce."

"*Red Mason?* Why she's not a patch on Dar! I can hardly believe it." But Jasmine's incredulity was overlaid with a revived fragment of memory. "Now I think of it, Dar asked me ages ago in a letter if I'd seen her, and what I thought of her. Well, well."

"It's finished more or less, I think. But best you know, even if Dar wouldn't thank me for telling you."

"Poor Dar. How she must have hated it! She's so proud. We all are I suppose." Jasmine smiled sadly. "I've had plenty of chances to imbibe humility myself and little enough has sunk in, believe me." Still smoking she stood up and began to move about the narrow room without direction. She reminded Dan of an animal traversing aimlessly its cage.

"It's hard to believe I won't see Robbie," she blurted suddenly. "His disappearing seemed so remote when it happened, because for me the whole family had, well, disappeared." She looked vaguely toward the easel. "Has anything at all been heard?"

"He must be dead," said Dan. "I can't think of any other solution, and it's the one everybody accepts. Even Dar, though she never says anything. She still feels it sharply, I expect. Twins have such a strong connection, starting out together so early in life."

"And Bayard?" Jasmine switched to a happier topic.

"Bayard's a rare old bird. In fact he's a positive phoenix. Having made and lost Blue Hills folks a fortune, he's become their revered intellectual and cultural authority. He gives luncheons: political, literary, ladies, and so on. To meet him you'd never guess he'd gone through all he has, or for that matter was ever a big-time money spinner. Jane thinks he and Ellen will get together now the war's over. I can't see it, though, not after all this time, can you?"

Standing in front of the old paint-encrusted easel, Jasmine scratched idly at a blob of yellow paint. "Chrome yellow," she murmured vaguely, before answering. "Ellen was quite a force in my life—a moving force, you could say," her smile twisted in irony. "But that's all water over the dam." She was wondering whether she'd forgiven Ellen or if in fact she should. Meddling morality. It was something to think about. "Ellen's too prudish for Bayard, if you ask me. For the whole family, as far as I can see."

"But they were crazy about each other." Dan, who had always been fond of Ellen, insisted plaintively, and getting no response, added drolly, "There's rumor of a new connection, though. Mrs. Ames out at Sextet Stud, Bigelow Ames's widow. She's bookish and horsey and she's plenty rich, and not bad looking either for her age, which must be near to fifty."

"You certainly do keep up-to-date tucked away up here. Are you putting all that in your family history, all the gossip and scandal? I ought to get a big fat chapter."

"I've saved the really big news," Dan went on, ignoring this. "Hot off the family press."

"Oh tell!"

There was a purposeful dramatic pause. "Chloe's getting a divorce."

Jasmine stopped picking at the easel. He had her full attention, but her response was less than gratifying. "Well I can't say I'm surprised. Jim Blount would bore any woman to death, even Chloe, though I admit I thought it a perfect match at the time. You never know, do you? And we never write," she hastened on, "we never got on together all that well." Still on her feet, she went over to the window and, sitting down on the window seat, looked out, puffing her cigarette in the old way, held between her forefinger and thumb. The lawn below was lightly scattered with leaves curling like old hands and turning stiffly brown, she noticed uneasily. Only the big magnolia retained its shiny bottle-green hue. "Remember those awful candlesticks," she said, brightening. She was still looking out the window. "It's odd isn't it," she added after a minute, "our lives had hardly begun then, everything was ahead of us, so welcoming and sure—and suddenly"—she smacked her palm down on the window seat—"it's over, behind us, kaput!"

"Childhood's over, maybe youth. That's all."

"I thought everything here would go on forever as it was, unchanged, and oh that seemed to me so boring!"

"A lot of it has. And it is I can assure you sometimes very boring."

"Oh but I loved, once I got away, knowing it was here and, as I believed, unchanged. I just never wanted to be part of it. I wanted to be of it but not in it, I suppose. The best of both worlds." She turned to Dan. "I'm sorry. I must sound dreadfully rude and self-centered. You've put up with everything." She cocked her head, looking sideways at him. "And funnily enough, in staying put, I believe that in ways you've learned a lot of things I haven't. Maybe travel isn't so broadening as people like to think."

"The point about Chloe," Dan said, returning to stiller waters, "is it's the family's first divorce, so of course it's causing quite a to-do. Papa and Jane are rather shocked. They think that having committed herself Chloe should stick it out. Papa may even have told her so."

"I bet he has, in spades," Jasmine wryly returned. She shook her head. "Even when powerless he can be horribly intimidating. That generation has a lot of moral loose change rattling around in its pockets, and to my mind its a dubious currency. Chloe has backbone, though. I'll give her that."

"She learned to do shorthand and typing at Camp Meredith during the war. She almost got to France, probably hoping to get away from Jim."

Jasmine's pert nose wrinkled. "France would have been absolutely lost on Chloe."

Instantly Dan recognized a flicker of the old Jasmine: arrogant and competitive, guarding her position, her imagined superiority, and he was glad. "What'll you do now, Jassy? Have you decided?"

"Get a job I guess. Like Chloe." It intoned the fall of the mighty into the lower depths. "I'm not incompetent, you know. I worked in an airplane factory for three years and I'm a damned good organizer. But in peacetime there are only three jobs open to women: school teaching and secretarial— the preserve of widows, and now it seems, divorcées—and shopkeeping for unmarrieds. I've been a shopgirl," she added ruefully.

"Won't you paint?"

"No, Danny, I won't paint."

A knock on the door and Ned's head popped around it. "Mrs. Douglas back. She say theys drinks at six o'clock and for ya'll to come on downstairs when you ready."

"Thank you, Ned." Dan smiled dryly at his sister. "We aren't a very demonstrative family, are we? Do you suppose it matters?"

"Oh, I long so to see Papa, but I dread it, too."

"You'll find him frail," said Dan. "He's over eighty, remember; he's getting old."

But the warning, impossible to fully register, failed utterly to prepare her; and entering the library at six o'clock, bathed, and dressed in a broad-shouldered navy dress, Jasmine, nervous but eager, was shocked as she went forward to embrace her father. How shrunken he looked standing before the fire in front of the old bearskin rug. He seemed literally inches shorter, the flesh hanging from his bones like an old sofa with all the padding gone. Hugging him she felt his fragile skeleton, now so alarmingly near the surface, and she was suddenly frightened. Her father's indestructibility, taken so far granted, had underpinned her life, given it a bedrock that so many people, most people—as she'd discovered—sorely lacked. It had given her too a singular outlook, stable and secure, salvageable in disaster.

Hamilton embraced her warmly and looked her sharply in the eye. The controlled smile and bright penetration of his gaze told her he was truly pleased to see her. "Welcome home, daughter," he declared with an animation bordering on gaiety. "You're looking pretty good for an old woman of thirty-seven." It said that all was forgiven, all forgotten. And deeply moved by the largeness of his response, Jasmine hoped that her own might prove equal to it.

As he spoke, to her relief, she found that the old strength of tone was there, and within minutes her eye had begun an automatic adjustment, blurring the sharply graven image from the past and producing in its place a revised and updated portrait that before long began to assume an easy familiarity.

"Is your room all right, dear?" put in Jane, giving her a kiss. "I had the curtains changed—they were in shreds—but everything else is just the same I believe."

From his wheelchair, Dan butled, handing drinks round, and Jasmine, sipping the well-chilled dry martini, suddenly felt an encroaching lightness of heart, absent since she couldn't remember when. Over the years her exuberance had ebbed by slow degrees mysteriously away, so that its loss was only keenly felt at the moment of possible restoration.

On the stroke of seven, the clock and dinner gong sounded their familiar and cacophonous duet, raucous and enduring noises from childhood.

"Now where's Bertha got to?" Hamilton demanded in what appeared to be a mild rebuke.

"On her way down, I'm sure," said Jane. "She stayed upstairs to have a chat with Stark and keep out of our way."

"Stark!" cried Jasmine in astonishment. "Is Stark here? In this house?"

"Yes but . . . oh look, here they are!" Jane left it unfinished, as Stark stood arm in arm with his mother at the library door.

Spontaneous joy wreathed Jasmine's face, and rushing forward, they exchanged a happy, easy kiss. "Where's Mary Ann?" she demanded, laughing. "I'm longing to meet her after all this time."

"She's a little unwell, I'm afraid," he solemnly answered, "but she sends her best."

A recollection of his dull side flashed and spun away. "Nothing serious, I hope," Jasmine politely noised, pleased she might have him to herself for a nice long chat after dinner. A bubbling effervescence was taking rapid possession of her, a sudden sense of genuine celebration, of homecoming.

"She's a mite queasy since the baby came, that's all," Mrs. Fenton supplied.

"Maybe like me she's allergic to them," Jasmine frivolously opined, with a knowing look at Stark. "Procreation," she reminded him in a softer tone.

"Let's get a move on," Hamilton interposed with something approaching heartiness. "I for one want to eat my dinner hot."

Throughout the meal Jasmine remained the tactful center of attention, though no direct questions were asked or any accounting for time past remotely demanded. In fact, the past was never mentioned. Talk stuck to the present and to Nashborough events, of which there was much to hear. Mention of Seneca's remarkable achievements on Okinawa in the final stages of the war were the nearest anyone came to acknowledging Frank, who had been killed by kamikazes there.

Jasmine's history, she began rapidly to perceive, was destined to be filed away and forgotten, a closet skeleton crumbling eventually into specks of dust ready for vacuuming. The salient point was that she was back, and Frank's death having been the enabler of her return, her family was, without knowing it, obscurely grateful, unconsciously relieved on all accounts that he was dead.

Hamilton's pragmatism and diplomacy glowed magnificently throughout the meal. Bygones were bygones, and instead of disappearing into his own thoughts, he kept up a lively conversation, retailing Nashborough gossip and making ironic even occasionally witty remarks. Enough anyhow that when Ned brought in the silver platter of meat, Dan, catching Jasmine's eye, whispered loudly, "What is it, veal?"

It took her a minute. "You know, I believe it could be," she beamed back, with an amused sideways glance at her father.

"It's lamb," said Ned, and Dan and Jasmine grinned childishly at each other across the table. What else would it be?

"Lamb in veal's clothes," Dan pursued, making a boyish face at his sister.

"We asked Dar and Seneca to come tonight," Jane said, "as a family celebration. But Sally's fiancé's arriving. They met down at Ole Miss, and would you believe it, her parents haven't laid eyes on him yet." She shrugged in mildly expressed resignation. "But as Miss Alice says, that's the way they're doing it nowadays."

Jasmine could just remember Sally, a naughty self-willed little girl with long unkempt brown braids. "Engaged?" she murmured vaguely.

"Her fiancé will have to run the Longwood gauntlet." Stark shook his head in amusement. "He'll be mentally black and blue and never know half what hit him."

"Alice Nash is sometimes too lenient," Bertha Fenton interjected, "especially with those grandchildren." She seemed to forget that they were Hamilton's, too. "Sally should have introduced the boy to her family *before* they went and got engaged. It's only proper." And getting no response, she added a trifle huffily, "Well that's my opinion, anyhow."

But the topic of headstrong engagements was, Jane felt, potentially unsettling, even after so many years, and quickly she changed it to one that, though also awkward, must of necessity be touched on. "Chloe's coming up next week with the children," she murmured quietly to Jasmine.

"Coming *here?*" Caught off guard, Jasmine's astonishment was laced with obvious displeasure.

"We'll open up two attic rooms for the children," Jane explained, assuming Jasmine's dismay was her concern for space and tranquillity. Unaware that she already knew of the divorce, Jane now faced its discreet announcement, potentially a red flag, in front of Hamilton.

Happily he himself moved the topic sideways. "This household seems to be growing instead of shrinking," he declared, helping himself to turnip greens, evidently not ill pleased by so unexpected an inflation.

"Yes, and luckily we've room for everyone," Jane gaily retorted. "Your chicks are coming home to roost dear, isn't it nice?" She smiled down the table at her husband for whom she did it all. "A family house should be full to bursting; that's what it's here for, after all." Then turning to Jasmine a moment later she added sotto voce, "Chloe and the children are moving back to Nashborough."

"So Dan told me," Jasmine whispered coldly in return.

"She's going to work for Stark." Mrs. Fenton, took it up with the speed of a dog grabbing at a bone. "She's going to be his secretary in the election run-up." She said it with a haughty pitch suggestive of table turning and a deserved Fenton triumph at long last, then polished it off with a dollop of patronizing gratuity. "Stark says she's a crackerjack shorthand-typist."

Stark, by way of response, looked at Jasmine and smiled, as he had been doing at intervals throughout the meal, meeting her eye, but conveying no special significance, a smile that, while well intended, was mildly vacant, even a trifle automatic. A politician's smile. But they couldn't really talk yet, Jasmine consoled herself. She wanted to very much, though about what she'd no clear idea. There was between them, however, the engaging pull that Stark had been a friend of both Mr. *and* Mrs. Noland; he alone had accepted her life in its entirety instead of picking out the bits that suited.

Suddenly and with penetrating clarity she recalled him standing beside the table where they now sat, on the day of Chloe's wedding, his hands thrust awkwardly into his pockets, the table burgeoning with silver and crystal and white damask in an almost barbaric display of trophies—and Dan's now portentous suggestion of its somehow being a tomb. She recalled she had been admiring that fresh picture of a wood signed J. Dinson, wondering at it. A moment of such casual and seeming insignificance, so light and superficial in its content, sparkling with ease and gaiety. And with a jolt of horror she saw that that was the precise moment her future had taken its first irrevocable step forward. At that seemingly inconsequential moment, the ancient sibyls who wove one's destiny, having agreed on the pattern, had purposefully taken up their looms. And now, just as suddenly, the thread was broken off, the pattern, the return, apparently completed—for she had come full circle. Yet had that haphazard episode not occurred, had she not seen that painting or asked to meet J. Dinson, had Stark not been on hand at that precise instant to answer her query, then her history would have gone very differently. How differently she could not begin to imagine. But that so much, so much of such importance—*her life*—had been largely the product of incidental whim, or of mysterious unseen forces outside her control and to no particular end, was profoundly chilling.

A sudden fear, an anxiety without precise location, rare and frightening, seized her fast-beating heart. She fought against its establishment in the same way her people always fought, with the stalwart push of a beleaguered swimmer battling upward toward the fresh air of a spirited gaiety, adamantly refusing to feel sorry for herself or to admit the possibility of a badly botched existence.

After all, here she sat, in exactly that same spot, as if it had never happened, as if none of it had ever taken place. That was the oddest part. Perhaps her family was right to dismiss it as a sort of dream. She had taken from that life all she was able—she might even have sucked it dry—but at any rate it was over. What had been the present, and so "life," in passing out of reality, might, like the dead, be buried and let go. There was a seal on it. Mourning, of course, was a necessity, a transition period for complete rewiring; but afterward, why not begin again? She'd accrued some advantages. She was no longer that silly arrogant girl, so cocksure, so famously high on herself, an assured world conqueror. Moreover, today everything, even the old things—her surroundings—looked so different. Recast in so many finer and more subtle shades, they were more resonant, both in their range and in their ambiguities—and so, more interesting to see and contemplate.

In youth her gaze was fixed instead upon the far horizon, which had glowed and beckoned, a fata morgana, wondrously blazing, like the campfires of far-off heroes patiently awaiting a victorious dawn. And she had yearned to be among them.

Oh, she had been right to get away, but not for the reasons she'd imagined. Know thyself, be thyself, express thyself, Frank always said. Well, she had made some small progress in that direction. And helping herself to Cook Anna's chocolate roll—Cook Melia's now—she began, like chestnuts picked out by quick fingers from a heated brazier, to draw forth the positive features of her life. Suddenly she felt happier. It seemed right that she had come home, where part of her must surely always belong.

After dinner, to her surprise, Stark didn't stay, but hurried home anxiously to his wife. Jasmine, so used to taking his interest for granted, saw that now she was like anyone else, not more or less important, and her new-raised spirits plummeted, while on his end of the plank Stark rode high, inescapably looked up to. His doggedness, his equanimity, even his lack of passion and imagination had paid off. Unlike her, he'd made a success of life.

"We'll put another leaf in the table tomorrow," Jane was saying. "My, how like old times it's getting to be." She had begun to lay out the backgammon board, and Hamilton, putting on his spectacles, pulled up his chair with interest. Bertha Fenton had retired and Dan sat under a lamp, in his wheelchair, reading the evening paper. The household had reverted with miraculous smoothness to its ingrained and familiar routine, the festive interlude leaving no ostensible trace. She had received a prodigious homecoming and that was that. It was assumed that she was home to stay, in Nashborough if not at Timbuctoo. In fact she had no plans, no job, and very little money, only Frank's small pension. She sighed a little, inwardly, watching this familiar family scene, sensing a nostalgic sweetness. But she mustn't allow it to close in and swallow her up. For the present she would live from day to day, and then some scheme would surely present itself.

Chloe's coming home was what depressed her most. It put them side by side on the same shelf. But though both had failed, Chloe's coming home was in its way a positive action, one aimed at producing a remedy, while Jasmine had been merely seeking sanctuary. She must pull herself together, become assertive, raise herself up and take life energetically by the horns, or even by the tail. But for the moment, stuffed like a jack-in-the-box comfortably back into a familiar cubicle, she felt, alarmingly, less energy to pop out again.

2

....

*O*ver at Longwood, another family dinner had been taking place, of a character peculiarly its own. For as Stark rightly foresaw, instead of open welcome, Jack Frazer, Sally's fiancé, was deputed, if unconsciously, to run a family gauntlet, testing his worth. Frazer had that morning traveled to Nashborough from Oxford, Mississippi, and Sally had collected him at the station, her brown hair swept up on both sides in a fashionable roll, her navy gabardine suit, piped in white, following to perfection the pretty curves of her body. Inwardly dreading Frazer's introduction to her fiercely opinionated family, though beaming radiantly, she was desperately summoning up her nerve.

A tall, solidly built young man, Jack Frazer's leathery face was pierced by great innocent blue eyes, his chin cleft by a deep dimple, his ears trumpeting at right angles to his head. A crop of sand-colored hair might have made him handsome in a screen-star sort of way, had not the army crew cut, beginning to grow out, created a ridiculous coxcomb on the top of his head. The son of a farmer, Frazer had grown up in southern Mississippi. Having survived four years of heavy fighting in the Pacific, becoming second lieutenant on an aircraft carrier, he'd returned to his final year of law school at the University of Mississippi, his fees taken care of by the GI Bill. He was twenty-seven years old.

"Pleased to meet you, ma'am, and I sure am mighty proud to make your acquaintance, General, sir." With an open grin and flash of white teeth, Jack had stuck out his paw, enthusiastically shaking those of his hosts. "I've read all about your exploits over there in the Ryukyus, General, and of course Sally's told me a thing or two." His grin swiveled toward his pertly adoring if uneasy fiancée.

Dartania, reared on the importance of "background," recoiled instinctively before the heavy drawl and countrified mode of speech. "How d'you do?" she coolly replied, at which Sally looked very downcast and then hard set in defiance.

Though spared the formality of granting his daughter's hand, Seneca proposed taking the young man for a walk on the back of the place. An informal chat would cast some light on Frazer's character and financial setup, though the latter was these days fairly unimportant. There were plenty of jobs about and any young man of reasonable intelligence could be expected to earn enough money to support a wife. Still the fellow needed sizing up.

They took shotguns in case Seneca's spaniel contrived to scare up some game, and marching in great strides along the gullied cart track, whistling occasionally to the itinerant dog, Seneca took the opportunity of scrutinizing the young man from the corner of his eye. He supposed that in a beefy way he might be thought good-looking, being blond and blue eyed. But to Seneca he was glaringly unexceptional. Seneca had hoped Sally would have had enough sense to attach herself to Pete Weaver, as any girl with her head screwed on would be bound to do. Pete Weaver had been Seneca's aide de camp, and Seneca was in every way thoroughly pleased with Pete Weaver's character and performance. The young man treasured what he'd been taught, he worked hard and diligently and had proved himself unflinching and reliable in battle. In short, he was all that Seneca had dreamt of in a son, and now Pete was a promising young attorney at Nash and Polk. But instead of admiring Pete's high merit, his daughters scorned him, claiming he was boring, a goody-goody, and calling him "Daddy's understudy." True, Pete was a mite scrubbed-faced, a mite overprinted with middle-class morality, but Sally's chosen spouse—trying to give young Frazer a fair chance insofar as that was possible, he avoided "cracker" and settled for "ordinary." Seneca was no snob but Frazer's marrying into the family unavoidably linked them, and if so superfluous an appendage must so needlessly be hooked on, then it must be brought up to a par with the rest of him—a job with all the earmarks of impossibility. This view was largely confirmed during their walk, but probably Jack was unlucky, and, in any case, the odds were solidly stacked against him.

First, climbing over a rickety wooden gate, a plank gave way underfoot, one end crashing to the ground and leaving a sizable gap. Jack tried to put the plank back in place but the rotten wood had given way at the nail, so there was no support.

"Always climb over a gate where the hinges are," Seneca ordered reprovingly. "That's where it's strongest. I thought you were a country boy. Now help me fix this so Samuel's cow and calf over there can't get through." He had removed the whistle from around his neck and was untying the leather thong that held it. "Hold that plank in place and I'll lash it to the frame. Samuel can fix it properly later on."

Jack did as he was told. The plank being rotten might equally have broken at the other end, though the rule about gates held true. "Yes sir, General, thank you for pointing it out, sir."

The boy seemed permanently locked into a cheerful cracker-barrel style that, despite Seneca's resistance, did somewhat mollify the blunder. Or did so for the moment, because very shortly after, just before they had reached the heavy scrubland, another challenge arose when the young spaniel suddenly got up a rabbit.

"He's all yours," Seneca offered as the animal streaked over the gullies in front of them. "Easy as a shooting-gallery target."

It was indeed an easy shot but Jack, though releasing in succession both barrels, stayed wide of the mark. The rabbit bolted into the undergrowth. "Looks like Brer Rabbit's gonna get his supper tonight, not make it," Jack drawled unperturbed, nodding his head as if in any case the rabbit somehow merited a reward.

Seneca said nothing, until, entering the long sage grass, they had to walk more slowly. "Sally tells me you want to marry as soon as you finish law school," he began, having, as he imagined, allowed his silent reprimand enough time to sink in.

"Yes, sir. I know we won't be real comfortable at first, not like what she's used to and all, but I think we ought to make out pretty good. My folks have promised us the downpayment on a house. They've saved a bit what with the government sending me to school and all. Of course, it'll be a right small house: no bigger'n a turtle shell, I speck."

This announcement, whatever else it achieved, lobbed the financial ball squarely into Seneca's court, where he chose to leave it unreturned. "Sally's a stable girl," he said in rejoinder. "She's fond of children and ought to make a good wife, if she'll learn to cook and can set her mind to looking after a house."

"Yes sir she is one fine woman," said Jack Frazer whose open smile moved as slowly but as surely as the rest of him.

To Seneca, his eldest daughter was a slipshod girl of average intelligence who wanted things her own way—innocently believing she deserved as much. But he was saved from stretching his mind to a polite response by the appearance of another rabbit leaping out of the sage and across the track. This time Seneca made no gentlemanly offers. Taking quick aim, he brought the animal down in a double somersault. It was still twitching when he picked it up, and Jack watched with cool admiration as Seneca clamped his teeth into the back of the rabbit's neck and with a sudden twist brought instant, pain-free death.

But the financial ball still lay with Seneca, who knew that he must serve it back. Only that morning, he had told his mother that he was giving Sally a check for three thousand dollars. He thought that very generous. But to his astonishment, Miss Alice had insisted on his offering the boy a place in Nash and Polk as well.

Seneca had balked. "Suppose he's no damn good," he blurted out. "A law firm isn't a charity for down-and-outs, and Sally could easily come home with an imbecile." To which was added somewhat pompously, "We have a professional responsibility to our clients."

But Alice Nash held her ground. "One for all and all for one," she said, quoting her family motto. "The boy's coming into the family, and he must be given a leg up. What on earth is a family firm for?"

"I had thought," said Seneca smoothly, "it was intended to provide the best possible representation before the law." But already he suspected he would have to cave in. His mother knew perfectly how to work him, and her lifelong affection and support were things he would never be able to sufficiently repay. Like Coriolanus he couldn't bring himself to cross her, and Coriolanus, he now conveniently reflected, had paid dearly for it. Nonetheless women were, he admitted, possessed of a vein of general wisdom, some kind of extra sensibility or perception that a man would be a damned fool not to heed, even when as now it rubbed against the obvious rational grain. However he had made no promises.

His mother was already making the most of Frazer's "background," the lack of which women found a particularly bitter pill, and was putting it about Blue Hills that he was kin to the Theban Frazers, a family everyone knew—though the precise lines of connection had remained opaque. "Well, everybody in the South is kin to everybody else," Miss Alice had offered airily in her defense.

Seneca slung the rabbit over his shoulder and, setting his jaw, pulled new breath from the air. "When you've finished law school, provided you make some decent grades, there ought to be a place for you at Nash and Polk. Unless of course you'd rather practice down in Mississippi."

"That's mighty white of you, General." Frazer's big smile opened the wider in a show of real appreciation. "I'm much obliged, sir. It's a fine opportunity and I aim to do everything I can to merit it. I think Sally'd feel awful boxed in down in Greenwood. Folks aren't real sophisticated back home like they are up here."

God forbid, thought Seneca, for whom the less said about Sally's education, let alone "sophistication" the better. They were approaching the Tebbit cabin and Seneca admitted grudgingly to a sort of solidity about young Frazer, whose slow easygoing manner reminded him of coon hunters he used to hunt with in the Chickasaw Mountains. Canny, reliable folk who knew their stuff but almost nothing else. Oh, the boy would probably do, but why on earth Sally couldn't see the superior qualities of Pete Weaver was beyond him.

It was unfortunate that marriages were no longer arranged. Nobody would set out on a serious business venture, not even on a vacation, with such slender and ill-digested information. But such was nature's trap and the current fashion was to sit back and let it snap shut, while in the past people had had enough sense to apply controls. He thought of his own marriage. He too would have resisted controls, and would not have listened to his parents. And really in the end there was no telling. The rate of success in arranged marriages was said to be about the same as for romantic ones. Just as for some equally mysterious, though more useful reason, about the same number of boys and girls were born into the world. But the fact of so much going on beyond a man's rational government was dispiriting, and Seneca, having resigned himself to the present outcome, let the subject rest.

The Tebbit cabin was now in front of them, its sagging tin roof hiked up at the ends as though pegged on an invisible clothes line. Mattie Tebbit was sitting on the rickety front porch, her legs and bare feet dangling over the edge, nursing another baby. Weight had filled out her body and face, so that, surprisingly, no wrinkles showed to mark her arduous and continuously fertile life.

Jack went a little red viewing this real-life madonna, but nonetheless smiled at her in a friendly way.

"Thisn's the last," Mattie said to Seneca in a regretful-sounding tone, as standing up, she removed the baby and pulled the open dress over her breast—as a woman might, on meeting acquaintances, adjust a hat.

Seneca, having shaken hands, paused till the commotion the dogs were making quieted down. "I'm afraid that gate down in the bottom pasture needs some fixing, Mattie," he said at last, holding the spaniel on a tight leash as two mongrels from under the house sniffed suspiciously at her. "It's patched up right now, but I'd be grateful if you'd tell Samuel for me. And ask him to save that leather thong it's tied up with. It's off my whistle."

Seneca had unslung the rabbit and now he held it out. "Something for the pot. Mattie's rabbit stew is famous," he added to Frazer.

"Lawsy, Mr. Seneca, that's a mighty big rabbit. Look more like a fox," said Mattie, taking the rabbit by its hind legs.

"This is Mr. Frazer, Mattie, who's going to marry Sally."

"Pleased to meet you," said Frazer. "I'm afraid it was me that broke your gate and I'm real sorry to put your husband to so much trouble."

Still holding the rabbit, but giving the baby to one of her children, Mattie leaned down from the porch and with her free hand shook Jack Frazer's. "Miss Sally is one sweet girl. I know ya'll gone be mighty happy."

"Why thank you," said Frazer. "We sure do aim to be."

Though Frazer didn't know it, this too was a test and one which, to Seneca's real relief, he had passed with flying colors. Mississippi boys were notoriously anti-Negro, but on this one point at least the young man proved exceptional. Sally was going to have to knock some corners off. The country style might reassure colored people and small-town Mississippi clients, but not rich Nashborough folk; and Frazer had no compensating assets of family, celebrity, or wealth to convert his backwoods style into mere eccentricity.

Without anyone noticing, a figure had been standing in the doorway, a dark shadow behind the closed screen door—and might have been there for some time.

"You remember Sammy," said Mattie, looking back over her shoulder.

Opening the door Sammy moved forward out of the shadows.

"I sure do," said Seneca. "And I'm glad to see you, Sammy, and to know for sure you never succumbed to snakebite or poor medical treatment."

Sammy smiled a little and stepped out onto the porch. He was wearing army trousers and thick-soled army boots, brilliantly polished.

"Sammy was over yonder across the waters too," his mother said proudly, "fighting them Japs."

Sammy looked from one man to the other, ducking his head slightly. "I tole em over there how you done save me from rattlesnake bite, sucked all the poison out, and I shown em the place on my leg," he said bashfully. Clearly some kudos had been gathered from this elaborated tale.

"Whereabouts were you stationed, Sammy?"

"Philippines," said Sammy. "Theys all islands, aint no real country at all."

"I was there," said Frazer, with something approaching instinctive camaraderie.

"Sho nuf!"

"Yep and I sure am glad to be home."

Sammy said nothing in reply to this.

"Sammy's working in Nashborough," Mattie softly explained. "Got a job in the shoe factory." She looked toward the young man, who again remained silent. "He give me a pair of high-heel, patent-leather shoes," she went on, grinning at him, "but I swan, I can't hardly wear em. Don't feel right toeing along like that. Them high heels is real pretty but I like to fall flat on my face downtown."

"You got to get used to em, that's all," said Sammy. "When ya'll come to Nashborough, you got to wear shoes. Everthangs concrete."

This time it was Mattie who was silent. She laid the rabbit down on a chair and reached out for the baby, who seemed comfortable enough where it was. "Look like all God's chillen got shoes, just like the song say." And Seneca noted that even the baby was wearing pristine white leather bootees. But he had taken note of Mattie's uneasy feint.

"Well, I better get the groom home before his bride comes after me with a stick," he told them in an easy drawl. It struck the right note and everyone shook hands and smiled and laughed. Then, the spaniel still on a leash, the two men continued down the dirt track without speaking, there being for the present nothing of further use to say. Autumn filled the air but the ground had remained parched and hard from lack of rain. The cotton stalks, brown and skeletal in the fields, were crested here and there with snowy tufts where shreds of fiber still remained after picking. In the distance was a silhouette familiar all over the American South: a man leaning forward into a plough behind his long-eared mule, as the sun slowly descended in a red fireball behind him.

"Samuel's hard at it," said Seneca, watching with a particular interest. He was remembering Mattie Tebbit's silent feint. "That scene's going to disappear pretty soon now, and for good."

AT DINNER JACK sat between Dartania and Sally, with fourteen-year-old Flora opposite, Emma being away at college in South Carolina. But despite the meal's prenuptial significance it did not last long, about twenty minutes, there being to Sally's acute dismay only one course, as at an ordinary family dinner—which this occasion very plainly was not. Delphine helped to draw things out as much as possible, taking the platters slowly around a second time,

"Isn't there any dessert?" Sally demanded incredulously.

Dartania instantly fixed on a solution. "There're some Hershey Bars in the gun room," she said cheerfully. "Go get them, will you, Flora, they're on the table just inside the door."

Sally's and Flora's eyes met in rapidly communicated shorthand as Flora obediently rose, returning with three Hershey Bars encased in shiny brown wrappers.

"About half a bar each," she said, removing the wrappers and carefully breaking each chocolate bar in two inside the silver wrapping paper.

Sally, glaring furiously at the silver paper, said nothing. If she did, she knew her father would side with her mother, even though he agreed with her, and the prospect of a family row developing, with everybody jumping in, was horrid. But it could easily happen. She tried to think of Sunday lunch next day at Cottoncrop, where she knew her grandmother could be relied on to put things right and mark Jack's introduction to the family in a civilized style suited to the occasion. How she hated Longwood, and how glad she was to be leaving. You always had to be on your guard, and now it was embarrassing to boot.

But Jack seemed not to notice. "Good ole Hershey Bars," he cried enthusiastically. "I used to dream about em out in the Pacific."

"There's some bubble gum, if anybody's interested," Flora reported deadpan. She had left her own chocolate, still in its silver paper, beside her plate.

Dartania knew the Hershey Bars would vex Seneca and she peered uneasily at him through the candelabra branches. Hershey Bars after all were perfectly edible, and anyhow Seneca was as happy eating hard tack in the wilderness as he was dining in any particular splendor. Nor did she care what she ate, and the boy had clearly been delighted. Why then make it an issue? It was of course his mother. Miss Alice personified Seneca's ideal of womanhood, and Dartania was expected to imitate her, which she never did. She greatly respected Miss Alice, but Miss Alice's way of doing things wasn't hers. And much that interested Miss Alice failed completely to interest Dartania, who couldn't see the point, so didn't give it her attention. It had never entered her head, for instance, to make any special provision for Sally's fiancé. Surely it was enough to have invited him. At Timbuctoo the norm was never departed from for any reason, and she could see no reason why things at Longwood should be any different. (The norm's being so much higher at Timbuctoo never figured into her equation.)

Seneca had been home for six months. When he had volunteered, Dartania was outraged, convinced she was being deserted, before she'd understood his motive. The war, he'd told her plainly, was the greatest event of his time on this earth, and he'd be damned if he was going to miss it. At which she had envied him his valorous opportunity. Moreover, she instantly perceived that going to war would put him out of Red Mason's reach—she hoped for good. And in this she had proved right.

In 1943 Dartania learned Red Mason had taken her children to her mother's house in Mobile and planned to live there. Dartania's inner life burst into sudden splendor. The angry obsessive thoughts, the searing injustices overlaying softer feelings and desires, miraculously disappeared. It was as if such feelings had never existed, becoming as difficult to recall as childbirth pains, their disappearance leaving a bountiful cup of overflowing hope. She began to live in tender anticipation. She was happy again.

When the war ended, and Seneca got off the train, a war hero, the reporters crowding around, she saw that he was looking past them, and as their eyes found each other, even at a distance, she knew instantly that it was all right. It was as if their love, frozen in some arctic glacier and thawed by an unexpected burst of sunshine, had been miraculously preserved intact. How right she'd been to hold on, not to let him go, and how wise.

Seneca felt much the same and that he had some making-up to do. He had learned in war what prisoners and regular soldiers knew all too well: What every soldier wanted, no matter how he'd felt about it before, was to get home to his family, to be one with it. And Seneca was no exception; Red Mason's image early on began to fade. When Seneca thought of her, he was happy, but increasingly he simply forgot to think of her. Older feelings were pushing forward, and Dartania's face now rose daily in his mind like a comforting badge. It even seemed she was standing beside him in battle, like an Amazon queen, as would have suited her. And though he never said so, not even to himself, her image became his good-luck charm.

His children too had been affectionately reincarnated. In a photograph sent by his mother, the three girls sat on a garden bench in summer dresses, with flowers in their hair, the older two grinning, well into their teens, and Flora, solemn and wide eyed, gazing out under her mop of curls. The image was sacrosanct, the thought of family and home charging his courage and starching his fortitude as he went about the dreadful business of an all-out war—at which, as far as any decent man could, Seneca excelled.

But in the months since his return home, the old pattern willy-nilly had begun to fall mysteriously into place. Petty grievances and repeated dissatisfaction raked and grated, to Dartania's persistent lack of comprehension. His children, no longer the budding adolescents in the photograph, and already leaving the nest, were unexceptional young women with whom he had little communication, though he admitted young Flora was something of an exception. As for Dartania, it was impossible to discuss anything with her. He knew she loved him, but why did she make no effort to do as he repeatedly asked, to simply do her job? He paid the bills, kept the ship well corked and comfortably afloat and got nothing for it in return. His family were all freeloaders. He tried hard to revive those wartime images, so nurtured and so nurturing in battle, so unexpectedly redundant in peacetime; but the precious icons had lost their sanctity.

The Hershey Bar episode, innocuous, even a trifle comic, had irritated chiefly on principle, however, and he accepted he ought to overcome it.

"We saw young Sammy Tebbit this afternoon," he said, making a determined social effort. "I believe he's planning to move his mama and papa into Nashborough."

"The Tebbits will hate that; they're dyed-in-the wool country people."

"Yes, it may be too late," Seneca agreed, "but they'll go just the same."

"What will become of the farm?" Sally inquired, trying to keep a conversation going. Her foot had moved over next to Jack's and was pressing hard against it, or vice versa, and swallowing hard, she smothered a rising giggle.

"We won't find another tenant is my guess. Farming was finished here sometime before you were born. We can't compete with the Midwest; our land's not good enough. And now that there are better jobs around, as Sammy obviously has found out, all the sharecroppers will go as quickly as they can." Absently he crumpled the silver Hershey foil into a tiny ball. "When you're my age most of this state will be second-growth forest. Just you wait and see."

"But a bold peasantry, the nation's pride, when once destroyed can never be supplied," quoted Flora in a tone hard to fathom.

"True," said Seneca approvingly. "Now tell me who wrote it."

"Oliver Goldsmith, 'The Deserted Village,'" Sally laconically injected. They had played these games since childhood in Seneca's random efforts to "put some furniture in their heads."

"Top of the class."

"Along with me," said Flora.

"Sally sure knows a heap of poetry," Jack declared admiringly, then reddening slightly, added, "I'm no bookie myself."

Dartania found this highly entertaining and looked toward Frazer for the first time in an amused and friendly way that was greatly pleasing to Sally.

"Daddy used to stuff us with poetry," Sally complained good-humoredly. "Remember 'Horatius'?" she asked her sister. "That poem is printed on my brain forever." She struck a mock heroic pose. " 'And how can man die better than by facing fearful odds, for the ashes of his fathers and the temples of his gods.' "

"Now that's a real grand way of looking at it," said Jack, expressing agreeable surprise. "Down in Mississippi, I guess we saw it more like this: 'Better go out there and get him fore he gets you.' "

Dartania smiled into her plate, and Seneca, feeling obscurely challenged, moved with some alacrity into the lead.

"The Chinese have another way of looking at it, a passive way, that's interesting. They say that if you sit by the river long enough the bodies of your enemies will come floating by."

"It's the darned truth, too," said Jack. "It happened just like that out in the Philippines. The rivers were full of em. But, mind you, we had a mite of help."

At this Dartania laughed outright, fixing her beautiful smile on Frazer, while Seneca reluctantly was struck by the possibility that the fellow, in his cracker-barrel way, might make a decent lawyer after all. He wasn't so easy to get around, he held his ground and did so in an affable, seemingly unconscious sort of way. "Would your father agree with me about the future of farming?" Seneca asked pleasantly, having remembered that Frazer's father farmed somewhere down in Mississippi.

"My pappy's a tree farmer," Frazer drawled. "Well I guess it's sort of what you were talking about—sort of a second-growth forest," he offered amiably.

"Growing trees must take a good deal of patience. Or do you mean he's in the nursery business?"

"No, it's grown-up trees, all right, and it's a slow kind of farming, like you say. Down home everybody calls it apple-pie farming."

"Oh, orchards," said Flora disappointed.

"That's a right smart guess, but no, it's sort of like this." He had laid his napkin down on the table and stared hard into the middle distance. "There's this big circle full to busting with trees, and every year goes by, you cut yourself out a slice, like out of a pie. I guess they could've called it peach-pie farming just as well."

"What happens when you've eaten all the pie?" Flora pursued impertinently, but with the full attention of her family.

"Well, by the time you get round to where the first slice was, it's full of grown-up trees again, so you just cut yourself another slice and keep right on going."

"That must be a fair-sized pie," said Seneca, restraining too evident an interest.

"Yes sir, it is, but Mississippi pine grows mighty fast."

For the first time that evening Seneca and Dartania's eyes met in understanding through the candelabra. Many square miles must be involved in such an operation. The boy's family must be big landowners. They might be very rich. A light of mutual comprehension edged with admiration and relief lit their shared gaze.

But despite Jack's steadily accruing assets, Seneca's first impressions were not to be so easily overturned. Frazer had failed on too many counts; he wasn't in the same ball park with the estimable Pete Weaver. "God knows how he survived the war," he told Dartania later that night, "the fellow couldn't hit a rabbit at ten paces." Seneca tossed his shirt across the empty birdcage and, getting into bed, reached out for his book on the table beside it. "Might be worse." He did not say that what rankled most was having offered Frazer a place outright in Nash and Polk. Dartania would instantly recognize, and deplore, the influence of his mother.

"You can take the boy out of the country but you can't take the country out of the boy," she opined, having opened her own book. "He's got a sense of humor, anyway."

"And I hope to God some money."

Both knew the difference money would make given the young man's obvious social drawbacks, but any elaboration of the point would have been crude. Sharing from birth the same cultural cradle, they had understood each other perfectly, however, and no more needed to be said. Once again a common heritage had worked to smooth and reunite, and they went to sleep with all their animosity dispelled.

AFTER DINNER FLORA had put her Hershey Bar into her pocket and gone up to the nursery. Miss Allen was sitting in her rocker reading the Bible, her sturdy black shoes, with their uneven soles, raised off the floor like a little girl's. As Flora entered, her nurse's blue eyes brightened behind the steel-rimmed spectacles and she smiled her innocent and warming smile, tinged with an unmistakable eagerness. Miss Allen had few visitors. Her meals were eaten alone, and her days, except for Sundays when she went to church, were lived out in the nunlike quietude of her room, a solitary confinement, suspended awkwardly between the socially well-defined worlds of masters and servants.

"I brought you a piece of Hershey Bar," said Flora, who knew Miss Allen's weakness for all things chocolate.

Miss Allen put the thin blue ribbon of her bookmark into place and closed her well-worn Bible with its soft black leather covers. "You never forget your old Miss Allie, do you, sugar?"

Flora handed her the silver-wrapped chocolate and, retreating to the other side of the room, perched on a cedar chest beside the door.

Miss Allen opened the foil and, breaking off a piece, offered it to Flora, who resolutely shook her head.

"Is he a nice boy?" Miss Allen asked, eating the chocolate square and, having closed the foil, was evidently intent on saving the rest till later.

"He's OK, I guess. Sort of country. Sally will bring him up to meet you in the morning and you can see for yourself." She waited patiently till Miss Allen, giving in, had consumed another chocolate square, and then she stood up. "Well I guess I better be off."

The latent plea in Miss Allen's blue eyes could not be missed.

"I've got to get back downstairs," Flora defensively explained, looking down at the floor. "I'll be back tomorrow, though. And don't forget you're going to meet Sally's fiancé," she tacked on brightly.

"You let me have that jacket tomorrow and I'll put the button back on it."

"OK," said Flora. "Night, Miss Allie." And closing the nursery door behind her, she went away looking if anything more downcast than before.

3

....

*W*hen the telephone rang at 7:00 A.M. on the Friday following Jack Frazer's visit, Seneca was eating his breakfast on a tray in the gun room, shoeless, a worn paisley dressing gown over his boxer shorts, his socks held up by black elastic garters. The rest of the family was still fast asleep.

"I wanted to alert you before the newspaper came," Hamilton began, his perpetually even tone making it difficult to know, without his wishing it, either his mood or, as now, possible degrees of gravity.

"You chose the right moment," Seneca cheerfully supplied, his curiosity mildly on the rise. "James has just gone down to the front gate for it." Already he was girding himself for whatever confrontation was to come, a cool alertness mixed with anticipation livening his senses in readiness.

"It's about Robin," Hamilton announced.

Seneca's interest plummeted. He had expected, indeed had hoped for, something immediate, and tucking the telephone under his chin he reverted to dismembering the first of two quails on toast that comprised his breakfast.

"You'll know how best to handle it with Dartania." There followed a pause, almost a dramatic pause, it seemed to Seneca, for whom an impatience to get on with his breakfast made it unusually long.

"Robin's been found."

Seneca put the quail leg down on his plate. Vigorously casting back in his mind, he sought to pull forward an event long submerged by the white-water rapids of time and, as was thought, permanently buried. Suddenly it seemed there was to be a funeral. "Go on," he said evenly.

"It's front page headlines. There was nothing we could do, it's interstate."

Still Seneca waited, a trifle impatiently, his consciousness now fully focused, however.

"He's alive." Hamilton's tone, unchanged in the utterance of such extraordinary and improbable news, made it impossible to know or even guess its impact on him. "Down in Florida."

Seneca's brow knotted but he said, "That's damn fine news and certainly unexpected. Has anyone talked to him?"

"We spoke late last night." Hamilton did not enlarge as to who had telephoned whom. "The press was already onto it." Again he paused, choosing the story's more pragmatic threads, those needing earliest action. "The Florida paper called Margaret out of the blue. She's in quite a state. It seems some friend of Robin's, one of those Collinses, found him by accident. But instead of keeping his mouth shut, the fellow blurted it out to a reporter friend down there, and the press were on it like a pack of hounds. We could have stopped it here in Nashborough, of course."

James had appeared in the doorway and Seneca reached out for the furled newspaper. With a nod of thanks he pulled the rubber band off with his teeth and, using one hand, shook out the folded paper. "Nashborough Man Found Alive after Ten Years," he read. And the subheading, "Mystery of a Decade Solved." There was a photograph of Robin taken years earlier and mildly out of focus. He appeared to be on a race course, the leather strap around his neck presumably supporting binoculars.

"There's a woman," Hamilton added impassively. "And a passel of children."

"I see." Seneca was engaged in rapid calculation. "By my reckoning he's only about eight weeks short of being legally declared dead. It will be ten years come Christmas Eve." Both men knew Margaret was counting on the substantial life insurance policy payable then. And both knew, too, that she was planning to remarry. "Could be tricky."

"Certainly the timing is disjointed," Hamilton confirmed, a hint of criticism fringing the solemn tone.

"How is he?"

"He sounded about the same. Maybe less so," he added cryptically.

"Dartania will certainly be pleased. She felt sure he was dead. We all did, I suppose."

"Yes," said Hamilton slowly, and without evident enthusiasm for this unexpected and sudden resurrection. "We all did."

Seneca said if Jasmine or Chloe came out to Longwood later and broke the news to Dartania when she was fully awake, it might be less of a shock. "If that's possible, I'll leave the phone off the hook and take the newspaper with me."

"Bayard would be best," said Hamilton. "He won't make a fuss or start on a lot of silly speculation. I'm about to call him, in any case."

There was another pause. Seneca wondered if that was all, but in fact Hamilton was face-to-face with the crucial nub. "There's another thing, and Margaret doesn't know it yet, but Robin and this woman are married."

"A few more weeks and most of this would have been water over the dam, legally speaking," said Seneca, aware the point was now somewhat redundant.

"Margaret has enough on her plate. I'd like to hold this back if possible till she's stronger and we know more. The newspapers don't know yet, or they've shown a most remarkable discretion."

"They'll know soon enough," Seneca rejoined. "Reporters must be running Robin to ground this very minute. I'd advise you to tell her as soon as possible. I'll have a word with Josh King, he's the new public prosecutor and a practical sort of guy, not morally or legally overzealous. But the real problem is likely to be in Florida, assuming that's where he remarried."

While talking, Seneca had read the newspaper article. It recalled the mystery of Robin's sudden disappearance and played up dramatically his chance discovery by a boyhood friend. Many men had disappeared in the Depression, it said, but that a man from so prominent a family should have chosen obscurity was indeed remarkable, the mystery not quite cleared up by the facts. The article claimed Robin worked as a fisherman in Daytona Beach and stated simply and without innuendo that he was married to the former Margaret Elsworthy and that they had two children. No speculation about the reasons for his disappearance were made, but Seneca could tell more was to come: The paper was baiting its readers, building up the human-interest angle and sniffing about for more ingredients. "We need to get going on this as quick as we can," he said. "The paper's set to build the whole thing up, and that could make more trouble legally."

"I'll handle the paper," Hamilton volunteered without enthusiasm. He would have to call the proprietor, and the story being already out would make it more difficult to cork.

For whatever reasons, no further developments appeared in the evening paper, but the element of coincidence effecting the discovery had seized Blue Hills' imagination, raising it from a fortuitous event to a fateful and ordained encounter, so that paradoxically Robin emerged in many eyes a man of destiny.

As the story emerged, a state of excited confusion permeated the Douglas clan, together with all the head scratching and false starts common to assembling jigsaw puzzles. An embarrassed Matt Collins had filled in details of the discovery, so that much at least was solid.

Collins, it transpired, had been in Daytona Beach on insurance company business and, after his meeting, was to dine with an old fraternity brother, now a newspaperman. On the way, he'd gone into a shop to buy some cigarettes. He was waiting to pay the cashier when his eye lit idly on the pack of cigarettes the man in front of him was holding. It was his own brand, Philip Morris. But as Matt came slowly into conscious perception, he noticed that the tip of the man's middle finger was missing. It made him think of Robin Douglas. It made him think, too, how surprising it was that so many boys grew up with all their fingers and toes, considering some of the things they got up to. Robin had lost his when a crate of hatchets the boys were trying to open had collapsed.

Vaguely Matt's gaze moved to the man's frayed cuff, ascending his rumpled suit to the bony profile and bluish eyes under graying hair. There was something familiar in the way he held himself, tilting backward slightly as he stood. But then the missing fingertip had set him thinking of Robin, and he shrugged it off.

Not till he was paying the cashier did the full mental photograph emerge as from developing fluid and, superimposed upon an earlier image, fitted perfectly. "Right down to the fingertips," Matt chortled, stuffing his change into his pocket, his eyes raking the pavement outside.

His quarry was crossing the street, he was already halfway over, waiting on the white line for several cars to pass.

"Hey," shouted Matt, flamboyantly waving his cigarette pack.

The man didn't respond.

"Hey, Robin!"

Startled, the man looked back, balancing on the white line, eyeing the waving packet of cigarettes with some confusion: It seemed to be meant for him. Then, recollecting himself he moved forward, despite the oncoming cars. But Collins, with the resilience of a rubber ball, bounced across the intervening lane, catching him up. By now he was pretty damn sure.

"Hey, old buddy!" He had clapped Robin on the shoulder and they could only go forward entwined like old chums toward the opposite curb. Robin said not a word, but his wry smile betrayed in a mix of complex considerations a degree of pleasure.

"Hey, I thought it was you. Who else could it be, I said." Collins waggled his finger. "Caught in the act," he grinned. "Remember?" and he clapped Robin on the back again.

"Matt Collins," said Robin finally, smiling slightly, "You bad penny."

"Me!" railed Collins, then, "It's great to see you, old buddy! But what are you doing here, man?" Matt's eye roved the surroundings then tactfully he shifted back into the safe and familiar territory of Southern superlatives. "This is swell. Just swell."

Evidently they were headed toward a rusty black Packard parked against the curb in front of a run-down bar. "What about a drink?" Matt offered, his exuberance becoming slightly forced; he had begun to wonder what exactly he was opening up. "We got to celebrate ole buddy."

Still smiling, Robin nodded toward the café at the corner. "What about a cup of coffee?" he said.

FORTY-EIGHT HOURS later a family conference was held at Timbuctoo, the first of its kind and a break with Hamilton's normally unilateral style.

As to Robin, his siblings knew only that he had been found, fortuitously, by Collins down in Florida; that he was remarried, had little money, many children, and worked, according to the newspapers, but improbably, as a fisherman. They knew, too, that Robin had begged Matt to say nothing, if that were possible—news that had wounded and confused them all. But Matt, believing in his newspaper pal's friendly priorities, had flubbed it. The Florida paper's scoop had caused Robin to call his father, before the story appeared in Nashborough.

Only Hamilton had spoken to Robin. Only Hamilton and Seneca, who denied it, had Robin's telephone number, and no one as yet knew of his pseudonym, Robin Kane, pinched from the Orson Wells film with an irony typical of Robin, whose own circumstances reversed that of Wells's protagonist, reborn to riches and power.

Dartania had tried hard to extract her brother's telephone number from her husband. Even if he had it, Seneca told her, there was the awkward chance, should Dartania call her brother, of getting Robin's new wife. And who then would Dartania ask for. Robin would almost certainly have changed his name. Did his new wife know yet who he really was? Did she know he already had a wife and children? The argument prevailed and Dartania was forced to wait.

By four o'clock, all the family except Margaret had been waiting for a full fifteen minutes in Timbuctoo's front hall. Punctuality, as ingrained as an inherited trait, was on this occasion augmented further by an eagerness for news and speculative exchanges.

As the library clock struck four, Hamilton entered the hall from his office across the conservatory, Seneca with him, and nodding to his brood sat down in a large Jacobean armchair with a heraldic crest of uncertain origin embroidered on its velvet back. Chloe, Jasmine, Dartania, Bayard, and Dan were already ensconced on the two facing sofas, and Chloe's children, hovering at the top of the stairs, had been sent smartly packing.

Seneca, who must respond to looming legal problems, among them possible charges of bigamy, sat on Hamilton's left, and another straight-backed chair, reserved for Margaret, stood on his right.

Jane, diplomatic as always, stayed near the back and, when Margaret arrived, hurried forward to greet her, whispering sympathies and encouragement.

Margaret, in a dark suit and navy pillbox hat with a short veil, kept her eyes on Jane and then on the carpet. The formality of the meeting mercifully prevented the need for further greetings, except to her father-in-law, whom she briefly kissed. The others, given license by her understandable failure to meet their gaze, could not resist making their own close scrutiny. What did she feel about it all, they wondered. Her insurance windfall almost certainly was lost (Matt Collins was trying to move heaven and earth down at Prudential Life). Might not she lose Tom Hepburn, too? As things stood, she couldn't possibly marry him in January, as planned. And what about her feelings for dear Robin, whom some awful woman had got hold of and kept a prisoner down in Florida? Maybe Margaret would take him back, and all would return to normal, as if it had never happened. This scenario engendered broad appeal.

Sitting in the grandiose armchair, Hamilton pressed his long fingers over the carved acanthus finials that completed the arms. He looked tired, seeming by his slow movements to wear his eighty-six years with Promethean endurance.

"I know all of you are glad to learn your brother is alive," he told his children as soon as Margaret had sat down. A slight hoarseness edged his voice. "But a number of problems are involved, including, as you know, legal ones that could be serious. There are also certain aspects concerning the family generally, to be considered." He said that being grown-up, his children would have individual reactions to Robin's discovery and how they chose to respond. But in fairness to Margaret and her children, they were in some respects obliged, as families are, to act as a unit. That was one reason the meeting had been called. Time was short, the matter a pressing one (the pun advertent or not was roundly acknowledged), and he was particularly grateful to Margaret for her cooperation at such a difficult time.

Eyes continued to flicker openly over Margaret, who, sitting very erect, kept up behind her veil a steady scrutiny of one of Hercules' labors depicted on the mural wallpaper.

"Among the legal questions are possible future claims on the family estate by Robin's children down in Florida, so the situation as you see is complicated in several directions. Much delicacy and perhaps some strenuous negotiation will be required."

"But those children are illegitimate," Chloe indignantly declared with a quick glance toward the stairs.

Dartania overrode this. "Papa, when is Robin coming home? When can we talk to him?"

"I know you all want to see him as soon as possible, but it may be necessary to delay his coming here." Hamilton looked toward Seneca.

"If Robin was remarried in this state," said Seneca, picking up his cue, "and there's some evidence to suggest he was, it would be dangerous for him to come here with a charge of bigamy riding on his head. We're doing what we can to stop any prosecution here and down in Florida. Nobody wants it, but the state must nonetheless be seen to do its business properly. Our own prosecutor won't, I am assured, ask for Robin's extradition, but if Robin were seen here or was known to be here he could be arrested. The police might have no choice."

"How could Robbie have remarried here?" Chloe's incredulity was mounting to impatience. "How is that possible? *Has he been living here?*"

"The facts are unclear as yet. But if he did remarry here, there are advantages. The state where he remarried is the one where bigamy charges would be brought, and it's a whole lot easier to suppress a criminal prosecution here than it is in Florida."

"You mean you might tell him that he can't come home?" Dartania looked at her husband with angry astonishment.

"I doubt you'd want to visit him in the jail," Seneca evenly rejoined, almost with a smile.

"I'm sure Robin is anxious to see you all, now the thing is in the open, as you all are to see him," Hamilton interposed. "But prudence and some patience may be needed. You'll have to hold onto your hats."

"I don't want to see him! I don't want him here!"

Every eye turned to Margaret, whose own gaze rested on no other face. *"Not ever again. I hope he never comes back!"* she cried, gripping the chair arm, her gaze raking the company without seeing them. "What he did is unforgivable. The horror and pain of it. Oh dreadful! All those years of not knowing, of keeping up hope and loving feelings for him, in case he were still alive. When all the time he was . . ." She swallowed, her lips set tight, attempting without success to bring her bitterness under control. "I hate him. I can never forgive him, not just for what he's done to me, but to his little children, abandoning them like that, just turning his back on them and . . . oh it's so cold . . . so irresponsible. It's so viciously weak."

Robin's siblings gaped in astonishment. In no way could they defend their brother's actions. His behavior had been cowardly and disgraceful, and as kin, his conduct was connected to theirs. But they felt no animosity. They loved him, and what Margaret, as an abandoned wife and mother had suffered, failed even now to penetrate their clannish skins. To them, Margaret was the outsider, not Robin, and Dartania for one still blamed her in part for what had happened.

"I spoke to Miss Alice this morning." Jane stepped swiftly in.

"You speak to Miss Alice every morning," said Hamilton jovially, trying with his wife for a more even keel.

"She feels, as I'm sure we ourselves do, that what happens now is up to Margaret and that for her sake and her children's we should all of us stick by her wishes."

"But he never wanted to be found; it's not his fault," Dartania blurted out softly. "Papa, you always said a family's first duty was to support its weakest members, that the strong will look after themselves."

"Robin is a grown man who has turned his back on every responsibility. His own family, who have become our responsibility, must take precedence over him."

"The prodigal son was forgiven," Dartania persisted.

"The prodigal son came home voluntarily. He asked for his father's forgiveness. Robin has done neither. In fact, he asked to be left as he is."

To this there was little answer.

"We don't have enough details yet," Hamilton continued, glowering at his nest of children, "but on the face of it, my view is that Robin can never formally be accepted back into this family." He said it would be necessary to discuss certain details with Robin, such as had been touched upon, and he knew there was much his children wished and needed to have filled in. "Whatever private relations you conduct with your brother will of course be up to you. But I trust they will be conducted *in strictest privacy* so as not to undermine Margaret's status in this family or upset her feelings and those of her children in any way."

Seneca proposed in lieu of Robin's coming home that a family envoy should go out to him. He suggested Bayard, whom he thought of as an inspiring example of a blotted copybook new-leafed. Moreover, Bayard's business head and open-mindedness could ably negotiate some workable solution.

"I'd love to see old Robbie," Bayard enthusiastically declared, "but I'm going abroad next week, sailing to England to see my wife and son."

This astonishing news, its timing cleverly arranged to stop a lot of questions, turned all heads from the serious matter at hand. Jane declared herself delighted, and Margaret, turning from her own domestic grief, produced an instant show of sympathetic hope. "Oh Bayard, I'm so glad!" she cried out in felt sincerity.

This view was not unanimous however. "Both our brothers married prigs," Jasmine exploded in a whisper to Dartania, sitting beside her on the sofa, "and it's no wonder they separated. They'd be fools to go undo it now."

"The Widow Ames had better get her campaign on the road," Dartania mischievously returned. "And if Margaret will let poor Robbie alone, I'm sure he'll move back home. She's what drove him away."

The meeting ended, despite its seriousness of purpose, like most Douglas gatherings, in banter and irreverent jokes. It would soon be cocktail time.

"WHAT AN INTERESTING family we are," Flora solemnly observed. She was settled at the foot of Sally's bed, her striped cotton pajamas, rolled up at the cuffs, giving her the appearance of a sailor boy. Her knees were scooped into her arms, her tousled curls boyishly capping large serious eyes, a pouting and unsmiling mouth.

Sally, very differently attired, eyed her dreamily. Propped up on two pillows in a black nylon nightgown, part of her trousseau being given a showy preview, Sally's hair paradoxically was knobbed in a coronet of rubber rollers for greater glory on the morrow. The Masons were giving her an engagement party.

"We've got aunts and uncles in every combination, a bin full of them," Flora languidly tapped a finger as she listed each. "There's a widow, there's a bachelor, there's a divorcée; we've got one who's estranged, and now there's a bigamist. Not a normal married couple anywhere."

"Well, there's Mama and Daddy," Sally offered, plucking admiringly at the black lace frilling her little bosom, "speaking for that generation as a whole."

"Henry and Eleanor? They're abnormally married." Flora was in the habit of calling her parents after the principals in one of history's stormiest marriages, Henry II and Eleanor of Aquitaine; and the practice, as with almost everything Flora did, was innocuously indulged. They were Henry and Eleanor to their faces, and they accepted it, probably with concealed amusement. "They're awful."

"Flora!" protested Sally, unable to repress the elder sibling's instinct for pseudoparental control. Sally was well aware that Flora and her friend Ginevra Tuttle repeatedly vilified their parents, denying them any shred of loyalty or respect. It was a postwar fashion, rearing up out of nowhere, and one she herself could not approve. "That's so disloyal," she predictably interposed.

"Loyalty's just a device for keeping underlings under. By our not complaining about them openly, they get to do as they please, that's all."

Though privately accepting this, Sally could not bring herself to show disloyalty. Her own sense of fealty was too ingrained. She was brainwashed, according to Flora.

They had had such conversations before and Sally, speaking with the superior force of eight years' seniority, always insisted that parents had a natural right to loyalty and respect. "Besides, everybody respects Daddy," she had pointed out, implying that any divergence would merely show abysmally poor judgment.

"Not as a parent, they don't. Name one thing Henry or Eleanor has ever done for us to deserve our respect. Name one thing they've ever done for us that the law hasn't made them do. They just order us around. They don't *care* about us. They only think of themselves. They think they're on the center stage and we should thank them for getting a walk-on part."

"But they're our *parents*, Flora."

"Having a piano doesn't make you a musician," the girl replied, widening her eyes slightly to accent this minor triumph of sophistry.

But Sally refused its acknowledgment. "They do care about us," she said. "Parents always love their children; it just happens."

Flora stared patiently at her sister. "I suppose you'll have a lot of kids." Her tone was one of resignation. "I can't think why anyone would."

"Oh lots," enthused Sally, "I love babies! I'm going to have four or five at least."

"They grow up," Flora ominously intoned, then shifted ostensibly the focus of talk. "Jack's really nice. But *they* don't like him, do they?"

"Yes they do, but they don't really know him yet. It's never easy when outsiders enter a family. Everyone has to adjust, including Jack."

Spreading her fingers on the white bedspread she looked admiringly at her diamond engagement ring, its three carats declaring her station to be of some importance while devoid of any vulgar ostentation. "It's true this family hates outsiders more than most," she admitted. "We're such a clan, somehow we just can't help it," she offered by way of an excuse.

"They're glad he's rich," Flora went on, threading a subliminal path of her own. "Is he very rich?"

"What a question Flora!" Sally tilted her head, absently twisting one of the rubber curlers. "I don't really know. His family's got all those trees. He says they're paper millionaires." She paused for Jack's witticism to sink in, but Flora remained impassive. "Trees are used to make paper, silly. *Paper millionaires*, there's a double meaning. Anyway, he hasn't got a lot of money himself. He has to make his own way, and he will, too. But honestly, money doesn't matter much as long as you've enough to live on and you love each other," she sagely opined.

"I wish I were rich."

"You do, do you? And what would you do with it, pray?"

"I'd run away like Uncle Robin and never come back."

"Well, don't come to me for a loan. One bolter in this family is enough."

"There's Emma."

"Emma? Emma's *at college.*"

"She's never coming back. I bet you anything."

Sally's incredulity was halted by a sudden high-pitched squeal, blurred but distinct and coming from the wall behind her bed. "Oh, what was that? It sounded like a little baby crying." With a mix of joy and alarm she half turned toward the wall.

"It is sort of. Come and see," offered Flora bounding off the bed.

THAT MORNING FLORA had taken the Greyhound bus into Nashborough and, circumventing the river warehouses, walked ten blocks to the city's pound. She wanted a dog, she told them, a little dog, a lap-type dog would do very nicely. The pound attendant, with a mole on her nose like a foothill, had taken Flora down a prisonlike corridor lined with mesh cages to see a new litter of puppies. The mother was part fox terrier, but the father's breed wasn't known, she said, the bitch having been dropped off pregnant on the pound's doorstep.

"Well, he mustn't get too big," Flora had reiterated, gazing uncertainly at the mound of puppies piled in a heap beside their mother. She chose the runt, chiefly to be on the safe side, but then her sympathies were for underdogs, and the runt very naturally lay on the bottom of the heap.

That afternoon, carrying a big cardboard box tied around with a red Christmas ribbon, Flora called, as every day, on Miss Allen in her room. Miss Allen sat dozing in her rocker, her Bible open in her lap, the white November light coming in through the window behind her creating a sort of icon, silvery and Russian.

"Hi, Miss Allie, are you awake?" Flora stood in the doorway holding her bulky parcel as Miss Allen opened her eyes, blinked, put on her steel-rimmed spectacles, and smiled with innocent sweetness at the girl.

"I brought you something, Miss Allie."

"Come on in, sugar," Miss Allen said. "What's that you're carrying?"

"It's a surprise," and stooping down, Flora set the box with a small thud on the floor beside Miss Allen's chair. An indistinct noise issued from inside.

"I can't get down there to open it," Miss Allen told her, leaning forward, suspicious at seeing Jack Daniel's printed on the box's side. Miss Allen was an avowed teetotaller.

Flora untied the bow and slipped the scarlet ribbon off.

"Don't throw it away," said Miss Allen, reaching out. "Save it for Christmas."

Flora handed it to her; then, reaching inside the open carton, she announced with a minute smile, "Get ready, Miss Allie!" And as Miss Allen rolled the red ribbon up neatly and slipped it into her pocket, Flora lifted the puppy out of the box. "Isn't he cute? He looks like a guinea pig, but he's really a dog." She put the puppy in Miss Allen's capable hands, and, like all Miss Allen's infant charges, it at once nestled inert against the warm solidity of her rigid corsets.

"Don't let him pee on you, he isn't house-trained yet."

But Miss Allen, either for reasons of experience or of deep concentration, continued to stroke the little black head with its brown muzzle, her own face glowing in a surprised and beatific smile.

"I think it's a Bonsai breed," suggested Flora in an upbeat tone.

"Bone's eye?" said Miss Allen. "What does that mean?" The puppy had rolled over to have its stomach tickled, paws up in the air, blissfully hypnotized. "You like that don't you?" said Miss Allen. "You like to have your tummy tickled." And to Flora, "Look at how he rolls over on his back to get his stomach tickled. I'm going to call him Roly. Roly," she informed the supine puppy.

"Roly po'ly," said Flora, looking dolefully at the little runt.

But Miss Allen, still gently stroking the thin stomach, was smiling into the black button eyes as she'd done into so many infants' eyes over the years, conveying her utter devotion.

"Holy Roly, then," Flora went on in an undertone, but Miss Allen did not respond even to a hinted sacrilege. It had begun to dawn that in her long years of nursing, only Roly of all her infant charges belonged entirely to her.

"Are you hungry, Roly?" she asked. "We'll go down to the kitchen in a minute and get you some biscuits and milk," she announced, having divined somehow a positive response in Roly.

For the first time in her life, Flora was able to leave the nursery unnoticed and without a pang of guilt.

NOW, TAKING SALLY into the corridor, Flora pushed open the nursery door a crack and pointed to the black velvety ball at the foot of Miss Allen's bed.

"What is it, a cat?"

"It's a dog," whispered Flora as she closed the door.

"What kind of a dog?"

"A well-bred oriental dog, a Bonsai," she risked again, looking Sally evenly in the eye.

"I think I've heard of them. Weren't they temple dogs somewhere out in China?"

"Don't let on to Miss Allie he's a heathen," Flora urged. "Just say that they're church dogs."

4
....

As the airplane drew to a stop outside the terminal building, great solid circles of air made by the whirling propellers began to dissipate, revealing at length the miracle of steel rotating blades. The morning sky from which the air was pulled so forcefully contained a presentiment of winter. The November wind was intense.

Behind the meshed-wire fence surrounding the terminal, a small group was huddled, and among them only Dartania, standing aloof, her worn beaver coat held together by crossed arms, seemed free of the propellers' hypnotic, mandala-like effect. Dartania looked around covertly. She thought she saw one of Sally's friends in a yellow hat, apparently with her mother. But the midtown set were unlikely to recognize Robin or to presume on small acquaintance to introduce themselves to her. In any event Robin would wear dark glasses and have his hat pulled down, and they would not acknowledge each other till they were out of the terminal building.

It was to be a flying visit in both senses, lasting only seven hours, only long enough for Robin to discuss legal and financial questions with Seneca, and to pay his father a perfunctory visit. Dartania was to be chauffeur, returning him to the airport promptly at four o'clock. Their other siblings would have to wait, as a chance recognition at this precarious stage could not be further risked.

As the hatch above the stairway platform opened, a trickle of passengers began their ambling descent. There were not many people on board, and for a moment, straining forward, Dartania was afraid that Robin hadn't come. The disembarking passengers, heads down, butting the November wind, frowned in discomfort after their stint in the Florida sun. Suddenly the hatch was empty except for a pretty stewardess waving at someone. Surely Robin wouldn't draw attention to himself by disembarking after all the others.

Then with a start she saw him, quite near, across the low fence, almost in front of her, and she could tell he had seen her. He carried no briefcase, but a brown paper bag; his mackintosh, not much protection against the cold, had the collar up. The dark glasses and tilted-down hat made excellent camouflage, but Robin's upright stance, leading slightly with his feet and looking therefore curiously blown back by the wind, was unmistakable, a defining outline any cartoonist would have emphasized at once.

Dartania beamed her excitement. A small tilt of her head welcomed and at the same time indicated the front of the building.

Arriving there, he followed her to the car parked a little way from the terminal exit and jumped in quickly beside her.

"Oh Robbie! Robbie!" She turned, facing him from behind the wheel, her face alight with pleasure, taking him fully in. "God, for a minute I thought you hadn't come! I couldn't see you anywhere," she laughed nervously, approving the success of his disguise.

"Hidden by two black eyes," he returned, taking the sunglasses off. The familiar crinkles of kindness around the eyes as he smiled back, beloved markings on a familiar map, brought home the adored and ever-whimsical Robin as, grinning like two children, they overrode for now the task of splicing together a ten-year separation.

But how worn he looked, the pale blue eyes like faded distant skies, a tautness unmistakable in his familiar thin-lipped smile. Would she have known him passing him casually on the street, she wondered. He looked so down-at-the-heel, so . . . seedy. A burst of sudden pity squeezed at her heart like an angry fist. "Let's get out of here," she said, starting the engine and casting a quick glance in the rear-view mirror. "Let's go get some breakfast."

They had an hour before he was due to meet Seneca.

The Krystal, a chain café famous for large coffees and minute hamburgers, its roof topped with a giant mosaic crystal ball, lay halfway between the air terminal and town, a hinterland where they were unlikely to be seen. Here, sitting across a speckled formica table over bacon and eggs, and away from the plate-glass window, they sought to erect the first span that would bridge the ten-year chasm.

"You haven't changed at all." He was smiling his new sad smile, the same smile, she saw with rising astonishment, as before, only now it struck her as sad, or wistful perhaps. Could it have always been so and she simply never had interpreted it correctly? The thought was impossible to pursue.

"I, on the other hand, am a sort of reassembly, a ghost in the machine."

"Oh Robbie, tell me what *happened?*" she pleaded, jumping passionately in.

"Delicious bacon," he said, as though that thought, already in his mind, must logically come out first. "I wish we had Krystals down in Florida."

She waited, lit a cigarette, puffed nervously at it. Never before had they needed the directness of a discussion, and both were at a loss, their old banter brutally inadequate to the job.

Nonetheless Dartania tried the familiar route. "I've missed you, you old so-and-so," she said playfully. "Everybody has."

"I'm sorry." He had taken it as an accusation, his head drooping suddenly on its stalk. "My leaving like that, without a word, it was an awful thing to do."

"It wasn't," she cried out in ardent defense. "It's just that we didn't know what to think. We still don't. But we're glad you're alive, Robbie dear, and we want you back."

"Poor old Margaret. Awful for her, anyhow. And for the children now. It would have been much better for them not to know."

"That wasn't your fault."

Robin smiled slightly and shook his head. "The truth is, all that seems a very long way off, it's like re-entering a vaguely familiar dream. Not at all like making a home run," he punned, to Dartania's great relief.

She lit a new cigarette with the old one. "Margaret drove you to it," she blurted out.

"Margaret's a very fine woman . . ."

Again Dartania leaped, blocking useless *politesse*. They had so little time. "You'll come back home, Robbie? I mean, when things are sorted out?"

He paused, gazing into the murky coffee, shook his head over it.

"Seneca will fix it up legally. There won't be any problem, you wait and see."

"I can't come back, Dar."

"But you *want* to! Is it that woman, Robbie? Won't she let you?"

"She *would* let me."

"Well then, when everything's cleared up legally, and a financial settlement or whatever is worked out . . ."

Robin smiled at her hopeful and innocent simplicity. "My life is finished here, Dar. It's over," he told her gently. "I've made another one, insignificant as it may seem looked at from your Olympian heights." There followed a flicker of the old ironic Robin. "Reverse pioneering you might say."

"Being a fisherman!"

He smiled again. "They got that wrong. As a matter of fact, I work at the public aquarium. You'd never guess what remarkable creatures fish are. Their personalities are as colorful as their skins."

"Oh Robbie . . . But that woman—I mean your new wife . . ."

"Myra."

"Is she . . . Well, who is she?" The note was plaintive, almost girlish.

"Who? Well, for one thing, she was my secretary."

It took Dartania a minute. "You don't mean all those years ago down at the Cotton Exchange!" She couldn't remember if she'd met the woman; she must have spoken to her on the telephone. "But you only got married five years ago, over at Mountain Springs, Seneca said."

Robin's fingers spread out over his thighs; he drew himself upright, looking vaguely before him, his mind evidently occupied by some inner scene. "Myra's family is from Mountain Springs, and like most mountain people, they're very religious and, when it comes to certain conventions, downright prudish. So when we visited them we did the 'genteel' thing and got married. There were small children by then to think about and it really did seem by that time to be another life. One that would stay separate."

"That it didn't isn't your fault," she again insisted. "But was your secretary—I mean Myra—was she the reason for . . . ?" Her amazement could not be hidden and Robin smiled with patient knowledge at the hierarchic social distinctions women found it so impossible to jettison. "Was that why you did it, Robbie? Because you fell in love with your secretary?"

"It hasn't been easy for Myra," he replied, picking a route of his own. "Taking on an inebriate who couldn't hold down a job." He paused as the waitress, wearing a tiny heart-shaped apron, poured more coffee and replaced the overflowing ashtray. "Myra saved my life."

This was so unlike Robin. It was also patently untrue: If anything, the woman had wrecked his life not saved it.

"Do you know what it's like feeling that half of you is missing when another person isn't there?" He said it quietly and without looking at her, examining the speckled formica surface.

"Something like," his twin morosely returned. It was the nearest she had come, even privately, to an accusation. The bridge was not being very successfully spanned.

"No booze has passed these parched lips in over five years now." The announcement implicitly awarded the credit to Myra. He had opened his wallet and, pulling out a worn photograph, handed it across the table.

Reluctantly Dartania peered into the eyes of a stout pudding-faced woman with a short twenties-style haircut, wearing a cheap cotton dress and surrounded by several children, one of them evidently walleyed, on her lap, all of them frowning into the sunlight. They stood on the porch of a run-down clapboard house.

Dartania could think of nothing to say, then noted with a small shock, "That one looks a little like Danny as a child." But decency called for more. "She's got a nice expression," she said weakly of Myra, who looked sheeplike and about as firm as a blancmange.

"She saved my life, and every day that passes, she continues to save it."

A strange isolation edging toward loneliness began to creep over Dartania. As Robin signaled the waitress for the bill, she handed the photograph back across the table. They went outside in silence.

In front of Nash and Polk, mustering gaiety, Dartania said, "We better not risk a restaurant for lunch. I'll get some sandwiches and collect you here. We'll have a winter picnic." As he climbed out of the car, she added, "Robbie, don't let Seneca beat you down. He can be pretty rough and it's not *your* interests he's representing, believe me."

"My interests are already taken care of," he assured her calmly.

Waiting outside the law offices, the packet of sandwiches on the seat beside her, Dartania tried to organize her impressions into a pattern capable of producing a unified response. In ways, Robin seemed such a stranger, the carapace recognizable but the contents so strangely altered. The old lightness of touch, the irony and dry wit, the clownishness that had set the tone of their affectionate camaraderie, except for rare glimmers, had disappeared. In its place was not exactly earnestness, such as Margaret or Ellen or even Chloe might effuse, but something almost—evangelical. Of course! It was the self-confessed tone of a reformed alcoholic: brainwashed, broken-backed and humble, lacking all pride and dignity, the antithesis of what a self-respecting man should be. But she held back from pity or disappointment. Her loyalty remained fierce, and when Robin reappeared, she knew that her allegiance, no matter what, lay unshakably with him.

They drove in easy silence down Elm Street and, after a few blocks turned west into the stone-gated entrance of Nashborough's public park, the first time either of them had been there. Dartania parked the car in front of the great bronze replica of Marcus Aurelius astride his noble steed, one arm outstretched, riding bareback and without a bridle.

Dartania laid out tuna fish sandwiches on the seat between them and produced two Coca-Colas and a bottle opener. Then, a little awkwardly, she opened her bag and extracted a small flask of whiskey, which, being politely offered, Robin smilingly refused. She took a sizable swig herself, relishing the prickly warmth as it went down. She had badly needed a drink.

"You see before you a uniquity," he told her, the old Robin briefly percolating up. "A remittance man without any remittance." Things had been quickly settled and without any disagreement. He'd simply signed a paper renouncing all future benefits from the family estate in favor of Margaret and her two children. Margaret would get a divorce at once, before any bigamy charges could be raised: She was going to Reno in a few days' time. He'd renounced the right to see or contact their children unless the children at some point should wish otherwise. "I'm as free as a lark and so is Margaret, or we shall be in a matter of days—to re-contract," for the irony wasn't lost on him. Matt he said had proved to be a useful catalyst. Only a week before, none of this unknotting and reknotting was conceivable, and legally, he had been very near to extinction.

"I'm only sorry Margaret lost the life insurance premium," he said. "That was bad luck."

When he had eaten half his sandwich, he added admiringly, "Seneca's quite a fellow. He was ready to pound me into a pulp if necessary, and he had the wherewithal to do it. As it was, we got on fine."

"Robbie, when you and Margaret are divorced and remarried, couldn't you bring your wife and family back here? After all, this is your home."

"This is Margaret's home now. Besides the air is too rarefied; it's as hard to breathe as on a Himalayan peak. You need to be born here to tolerate it, and even then not everyone has the lungs. I never did, and poor Myra would suffocate on arrival."

He was gazing through the windscreen at Marcus Aurelius high on his concrete plinth. The emperor's arm seemed to be extended in benediction over them.

"I'm a poor man, materially speaking, but the truth is—and you'll find this very hard to believe—I'm happier than I've ever been in my life." He threw her a quick look, moving only his eyes. "Before, I was a sort of row vegetable sprouting in a very superior patch. But something was wrong, some ingredient was left out of the compost. I always felt that, you know. And for a time alcohol just about replaced it."

"What *ingredient*? You were happy, Robbie, it was always fun," Dartania cried out with passionate resistance.

He smiled his old or new sad smile. "What are we going to do for happiness today?"

"Well what's wrong with that? Life should be fun, why not?"

"Should it? I don't really know what it should be. I only know when it's not in working order for me, or when I myself am not in working order. Dear old Cal was better off than me, and I think he knew it, too. I always sensed he felt a little sorry for me." A small spasm twitched the corner of his mouth. "He must be dead."

"Yes, a long time now."

Robin said nothing for a minute, but sat still in sad repose. "The finest gentleman I ever knew, the finest gentle man."

They had begun the drive to Timbuctoo; passing by rows of neat, eclectically built midtown houses, their architecture suggesting that indecision had warred with a resolved stability. Gazing out at the largely unchanged scene, Robin kept up his fragmented and moody reflections. "Most people seem to bumble along in their inherited patches, making the best of it. They don't want to run away to sea or to another town or even to another life. But if a chance for some real happiness comes along, shouldn't they jump at it? Is that cowardly, or is it cowardly not to? Is it worse to be thought a coward than to plod along day after day in an ill-fitting harness? Papa would say, maybe will say, that it is, and I expect he's right. I expect duty is a very high virtue." He lapsed again into silence, looking with concentration through the window as they skirted the outer precincts of Blue Hills, turning right onto Auntie Nell Pike.

"When I married, I knew nothing about life, only that I was a bit uncomfortable in my vegetable patch. Margaret was wiser, a more grown-up, definite character, and that may well have had its appeal. But I only felt more boyish and unformed than before, which wasn't her fault, of course." They had stopped at a newly installed traffic light and he looked over at his twin, briefly meeting her somewhat embarrassed gaze. "But I've found my niche now. It isn't prominent but it suits me and it's real. I go to the aquarium, I feed the fish, I watch them go about the business of survival with their greedy snapping mouths and unenviable aggression. I come home to a plain meal, to quiet well-behaved children, and above all to a wife, who, without complaint, will endure anything on my behalf. What more could any man want? What more could a man like me want, that is?" There was another pause. "And having known affluence I don't feel I'm missing anything."

"Oh Robbie, I really can't make you out! You had everything, you did whatever you wanted, and everyone loved you so. They still do. I know you hated the Cotton Exchange but it wouldn't have gone on forever." With a kind of exasperation she shifted gears downward, making a rasping noise. "It's not too late to put things right again, the way they were."

They were approaching the winding drive at Timbuctoo, and driving slowly over the cattle guard between the gateposts, the familiar bumps of themselves announced their destination. Almost at once the house arose in all its grandeur, its elegance and grace—in all its overwhelming welter of associations.

Robin gave a visible start. Like a scene change in a play, another reality was ringing down, blocking what had appeared to be a fixed backcloth, a firmly entrenched existence, as the compassing aura of Timbuctoo closed in. It seemed for a moment he had never left it. Suddenly panic raced crazily through his limbs and his heart beat wildly as the great shell of the past closed over him, Jonah swallowed by a whale, blacking out all other existence.

"If there's anything left in that flask, I think one swig would put me right," he murmured apologetically. "Hair of a dog long dead."

Almost with relief Dartania handed it over. She knew what he must be feeling: the terror of an interview with a judgmental father whose reprimand need not be stated to be made effective, whose disappointment in him would be received in a confusion of shame and tender filial devotion.

They had stopped in front of the house. Robin capped the flask and handed it back.

"I'll trot down to the springhouse or something," she said, "so if I'm not here . . ." Empathy lit her delicate features with sisterly solicitude. She patted his arm, "Good luck," adding on the upbeat, "It's not the end of the world."

Neither father nor son ever spoke to anyone of what went on. Jane met Robin at the front door and after a warm and welcoming hug directed him toward his father's office, for Hamilton had in no way altered his routine, meeting his son at an appointed time, after his daily siesta. One of Chloe's children, however, a little girl playing behind potted palms in the conservatory, claimed that when Robin came out half an hour later he had sat down on a bench behind the aviary and wept. She had seen him blowing his nose with a pocket handkerchief. No, it wasn't a cold. He was crying; she was old enough to know the difference.

"He was very civil," said Robin quietly. He had found Dartania leaning against the springhouse wall, sheltering from the wind. "He already knew Seneca had sorted things out legally so there wasn't much left to say, about anything. He looks so old." Robin's voice faltered slightly. "I hadn't expected that. Intimations of mortality."

In fact, Robin had been deeply hurt, his vulnerability increasing as he felt his father's criticism, so powerfully implied; and for the first time, the gravity of his misdeeds came guiltily home. He had let them all down. He had caused inordinate worry and pain and cruel despair. It had been necessary for his father to shoulder his abandoned responsibilities to Margaret and her children, and now they must have priority. Robin therefore was and must remain a pariah.

No syllable of any of this was uttered, but Robin read his father loud and clear. When, after the interview, he sat down on the stone bench, where some fifteen years before, champagne in hand, he had so airily engaged himself to Margaret, he was struggling hard to find a pocket of moral air in which to breathe. Shouldn't a man have certain obligations to himself that came before everything else? Hamilton would say no: Man was a social animal and must conduct himself in that context first and foremost and to the very best of his abilities. Robin had run off, not broken off, which might, he now saw, have been deemed more manly. But he had hoped in doing so to spare others' feelings. Surely not all was debit. He had built a new life, a new identity, out of nothing but his feelings for a woman, and with her support it had been made to work. He'd sought neither aid nor discovery. Could not he then be said, second time around, to be standing solidly behind his actions, to be taking a manly responsibility for them? Was there not worth in this, he asked himself, trying hard to build a makeshift raft of self-respect. Not to feel himself a worm.

The flask was lying on the car seat. "Might as well polish it off," he said, holding the leather-covered bottle out to Dartania. She shook her head and Robin unscrewed the top, put the flask to his lips, and opened his throat up wide.

Dartania felt a sudden alarm. If he returned home tipsy after a five-year break, she would be partly to blame. She pictured the anxiety and resignation masked so unsuccessfully on his wife's plain face as they began again their Sisyphean struggle. And for the first time in her life, Dartania shivered in the realization of how fearful a thing life could sometimes be: For no good reason at all, no reason you could put your finger on, it could suddenly veer wildly, insanely out of control. And yet, what was strange to her was that Robin's problems had never been crucial ones: He had enjoyed good health, he'd had enough money, he'd even had a workable marriage. His problems had come from vague dissatisfactions, obscure uneasiness; and he had sought relief in drink. Probably his going off with another woman was simply giving in optimistically to another panacea. Probably it was cowardly and weak willed, but in her feelings for him, none of that mattered. What mattered was his becoming so unreachable, so exasperatingly passive, and that they had so very little to say to one another. All day, the gap had been widening, when she had expected a perfect knitting together after their quick retrieval of lost stitches.

"When will we meet?" They had reached the airport and once again Dartania stopped the car well beyond the terminal entrance. She was thinking that no relationship could be repaired in one go. The less people saw of each other the less they always had to say at first. It stood to reason. They had to reestablish some common ground, and that took more time.

"We'll work out something."

"Once Margaret's remarried, Papa's responsibility will be over, and that's the real impediment," she maintained. "We'll fix it all up then. I know we can. Things will fall into place."

Robin nodded vaguely and, looking at his watch, opened the car door. "Oh, sunglasses." He tapped his coat pocket, pulled them out, and put them on. He felt himself to be dangling perilously over a precipice, anonymous, without an identity, and again the panic mounted. If he could only hold on till he got home, he told himself, then Myra and time and his familiar routine would be sure to put things right. He'd be back where he was before. He would be Robin Kane again, a quiet and reasonably happy man, without a past to consciously brood about. But right now, he was nobody at all, suspended between two worlds, a ghost with no name rattling frantically in a broken machine and desperately wanting a drink.

Dartania watched him walking off in his shabby mackintosh and with a paper bag, the contents of which she never learned. His crinkly-eyed, wryly smiling image, tended on her private altar for so many years, was leaving with him, like a man's shadow mysteriously retrieved. In a way she had lost him more truly than when she had believed him dead. As he shrunk into the distance, suddenly she wanted to call out, to find out what he had meant. What was the ingredient, Robbie? You forgot to tell me. But it was too late.

Dartania put the empty flask into her bag. She sat there very still, her slender hands resting lightly on the steering wheel. In reality, in real life, nothing had changed. It was all going to be just fine. She had no serious worries and on no account could she complain. A woman with her advantages had no right ever to complain. It was a matter of noblesse oblige.

In front of her, in the distance, the Nashborough horizon was in place looking like a gray cardboard cutout. The cold wind had died down and the sun was tentatively shining.

Dartania watched the airplane moving slowly toward the runway, the propellers beginning to race, the speed increasing as it reached the concrete path and the airplane lifting suddenly like a featherweight in the air, defying gravity.

For a moment she, too, felt groundless, afloat, uprooted like the plane. She looked at the jagged Nashborough skyline. Behind the cardboard cutout a familiar reality loomed: the downtown buildings, the houses—Timbuctoo, Longwood, Cottoncrop—her family, a world where she belonged. She took a deep breath, it was almost a sigh, and across her mind, of an instant, there flitted the twins' familiar litany, "What am I going to do for happiness today?"

Leaning forward, Dartania turned on the ignition.

5

....

*W*ell!" breathed the widow Ames with considerable emphasis, sinking into a velvet *bergère* beside the fireplace and fixing her cool gray eyes on Bayard, recently returned from Europe. The word, meaningless in itself, on this occasion brimmed with content, forming by inference an oblique inquiry resonant of past and present, and at the same time subtly soliciting explanation, or at the very least, elaboration. Finally it declared quite simply, "Here we are again; what next?"

Madeleine Ames was a small-boned woman with finely molded features. Her dark hair pulled tightly back in a chignon, was streaked with gray. Her gestures, self-possessed and elegant, suggested something or someone larger than her delicate presence and the space she occupied declared. She had thrown out her inquiry as Bayard crossed the room, his back to her, toward the silver tray on which a number of bottles clustered like minute skyscrapers.

Bayard had returned four days ago after two months, as he put it, "recovering England and France," and Madeleine Ames was busily sounding depths and measuring tides prior to embarking on possibly choppy seas. She had arrived before the other luncheon guests for this specific purpose, aware that an assessment must be made and that in all likelihood it could only be made obliquely, through careful testing of the atmospheric pressure. Bayard, indirect by nature, and diplomatic, even cagey, by training, was pronouncedly mute in any matter pertaining to private life. Nothing would be directly stated: There would be no broad strokes or primary colors, no graphically printed signs, no defining outlines or directional arrows. But despite high hopes for the continuation of affectionate habit, she half-hoped, too, for news of his domestic restoration, should that be what he wanted; and she believed herself fully prepared for it—or had been till she saw him.

"Europe is inexpressibly sad," he said, pouring out twin whiskeys and adding equal amounts of water from a crystal jug. "Our allies have had a miserable time and now that the elation of winning is wearing off, they're staring austerity squarely in the face." London was derelict and shabby, the buildings peeling, the streets of terraced houses snaggle-toothed where German bombs had fallen. It was painful to see. "The great thing is, there's plenty of hope *and* there's plenty of work. A brand new future to run up, and it's my view a good shake-up always does England a world of good."

He'd gained a little weight. Even in times of austerity, deluxe hotels managed mysteriously to provide. "And Paris?" It followed logically, shading her larger purpose.

"Harder to tell. The mood's different. People are hungry, scores are still being settled, and some consciences are, I suspect, badly in need of scouring."

"At least those magnificent buildings have been saved. That's something. I shouldn't like to see it right now, though. It would be like visiting an aged beau one hadn't seen since he was in his prime." Madeleine, a Virginian, had spent four childhood years in Paris, playing in the Luxembourg Gardens under the watchful eye of her French *bonne*. Her father had been the American ambassador. Her husband, twenty years her senior, whose flour all America baked with, and whose sprig-printed cotton flour sacks, made into dresses, still clothed the Southern poor, had died of a heart attack before the war.

"We were surprised how *normal* Paris is. Only eighteen months ago the Germans were skedaddling and the Americans and de Gaulle parading like Roman conquerers down the Champs-Elysées. Now it's business as usual. There are factions, of course, but they're less from divisions during the war than from political extremes. If there's trouble, it's my view that's where it will be."

She had been wise to give him his head. Spotting the minnow of a "we" swimming (purposefully?) in his narration, she fished it neatly out. "Ellen went over with you," she murmured, half between a question and a statement, wondering if he was making it easy, wanting her to know, without raw crudity, how it was.

"Yes." Bayard moved toward the chair opposite her. "And young William. The boy's seventeen years old. Incredible, isn't it?"

She sat still, giving a loose rein. "Tell me about him."

Bayard settled comfortably back, resting his drink on his knee. "Handsome in an exotic sort of way: dark hair, black eyes, thin, not too tall. Sharp as a briar." He paused. "Also very exploitive and self-willed. He loathes Eton, which may be no bad thing, and of course he's been spoiled rotten by a doting mother and overly indulgent grandparents. You know, don't you, that Ellen's only brother, Tom Ferris, was killed in the war?"

"Does that mean . . . ?"

"No, it doesn't." He instantly took up her point. "English inheritance descends through the male line. That was a big surprise to William. He'd assumed Tom's death made him, as next of kin, the heir. But worse was to come. You see, Ellen's elder sister had a Scottish title, inherited through the female line. Poor Elisabeth died the other day. She never married, so the title goes to Ellen, and William normally would become her heir. William got very excited about being the future Earl of Glengarth. He thought that capped becoming Lord Ferris. But the plain truth is, adopted children can't inherit titles." Bayard sipped his drink reflectively. "So there was no way round it but to tell the boy the truth. Ellen never wanted William to know he was adopted, and with hindsight that was probably a mistake. It's come out at a difficult age, and tied to losing an inheritance, is a nasty double blow.

"What's more, the minute Lord Ferris dies, his family will have to vacate Elderest. It and the title will go straight to a cousin, whom no one likes, or ever sees, as far as I can tell."

"How very hard for Ellen, if she's going to stay. But if they move back here . . ." The widow did not go on, the pavement was now laid and they must walk upon it to the end.

Bayard chose his own pace. "William's a dyed-in-the-wool English boy now, though one that's a renegade at heart, and finding out he's adopted only exacerbates it. But Ellen is hell-bent on sending him to Oxford."

"And Ellen?"

At last she had it. "Ellen will go on as before. Her parents are old and recently bereaved. She's a great comfort to them and feels it responsibly."

So the coast was reasonably clear. There would be more to go into, a pattern of deeper responses, but for now there was enough. She looked at her watch and, taking up her glass, gave Bayard a warm and cheerful smile. "What's the *ton* at lunch today: Literary? Philosophical? Witty and amusing ladies?"

"It's political, or I hope it is. We want to put Seneca back on the Washington road. Senator Beany's retiring in 'forty-eight. Mind you, Seneca will have to button up some if he's going to win. He was a fine general, but his views are far too liberal for voters here, rich and poor. He could grab the Negro vote, such as it is, but he'd need to do it without losing all the whites."

"Is Dar coming?"

"I didn't ask her. She hates politics and would sabotage the lunch, even if in doing so she made it a lot more fun."

"Stark's coming and I did ask Mary Ann. She keeps up with things and can be surprisingly perceptive. But she's got some sort of depression. So we'll be five not six."

"Postnatal depression," Madeleine lightly explained, "and sometimes it's quite serious. Who's the fifth?"

"I've asked Jasmine. She's not political but I wanted her to meet you, as a grown woman, I mean."

"That's very flattering. She was engaged to that boisterous painter when I saw her last. It's been that long. But why on earth to meet me?"

"Jasmine's in a cul de sac, doesn't know what to do with herself, and I thought you might help her along, give her some sort of focus." There was the sound of crunching gravel in the drive and Bayard set down his drink and, standing up, moved toward the door, where Albert, in a white coat, was also headed.

"I'm glad you're home," Madeleine offered warmly as he retreated.

He half-turned, his expression, for Bayard, was a smile. "So am I," he said.

Left alone, Madeleine got up to examine a new picture, a vividly colored still-life by someone called Matthew Smith. So Bayard was still collecting. Rumor had it that a number of his pictures had been sent to dealers in New York, but Picasso's family of acrobats stood in its desert background above the mantelpiece and Klee's colorful platter of fish hung over the drop-leaf table.

The house though small was tremendously comfortable, the twin *bergères* the only French furniture in the room. Whether Bayard had sold the grander things or was keeping them in storage for Ellen, no one knew. They might never know, he was such a secretive man, so Victorian in his pronounced discretion. But it had advantages.

Stark arrived with Jasmine. He had left his own car at Timbuctoo for his mother, and en route the pair had for the first time talked *à deux*. The topics were inconsequential, as must be so on short trips, but they were laced with an evident if bantering affection.

"You've become eminent," she told him with conscious gaiety. "I used to tease you so when we were young. I don't know why. Chloe tells me you can be quite formidable."

He smiled, noting that her tendency to tease remained but that all the thorns had gone. "Chloe's doing a fine job," he said, letting the subject drop.

Jasmine wanted to tell him that he was her only ally, her only truly sympathetic friend, but it was out of character and certainly the wrong moment.

So she confided that starting in January she was going to teach French in a girls school, Miss Harper's, where she herself had been a student.

"Why not teach them how to paint?"

"I'm no painter and I wouldn't know how to teach it."

It refused discussion so he said that by January he expected to be back in Washington; he was only waiting for Mary Ann to get better.

"I'm longing to meet her," Jasmine reiterated, mildly curious, but mainly sad at the impending loss of her good friend.

"We'll be back and forth," he said. "After all, there's Seneca to set on the political track. I believe it's the point of this lunch."

"For me, it's gleaning what's happened about Ellen," she impishly declared.

"I doubt even Sherlock Holmes could find out something Bayard didn't particularly want him to know," suggested Stark with a smile.

Jasmine laughed. Really he was more substantial and had a greater range than she'd remembered, was altogether easier and, in being successful, more at ease. "I plan to fix my guns on Mrs. Ames, because she'll know, she will have found out. Dar says she's our sort—and Bayard's—and she's rich to boot.

"The truth is we're glad Margaret and Ellen are out of the family, and it's for good, we hope. They're such prigs. And Dar thinks once Margaret has remarried, especially if they move to South Carolina, Robbie will come back home. Oh I should love to see him so!"

"You'll say I'm priggish, too, but I think they're both of them fine ladies," Stark maintained genially in a double defense.

Of course, thought Jasmine, Mary Ann would be the same sincere and humorless sort; she was almost bound to be. "We Douglases are such barbarians," she half-apologized. "For some reason too much polish and high-mindedness puts us right off. I can't think why."

"At any rate you're an extraordinary family," he conceded.

"We survive." Taking out a cigarette, she smiled pleasantly at him. "And generally speaking we're very good-humored you know."

EVEN WITHOUT DARTANIA'S presence, politics got short shrift, derailed by issues that, in the enthusiastic interest they produced, overtook everything else. It started with Mary Ann. Madeleine Ames hoped, with a show of feeling, for a quick recovery. "It's hard for anyone who hasn't experienced deep depression to comprehend it," she said, aware it was as foreign to Nash and Douglas natures as a snowstorm blanketing Mexico. Her own husband had known bouts, however, and she had been close enough. "It's so intangible. If you burn your arm, the pain's there in that spot, but with

depression there isn't any locale, you can't pinpoint the pain and yet it's terribly real."

Stark was grateful for Madeleine's support. He knew the others thought
Mary Ann should simply pull herself together—pull her socks up. "It may be
necessary to see somebody in Washington," he said. "I doubt Nashborough
runs to a psychiatrist yet."

"Praise God for small blessings," Seneca warmly declared. "That stuff's a
lot of hooey, if you ask me."

Stark shrugged his agreement. "In extremis you try all sorts of things."

"I doubt you'd try voodoo if they suggested that." Seneca's Emersonian
self-reliance, once challenged, was not so easily pulled up. "Psychiatry's not
much different: Instead of casting out evil spirits, it finds scapegoats—one of
the ugliest and to my mind base instincts in human nature. Psychoanalysts
tell people it's not their fault, it's somebody else's—they can blame their
difficulties on others. People grab the crutch and end up permanent cripples, weaker not stronger characters."

"You ought to read Freud, nonetheless," said Bayard. "His theories may
not be to your taste, but he's a fine writer, and a really first-class observer of
human nature."

"Mind you, Seneca," said Madeleine Ames, "with respect, when chloro-
form and morphine came in people were against that; they said character
was made by grinning and bearing pain. Nobody would say that now, or
resist a whiff of ether, ghastly smell though it has."

"I'm with you a hundred percent, Madeleine, and if you give me a drug
for depression or anxiety or whatever I happen to have," he motioned
vaguely in the air, "I'll take it like a shot, so long as it doesn't turn me into
some kind of lotus eater. But that's different from putting the cause of problems onto others, turning *them* into evil spirits. Not only is it back to
witchcraft but it removes personal responsibility, which frankly is the only
gauge of maturity I know."

Bayard let political tinkering rest for the present, throwing instead a seasoned philosophical log on the debate. "Stopping pain by any means must
be seen as part of a drive toward happiness. And yet the absence of pain
rarely results in the presence of happiness. They seem almost to be at opposite poles, and we to live largely in between, fleeing the one and seeking the
other, but mostly flailing about in the middle."

The little log blazed up furiously.

"The French have a pragmatic approach," said Jasmine with some feeling.
"Their very word for happiness contains it: *le bonheur*, literally, a good hour.
But in America happiness is supposed to be a way of life. We expect it.
While the French expect at best a welcome interlude, maybe only a blessed
release from pain."

The widow joined in indirectly with her support. "We've got it all wrong over here, as Jasmine says. We expect automatically to be happy. We even weigh things on a scale of perfect happiness. Why, our right to it is inscribed in the Declaration of Independence, as a primary goal."

"I agree we expect happiness," admitted Stark, "but the Greeks, who after all started this debate, settled very firmly and after much thought on the superiority of reason. The happy life became the reasonable life, reflective, balanced, devoid of unsettling passions. In a way, the middle ground Bayard mentioned."

"But feeling is how you know that you're alive!" insisted Madeleine, dismissing out of hand the overthoughtful Greeks. "And it's the only way you learn. All experiences involve feeling. Happiness is itself a feeling," she added, brightly capping her point. "The difficulty is to make it last, which, as Jasmine says, the French believe is impossible, and they may be right. We Americans are innocents, hopeless babies, really."

"I'm in your boat, Madeleine," Seneca told her. "To live you must involve yourself and not only with good feelings. A man is born into a given time and he's obliged to live in it to the very best of his abilities—to the fullest he can, whatever feelings that incurs. Willpower is his means of doing it."

"For me," said Bayard, rearing back with a show of mock pomposity, and capturing all attention, "happiness is the preservation and culture of one's individual mind and character. I put self-knowledge where Seneca so characteristically enthrones willpower and action."

Seneca wasn't surprised. He thought Bayard could have done much more with his life. After the collapse of Douglas House he was still a young man. He had thrown in the towel too soon. Leisure to Seneca's mind should be a part-time activity and not a way of life. But he greatly respected Bayard's battle scars and his endurance in past trials, and he thoroughly enjoyed his company. "A man must get out and do things, face what comes his way and try at the same time to make the world a better place. That's my philosophy pure and simple. It can bring occasional and very real satisfaction, but looking for happiness isn't a stable goal."

"Hear hear," said Stark approvingly, raising his glass. "Our next senator."

Jasmine smiled inwardly. Seneca's forthright manner brought to mind Frank's thrusting and often brash assertions. Both men were fighters, pursuing goals that required a certain blinkering to get on with. Frank had seen more deeply into hidden realities, if not himself, but Seneca had a more coordinated and pragmatic style and operated from a less defensive position. He was a natural aggressor who was determined nonetheless to make himself into a decent man. The result was a solid, even touching, grandeur.

"The difference between us," Bayard continued, bestowing on Seneca his wily bird's-eye penetration, "is that I'm Athenian at heart and you're Roman. The pleasures of art, of aesthetics, if you will, of good living and of introspection are replaced in you by high civic responsibility, empire build-ing, and a uxorius family life."

Everyone knew Seneca didn't have a particularly uxorious family life, but they knew, too, that he would have enjoyed it mightily if he had. It was per-haps this thought that caused Madeleine to say, "But it's true we're much too focused on happiness nowadays, we have been since the twenties. And what most people mean by it is simply having a good time. They don't think much beyond that. When chance and attachments are really what make a life. The challenge is to do with them what you can. Maybe willpower is, as Seneca claims, the essential tool."

Laying his fork down, Stark slowly wiped his mouth with his napkin, his eyes resting thoughtfully on his plate before looking up. Jasmine thought it a consciously developed style and was impressed. "I think what people want above everything else is security, to feel that they are safe, and therefore the thrust of modern liberal politics is and should be to provide it; because if we don't socialism will."

"That, Congressman, is where liberalism and I part company." Seneca's good humor trickled lightly across the bed of rock-solid disagreement.

They had fallen onto politics at last, and the women began to concentrate on their food.

"Liberalism to me," Seneca pursued, the bit now firmly between his teeth, "means increasing people's opportunities, giving them more freedom of choice. They may think they want security but they don't, any more than a child really wants to eat a gallon of ice cream." Like Stark he too had laid down his knife and fork. "Look at history. Evolution has fashioned mankind to live on the edge, women through the repeated dangers of childbirth and the worries of rearing children, and men in the hazards that come from pro-tecting and feeding them. Shave all the edges away and people don't know what to do with themselves, so they end up creating new problems, often silly ones, like becoming self-obsessed or anxious and wanting to talk end-lessly about themselves to a psychiatrist.

"Of course, what people think they want is highly tempting for any politician to offer, as our astute Congressmen knows well. But I'm against giving it to them, myself."

"Do I detect an undemocratic and despotic note?" Stark's simmering glee was undisguised.

"You detect the philosophy of Edmund Burke. The people elect their rep-resentatives to do what's best for them, not to consult them on every issue."

Jasmine wanted to get off politics and back to moral issues. "We've been discussing happiness entirely from a classical-humanist tradition," she inter-jected, "but what about the Christian ethic, the place of love? It's a unique contribution to human civilization."

"Love is fine," Seneca replied offhand, "but it's no more permanent than any other feelings, unless you're some kind of saint. I'm still in Madeleine's boat: We've got the focus wrong."

Madeleine also preferred to keep off politics. "You mention evolution," she said, examining this beguiling new thread. "It occurs to me that doing what nature has biologically decreed must, in evolutionary terms, have some happiness built into it, if only as a carrot to make the system work. So as pawns of evolution we might be wise to look for payoffs there."

"You must mean family life," said Stark. "Human survival is, and always has been, built around the family."

"But all that's changing," said Madeleine, "so we may be getting further from happiness."

"Yes, and Christian values have a lot to answer for, that and Dr. Spock," said Seneca with a nod to Jasmine. "Families are becoming a tub of mutual consultation—kind and loving parents soliciting their children's views. What a family needs is stability—that's a form of security I'm not against— but stability means knowing what the rules are, and seeing they're enforced, not consulting children about whether they like them or not, which produces God knows what."

Stark stepped smartly in. "It will produce happy, well-adjusted children whose sensibilities and talents are developed instead of repressed or ignored. What's really extraordinary is how long Old Testament values have managed to rule the family roost. Patriarchal systems were thrown out of the political arena ages ago, and it's high time they were ousted from the family."

"That's a lot of tripe, Congressman. A family can't be democratic. It needs a head for the same reason that a state needs one. But for obvious reasons the head can't be elected. Enlightened despotism would be my choice, with rules imposed by fear." He shot an amused but challenging look at Stark. "Children are self-regarding little savages who want their own way. And with Dr. Spock's help and showerings of Christian love, it looks like they're going to get it. The power structure is moving into their hands, and that means chaos and rebellion."

"I hope you'll keep domestic affairs under your hat on the campaign trail," chuckled Bayard. "Not that I disagree with them." He turned toward Jasmine. "It's women who're changing the whole setup and I don't know why. For the first time in history a woman who can afford a nurse chooses to rear her own children. Now that to me is an extraordinary thing."

Jasmine shrugged. "Maybe we haven't got enough to do, so it's tempting to make our children into a project. Also, since there are fewer children, they can be brought up as individuals. In patriarchal families, whatever else their merits, the individual is sacrificed to the whole." She was thinking bitterly of herself and Robin.

"Well, it's my view children need some distance from their parents," said Madeleine. "And vice versa. Traditionally it was grandparents who looked after them, an arrangement that I suspect made everybody happy."

A spontaneous "ah" sounded around the table, as Albert entered with a Baked Alaska flaming blue like a neon sign.

"Papa was once served Baked Alaska in New York," Jasmine laughingly recalled, "and he highly disapproved. He told them that where he came from they always did the cooking in the kitchen."

Albert, enlarged from chauffeur to cook and houseman, set the plate down on the sideboard and, the flames having subsided, began to slice through the hot brown crust to the nugget of ice cream inside. "I doubt Mr. Hamilton ever been inside a kitchen," he observed.

"Nor you till recently in any useful way," Bayard promptly returned, getting in the last word, or believing that he had.

"I turn up where I needs be, don't waste time taking up space."

"Einstein I'm sure never put it better," Bayard rejoined with obvious pleasure.

Madeleine helped herself to a slice of Baked Alaska. "You know, we've sat around this table talking about happiness as though it were some undiscovered country God knows where—when we're right in the thick of it, eating and drinking well and talking to our good friends." She raised her glass in a toast. *"Le bonheur,"* and giving Jasmine a smile of particular kindness, added, "French wisdom. Right now, it seems to me they got it right."

"To Bayard's excellent symposia," toasted Stark. "The best conversation in Nashborough."

"I'm so glad it hasn't been a political lunch," Jasmine ventured amid the general elation. "I don't care for politics one bit."

"You should give it a chance," said Stark. "Mary Ann once felt the same I think."

Seneca, leaning back, responded with a stentorian flourish, quoting from Pericles' great speech in honor of the Athenian dead. " 'We do not say here that a man who has no interest in politics minds his own business, we say that a man who has no interest in politics has no business here.'

"One of the things I liked about Frank Noland," he went on, "was his political commitment. Ours by comparison runs pretty thin. We're 'improvers' or at best we hope to be, but he was for going the whole hog right away."

Frank's name had at last been uttered, and Jasmine, deeply touched, was thankful to Seneca for his open-handed tribute—pleased, too, that he'd glimpsed something of Frank's exceptional worth.

"Come down to Thebes with us in February," Stark urged Jasmine. "You can see some politicking and meet your brother's namesake, the Reverend Robin Douglas. He's a pretty important fellow in this state, and we're hoping he's going to deliver us the Negro vote. Chloe's coming," he added, as though propriety might be at issue. "Who knows, the political bug might bite."

"Telephone, Mr. Seneca."

"Who is it, Albert?"

"Didn't rightly say." Albert's vagueness was such that getting up Seneca looked at him hard. As they entered the library, Albert suddenly volunteered in a whisper, "Sound to me like Mister Dan."

Puzzled, Seneca sat down at Bayard's desk, and when a few minutes later he replaced the cone-shaped receiver on its upright stand, both hands continued to grip the telephone's two pieces. Then he went to the dining room and called Stark out. The action, though seeming casual, produced a little hush of curiosity that Bayard diplomatically filled with the suggestion they move into the living room for coffee. As the coffee had not arrived, however, they milled vaguely about till Seneca reappeared, alone.

"I'm going to drive Stark into town," he told them. "There's been an accident."

Bayard, as host, moved quickly to accompany the two men outside and to offer any assistance. Caught up in a never-never land of waiting, the women could find nothing to say till Albert entered almost on tiptoe with the tray of coffee.

Impatient, Jasmine breached a solidly entrenched line of etiquette. "What is it, Albert? What's the matter?" No one else could have quizzed in this way another's servant, but she had known him since girlhood and this gave special license. "Who's had an accident?"

He dipped his head and set the tray down carefully on the drop-leaf table. "Mrs. Fenton, I believe Mr. Seneca said," he murmured vaguely, without looking up.

"Oh God, Stark left her his car; she had some errands to run," Jasmine exclaimed to Madeleine, standing in front of the fire. Mrs. Fenton was nearly eighty and Jasmine had never liked her, but at the prospect of a grisly accident, she was consumed with horror. "A woman her age shouldn't be on the roads," she added in blind accusation. Then, "Poor Stark!"

Bayard came in, slammed the front door, called for Albert, and, entering the living room, looked sharply from one woman to the other. A car could be heard moving swiftly down the drive, the gravel spraying as it braked to turn into the road. Bayard sat down heavily in the chair. "Some brandy, Albert," he ordered, "and some brandy glasses."

"Is it Mrs. Fenton?" Jasmine ventured lightly, as if it were a guess.

"Yes, it is," he heavily replied. He seemed beyond surprise, showing no reaction to her fine lucidity. "It seems she's done herself in. I don't know any of the details, but it was pills, I think."

"Good God, Mary Ann!" cried Madeleine.

Wearily Bayard shook his head. "A fine woman and an excellent wife to Stark . . . It's incomprehensible."

Jasmine looked from one to the other as the news sank in. "I never met her," she said feebly, bewildered, assailed by an obscure guilt.

"Poor poor Stark! And oh those poor little children!" Madeleine Ames threw up her hands. "Oh, how fate can strike! Quick as a cobra. Here we were, eating and drinking and debating happiness so frivolously—enjoying every minute of it. And all the time she was sitting there thinking of . . . was preparing to . . . Oh, it's horrible."

"Stark, a *widower*," murmured Jasmine, but in truth she had never really known him as a married man.

LATER THAT AFTERNOON Madeleine Ames, preparing to leave for home, returned to practical matters. "Jasmine is charming," she told Bayard, "but I don't know how she's going to fit in here. She's seen so much of life and the world, and she's still young. I suppose she has no money." The widow, whose white plank fences ran for two miles, knew well how it enlarged one's options. Leaning forward she collected her gloves and cigarette case from the table. "Forgive me for rushing ahead with what will sound vulgar and insensitive right now, but Washington, I suspect, would suit her a great deal better than here."

Bayard took this easily on board. "Stark was never lively enough for her. But as they say, the surest aphrodisiac is propinquity—that and nothing much to occupy the mind."

"How very true." The widow bestowed her sweetest smile and stood up. "It's dreadful your beautiful lunch was marred by so much horror but it helped greatly to fortify us when it came."

He took her arm in his, leading her with gallant intimacy to the front hall where he held her coat for her.

"You'll come and see me tomorrow, won't you?" she said putting it on. "Usual time?"

"I shall look forward to it, my dear."

6

....

*M*ary Ann's funeral produced a great assembly. The mighty phalanx of Blue Hills, clothed and crowned expensively in black, stood in the front pews, while behind them a flock of devoted East Nashborough constituents were grouped. Both senators had come down from Washington, and Senator Beany appeared the next day in a newspaper photograph grinning and shaking hands with Seneca. It looked like an endorsement, which to Senator Beany it most certainly was not. President Truman's condolences had been received that morning, telegraphed from an evidently on-the-ball political office.

As all the world knew, or most of it anyhow, Mary Ann Fenton had died very suddenly of a cerebral stroke. Suicide in families, always hushed up, was more needy of suppression when a politician was involved, and the cover-up was accomplished at high speed and with maximum efficiency.

Miss Alice Nash, making a rare appearance, and swamped by well-wishers, was rocked precariously on her symbolic pedestal by energetic handshakes. Christmas was only two weeks off and for the first time there would be no Christmas party. A hallowed but taken-for-granted custom was to be abandoned. "I'm too old and so are all my servants," Miss Alice had let them know, and had simply turned her back on it. But society felt bereft as of a natural right and people were appropriately dismayed. There were so many new people moving to Nashborough that it was more important than ever to stick together and to keep the old traditions going. Couldn't Seneca and Dartania be persuaded to take it on? But everyone knew Dartania wouldn't touch it.

Standing beside her father in the Presbyterian church pew, Jasmine gazed in bewilderment at the grandiose coffin, its chromium plating vaguely reminding her of a brand new car. She thought of the dead body inside it that had been Stark's wife and who, for Jasmine, had never had a stronger reality than now. Life could bow one down to the ground, could flatten, could take the breath away and break the heart. She had experienced all that, but always some inner resilience had picked her up and shaken her out, as if she'd been restored to the whimsical care of invisible owners. Evidently this had not been so for Mary Ann.

"A schoolteacher, third grade," Dar had quipped years ago in a letter written to Paris. How dull that had seemed and how remote, how inferior to the intense excitement of her life in Paris. Now Mary Ann was dead and Jasmine was to be a schoolteacher, surrounded by callow girls and by a staff of stoical widows and irritable and deprived old maids. At Bayard's lunch they had talked so airily of happiness, and despite what she herself had said about the French, like most Americans she, too, expected to have it on a permanent basis. Instead she was pitted against her longtime phobia of ordinary existence, its imposed repetition a terrible treadmill with little and, for some, no hope. How to make limited opportunities endurable? It must be the simplest art on earth, as so many seemed to achieve it, but it eluded her. She looked at the coffin and thought of the woman inside it with sympathy. Mary Ann's life had, for whatever reasons, became unendurable, and she had made an intractable decision. She had sat down in a chair and taken a great quantity of pills. It must have required enormous courage. Suicide was by no means always a show of failure. It could have the dignity it once had in Rome, where it was noble to get out if the going became impossible, or wasn't up to an acceptable mark.

If a suicide note existed it had been kept secret, but a note surely would have been a kindness, some exonerating explanation to make it easier for those left behind. But maybe there was nothing to say. Maybe it wasn't a Roman suicide at all, only a state of mind severely altered by disease—a mind turning murderously against itself.

In front of Jasmine old Mrs. Fenton clutched Stark's arm like a sparrow hanging dizzily on a branch. Mary Ann's children would now come more often to Timbuctoo. Jane would encourage it. But as soon as Jasmine had earned some money she would move into a small apartment, a little box of her own, she thought, looking at Mary Ann's again with feeling.

The minister, having enumerated the virtues of the deceased and intoned the sympathies of friends and family, was announcing the closing hymn—predictably "Rock of Ages." And as the organ thumped out the opening chords the congregation took it up in a straggling tide. Hamilton sang in a firm impersonal voice. Who knew what he was thinking? But Miss Alice, on his other side, looked sad. These two great rocks towering so reassuringly above Jasmine's generation were themselves not far from dissolution. What must they think of willfully obliterated youth, of obligations so casually left behind? At least Mary Ann, unlike Robbie, wouldn't have to face reproach for letting her side down. Jasmine could hear Seneca's voice strong but off-key in the pew behind. Soon he would be the sole remaining rock. And despite her fiercely held sense of independence she felt deeply grateful he was there.

7

....

*L*ate in March on a blustery afternoon, raining and getting dark early, Seneca, Jasmine, and Stark set out in Seneca's dilapidated Ford for Thebes. Chloe had stayed behind to look after Stark's children, taking them to Timbuctoo with her own. Jasmine was pleased to be off, pleased to be leaving Nashborough and the environs of Miss Harper's school. Teaching some of the children, especially the beginners, was enjoyable; they learned quickly; but getting the slow and apathetic ones interested exceeded her ability and patience. Clearly, teaching wasn't her line, but she was at a loss to know what was. Moreover, wasn't the first lesson of "ordinary life" that of relinquishing choice, just putting one foot in front of the other and getting on with it? As the car sped down the highway, she cheerfully turned her back on such unpleasant questions and entered wholeheartedly the present.

Stark too was intent on leaving heavy burdens behind, and when they stopped for supper at a roadside diner near Allenstown, he and Jasmine were in high spirits. Like a pair of new-molted cicadas, Seneca thought, marveling at life's serendipitous, if transitory, offers of respite. They all laughed a lot, drank beer, and ate big plates of fried country ham, turnip greens, and yellow pan-baked corn bread. Even the coffee was good.

Travel was such a wonderful tonic, Jasmine declared with some passion. She had forgotten how reviving it could be. She told them she had received an invitation to stay with friends in Paris that summer, and this very minute had made her mind up to do it. Instead of moving into an apartment she would hang on a bit longer at Timbuctoo and save her money for the trip. Some of the transatlantic liners were not yet reconverted from troop ships and she might even get a cheap fare in one of the dormitories.

Seneca said Nashborough was facing a potential diaspora. He himself was going hiking in the Pyrenees that summer with Pete Weaver. He said Jasmine and her friends would be most welcome provided they were decent walkers. Some fluent French would come in very handy.

The proposal caught fire instantly, enveloping Stark in its conflagration.

"Oh, yes, you must come," Jasmine cried. "It will do you a world of good. It will do us all a world of good!" A mental picture had begun to form in her mind, blurred but luminous: the outline of a plan—something appealing she could look forward to.

"Shake the dust off, old man," Seneca tactlessly insisted, and Stark, evidently attracted by the proposal, said that he would see.

It was nearly midnight when the euphoric party checked into the Palace Hotel, trooping into Stark's bedroom for what was unanimously declared deserved nightcaps. Nobody wanted the evening to end.

"We need to keep in good with the Baptists." Seneca, sitting on one of the beds, was pouring out whiskey from a bottle produced by the night porter, still in its brown paper sack. "Southern Baptists are the fastest-growing religious sect in America, and it's the Negroes' favorite church." He handed the glass to Jasmine, propped up on the twin bed opposite in her stocking feet. "Even though Baptists don't drink, or aren't supposed to, I believe."

"Or dance." Stark, sprawled in the low armchair, comically tapped his feet, then sat bolt upright. "But especially we need to keep in with the Baptist preachers. The Negro listens to his pastor. Pastors have the sort of clout European clerics had in the Middle Ages, and in some ways they're more useful right now than the NAACP." The congressman had failed to make it clear to whom.

Talk had taken this turn because a meeting with the Reverend Robin Douglas was fixed for the morning, and before the pint of whiskey was emptied, it was agreed that for politeness' sake Jasmine should be passed off as an amanuensis, albeit a voluntary one. She left half an hour later, shoes in hand, vowing to buy a notepad and pencil next morning in the hotel book shop. "But don't expect me to write anything down. I don't know a word of shorthand, or for that matter how to type. It's too bad Chloe couldn't come."

Like the Palace Hotel, the Thebes Baptist church where they were to meet Robin Douglas was downtown near the river. But it was south of Pear Street, and leaving the modern city abruptly behind, they entered, as behind a curtain wall, a landscape of run-down wooden buildings. Tenements of four or five storeys with gap-toothed exterior banisters lined the riverbank, housing the poorest, the down and outs, the indigents, the prostitutes, the drunks. These were succeeded by several streets of low clapboard houses one room wide, the other rooms connected from behind "shotgun" style, the buildings' narrow ends sensibly to the street, where, as Stark pointed out, land cost more. Everywhere, chimneys smoked, the firewood piled neatly in a corner of the porch. But the houses badly needed paint, and their porches drooped like crestfallen faces. In the front yards the earth had taken on a terra-cotta burnish under children's bare feet. In some yards an old tire hung from a tree to make a swing. In some yards too a derelict car reposed, either beyond repair and vainly trumpeting former glories, or else carefully set up on blocks in the hope of better times ahead.

Rounding the corner at Green Street, the new Baptist church rose up spick-and-span, its red rough-surfaced brick emphasized by thick joins of cement. A columned portico declared its rapport with Southern tradition, while at the same time a pristine steeple pointed a reminding finger up to God. Reverend Douglas was in town for its inauguration.

The church was cold, the heating not on. Behind the central pulpit a choir of blond varnished wood rose like a minute amphitheater. Stark pointed out the baptistry behind it, the oblong pool constructed above floor level so that anyone standing in it could be seen from waist up in the pews.

Seneca and Jasmine climbed the baptistry steps to have a better look. Both had seen Negro baptisms in local ponds as children, the dark-robed preacher standing sedately in the muddy water, the initiate, shrouded in white and wearing a white bandanna, bent over backward, nose and mouth covered by the preacher's hand, then brought up again to joyful hallelujahs and happy rhythmic clapping on the bank. This was an altogether more refined arrangement, the pool built by a local swimming pool company, the blond shiny pews grouped in serried rows before it. But the ceremony would be the same.

"You *would* feel something significant had happened," whispered Jasmine, looking down into the pool. She had been baptized wholesale with her brothers and sisters, the bishop sprinkling a dab of water parsimoniously over the lot of them.

The chancel door opened unexpectedly and Robin Douglas, as he came forward, showed in his expression mild reproach. Though in his mid-thirties he looked older by several years. He wore a sober black suit and dark funereal tie. Of normal height, his figure was thick, inclined to portliness. Most striking however was the largeness of his head, the face flat, moonlike, the lips thin, the sharp eyes uptilted in an oriental way. His whole bearing registered, and every movement reinforced, a momentous and dignified reserve.

"Reverend," Stark called out genially as the other two, in effect caught spying, quickly descended the baptistry stairs.

"Congressman. General Nash." He greeted them each with a firm handshake and fixed, somber demeanor.

"This is Mrs. Noland," said Stark. "She's helping on the secretarial side, taking some notes for us."

Jasmine came clean in one respect. "I'm so glad to meet you, Reverend Douglas," she cried, warmly shaking his hand. "I loved your grandfather so. In fact he practically raised me. I'm Mr. Douglas's daughter." And reddening with embarrassment was forced to add, "Mr. Hamilton Douglas."

To this, Robin Douglas made no other acknowledgment than "Yes," upended very faintly into a question. Then changing the subject he asked them to come into the office where it was a whole lot warmer.

They sat down around a table made of the same blond wood as the church pews, some sort of ply. A stack of new hymnbooks was piled in one corner, and a vase of artificial flowers stood on the windowsill. The room smelled faintly of paint. "What exactly can I do for you, gentlemen?"

Seneca, who hadn't seen Robin Douglas since the civil rights conference before the war, was impressed by the bulking out of his presence. Before, he'd been little more than a boy and was unwittingly patronized as such, young Douglas putting it down resentfully not to youth but to ingrained color prejudice, in which there was also some truth.

Seneca passionately wished to help secure black people's legal rights, but he privately believed that socially and culturally they still had a long way to go. "Why don't we begin, Reverend," he suggested, "by you telling us what your own political priorities are, those with a reasonable expectation of success in the foreseeable future."

Douglas looked unwilling, even mistrustful. "I do not expect the kingdom of God to appear on earth tomorrow, General Nash, but desegregation does not seem to me an unreasonable demand in a country where equality is every citizen's constitutional right."

"Most certainly it is not unreasonable." Seneca answered, speaking slowly in an easy informal drawl. "But like the kingdom of God, I'm afraid we can't expect its arrival in the South tomorrow." He smiled pleasantly at Douglas.

"As you know, Reverend," Stark intervened, "we're pressing hard right now for poll-tax reform. That has to give soon." The poll tax, designed to keep Southern blacks from voting, required, in order to vote, payment of a poll fee some months before the election. Stark said President Truman's committee on civil rights would shortly publish its report, and it would take a tough stand on the issue. "Wherever the federal government has clout it's going to use it to achieve desegregation. The president will personally back his committee's recommendations, but the proposals must then be got through Congress. You know I will support them to the hilt, and so will General Nash if he is in the Senate. But it's up to us to put him there in time."

The reverend locked judgmental eyes with Seneca. "Can we rely on you to publicly back the committee's proposals in your campaign?"

"No, you cannot." A chilly pause ensued. Despite Seneca's easygoing manner, his reply conveyed unmistakable finality. "As I'm sure you'll appreciate, Reverend," he continued, "our party can't afford to lose white votes before we've secured an equivalent Negro backing, and that won't come, even with your own vociferous support, till after the poll tax is repealed. Then colored people will be able to vote en masse. But openly to support you meantime would be impolitic to the point of frivolously committing hari-kari." Seneca was sitting back comfortably, one ankle resting on the opposite knee. "However you have my word of honor, and I hope you will let others know of it, that if I'm elected to the United States Senate, civil rights reform will be my first priority. I think the Reformed Democrats' main plank of voters should eventually be the Negro community. We are their best bet. But we need to get their votes before we can risk losing others, or we shall get nowhere."

"It's true your party is our best bet, as far as *white* representation goes, but why is there no Negro candidate on your ticket? Not for senator—we wouldn't stand a chance there—but in a black congressional district. Are you prepared to support that within your party?"

"I am indeed. But again, to do so before poll-tax reform would knock the possibility of its repeal squarely on the head with a sledgehammer. You know what things are like down here. Best to hold your horses for a year or two, then, when the poll tax has been abolished and the civil rights bill passed—when there's nothing more to gain immediately in that line—then sure, go ahead and rock the boat just as hard as you want."

Although his face remained impassive, a deep anger under supreme control could be seen in Douglas's fists pressing hard against each other on the table. *"In other words be patient."* The sentence sprayed like bullets. "How long and how often have we heard those words. I tell you, General, the white liberal is sometimes the most disappointing man of all to deal with in the South. He gives us his verbal support but most of all he wants to keep the peace—not 'rock the boat' as you put it. In short, he prefers order to justice and he fails to see that in doing so he is setting a timetable for another man's freedom. Sometimes the shallow understanding of people of goodwill can be more desperately frustrating than the absolute misunderstanding of those who wish us ill."

Seneca was unperturbed. "Politics is the ugly underbelly of democracy, Reverend, and like a trading bazaar everything on the table has its price for barter. But outside this imperfect setup, what have you got? What tools, what weapons, what real power? In any battle, if the opposing force is bigger and better equipped, and I'm afraid it is, then you have to find a way to morally undermine or else outsmart it—set a trap, for instance, build yourself a Trojan horse. Why not let your supporters, men like Congressmen Fenton and myself and Governor Sayle infiltrate the established political order as broadly and as quietly as possible and work on your behalf from the inside? Then when your ranks are big enough and well enough organized, call up your troops and move right in."

Douglas looked very carefully at each of them. He seemed to be making up his mind about something. "I came down here yesterday on the Trailways bus," he said slowly, "and on the way, it filled up to where there were no places left up front for whites to sit. So the conductor ordered me and an old lady with her grandchild to give up our seats for some young men." He swallowed and breathed in sharply. It was not an easy tale to tell. "Of course, I objected strenuously, but what could I really do? The law in this state was on their side. We had to stand. Can you imagine the sense of impotence, of moral injustice—the frustration of having no redress?" His voice corrected itself, moving again into a more even tone. "I had brought some sandwiches with me because there are no cafeterias for Negroes at rest stops. I ate my sandwiches in the colored waiting room. It made me right thirsty and I went outside to the water fountain, but it was bust. The whites' water fountain was not, but I could not use that, so I went thirsty. I am still thirsty, *thirsty for justice, General Nash!* I do not want to leave this earth without having enjoyed one day of real freedom, of proper justice, in my life, without being accorded the rightful dignity due to all human beings. I am flesh and blood and yet the world I live in tells me this is an illusion, that in fact I am only a white man's shadow." He paused and drew breath, beginning again more quietly; his voice deep and mellifluous, contained the hypnotically rhythmic cadences of fine religious oratory. "What I describe is the life of all Negroes in the South. You know that. The social and moral deprivation we are handed fills us with anger—and it fills many, too many, with the belief that they are indeed inferior. They are brought up to think so, and they in turn have to explain this demoralizing system to their children, to teach them their inferiority early on, so that they may survive by keeping to the shadow world of being black."

"I don't believe I would have had your courageous forbearance, Reverend," said Seneca with real respect. "I'd have got in a fight on that bus and gained nothing but some broken bones." Privately he believed that without freedom, he actively would have chosen death, would have died fighting for it, but then he had started from a more privileged rung in life and was used to freedom.

"You would have been a dead man and so a useless one," the reverend solemnly observed. "A live dog is better than a dead lion, the Bible says, and when it comes to helping others and to changing things, it is certainly true." The point was plain enough and Seneca for the first time spied a golden thread of honor subtly woven into the rough sackcloth of humility.

"What we'd like you to do right now, to answer your question, Reverend," said Stark, "is for you to come with us this afternoon and introduce General Nash to some of the leading Negro citizens here: preachers, NAACP officers, local businessmen. Give him a chance to talk to them and hear what they have to say, and give them a chance to hear him. You know the community, so we're riding on your coattails is what it amounts to."

"They'll be proud to meet a famous war hero, and they will hope your campaigns, if you reach the Senate, General, will be as successful as on the battlefields of Asia." A faint smile flickered, then, like a match struck in the rain, went out. "In fact they will expect it." He had stood up and the others followed. "Federal legislation is of course invaluable," he continued, "but lobbying the big industrial companies could be productive, too. Dupont, Firestone, General Motors—they all want to build factories down here. They want our cheap labor, black and white. Pressure could be put on them by liberal Northern stockholders to make some guarantees if they come South, hiring on an equal basis for instance—it needn't be just government contracts that have strings attached."

"A good point," said Seneca firmly, aware that such companies would never upset the status quo by backing any change in local customs. But he showed himself a politician by agreeing to look into it.

They had reached the church porch.

"I haven't lived in the South in a long time," Jasmine said with some feeling, turning to Douglas, "and what you tell us is really distressing. But I so hope that at least you're able to glean a degree of happiness in having so much useful work to hand."

"My work does have moments of satisfaction," Douglas answered gravely, "But as to happiness, Mrs. Noland, that comes entirely from the love of God."

STARK WENT TO dinner that evening with a fellow congressman, the announcement stinging the unsuspecting Jasmine like a bumblebee. The engagement was long-standing however and Stark felt sure he could meet them for a nightcap later on.

Gallantly Seneca proposed dinner at the Grand Meridian, the hotel's rooftop nightclub. Jasmine had no suitable dress but that didn't matter. What mattered was finding something to talk to Seneca about for several hours. Though humorous and relaxed, he was strongly disinclined to chat, and though she had known him for many years, she now saw that as a person she knew him not at all. He was part of a constellation, fixed and useful, taken for granted in the family galaxy.

The glassed-in roof terrace was predictably candlelit and ringed by seductive red velvet banquettes. Little tables *à deux* framed the parquet dance floor where a band in pale blue tuxedos played foxtrots and popular romantic songs. It was Saturday night, crowded and very gay.

Jasmine should have joined them that afternoon, Seneca told her, sitting down at one of the small tables (she had gone to lunch with a friend). She would have seen some political bargaining at work.

Feigning interest she feigned, too, her regret. Had they got the support they wanted?

Seneca said the NAACP had some fine horse traders. They'd let him know at once how useful from time to time free legal advice would be, since their objectives were currently being pursued almost exclusively through the courts. "Old Stark agreed on my behalf even before I did," he chuckled.

"He's become political in the best sense, hasn't he?" she said with open pride. What had his wife been like?

"A woman of backbone and character. Very supportive and very proud of Stark. Very womanly. She was pretty too. Suicide was the last thing I'd expect." He signaled the waiter. "Stark's doing as well as any man in his circumstances can. He's been knocked flat and he's putting up a damn good front."

Unnerved by this response, Jasmine, who felt she too was putting up a damned good front, eagerly switched the subject. Wasn't Reverend Douglas unbending, and so humorless; wasn't he unforthcoming about dear Cal? "I suppose he thinks of him as an Uncle Tom. I suppose to him he was." She dropped her voice as the waiter approached. "If you ask me the reverend's got a sizable chip on his shoulder."

They had left a bottle of gin at the bar and Seneca ordered two dry martinis. "I thought he was a pretty impressive guy all round."

"Can you see him whooping up a Baptist congregation every Sunday? I can't."

Seneca said the reverend's church was mostly middle class. It was in Zion, an up-and-coming Negro quarter in Stark's congressional district. "I imagine the spirit of desegregation comes in equal parts with the holy one," he added.

"What he has to put up with is a perfect nightmare, and yet what he said about happiness, and so solemnly—about its coming from the love of

God—you could see he really felt it. He's got something there we haven't, a developed spiritual life, and frankly I envied it."

"You lost your own chance through education and an affluent background," said Seneca, pausing while the waiter set the drinks down on little cocktail mats. "Education usually makes faith hard to swallow, but then affluence reduces considerably the need." He picked up his glass. "As a palliative for the oppressed however I'm glad to say religion still delivers the goods, and I would pity colored people all the more without that useful nourishment to their souls."

"But doesn't everyone in adversity make little pacts with God? I know I do. When you were in the war for instance, didn't you?"

"I was mainly preoccupied with getting men over a metaphorical Hindu Kush when they wanted to stay in bed on the oasis. I may have made some pacts. I see it as a weakness, though—a cry for magical assistance, which is foolish. I'd like to think I was beyond that belief or need."

Leaning on her elbow, her chin cupped in one hand, Jasmine gazed rapturously across the room. "I think to live in a spirit-filled world would be marvelous. I'd love to believe that there were genies hovering in the air, ready to look out for me, and keep harm from my door. Nowadays that sort of power is in the hands of life insurance companies and courtrooms and the police. They may be more efficient, but all the magic, all the thrill, is gone—in other words, the spiritual dimension. I miss that."

Seneca found this charmingly feminine, but clusters of fairies whirling helpfully overhead had not the slightest appeal. Power reposed in the proper exercise of individual will, in self-reliance, and in concerted civil behavior—in short, the real world. "In my view a man must stand on his own two feet," he told her lightly, "even if it means crushing a lot of cavorting pixies underfoot."

"But life can be so dreadful, and so beyond a person's ability to change it. What Negroes put up with, for instance."

"Now the war's over we can concentrate on the remedy. The Negro's plight is the great issue of our time, at least here in the South, and I'm going to do everything in my power to put it right. It won't be easy though. Prejudice is every bit as hidebound and cocksure as religious faith." He smiled good-humoredly. "You could argue that the law provides us with salvation from the excesses of both."

Jasmine wished that like Seneca and the Reverend Douglas she could deliver herself up selflessly to a worthwhile cause. She envied their dedicated commitment. "I suppose it's selfish and narrow but I don't seem able to involve myself in things that don't concern me directly. I couldn't with Frank's political interests either. I don't know why." She pulled out another cigarette, leaning forward for a light. "I haven't told anyone this—I've only recently told myself—but I gave up painting because I discovered I wasn't really interested in that either, though I had thought I was. What really interested me was entering an imagined glamorous world, being famous, making a splash. That's what I really wanted, not to be a painter. I imagined painting would provide the entrée." She drew in on the cigarette, exhaling with a sigh. "Frank was a real painter; he had that mysterious commodity called talent: It's a divine gift." Noting Seneca's skeptical frown she laughed softly. "I guess the muses are the last members of the spirit world to survive in modern life."

"I don't know much about artistic talent as against solid ability," he replied, uneasy at the thought of such powerful and mysteriously imbued advantages, "but all ambitious young people want to be famous; it's the crankshaft of every driving will. When it occurs, of course, assuming it's the result of real achievement, it usually means very little." He put down his drink. "Come and dance."

The band was playing "Fascination" and couples were gliding in little circular patterns on the floor, smiling vacantly over each other's shoulders. "Oh dear I haven't danced for ages," Jasmine cried, more in gaiety than alarm as they wheeled gracefully around the floor. But the next tune, a jitterbug, returned them to their table. Seneca ordered two more martinis and they both chose filet mignon from a menu of truly grandiose format. "Anything but lamb," insisted Jasmine, for whom steak was still an enormous luxury.

The hotel's photographer was meandering like a firefly among the tables. He knew Seneca and they greeted each other warmly. "Be on the safe side, General, and get yourself fixed up right now with some immortality." He indicated the camera. "No need to wait till you get to heaven, when it only costs a dollar and a half right here on earth."

"Immortality is a mighty agreeable notion, George, and it's a bargain at a dollar fifty. You've got yourself a deal. Besides, no matter how you look at it, heaven is a pretty shaky proposition."

"Sho nuf!"

Seneca and Jasmine drew closer as instructed, laughing, Seneca's arm around her chair.

"Hold it! Now that's a good one. Be ready in an hour."

"We had a rough time in Detroit," Jasmine suddenly volunteered when the thick bacon-wrapped steaks were set before them. "But I enjoyed working in that factory. I suppose it was an escape of sorts, a kind of limbo, and I needed the money." They ate in silence for a moment. "I don't know where Frank and I would have gone from there, after the war." She said it vaguely, as if addressing a distant problem, or even someone else's. "It turned out I wasn't at all the person I had thought I was."

"It's my observation that nobody's life is ever what it seems," he answered reassuringly. "Everybody is full of proudly hidden shortcomings and intractable disappointments. You're a very attractive woman," he said, "and in some ways I think you've been the most adventurous of your brothers and sisters."

"Oh no," she protested, secretly very pleased. "Robbie's that. I know everyone says he's a weakling and you probably think so, too, but he went out and reinvented himself. I suppose that's what I was trying to do, but I wasn't successful. I so hope he is.

"Isn't it odd?" she added after a minute. "Robbie is now someone called Robin Kane, who's a stranger, and Robin Douglas is—well, to use his metaphor in reverse—becoming the reality, and our Robbie's falling into the shadows. But Dar's the really courageous one. Nothing ever scares her does it? You did well," she tacked on flirtatiously, "and so did she. You know you positively exude security. If the hotel caught on fire tonight, I feel sure, without my having to call on spirits or the fire brigade, you'd get me out unscathed."

"I'd make a damned good try at it," he laughed.

"I guess your soldiers must have felt that too."

"I won't tell you how many of them I lost." He said it lightly, as of half-remembered events, casual casualties, but underneath there was a solemnity, a glimmer of distress toughly plated over, and for a fleeting instant she perceived a bruised schoolboy biting furiously his upper lip.

The bottles of gin and whiskey left by customers on arrival were rapidly being emptied as busy bartenders filled repeated orders. Spirits produced spirits and the band, keeping up with the psychological pace, had increased its tempo. "Maresy Doats" was followed soon after midnight, as a finale, by "Roll Out the Barrel," with everybody on their feet singing and clapping and one couple, to the admiration of all, dancing crazily on their tabletop.

Among the last to leave, Jasmine laughing and a little drunk, hung lightly onto Seneca's arm as they traipsed, weaving slightly, down the thickly carpeted hotel corridor. Life seemed to bud if not exactly bloom, the evening having so unexpectedly been a success.

"Can that night porter you're so thick with produce another bottle, I wonder?" she amiably proposed. "We promised Stark a nightcap, after all."

"I'll see what I can scare up and bring it round."

"Oh goodie, and I'll call Stark."

Draped against the doorpost, she waved vaguely at Seneca's back, then in the bathroom dabbed water on her temples, combed her hair, and carefully repaired her makeup. If not exactly sober, she was wide awake, and leaning forward, she smiled conspiratorially at her image in the bathroom mirror. "Not a bad-looking girl."

At that moment a loud thump sounded inside the bathroom closet. Startled, Jasmine stepped quickly back to the bedroom threshold. The thump was repeated, this time sharper, more insistent. If need be she could run into the bedroom, slam the bathroom door, lock it and make for the corridor. But she was damned if she'd retreat quite yet.

A long-handled bath brush lay on the rim of the tub. She picked it up and, with a deep intake of breath, stepped cautiously forward, the brush raised over her head. Then boldly she flung open the closet door.

Inside in the dark stood Seneca, smiling patiently, holding a bottle and some glasses. "We have adjoining rooms," he said. "I know this old place pretty well."

"Oh for heaven's sake! I thought that was a closet." Still foolishly holding the brush, her other hand pressed against her jumping heart, Jasmine laughed outright, recovering her wits. "As they say, you certainly are very widely informed. Come in, come in. I'll call Stark—whoops." The bath brush had caught on the towel rail and she let it go, clattering on the ceramic tiles. "We're a good trilogy, aren't we, or do I mean trinity? Not triplets, anyhow."

"Triumvirate, perhaps." His back was to her as he set the bottle and glasses down on the writing table.

"Threesome," she happily declared, and sitting down on the bed picked up the telephone. Pausing, she put it down again and looked at her watch. It was half past twelve. "Perhaps it's too late?"

"JE T'AIME. JE *t'aime*." Jasmine repeated the words huskily and with feeling.

"*Je t'aime*," the tenth-grade girls repeated giggling and looking interested. "*Je t'aime*." They made eyes foolishly at each other.

"*Je vous aime*."

"*Je vous aime*." One or two patted her neighbor facetiously, "*Je vous aime*." Jasmine had them hooked, but for once she didn't give a damn. She wanted the day over and done with so that she could think, but the minutes were moving along like spilt glue.

Driving back from Thebes four days earlier she'd felt so carefree. What had occurred was delightful, but it had happened in another country and was indubitably a thing apart, without any expectations or the need of them. On parting, both had felt a special warmth, the intimacy of friends who shared a secret, were covertly bound by it to an extent, but nothing more. That in itself had been enchanting. Then as the week drifted on, she'd found herself dipping repeatedly into a fountain of happy reminiscence, which was now in danger of spilling over into myriad channels. She mustn't allow it to happen. Creating a network of happy associations might end up with it insidiously taking possession of her mind.

But the sharp yet melting wakening of desire had been so unexpected—the more marvelous perhaps because of it. Yet the event must not be foolishly twisted. That wasn't practical. She had been very tipsy and what transpired was almost entirely of her doing. She had been the instigator, and she was proud of it. If looked at squarely there should be no complications; it had simply proved that she could live again, and the rediscovered pleasure of that, of being raised up so miraculously from the limbo of the consciously dead, was reward enough. She wanted no more than that.

"Je suis content," she told the class, smiling and writing the sentence in large letters on the blackboard. Together they repeated it in all the personal pronoun forms.

8

The white plank fence encompassing Sextet Stud bordered the road for half a mile before the drive appeared. The widow Ames had said to come at ten o'clock and they could have a swim before lunch. "I must stop calling her 'the widow,' " Jasmine chided herself, aware that she herself might equally be called that. Then her mind returned to its purposeful preoccupation.

On both sides of the oak-lined drive there stood at regular intervals three brick cabins fronted by white Dutch doors. Originally slave quarters, each now housed a thoroughbred stallion, and from one or two of the windows, a finely shaped head looked out in eager anticipation. But Jasmine, busy rehearsing, saw little. She confronted a mix of wishes wrapped in a single purpose, but among the mix, most surprisingly, was her desire—as once in the distant past—for a confidante. She wondered mightily at it.

Jasmine drove around to the back, to Madeleine Ames's office—a tack room of sorts in one corner of the big brick barn. The office was covered with photographs of horses being led by grooms or by Madeleine herself wearing an elegant hat; many carried jockeys and a number were garlanded in the fat floral necklace of a declared winner. The name of each horse was neatly printed under the photograph.

Madeleine was in jodhpurs but on seeing Jasmine's summer slacks asked, "Foot or horseback? We can do either."

"Oh horseback. These slacks don't matter. They're almost as old as me." In truth she no longer owned any riding breeches.

The two women had met only twice since Bayard's luncheon party, but there was a certain rapport between them stemming from generally wider horizons, and also perhaps their mutual status as widows.

It had been Madeleine, who, sensing the younger woman's lack of focus, had coaxed the wavering Jasmine to go to Paris. Everyone had joined in, in a humiliating chorus of pity, pressing her, and also Stark, to breathe some fresh air, even if of a foreign concoction.

"Go hiking with Seneca, if you can bear it," Dartania had urged. "None of his family will. It's too much like the army. But he likes to have a platoon around him, and his French is execrable."

And Jane, with or without consulting Hamilton, had given her on the quiet a hundred dollars toward the trip. It made her miserable to connect it with the dubious financing of her earlier voyage.

"France obviously did you a bushel of good. You look blooming," Madeleine pointedly declared. "I hope you aren't sad to be home. I can't say that you look it."

"No, but I'm very glad I went."

A groom had brought around two horses, a chestnut and a gray mare that kept on baring her teeth and stretching out her neck. Madeleine took the latter, and as Jasmine adjusted her stirrup length, the groom opened the gate to a track behind the barn. The pastures on either side were toasted brown in the caustic July heat. Here and there under an umbrella of trees a few brood mares were sheltered, heads down, lower lips stuck out, whisking desultorily at flies. Old women visiting.

Beyond the pastures, taken at a trot, the dark eye of a stream-fed lake appeared, embedded in a sloping bowl-shaped dell. At the far end was a little beach with real sand and a couple of changing cabanas, and beyond it a low-lying beach house, its screened-in veranda fronting the glittering lake.

Jasmine had said very little and evidently Madeleine saw no necessity either. Both appeared to be waiting, sizing each other up, but for what?

"I won't ask you how Paris was," Madeleine finally began. Having tethered the horses, she was pulling their swimsuits out of her saddlebags. "I've had it repeatedly in great detail from Bayard. And as for the 'New Look,' our own magazines are full of nothing else." She handed Jasmine her wool swimsuit stuffed inside a rubber bathing cap. "Did I hear you'd stopped over in Washington on the way home?"

Saying she had, Jasmine quickly changed the subject, enthusing if banally on the beautiful setting.

Madeleine held her horses, as it were.

Half an hour later, as the two women lay stretched out on bath towels, their eyes closed, perfecting fashionable tans, Jasmine suddenly sat up. Swiveling around to face her hostess, she gathered her knees in her arms, her bathing cap falling into the sand. It was abrupt and startling, but she could wait no longer. She had to get it over with or she would lose heart altogether. "Madeleine, there's something I want to ask you, something very private; it's a favor really, but an awkward one, and even my asking may embarrass you. I don't know how to begin exactly, but please excuse me if I sound presumptuous."

Madeleine removed her sunglasses and shielding her eyes turned her head toward Jasmine. "There's a table under the trees. Wouldn't you rather sit down? I can produce some cold martinis in a jiffy."

Jasmine, so evidently ill at ease, was grateful, and towels over shoulders, they moved to canvas chairs on either side of a square weathered-gray table.

As she extracted a thermos from the saddle bags, Madeleine threw out over her shoulder another lead. "Is it something to do with your stopping in Washington?"

"Yes, something. But no, that's not it really. You see, well, you see something's happened." Waiting for the martini to be poured, she took a calming sip, and then another. "Forgive me if I sound ridiculous, Madeleine, but I don't know how else to say it except to say it outright. The fact is I'm in love, very *very* much in love and it absolutely must be kept hushed up."

"Is that partly for political reasons?"

"Partly, yes. And asking your complicity is probably very unfair. But, well, we need a place to meet that's safe. We can't go to a hotel or to one another's home." She took a deep breath. "You know what this town's like." She glanced at the older woman, trying automatically to gauge her sympathy, but without success. "I wondered if we could possibly use your beach house here on the lake to meet? Not that we can meet that often."

"I see." Evidently taken aback, Madeleine Ames stood up and, hands behind her back, paced up and down in front of the table, ignoring Jasmine and gazing from time to time toward the beach house. Jasmine felt like a naughty child awaiting a deserved punishment.

Sitting down again Madeleine reached for a cigarette and lit it. "I'm sorry, Jasmine," she breathed, "but I can't do it."

"Oh, it doesn't matter," Jasmine threw out lightly, embarrassed, but glad that if that were the case, her story had got no further. "It was just a thought."

"It's not that I disapprove, please don't think that—on the contrary. But the fact is"—she inhaled the cigarette deeply, fixing her sharp dark eyes on Jasmine's—"the fact is, the beach house is preempted—by myself." This confidence, offered so gratuitously in a show of easy grace, deeply touched the younger woman with its open generosity. Of course, everyone suspected the truth about Madeleine and Bayard, but no one knew for sure; they had always been so beautifully discreet.

"There's a cabin in those woods that might do, though," Madeleine added casually. "I did it up when the tenants left last year. It's private, can be approached by two routes, and it's empty. Would you like to see it?"

"Oh I would!" But her hostess's kindness, measured against her own lack of veracity, stirred uneasily. "Madeleine, before you commit yourself, I'd better tell you exactly what . . . you may well want nothing to do with it."

"I think I know who it is, so you don't have to tell me."

"I don't think you do," Jasmine solemnly returned, examining her hands interlaced so tightly in her lap. She pulled her head up. "I must tell you even if you find you'd rather not have known."

Madeleine looked a trifle disappointed. "Ah then it's not . . . I had hoped . . ."

"Jigsaws rarely fit together perfectly in real life, do they?"

Rapidly Madeleine surveyed possible runners across the field of propinquity. There was not a big turnout. Then she thought of France. "Oh Lord!" Emptying her drink in a swallow, Madeleine looked at Jasmine in amazement. "What a tangle. Is it serious?"

"The most serious thing that's ever happened to me in my life." Tears welled up and yet she was smiling radiantly.

The devil is beating his wife indeed thought Madeleine Ames.

"I don't want to pull you into an embarrassing conspiracy, so if you'd rather not . . . There's danger in so many directions: There's the primary next year and . . ."—she shrugged helplessly—"family. Oh Madeleine, I suppose it shouldn't have happened and it's entirely me who's to blame. But I can't wish it otherwise, I can't wish it undone. It's brought me to life again. Do you think me horribly selfish and immoral, and grossly disloyal? I suppose I must be, but I can't say I feel it. I'm much too happy."

Madeleine had seen a good deal of Dartania through horses. She was by no means a conventional woman, and Madeleine had always liked her for it. Nonetheless she found it impossible to hold a conversation because Dartania either dismissed a topic outright or she turned things into a joke. It was a curiously isolating strategy, the effect of which was to cut off the interlocutor and with it the establishment of any felt connection. Nor had Dartania a domestic side, and Madeleine now recalled Bayard's claim that Seneca was therefore easy fodder. He said Dartania wanted her husband to do what their father did, hold a big umbrella over her head, adding, "If he ever falters Dar will kick him in the shins." A man wanted something else in return for his protection, he said, "and a man like Seneca will look out for it."

Madeleine pulled the towel more closely about her shoulders and looked keenly at Jasmine. "You will, as you say, have to be very careful my dear or you're going to blow your family to smithereens and Seneca's political future with it. You're skipping along in a minefield you know, not a bed full of roses."

"I do know, but there it is Madeleine; my life is suddenly miraculously complete. I wouldn't have believed it possible, but as it exists now, it's everything I want. It needn't be more—conventional." She paused, smiling softly. "Though I myself am more conventional than I ever dreamed. To love someone, to have his company and tend his needs, even part-time, completely satisfies me. All the old ambitions have simply evaporated." She gestured gracefully in the air.

Madeleine knew that what was wanted at one moment from love's cornucopia could change, but it was useless to say so. "To a degree we're in the same boat," she pleasantly returned, "which is partly, I expect, why you came to me."

Lying on the sandy beach after another swim, Jasmine poured out her story, or at any rate an edited summary of it. She nearly hadn't gone to the Pyrenees when Stark couldn't come, but her Parisian friends were keen to go and it had been a great success. They'd kept pace with Seneca and Pete Weaver on the trails, everybody was good-humored, and her friends, though they spoke no English, had admired Seneca no end. Clearly, character required no common language to be accurately perceived.

When her friends had returned to Paris, she'd lingered on for a few days in the south. That was really when it had happened, though all the time, it had been growing, if not consciously so. In the end they had sailed home on the same ship, with Pete Weaver, short of money and obviously in the way, languishing in steerage. But Pete was devoted to Seneca and would in any case be absolutely discreet.

Jasmine confessed she had stopped off in Washington as a feint, so they wouldn't arrive back in Nashborough together. Her careful summary omitted, however, the earlier episode in Thebes, which might have put a different slant on the affair's development. Nor did Jasmine mention Dartania. Madeleine rightly supposed that, because it was a family matter, it was, therefore, to any Douglas, private. But Jasmine did mention her own marriage. She said her feelings for Frank had been intense, all-compassing, but that they were seeded in complete ignorance of herself and of the world, and so ultimately had proved to be fantastic. This was something solid. So much was automatically shared and understood between them, and of course, she herself was so much older and wiser. At which, Jasmine laughed, "Or just plain mad I guess. Love is a madness isn't it? A divine madness, like they say—and yet it brims with lucidity. I believe it's what, if anything, we're here on earth for, because it feels so right, because it fits."

She reached out for the bottle of suntan oil lying in the sand. "Anyhow I've bitten the apple, Madeleine. It's delicious and it seems to me worth any consequences."

The promised cabin stood in a grassy clearing. Built of unpainted planks, the shiny tin roof swept down gracefully over the front porch. The living room had a big stone fireplace, and a rudimentary kitchen filled one corner. A pump brought water in directly from the well, and Madeleine proudly pointed out the curtains she had made herself, sprigged flour sacks lined with calico. There was a small bedroom and a tiny bathroom with a feeble shower.

Jasmine was enchanted. "It's really charming! You've done a marvelous job." She sat down on the chair arm and took in the "feel" of it. "Why, it's perfect Madeleine."

Having once dreamed so intensely of European grandeur, a glittering golden life of high polish, urbanity, and celebrated notoriety—how strange indeed that much of the happiest period of her life might be spent in a former Negro shack four miles from Timbuctoo.

But despite her profession of joy, Jasmine's heart lay far from perfect ease. Her anxiety wasn't to do with Dartania however but with the measure of Seneca's attachment. He was a gallant man, one who, as their Theban adventure showed, was unlikely to turn a willing woman down. But in France a genuine bond had formed: They had found keen pleasure in each other's company, together with a passion that struck fire, and their mutual sympathy had been fully focused.

But in Nashborough things would be different; they already were. Seneca, unlike Jasmine, had much to entertain his mind and to excite his interest and imagination. A busy challenging life daily presented itself in work and politics; and there was too his family. When jogged, his memory would no doubt produce a pleasant, even a desirous smile. His interest was real enough, his wish to continue seeing her. She had obtained residence in a small compartment of his mind. But the key to his heart and a free run in his protean imagination she did not possess. Moreover, the thought that he had discovered the woman of his life, as she had discovered the man, she rightly guessed never once crossed his mind.

As to Dartania, Jasmine was curiously unperturbed. There had never been anything but affection and a sense of fun between them. Douglas family attachment, rooted so early and so deeply, lay beyond the reach of threat. Subsequent attachments coexisted but they could neither displace nor dig up family ties. If anything, clan feeling *decreased* in Jasmine's mind the possibility of wrongdoing. She knew her sister's marriage wasn't a success. Dartania was not domestic and the couple's mutually independent styles had failed to merge, so that an element of mere convenience had entered their relations. Jasmine could not believe that Dartania would, should she find out, really mind too much; though it was best all around of course that she did not. In France it had seemed a simple matter of enjoying parallel lives, laying down a new track alongside the existing ones and maintaining, thereby, a smooth and untangled existence, without any collisions. Now at close range Jasmine could see no reason why, if managed carefully, that plan could not be made to work.

9

S ally Nash's wedding set for late July had at short notice to be post-
poned. On Sunday morning two weeks before the event, Jane Douglas,
calling to her husband in the opposite bed, got no response, or, as she soon
learned, ever would. Sometime during the night, Hamilton Douglas, with
the quiet dignity that characterized his firm and austere nature, had, in a
sleep deepening into death, been divested of his mortal coil.

The announcement fell to Dan as senior male in residence. Rippling
in cold eddies through the family, it ricocheted over to Cottoncrop, then
spread across Blue Hills, and by evening had reached all Nashborough
via the evening paper. "Renowned Citizen Dies in Sleep," the *Herald*
reported, bending much space and many words in a eulogy of the "venerable Titan" who had left his mark graven so deeply on the town, and his
high virtue, it was to be hoped, imprinted with an equal depth upon on its
citizens.

By afternoon Timbuctoo was full of people paying their respects, and the
Greengage Flowers van came and went with the frequency of a rush-hour
bus. Chloe cataloged the cards attached to flowers while Dan, lodged near
the front door, formally greeted callers on the family's behalf. At first, voices
were kept to a murmur, as though Hamilton's overdue repose might be disturbed into unwanted consciousness, but as the afternoon wore on, the
event increasingly took on the ambience of a cocktail party. Cook Melia and

Ned served drinks from a sideboard in the hall, and conversation fell along lines typical of Blue Hills social gatherings.

A small handful of intimates went upstairs to commiserate with Jane, but Miss Alice wasn't among them, having sent her excuses. She was too old to visit the living or the dead, she said: Her legs were calling the show and today they had gone on strike and were refusing to carry her.

Only Dartania, smoking nonstop and moving vaguely about, but talking to no one, had a nervous, frantic look. A taproot had been severed and she felt it as a physical amputation.

The more general view was that Hamilton had led, in eighty-seven years, a full and worthwhile, if by no means easy, life. And though losing his fortune and that of others who'd depended on him, he had retained his foothold on the premier rung of social respectability. Moreover, he had died an enviable death. Few contemporaries remained to mourn him, however, so that for those present, it was more a case of lamenting a statue fallen from its pedestal or a great oak sundered by a bolt of lightning than the felt loss of a friend.

Word soon got around that there was to be no funeral. Hamilton's instructions in the matter were clear. He was to be buried in the family plot beside his wife, with space for Jane on his other side. The family could attend if they wished but there was to be no ceremony—at most the reading of a short poem chosen to convey his sentiments on death. His tombstone should give his name and dates of birth and death, but nothing more.

Seneca was politicking somewhere in the northern part of the state. Pete Weaver managed mysteriously to contact him, however, and brought the will over to Timbuctoo on Seneca's instructions. Jasmine, reached somehow at the widow Ames's, where she had recently taken up riding, turned up late that evening—and Seneca soon after. Meantime Dartania had telegraphed the news to Robin in Florida, and he had called back to say that he would be there for the burial on Tuesday.

Hamilton left everything to his wife, with stipends for the remaining servants. His deeds and stock certificates were in his office safe, the combination given in the will, together with reiterated burial instructions.

Two days later, gathered around the open grave, Bayard read William Savage Landor's short poem from Hamilton's underscored copy of his collected works.

> *Death stands above me, whispering low,*
>
> *I know not what into my ear;*
>
> *Of his strange language all I know*
>
> *Is, there is not a word of fear.*

The family watched dumbly as the polished mahogany coffin was slowly lowered into the ground. There were no tears. Hamilton had for some time been growing visibly into death and wisely his wife and children had prepared themselves. But the great umbrella was furled.

Looking up, however, the sky, though gray, did not portend rain. Moreover, Hamilton's offspring were all sufficiently rooted in and by fixed patterns of existence that vulnerability, where it existed, shifted largely to the unstructured futures of their children, whose fragility they themselves of course did not suspect.

Robin wasn't present. His wife had called Dartania that morning to say he was ill, a message taken unanimously to mean that he was drunk. It was the first time the two women had spoken.

"What did she sound like?" Chloe asked suspiciously.

"Sort of country—mountain country—and sort of submissive. But Robbie must be taking Papa's death very hard. He'd feel much better if he were here with us."

When, after the funeral, the family sat down to lunch, the place at the head of the table had been laid, but Jane did not appoint a successor. It was Flora, who, hoping to bring the issue to a head, asked Ned outright who was going to carve.

"Fried chicken don't need no carving," he portentously replied.

With admirable foresight Jane, by nature no king-maker, had sidestepped a highly symbolic decision, and her instinctive diplomacy struck an impressive note all around.

"Who's chicken?" Flora quipped. But the pert double entendre passed unnoticed, or was ignored.

Youth however could not for long be overlooked or ignored. The conveyor belt was moving inexorably, carrying the younger generation nearer to center stage. And those who had held that place for what seemed to them so brief a space were in turn moved nearer to Hamilton's void, receiving the first hints that they too would be marginalized. *Memento mori* shouted the empty place.

Remember the hopes of youth! might have been the response when, one month later, wearing a white satin dress and her great-grandmother's *rose pointe* veil, Sally Nash, buxom and smiling, on her father's arm, walked with easy assurance through Cottoncrop's triple parlors. The bridegroom awaited her on the spot where the Christmas tree always stood.

Sally was preceded by sixteen-year-old Flora as maid of honor, the full skirt and peplum of her turquoise dress proclaiming Dior's New Look, and less overtly Flora's own—her footing on the threshold of womanhood being suddenly apparent to any interested eye.

She was Sally's only attendant, as Emma was somewhere out in Australia and, rumor had it, going to marry a sheep farmer. ("I told you she wasn't coming back," Flora had trumpeted, opening the present of a sheepskin beautifully cured by Emma's antipodean inamorato.)

Small family weddings were a tradition at Cottoncrop, and Seneca, with three daughters, thought it a very great blessing. "Look at all the money lavished on Chloe's wedding," he was heard to say, "and it came to nothing. Another bad investment."

After giving the bride away, Seneca joined his wife and Miss Allen, flanked by Jane Douglas and Alice Nash who sat together on a little gilded settee. In the row opposite, Mr. and Mrs. Frazer smiled and wept, respectively. No one knew the Frazer family's size, but only the couple themselves had been invited, the inference being that in the wake of Hamilton's death, festivity must respectfully be downplayed. In fact it was believed, though no one said so, that the lower the profile presented by the Frazer family the better. But when the couple had arrived in a gray chauffeur-driven Rolls Royce, the first one seen in Nashborough since the Depression, Sally's in-laws shot up a notch or two. The vehicle's somber opulence (Flora alone wondered if it was hired) offset Mrs. Frazer's pink lace dress, far too girlish for her plump figure and gray hair, and Mr. Frazer's string tie, Texas style, worn with his morning coat. But then, so much that was Frazer seemed to Nashes and Douglases, not disappointingly, like Texas.

The "turtle shell" of a house, instead of being in the local "stork hollow" near the railroad tracks, was smack in the center of Blue Hills, opposite the golf course; and though small, being one-storeyed, was in a pretty French country style. The front yard was a mere strip separating house and street, but in the back a mature flower garden meandered for over an acre beyond a large brick terrace.

Set against the repeated suggestion that young Frazer lacked background, Dartania now opined affectionately that at least he had backyard. But the new rich, she and Seneca agreed, tended to spoil their children, giving them right off all the things they'd never had themselves; while in established families children were a mere adjunct, taught the house rules, kept on a short lead, and receiving no special attention, were expected to get on naturally with growing up. Seneca kept on saying the pair should start out like other young couples, but secretly he thought the house would do young Frazer good in terms of reassuring clients.

There being no recessional, Sally and Jack turned and greeted their guests informally on the spot, in front of the velvet covered prie-dieu. The servants having slipped out immediately, trays of champagne were soon in circulation, and smiles and fans fluttered like butterflies in the August heat.

Alice Nash and Jane Douglas did not mingle but as senior dowagers remained enthroned on the gilt settee. "I really can't see how I'm going to make ends meet," Jane, having voiced her praises of the wedding, confided. "If it were up to me, I'd sell Timbuctoo tomorrow and move into an apartment." There were however three of Hamilton's children, several grandchildren, and Jane's elderly sister, Bertha Fenton, to think about.

"Surely things aren't as bad as that," Alice cried out in protest, aware Jane was a level-headed woman and not generally given to exaggeration.

"I'm afraid they are." Jane reminded her that Hamilton's electricity board income had stopped the day of his death—a thousand dollars a month. She said there wasn't much else. He had, rightly she was sure, eschewed the stock market after the Great Crash. And now the town limits were about to engulf them, and the taxes on Timbuctoo would be colossal.

"Well, my dear"—Alice Nash patted her neighbor's arm—"go on and sell. The children aren't stupid; they can fend for themselves." She thought it dreadful to break up a family house, but Jane's true motivation having lapsed, so, understandably, had her energy and will. And gazing vaguely around the high-ceilinged parlor, Alice wondered, not for the first time, what would eventually become of Cottoncrop.

At the end of the hall, Flora, hurrying forward, stopped her old nurse at the foot of the stairs. "What's wrong, Miss Allie?" Tears were brimming in Miss Allen's blue eyes behind her steel-rimmed spectacles. "Is it old Sally? Because she couldn't be happier, fool though she may be." In fact, Flora knew what it was, that was why she was there.

"Do I look all right, honey?" Miss Allen's eyes shimmered like two windswept ponds.

"Why, you look great, Miss Allie." Like her nurse, Flora had overheard the little boy demanding loudly of his mother who that "dwarf in the funny clothes" was, and Miss Allen's unprotected heart had suffered a ripping wound. She had believed that she was looking her best and had taken her place in the front row as an honorary parent with great pride. Sally, after all, was her first baby, and Miss Allen loved her as her own. She was mortified to have let the family down.

Flora, whose own heart bled in silent and indignant anguish, searched frantically for a remedy. "Grandma Douglas said you had on the best dress at the wedding," she fluently lied. "I told her you'd made it yourself and she was really impressed. But if she asks you to make her one, don't you do it. You put yourself out too much for others as it is."

Miss Allen's sweet smile hesitated between light and shade. "I don't want you-all to feel ashamed of me. I don't want to embarrass you-all."

"That's the craziest thing I ever heard, Miss Allie! You could never embarrass us. We're all so proud of you." Flora, devastated by such humble abnegation, gave her nurse a big hug. "Come on, I'll go upstairs with you. I bet old Roly's getting lonesome after all this time."

But the bride and groom were advancing like new-crowned royalty down the crowded hall. Sally, her train looped over one arm, a champagne glass in hand, leaned lightly with her free hand on her husband's arm. "Oh there you are, Miss Allie," she called out gaily. "We've been looking all over for you." Flora could have kissed her. She could have kissed them both, for Jack at once piped up, "I want my family to meet you, Miss Allen, if you have a minute. I want them to know who made such a good job of my Sally here. They'd be mighty proud to make your acquaintance, if you can spare the time."

"Go on, Miss Allie," insisted Flora.

Eyes misting over for very different reasons, Miss Allen walked, leaning on Jack's other arm, down the hall toward the front parlor, her bruised heart plastered over, her head held almost gaily to one side, and beaming like a child. The other guests made way, smiling in broad beneficence as people do at weddings, and making a wide corridor for the central stars.

Dartania, passing through the triple parlors in the opposite direction, made a beeline for Bayard. He scrutinized her over a pair of half-moon spectacles that had recently replaced the old-fashioned pince-nez and sardonically raised his glass: "The mother of the bride."

Dartania made a face. "I feel like the mother of all living. We drank about fifty toasts last night. Those Frazers must have Russian blood; it didn't faze them one damn bit. They're really quite a pair, and the old boy's got a twinkle in his eye."

"The *on dit* is Sally's landed on her feet."

"Well the rest of us are about to be knocked off ours," she said with some vehemence, maneuvering her portly brother toward a corner despite his strong reluctance to being cornered. But her purpose was not as he had feared. "You aren't going to believe this but Seneca told me last night that Jane is thinking of selling Timbuctoo!" Her tone implied a consciously planned act of desecration.

"I believe she's very short of money," Bayard languidly replied. "Upkeep and taxes are high and they're going up."

"But to sell would be awful. We must stop her."

"Have you got the money? I haven't. You know, it's too bad Timbuctoo isn't older. It could be a museum. I'm serious. There's a plan afoot to turn Blue Hills House into one—make it a model antebellum house and give the Blue Hills crowd a sort of shared past with which to face down newcomers. They'll all invest in it, you'll see."

"That's nice for you, and Miss Alice," Dartania said shortly.

"Blue Hills Ladies Association is behind it; they'll be passing the cup your way pretty soon."

"Blue Hills has nothing to do with me; they won't get a nickel. But, Bayard, we must keep Timbuctoo. We have to save that. Jassy and Chloe and Dan, and that godawful Mrs. Fenton will have to start pulling their weight, that's all. Chloe's working and so is Jasmine, and Dan's book is making a little money. They ought to contribute something on a regular basis and not just sponge off Jane, which is what it amounts to now that Papa's dead."

"It was all right to sponge off him?"

"You know what I mean. And Jane isn't really kin; she doesn't understand what Timbuctoo means. She can't."

"You mean a respectable hotel for freeloaders? I expect she understands it perfectly. But isn't that what family homes have always been?"

Dartania ignored this. "I'm damned well going to stop it. I'll talk to Chloe and Jasmine today. They'll have to fork up. If they don't they're going to find themselves in the street." She nodded to emphasize this impeccable logic.

At the opposite end of the parlor Jasmine, aware every single instant of Seneca's whereabouts, was complimenting Sally on her dress and, in a friendly whisper, on her handsome husband. Jack's crewcut had grown out and people were beginning to say he was the spitting image of Burt Lancaster and sounded just like Jimmy Stewart. "I keep on meaning to tell you," Jasmine went on, "that when I was in that factory during the war, I met someone who knew you: Delphine Brown."

"Good heavens, Little Delphine!" Sally cried out in amazement, a mild embarrassment etched into her surprise. "I always wondered what became of her." She had indeed wondered, but at the same time, for some reason that she was unable to fathom, she had never asked Little Delphine's mother for any news.

"She'd lost her husband, and not in the war, and she had some children to support. She told me you two once got in a fight and she hit you with a brick," Jasmine laughed.

"She caught hell, poor thing." Sally giggled sympathetically, turning to her husband. "Fortunately I've improved a bit since then. I've stopped beating up my friends."

Pete Weaver had come up, his sandy hair and freckled face, unusually boyish on such a tall young man, were offset by penetrating if pale gray eyes. Jasmine gave him a brilliant smile in which was embedded more than a hint of camaraderie.

"Oh I forgot you two were in the Pyrenees together." Sally exclaimed, adding caustically, "How was it? Forced marches every day, hardtack dinners? None of his family would dream of going anywhere with him."

"Your father is a fine outdoorsman. He outwalked the local mountaineers," Pete answered proudly.

"Praising Daddy's pedestrian virtues?" Flora blandly inquired, showily smoking a cigarette.

"I'm praising his ability to come in first," Pete defensively replied.

"Oh sure, you can count on that. He'd come in first in a slow bicycle race."

"What does that mean?" Pete sensed it was no compliment.

"In a *slow* bicycle race, to win you have to come in *last*."

Pete found Flora exasperating. Instinctively she undermined the better values, and yet she fascinated. She needed besting, and the challenge wasn't easy; she was a tricky customer.

"So, how's Nash and Polk?" she asked him indifferently.

Pete trod cautiously, suspecting a covered pit. "Great, flourishing. Your father's a brilliant lawyer even if by your lights he's no great shakes as a cyclist. And Jack's settling right in," he added with just a whiff of patronage. "Though I doubt he'll take up courtroom law. He'll probably go in for the corporate side."

"Are you a courtroom lawyer?"

"I'm getting to be I hope. Why don't you come down and see sometime? Have you ever seen your father try a case?"

Flora had not, nor had she any wish to watch Pete Weaver mimicking his performance. "I see enough of him as it is, thank you," from which might have been implied, as her eye began to wander, and more than enough of you.

Jasmine perceived Seneca was turning, gazing about the room, perhaps about to move in her direction. But instead he nodded surreptitiously toward the garden, and with equal discretion, she acknowledged receipt of the message.

"Can I get you something to drink?" Pete courteously proposed to Flora. "A Coca-Cola, or is that water you're drinking?" He nodded at the nearly empty glass.

"You can get me a martini on the rocks," she told him flatly.

Pete stared in surprise if not exactly disbelief. "How old are you?"

"None of your business. Don't you know better than to ask a woman that? Well, are you going to get it or not?"

Rapidly Pete made up his mind. "OK, but you better drink it on the QT, and for God's sake, take the olive out."

Flora, following him toward the bar, stood at a distance while he placed the order. She didn't think Ben, if he knew, would agree to give her another.

Jane Douglas, exercising a widow's prerogative, had departed soon after the ceremony, and shortly afterward, Miss Alice Nash, greatly fatigued, went quietly upstairs. She lay down fully dressed on the big tester bed. How tired one got doing nothing at all but sitting. She had greeted innumerable people but spoken to no one, really, except Jane. Her role was now largely ceremonial, like that of an icon paraded through European streets on feast days, venerated and returned to its solitary niche until required again. But Alice accepted the redundancy of age without complaint. Better to have a symbolic presence than none at all perhaps.

The noises coming from below resounded at the decibel of success. The ceremony had gone smoothly and the young couple were certainly happy together. They were pleasant and good-natured into the bargain, which was a blessing. But who could tell what would become of them, or how they would cope when one day life delivered a knockout blow, as it was sure to do. At least money would be no problem and money, enough money, was more important than people cared to admit. But disaster could come from so many different quarters, and saddest of all, wantonly, foolishly, it could be self-imposed. Dartania and Seneca, though undeniably the cynosures of their generation, had failed so miserably in their marriage. Estranged and unbending, neither of them was able to give an inch. The trouble was that nobody worked at marriage anymore and you had to work at it. It had to be the main thing.

Birth, courtship, marriage, the rearing of children, and death. From the beginning of time that was the desired and necessary course of life, a linked chain of continuing progression and renewal that made up family life, that rooted individuals reassuringly in a past and future and built some purpose into their lives. Now suddenly there was divorce. It would shatter the chain into irreparable pieces. It could not do otherwise. And what then would become of families, and so, likewise, of individuals?

The young talked endlessly of happiness, and Alice thought it a sadly trumped-up mirage. Her own generation had never thought much about it. They had thought about survival and the improvement and development of good character. They had relished happiness when unexpectedly it came along, relished it heartily. But it was not a continual expectation, a daily gauge of one's condition, like taking your temperature. Hamilton's marriage to Flora, for instance, was probably the greatest happiness he had known. Yet had she lived, Alice believed that would have changed. Flora, though attractive and fun, was ultimately rather a light woman. Jane had been better for him and she had given him some peace—a kind of happiness.

In any case Alice suspected it was on the whole an innate capacity: You either had it or you didn't, so it shouldn't be made too much of. The doctor had had it but even he used to get depressed. Probably it was a question of chemistry. She had known cripples, Dan Douglas, for instance, who were happier than people who could somehow never actively feel their blessings, but saw them merely as the marker to some new achievement.

The younger generation was chasing phantoms. The Prince of Wales had set the pace, throwing up everything for love. The man must be a fool. And poor Robin Douglas had repeated it. He had traded one set of problems for another. Drink remained his only hermitage, and word had it he was often in retreat. So too Red Mason down in Mobile, they said.

A whoop of laughter sounded from the garden below. Weddings always made people happy. Even those who wept enjoyed themselves. A wedding revived such optimism and goodwill. As a couple nailed their colors to a mast and set their sails, a collective hope arose like a fresh breeze that this particular ship, setting out so buoyantly in uncharted seas, eventually might sail proudly into port carrying a wealth of well-earned personal treasure. Miss Alice sighed with resignation. Nowadays, sighting the first sunny-looking tropical island, couples jumped overboard and struck out for it. Or one of them did.

Yet paradoxically the old ports for the shipwrecked were being dismantled. Timbuctoo would go soon, while Cottoncrop's only use outside the ceremonial now seemed to be as her interim coffin. The old places had served their purpose. Families were scattering, generation fleeing from generation, man from wife, and nobody wanted a big house anymore, spreading its sheltering wings out like a mother hen. Alice sighed again and closed her eyes.

Downstairs the windows and doors were opened wide, and though the high ceilings made it cooler inside than out, people still spilled onto the porches and strolled, glass in hand, about the flower garden, even though there wasn't much to see in August and the front lawn had become a parking lot.

Dartania went outdoors in search of Jasmine, to suggest in the friendliest way the sacrifices needed for Timbuctoo's salvation. Half a dozen people were gathered on the front porch, but Jasmine wasn't among them. Looking about, Dartania held the screen door open for a little boy in white shorts and a ruffled shirt carrying a plate of sliced ham.

"Can I let my dog out of the car and give him something to eat?" the child asked in a small high voice.

"I don't see why not, so long as you stay with him and take that plate back to the kitchen afterwards."

"Yes, ma'am. Can he have some too?" the boy nodded toward Roly, not beneath dancing on his hind legs in the hope of getting some ham.

Dartania nodded absently; she had spotted Jasmine; and the little boy, holding the plate carefully with both hands, stepped gingerly down the front steps, Roly scampering alongside.

Jasmine was walking in the direction of the house and Seneca was with her. But what struck Dartania almost unconsciously was the extraordinary slowness of their pace, so unlike either of them. She was about to signal but the pair were speaking with such evident intensity, not looking up or at each other.

When Jasmine did look up, however, Dartania, seeing her expression, almost smiled. She knew that look so well. She had seen it on countless women under the spell of Seneca's personality. As he liked them to be. Chloe, even on her wedding day, had had it. It always amused Dartania and made her obscurely proud, though it surprised her that the critical and independent Jasmine should fall sway.

The impression had no time for further penetration. A fierce growl cut through the heavy afternoon humidity, and from the porch, Dartania turned in time to see the Spencers' Doberman lunging forward like an unleashed panther, as Roly, a large piece of ham in his mouth, trotted blithely away from the plate set down on the lawn. The little boy was knocked flat as the enraged animal pounced from behind upon the unsuspecting Roly.

Dartania was running before she was conscious of it. One high-heeled sandal jettisoned, the other one still in her hand, she sped down the steps and toward the parked cars with Amazonian grace, barefoot, her blue summer dress billowing out behind. "Get away!" she shouted furiously at the Doberman. "You leave that dog alone!" No conscious thought entered her head. She was embodied instinct: sure and swift and unafraid. But coming suddenly within the animal's range, becoming herself a target, she recalled Seneca saying to get your forearm in the back of an attacking dog's mouth, then he couldn't bite. How to get past the teeth? There was no time for reflection. As the Doberman attacked, so too did Dartania, the two springing at one another like a pair of matched and graceful fighters. There was an aesthetic beauty about it, a harmony of balance and color overriding all barbarity and danger. Then at the moment of contact, human inspiration triumphed. With all her strength Dartania rammed her sandal into the open snarling mouth. The impact of collision knocked her backward to the ground, but the deed was done, the Doberman wheeled, frantically tossing its head, trying to dislodge the shoe.

Then Seneca was beside her. He was picking her up. Others were flowing forward like extras in a film, and the little boy, his white suit badly stained, was shrieking for every conceivable reason.

Seneca put his arms around his breathless wife, then after a minute he held her from him at arm's length, a look of admiration in his eyes, a look of tenderness as, badly winded, she laid her head again upon his shoulder.

Jasmine, standing at some distance, watched, assailed by feelings she had not dreamt possible. Always she had said Dartania was the best. She had felt it generously and without the faintest tinge of envy in her heart. Yet as she witnessed this unexpected tenderness between man and wife, a fierce antagonism blazed, a sharpened flame of putrifying jealousy that was close to outright hatred. Dartania did not deserve her husband. She neither knew nor needed him. All his excellent qualities were lost on her, and she added nothing to the contentment of his life.

Then, with frightening clarity, Jasmine perceived suddenly that Dartania, though wild and untameable, paradoxically was in a cage. But the cage was somehow necessary to her, for the door was certainly open. Yet instead of escaping Dartania paced nervously up and down inside, from one familiar corner to the other, without evident purpose. It was remarkably like a tragedy and instantly Jasmine's sympathies for her sister were revived. Now however with the protection of her anger gone, there opened before her what she had sought to hide: the terrible suspicion that where Seneca was concerned she would always be peripheral, skirting desolately about the edges, waiting for a crust.

Two men had prized Dartania's sandal from the Doberman's mouth and the whimpering animal was led back to the car by a shaken and apologetic owner. There was talk of rabies, of rabies shots, and of shooting the Doberman on the spot. But Dartania protested strongly on that score. The animal wasn't mad, he was merely indignant, she said—and rightly so. He had suffered loss of face together with a substantial part of his dinner.

Flora too finally came outside. She was carrying a red silk shawl, some of its long crimson fringe trailing on the ground, as quietly she maneuvered through the talkative throng. Stooping down, she gently wrapped the shawl around Roly's inert form and, standing upright again, slowly carried her bundle back into the house as patches of red darkened in blotches on the crimson silk. No one took any notice. Attention was elsewhere. It was all for Dartania.

Jasmine had retreated too. She needed to be alone and to collect herself, to control the welter of passionate feelings and ease somehow the biting fear that she would never be of much importance to the person who was everything to her. Seneca and Dartania were more deeply bound than she'd allowed herself to believe.

In the front hall she encountered Stark, who, seeing her face, assumed the dog's attack had badly shaken her, since evidently something had.

"I could do with a drink," she admitted meekly, covering up her misery as she took his arm, glad in some corner of her mind for a friend's support.

Stark took two whiskeys from a tray. "I've been wanting to talk to you all afternoon," he said. "Let's go in here." He nodded toward the empty library. A suppressed intensity colored his tone, though she hardly noticed it. "About something pretty important." At which a mild sense of déjà vu—the parlor at Timbuctoo all those years ago—faintly raised Jasmine's apprehension. There had been a baby asleep, but which baby she could not recall, only that Stark had suddenly and without any encouragement kissed her. But had she recently given him any encouragement? She had felt such warmth for him, being herself so isolated and alone. Could that have been misinterpreted? She saw instantly that stopping in Washington was a mistake. In doing so, she had used him, and almost certainly she had misled him, too.

Having handed her the whiskey, he waited while she sipped it greedily.

"What I want to say may well strike you as highly premature," he began, his gaze scanning absently the dark rows of books as he thought out the details of his speech. "In ways it is premature. But if there's one thing I've learned in politics, it's to seize the moment and not to hang about hoping things will fall into place of their own accord. Besides, I go back to Washington next month in time to put the children in school, so I can't afford to beat about the bush."

They had remained standing, away from the window but well within sight of the open door. Jasmine, whose attention to what he was saying was incomplete, could not help wishing that Seneca would pass by and see them together in intimate talk, standing inside the open door. It was a despicable and small-natured thought, which she sought desperately to banish.

"I'm a rudderless man," Stark was saying, "which no man ought to be if he can help it, especially a politician, and most especially a man with a young family."

She seemed to have missed some of the beginning, but given the ease and fluency of his delivery, she judged it a better speech than he would have managed in the past. She began to cast around for a response to what was coming. The truth of the matter was, he was too late, but she could not say that.

"Mary Ann and I had a very happy marriage and we loved each other. I believe everyone knows that. Her death has left me horribly shaken, and I confess profoundly bewildered too. I still can't understand it and I don't suppose that now I ever shall. But I have to get on with my life. I must plan my future and that of my two children. I've been thinking about it a great deal lately and, well, to come to the point, today I decided to act. Not on the spur of the moment, mind you. I'd thought it all through carefully. Do you know I even chose in advance this very room. Everything was planned."

"Stark . . ." Jasmine interrupted, trying to stop him, hoping it wasn't too late for the subject somehow to be successfully diverted.

"No, please, hear me out. In ways it's premature, I know," he went on, believing apparently that he had read her thoughts. "But I very much want and need to marry again. And frankly I think if it took place quietly then it oughtn't to cause a rumpus."

"Excuse me?" Watching the door and thinking of Seneca, had she missed an outright proposal? She felt enormously flattered by his determination, it bucked her up no end, but ultimately the encounter was embarrassing, and she feared for a future awkwardness between them.

"I had such a crush on you when we were young. All your verve and arrogance and intelligence. You were like the princess in a fairy story, leaning out of some high tower, throwing out such big challenges. And nobody, nobody from here, anyhow, could manage to scale the walls or discover the password, if there was one." He paused and smiled almost wryly. "I very much wanted to. I dreamt of it often enough."

Jasmine had sunk onto the arm of a chair beside the window.

"Reality takes years to accept, doesn't it? And even more time to come to terms with, to know oneself enough to set realistic sights and accept a direction that will work and be compatible."

"And then two people also must agree."

"Ah, they must indeed." Again he smiled, and this time it was broadly. He even took a little turn about the room. "Well then, it is agreed."

"I can assure you it is not!"

Stark looked taken aback. "But surely you've noticed something," he managed awkwardly in response. "I'm told everyone has."

"I think you'd better come to the point, Stark," she almost rudely declared.

"The point is," he said, his surprise woven with obvious bewilderment, "I've asked Chloe to marry me and she has accepted."

At last he had her full attention.

"I don't know how I could have coped these months without her help and kindnesses. She's been so good to the children, they're genuinely fond of her, and she's helped no end in sorting out my office."

Jasmine had gone very pale then very red. Shock was being piled on shock. "No," she managed stiffly. "As a matter of fact I hadn't noticed anything. I must be singularly unobservant. But this is wonderful news!" Good manners were rescuing her, and pragmatism, never far away, inspired her next inquiry, "Who else knows?"

"No one else, I think. Chloe wanted to tell the children first." He was suddenly more relaxed and at ease. "But since there's such a special friendship between us I wanted to tell you myself, and Chloe readily agreed, of course."

The absurdity of Jasmine's assumption was becoming plain, and with it the rightness of the impending marriage, which began almost to seem inevitable. Old Chloe was quite a trooper. She had stayed in there slogging away and it had brought its reward. Wormed her way in, thought Jasmine uncharitably. Then pulling herself up, she kissed him on the cheek and cried, "Oh Stark, I'm delighted. You always belonged in the family, we always felt that. But Chloe's been hiding her light under a bushel and I must go and congratulate her." Jasmine was suddenly glad, her natural optimism was returning.

At that moment Dartania put her head inside the library door. "What a to-do," she cried dismissively of the recent canine drama, but there was undisguised exuberance in her voice, and she was still barefoot. "Jassy, have you got a minute? I need to speak to you about something."

Jasmine, offering a bundle of excuses, fled through the other door.

BY SIX O'CLOCK the bride and groom had changed and were standing in the front hall as Ben carried their suitcases to the waiting car. He would drive them to the railway station and they would stay the night in Thebes before continuing to New Orleans the next day. Amid laughter and much merrymaking the young couple were followed out on to the front porch, where little gauze bags of rice were being distributed. Alice Nash's Cadillac was at the foot of the steps, and Ben, having stored the suitcases, opened the rear door, smiling broadly as the newlyweds prepared to descend. Sally, wearing a pink linen suit, still carried her wedding bouquet. She intended throwing it as an affectionate tease to her little sister who so vociferously despised the institution of marriage. But where on earth was she? Discreetly Ben glanced at his watch. Everything was suspended while they looked for Flora. Then Rosetta murmured to Seneca that she believed Flora was upstairs, with the little dog.

Seneca mounted the stairs two at a time. Outside the nursery, Flora sat huddled on a step, her back resting against the nursery door, her face desolate and pale. Inside the room the creak of Miss Allen's rocker could be heard, together with a repeated keening, as, holding her precious bundle in her arms, still wrapped up in the red shawl, she rocked back and forth, back and forth, back and forth. It sounded like the ticking of a clock, against which could be heard the steady low-pitched moan of anguished grieving.

Flora looked frightened when she saw her father.

"Let's get the show on the road," he called out impatiently. "You're holding up your sister's wedding." And seeing her wretched face, guessing the cause, his irritation congealed into an inchoate rage incomprehensible to Flora.

But shuttering across Seneca's mind, mangled corpses and horribly wounded men lay on a bombed airfield. Hoarse and agonized shrieks and desperate pleas for help sounded accusingly in his ears. More could follow, much more, but he willed that it did not. "You heard me!" he shouted furiously. "Now get a move on, and stop crying like a damn fool over nothing!"

Slowly Flora got up, her tears frozen at their source.

"On the double! And for God's sake wash your face."

When Flora came downstairs traces of tears remained, and Sally, laughing when she saw them, gave her sister an affectionate hug. "You little idiot," she said. "I'm not going very far."

"Yes, you are. You're going to another planet," Flora answered grimly, and she believed it, too.

Sally shook her head gaily, and smiling brilliantly at Jack, the two descended the steps, ducking under a shower of rice and bon voyages. Then turning suddenly at the bottom Sally, laughing out loud, roguishly threw her sister the bridal bouquet of lilies.

Everyone clapped and cheered. "You'll be next," they predicted.

Mournfully holding the bouquet, Flora watched the couple climb into the car, waving joyously from the open window as Ben shifted into first gear and the vehicle moved slowly forward.

But Flora had arranged to have her say. The car was trailing a rattling tail of tin cans, but instead of "Just Married" a big sign above the bumper read "The End."

Under the Sun

The early 1950s was a deceptive period in America, a time looked back on with benign wonder at its peacefulness, its spiraling prosperity, and its easy, taken-for-granted security. Nobody locked their front doors or took their car keys out of the ignition. The streets were safe and murders rare enough to flabbergast the nation, feeding columns of copy to an eager press. Moreover, people were getting richer and the promise of a chicken in every pot had given way to that of a new car in the driveway, every year. There was a subscene, of course, but it was swept neatly under a grassy carpet of new dollar bills.

Becoming almost overnight the richest, most powerful nation in the world, ours was an early inheritance, for the country, a most astonishing prodigy, was as yet still in her teens. And Europe responded with all the condescension and mistrust that elders feel toward a disobliging adolescent who is blithely kicking over the traces and casually brushing aside a proffered treasury of mature and worldly guidance.

Nor, it's true, had we much of a developed national culture. What we had came largely from what, given half a chance, people found they could do best: in the broadest sense, getting and spending. Our great consumer society, the future centerfold of our national ethos, had already opened wide its infant mouth. But we had too our own indigenous art forms. Chiefly modes of popular entertainment: music outstandingly; paradoxically the voices of poor people, rising up out of decades of Negro misery and upcountry Southern white deprivation, creating blues and ballads and that upbeat song of the oppressed survivor, jazz. As with so much that we produced, it was to sweep the world.

But more important at that time, of course, was Hollywood: purveyor, guardian, perhaps to a degree even inventor, of our moral outlook. As celluloid good guys fought celluloid bad guys on Wild West prairies or Chicago's gangster-infested streets, epic myth was reenacted—but with a special American twist: Always it ended in the prescribed American way—happily. Always virtue triumphed over vice, to be rewarded by boy winning girl, a pretty, housewifely, childbearing sort of girl, who, the audience knew, would move into a well-run orderly house and reproduce happily ever after. For optimism in America was and is a positive religion, and the triumph of natural justice a central pillar of our national belief. Moreover, having recently freed Europe in a struggle of good and evil, peculiarly Hollywood-like in its clear-edged moral print of right and wrong, we believed ourselves to be a righteous nation of good people—even uniquely so.

The South still clung to its traditions of landed values and courteous courtly manners descended from ancient feudal societies. Reverence for pedigrees, bravery in men and a flirtatious boldness in women, but above all, for honor. This venerable currency was becoming so much loose change as the divides of hierarchy on which it had depended blurred into nonexistence. Sharing in the economic boom (most senior senators were Southern Democrats and wangled huge federal outlays for industrial development in the South), merchant values were trickling south together with new money, and for the first time since the Civil War the well-off turned to the Republican Party to protect their interests.

There was unprecedented national cohesion. As each family labored to keep pace with next-door neighbors in the subdivision, America's new oasis, there was little or no wish to better them or cock a snook. For to be like everyone else was what, in the 1950s, people wanted. They wanted, I suppose, to belong together as a family.

Of course cohesion requires that different alloys bind congenially together, or, socially speaking, that the mordant of a common enemy be found. Fortuitously it was supplied by Communism.

There were hardly enough Communists in America to stand on the head of a pin, and most of them were idealists—egalitarians to a degree the country thought went much too far. But Senator McCarthy preached a pernicious plague, and taking his witch-hunt to Hollywood, he exorcised America's temple of moral and ethical culture. What he achieved was largely an acceleration in the spread of mediocrity—the blood money I suppose of peaceful times.

A bland sameness descended over the nation, the result of, some might say, too much fear, others too much majority rule or too much assured self-rightousness, too much seen in terms of black and white. The unusual, the extraordinary, with all its blemishes and inherent threat, was being culled systematically from the munching herd. Though happily, a few specimens, a few monstrosities, if you will, survived. While under the grassy carpet of new dollar bills, hairline fissures of discontent were opening. Not everyone was in the money or even equal before the law. And deeper down small volcanoes had begun to rumble—nowhere more so than in the South. But in the early fifties all of this was merely distant thunder.

SOME TWO YEARS after Hamilton's death, and despite Dartania's vehement protests, Timbuctoo was sold and the furniture, most of it too large for modern use, auctioned. If truth be known I think only Dartania really minded. The rest of us felt Timbuctoo had largely served its purpose and that a change would do us good. Moreover we were amply compensated by the amount of money we received.

The estate was bought by a man who'd made his money in cement. He sold off the surrounding land, except for four acres, to a developer, who divided the property into a grid of neat half-acre lots. The developer named the new subdivision Timbuctoo Woods—though when it was finished there wasn't a tree in sight. Instead, two hundred lookalike houses were set like checkers across a grid of new-seeded lawn, and what had been the domain of under a dozen became home to some five hundred people. The Douglases left behind a sort of ghostly presence. The old house was separated from the new development by Douglas Drive, while Hamilton Terrace marked the subdivision's entrance.

Jane, willingly I think, found an apartment in a new building opposite the country club. Dowagers' Destiny it was locally called. But now that houses were smaller, the elderly had to go somewhere, and in Blue Hills it was thought the nearer to the country club the better.

Bertha Fenton having died shortly before the move, Jane generously offered her two spare rooms to me. But my concise history of the state, having just been published, and with some money to hand from Timbuctoo's sale, my sights were fixed on the building's little penthouse, overlooking Blue Hills Boulevard and the peaceful shady streets that opened off it. I am writing this memoir there.

But I return to the moment at hand.

In 1948, to avowed Blue Hills' displeasure, Seneca had been elected to the United States Senate. A bad year for the Democratic party generally, Seneca's wartime prestige, and the fact that he'd kept quiet on civil rights, and kept his private life private, saw him through. Besides, Americans love a celebrity, and Seneca was a big one in this state after the war.

Years earlier Dartania had put her foot down about Washington, and after the election, she stayed put at Longwood, and Seneca came and went.

Taking a page out of Chloe's book, therefore, Jasmine slipped in quietly up in Washington, ostensibly as Seneca's research assistant. She even learned shorthand and typing to be useful and to look convincing.

Traveling between two towns and two women, Seneca somehow managed it, so that what might have caused much heartache, even a family dissolution, became at worst a potential misfortune, to which was attached certain practical benefits for all concerned. At least until 1954.

At Cottoncrop Alice Nash held on with infinite patience in an increasingly silent world. Few friends were alive to telephone her with news and gossip, but Blue Hills was fast slipping from her realm of interest. "My friends don't know who they are anymore," she said of those few who remained alive. "But nobody else these days seems to, either." Hers had become a waiting game, inevitably a solitary one.

Miss Allen had died the year before and, according to Flora, been buried in a cardboard box, which was how she viewed the simple coffin chosen by her parents and suitable in Flora's mind to a pauper's grave. Flora was enrolled at Nashborough College and doing little above the minimum, if that. Pete Weaver still tried to get her attention and from time to time she went out with him, making Seneca think she might yet achieve a responsible place in life. Though what an able fellow like Pete saw in the lazy unformed snip of his youngest daughter, he could not imagine.

At Nash and Polk, Jack Frazer and Pete surprisingly were running neck and neck. Jack had also chosen trial law, and his easy country style and cracker-barrel homilies inspired in juries likability and trust. They believed in him and therefore in his client. Jack and Sally had moved into a big brick house on Blue Hills Boulevard and Sally was busy rearing their four children herself. But she drew the line at cooking and cleaning, which she could afford financially to do.

"Your offspring are even worse than your mother's were," Bayard told her, confronted with Sally's tumbling noisy brood. "They should inhabit Borneo or New Guinea. 'Uh huh' may pass for 'please' and 'thank you,' or even 'yes sir' there. But it is not so here. I am prepared to finance transportation myself. One way, since discovering their true niche will remove all future need of reinstatement."

"Yeah, yeah!" shouted the enthusiastic foursome. "You just give us the money, Uncle Bayard, and we'll get the tickets. We don't want to put you out."

"I sincerely wish that I could say the same."

Bayard, like Seneca, was leading a workable double life. Relations with Madeleine continued, but each summer he traveled for three weeks on the Continent with Ellen. No one knew the details of this unorthodox relation,

but it was generally assumed, despite their being man and wife, to be pla-
tonic. Madeleine wisely deemed the trips of small importance, so long as no
unpalatable facts were set upon her plate, and predictably Bayard's reports
kept to general descriptions and random impressions of a politically uneasy
Europe.

Similarly Dartania showed no interest in Seneca's Washington life. She
behaved as if his existence ceased on leaving Longwood until his reappear-
ance, at which point they took up exactly as before. The arrangement, if for
different reasons, suited them both.

Mulling this, Jasmine decided that her sister, to whom she remained most
devotedly, if a trifle guiltily, attached, wanted no part in any reality involving
change or inconvenience. "I would suffocate without some new input," Jasmine told Bayard, examining aloud this intriguing mystery, by which she
herself had profited so much. "But Dar wants everything to stay just as it is.
Or as she thinks it is."

"Maybe, but the fact is we don't know, do we, really what she wants or
thinks, and I doubt she's ever going to tell us."

1

....

*B*ayard folded the letter and placed it thoughtfully in his jacket pocket. A mottled sky filled the window behind his Chippendale desk, and a coal fire, unusual in May, blazed in the iron grate opposite. On the whole he decided he was pleased. There would of course be problems: problems of providing sufficient amusement, the undesirable rupture in his routine, and, more challenging, the problem of bridging a prolonged estrangement. That was the trickiest part. Still, on balance he was pleased, or rather he was interested and looking forward, even mildly excited, as his imagination had been stirred.

Ellen's tiny handwriting, carrying to a third page, displayed an epistolary style developed in English schoolrooms. In other words she did not go bang to the point. Rather she began with generalities, filling out and embellishing the central point as it unfolded in fits and starts, as from a chrysalis. After touching on the weather and the garden, she made a brief allusion to her father's health (Lady Ferris had died the year before) and noted that she herself was well. The point began in paragraph two, yet that short paragraph did not contain it. Rather it brought the topic, which was William, forward in an introductory way.

For Bayard this was a complex topic. He was fond of the boy, whom he believed to be suspicious of him—perhaps rightly so. William could be difficult and abrasively irritating, but he was sensitive and clever. He was also manipulative. But he had lacked a father, and here Bayard felt himself to blame.

Having been cajoled into Oxford University by his mother, William, after two years, had checked himself out, as from a hotel, announcing an intention to go on the stage.

"A player!" Lord Ferris's very word on hearing the news spotlighted the frivolity of such a career, its impropriety in a gentleman. It was a career built on pretense, the pretense not only of being other than oneself, which was spurious enough, but the pretense of impersonating others, often famous people, and so, through imitation, stealing undeservedly, through a sort of sleight-of-hand, their credit. But he loved William and in the end had paid his fees at London's prestigious dramatic academy, RADA. Perhaps he could learn to act, and even make some success of it.

This was also Bayard's view. The boy had undisputed presence, and though slightly built, a sort of electricity emanated from him, such as the small and lean do sometimes so mysteriously exude. He moved with a lithe and easy grace and the quick agility of a ballet dancer. He spoke clearly and in a voice pitched deeper than for some reason one expected to issue from that small frame. And within a year of leaving RADA, he had secured a few small parts.

A kind of arrogant nerve inspired William to go for roles beyond his experience and to call with brazen insistence on theatrical agents. Then suddenly he had the proverbial actor's break. He had understudied Paul Scofield in *Hamlet* and, due to a throat infection, played the part in London for two nights. His extreme youth, his brooding sulks mixed with witty levity, his cockiness streaked with a youthful and perspicacious insecurity, his dark good looks and sheer unpredictability, successfully snared the audience, despite his unevenly mastered diction. The upshot was a paragraph in the *Daily Telegraph* saying that he showed some promise.

Ellen, having touched upon this recent success (the review was already in Bayard's possession), approached in paragraph three nearer to her point. She informed her husband that William had been seen in *Hamlet* by someone called a talent scout, who had invited him to come out to California for a screen test—with a view to being in the cinema, she added by way of illumination. Most wonderful of all the studio was going to pay his fare.

The letter's real purpose emerged in paragraph four. William had many relations in Nashborough and it was only right that he should strengthen and develop these connections. If therefore Bayard would take the boy for a week or so, en route to Hollywood, she would be truly grateful.

The impression behind the bars of minute writing was that if Bayard agreed to it, then so would William. In other words she was going to broker them into it.

Bayard refolded and returned the letter to his pocket. Madeleine would know how to manage the youngster and keep him agreeably occupied. A worldly and elegant woman could do much for a callow and egotistical youth—give him a spot more polish and self-knowledge. William had been overpraised and overindulged by much doting and by dotage. He could do with a bit of ironing out.

Albert, opening the door after a perfunctory knock, brought in the evening paper and, laying it on Bayard's desk, went over and gave the coal fire a gratuitous poke. This was the moment when Bayard normally read the headlines aloud, provoking Albert's commonsensical responses, which he himself then commented on, and they would often argue about. Both men relished these exchanges as part of a general tussle through which their mutual affection and competitive spirits found an expressive outlet.

Today the headline took up half a page: "Supreme Court Orders Deseg-regation with All Deliberate Speed."

Bayard turned the newspaper face down on his desk. "We're going to have a visitor," he said, leaning forward on his elbows.

"From over across the waters," Albert, checking the coal basket, half-opined half-inquired.

"How the devil do you know!" Bayard smoothed over the newspaper with his hand. Perhaps Albert could read after all.

"That's where visitors come from," Albert, having seen the letter's foreign stamp, categorically observed.

Marveling, Bayard divined a need to add exactly *who* was coming from across the waters. But Albert's clairvoyance proved complete. "It Mr. William," he ventured evenly, picking up the half-empty scuttle. "Bout time too."

It was not clear whether this reproof was aimed at father or son, but the fact that Albert did not for a minute think it might be Ellen who was coming implied a view about the finality of Bayard's marriage that made him wonder if his own thinking on the subject was quite as clearly set out.

Not until Albert had left, ostensibly to refill the scuttle, did Bayard again pick up the paper, devouring the front page article with deep interest. The cat was among the pigeons at last! He would telephone Seneca in Washington that evening to get his views on the ruling's immediate outcome. Blue Hills must be hopping mad, the whole South must be; and suppressing a smile that was for Bayard broad, he peered at his watch and again his thoughts reverted to the impending visit.

*   *   *

JASMINE WAS IN the kitchen of Seneca's apartment, cutting up mushrooms, when the telephone rang.

"Isn't it marvelous?" She had instantly guessed her brother's purpose. Seneca was still at a meeting, she explained, and as they chatted, she was strongly tempted to mention the letter received that morning from New York. Her brother's advice would be invaluable. But she held back, saving it, like every special morsel, to share with Seneca first.

So Bayard filled the gap with news of William's impending visit. Jasmine was astonished to learn the boy was twenty-five; she had thought him about sixteen. Mention of Hollywood however met reserve. He might just as well have said the boy was going to be a nightclub entertainer. But at once Jasmine corrected herself. "It would be wonderful to have a star in the family," she enthused. "We'd be in a lot less danger of eclipse."

Returning to the preparation of her coq au vin, she reflected, turning the chicken pieces in the pan, that prejudice, such as she had just displayed about nightclubs and Hollywood, represented, in her case anyhow, a kind of snobbery, an instinctive shoring up of superiority along the lines laid out in her upbringing. There had been numerous others to get over—among them: class, color, even cooking. Moreover she was by nature a judgmental person, and where judgment and prejudice parted company, if in fact they ever really did, was not always possible to know. Only where Seneca was concerned was she beyond conceivable criticism. He alone, being the standard from which she took for everything a bearing, could do no wrong.

Jasmine was immensely happy. She had got by degrees what with all her heart she wanted. Not for the first time, but now it came when she was old enough to treasure it and, grasping its rare value, give herself up entirely to its nurture. All her interests were now bound up in Seneca's, were spawned by and developed out of them, so that what action might be selfless and what selfish was beyond definition, the two being indistinguishable.

In the face of such profound and uncritical devotion, eventually Seneca had let his own heart fly, for he was capable of it. He had even come to feel that Jasmine was a part of himself, even his best part, and he wondered mightily at it, marveling at the rewards, so unexpected, of a totally dedicated affection—its inherent vulnerability, so against his philosophy, being inevitably a part of the deal. In the truest sense theirs was a love affair, and the hothouse phase now past, the sacred plant flourished in glossy evergreen luster out of doors, blooming continuously.

Hearing the front door open, Jasmine hurried into the vestibule. They embraced as if they had been parted for days, not merely for a few lean hours, her own news producing an underlay of almost visible excitement as she drew him into the living room and mixed their drinks. But she spoke first of Seneca's day, and there was much of significance to hear.

Seneca was tired. He said it would take a long time for the Supreme Court ruling to be successfully applied. It would be a protracted fight at best. The South was bound to raise unshirted hell, and not for the first time either.

"And the meeting?" Jasmine waited breathlessly.

Several liberal party stalwarts had that afternoon assembled to initiate a discussion that would, they hoped, advance Seneca's name as a presidential nominee in 1956.

"A number of reservations were raised, which on the whole were highly sensible. The Dixiecrats may or may not disappear," he said of the break-away Southern faction. "But if they don't, a Southern candidate could save part of the Southern vote—so long as he doesn't appear too liberal. I thought about it on the way there, after the Court's decision was announced. Could I go through a presidential campaign and keep my mouth shut on questions about race, just dodge them all? Would I be able to do enough once in office to justify that reserve? Truman couldn't swing it." Seneca sipped his drink reflectively. "Sir Thomas More is a great hero of mine. He tried hard to avoid the issue of Catholicism and to get on with his career, but when it landed on his plate, he felt he had to take a stand. Doing so cost him his life. It would only cost me a few frostbitten laurels."

Jasmine felt both proud and disappointed. "Wait and see," she told him cheerfully. "You could be up there with Roosevelt and Lincoln. It's what this country needs." She drew her feet up under herself on the sofa, settling into a corner. It was her turn now.

"I had a letter today from somebody in New York, an art dealer who says he met me once at a Smithsonian do."

"Does he want you to persuade Bayard into getting richer?" The importance of Bayard's collection was becoming more widely known. He had sold a few pictures recently, and dealers were avidly hoping for the release of more.

Jasmine reached for her drink. "As a matter of fact it was about Frank."

Seneca seemed not to know for a minute who she meant.

"The man wanted to know if I had any of his pictures. He said Frank's work is attracting attention, and he was wondering if enough paintings existed for an exhibition. I didn't know this but there's a movement in Detroit to preserve all Frank's murals. Isn't that wonderful!"

"That's swell," said Seneca without enthusiasm.

Instantly Jasmine perceived her mistake. Seneca would never want Frank resurrected, especially famously. It was not in his nature. If it was to happen, therefore, she would have to manage it quietly and tactfully, without its intruding on their life in any way. But secretly she was thrilled. Frank might prove to have been a genius after all, and she the first one to have recognized it. That particular prejudice might turn out to be a correct judgment as well. How it would rejuvenate those years now thought of as a largely wasted adolescent dream, almost as the life of another person. Next week in Nashborough she would examine the crates stored in Madeleine's barn. There was easily enough there for an exhibition. More.

"When I see your mother next week, I'm going to warn her that her son could well be our next president," she told him.

Whenever she went to Nashborough, Jasmine always called on Miss Alice. Sitting beside the canopied bed, holding Miss Alice's hand, Jasmine talked to her of Washington life, but really she talked of Seneca's shining attributes, of his success in politics and of the respect with which he was held on both sides of the Senate, of his hard work to topple Senator McCarthy. Now she would be able to confide that he might be president of the United States.

Miss Alice had been quick to perceive the depth of Jasmine's attachment and how intensely she desired to please and cosset Seneca, who needed to be pleased and cosseted, and adored by a loving woman. Miss Alice had perceived all this with real relief, and though she did not speak of it directly, she had squeezed Jasmine's hand. "There never was a man who needed the devotion of a woman more."

But Miss Alice had her reservations, too, and at the prospect of her son becoming president, they increased. He had been blessed with personal happiness, and that was the most important thing in life. Miss Alice was immensely grateful to Jasmine for it. But how could Jasmine, whose policy was to agree with him in everything, provide the subtle guidance that from time to time he so badly needed and that only a wise and loving woman could provide? It was a vexing problem, and possibly one without any solution. Seneca hated to be crossed, most especially by those nearest him. Though merciful to a defeated opponent, family rebellion was like a stab in the back: He raged, counterattacked, and could not forgive. His mother's counsel penetrated only because the pattern was so early set. But with Jasmine, when such a need arose, mightn't he feel betrayed? Mightn't it badly backfire? Miss Alice patted Jasmine's hand with resignation, choosing to be grateful for benefits already solidly in place.

2

William Douglas's impending visit attracted even less notice than had his initial entry into the Douglas clan. Nobody knew him or really felt that he was kin, but when news of a Hollywood screen test got about, the young at least picked up their ears, and seeds of romantic curiosity were quickly sown.

William's interest in Nashborough was on a par with Nashborough's interest in him. He did not want to visit his father, who was not his father, and toward whom he felt a mild hostility—or was it uneasiness? He did not wish to meet strangers who had obscure and artificial claims on his attentions, pretending, like Bayard, to kinship—if in fact they did. But pretense being the core of his profession, he had firmly determined to play his Nashborough role with the same panache as if it were a major theatrical stage.

Meeting his son at the airport, putting forth his hand, Bayard experienced a sudden rush of kindly, even paternal, feeling mixed with an unexpected hope of congeniality.

Albert was introduced, and, noting the chauffeur's cap, William did not shake hands. In England one did not shake hands with servants, nor were they introduced. But he would have liked to shake this affable old man's hand, and handing over his baggage tickets, he smiled warmly at him. "There's rather a lot I'm afraid. I'd better give you a hand."

"Rather a lot" referred to a brass-bound wardrobe trunk on which considerable excess charges must have been paid. But William's hankering for clothes, or more correctly, costumes, was persistent and immense. His present attire, a white panama hat and three-piece vanilla-colored suit subtly tapered at the waist, though modern and probably from Savile Row, suggested a turn-of-the-century Southern planter, and passersby stared unselfconsciously at this more elegant and exotic version of themselves. Already William was easily turning heads.

His eye quick to rove and absorb, William stared with unconcealed disgust from the car window at the plethora of neon signs and plate glass lining the boulevard into town. The glittering mosaic ball above the Krystal amused him as unadulterated kitsch. But Blue Hills, its sprawling showy houses built in a mix of phony styles, struck him as vulgar and distastefully new-rich. It was the first suburb he'd ever seen.

Only on arrival at Bayard's white clapboard house, its picket fence and delicate fretwork veranda framed by a brambly arch of old roses, the shutters suggesting midnight at noon, did William finally smile. Here was manifest charm. Inside, the furniture's elegant simplicity bespoke a refined and unpretentious comfort, and the polished silver, muted chintz, and many fine pictures confirmed an optimum human scale of domesticity, at once graceful and devoid of any ostentation.

So that by the time Albert and William got the big wardrobe trunk into the upstairs bedroom, its maple four-poster bed covered with a pretty patchwork quilt, William had begun to experience a palpable lightness of heart. There was so much freshness in it all, yet there was a fine patina, too.

Reaching into his pocket, he gave Albert five one-dollar bills. It was the biggest tip Albert had ever got in his life and instantly secured his high approval of the young man, but not entirely for the obvious reason. A five dollar bill might have meant the young foreigner had made a mistake, and Albert would have felt obliged to give it back. But five ones settled the issue with exactitude and in the way it was obviously meant to be.

Although aware that his mother and Bayard, as he called his father, had in their youth collected pictures, William was astonished by their modernity and that so many were by truly famous artists. As he looked and asked questions, as the afternoon sun, pouring in through pretty chintz-framed sash windows, softened further the quietly elegant living room, and a tea table, gleaming with old silver and fine eggshell porcelain, was unexpectedly laid beside the fire, William's guarded reserve, his sense of coming from a superior metropolitan world into the provinces, began to thaw and break up like pack ice moving inexorably into warmer seas.

Madeleine Ames came to dinner, creating a welcome buffer since, despite their agreeable circuit about the house, father and son remained far from easy in each other's company.

Adroit and tactful, Madeleine focused first on William, as more likely to need it, though this was by no means evident. Actors had often been guests at the embassy in Paris and she recounted her childhood memory of meeting Sarah Bernhardt there. She had never forgotten, she said, the magic that Bernhardt conveyed through her sheer presence. It was something exceptional.

"What in retrospect do you put it down to?" William wanted to know, his imagination moving eagerly into a scene of the aging tragedian and tiny American girl greeting one another in the palatial embassy hall.

"Well it certainly wasn't because she was famous. I didn't know that till later. I think it was that she showed such remarkable serenity, the serenity of the truly powerful and secure, which is rare, and yes, awfully heady too. She made me see her as a great and indestructible queen, and it's my view that at that moment she believed it herself—and that's why it was so successful."

William was delighted by this answer. "You mean, she willed it!" The idea suited admirably his philosophy of acting, and to a degree also of life. But he too was falling under a spell, one of charming and unexpected civility, to which Albert's Beef Wellington and Bayard's 1937 Haut Brion (he was giving the occasion its due) added a rich texture of fine sensual pleasure. Perhaps the town wasn't such a backwater after all, and given Bayard's description of Sextet Stud, there was more than one horse in it too.

"When I was young, people didn't travel much." Bayard lit a cigar from one of the candles, now burning quite low. "But plays and ballets used to come to us on tour. Bernhardt came here. I never saw her; my parents did not go out. But I saw Nijinsky once and it seemed to me that he defied Newtonian physics. He hung suspended for what seemed ages, in midair, and we all held their breath as though we were underwater and he alone was in the air. It formed, I think, part of my attraction to the *Bateleurs* (as the Picasso in the living room was properly called).

"Nowadays plays no longer come to us; we must go to them, and I'm afraid not enough of us do."

Talk moved on to Europe and General Marshall's proposals to help the ailing continent back on its feet. Then Madeleine took her leave, and Bayard, pouring two brandies, pointed out to William which pictures he and Ellen had chosen together, and in William's view, they were some of the best.

"We were pretty well-off back then, and most adventurous painters were very poor: The scales were badly loaded against them. Today they have bigger promoters, and there's much more money in it."

William's Aunt Jasmine was in a fine position, Bayard explained. "She married an artist back in the Depression and they lived in Paris for a bit. Like most young painters, he never sold anything, so pretty soon they ran out of money and had to come back home. He was killed in the war. Now all of a sudden, his pictures are in demand. A dealer is backing him and there's going to be a big show in New York. So you see, life takes some unexpected turns. Back in the thirties he was a failure; today he's a much-sought-after precursor of abstract expressionism. His hour has finally come round."

"Without him, unfortunately." William didn't like that part one bit. Fame, like money, was to his mind chiefly utilitarian. It expanded power and therefore freedom. Who wanted to inherit money posthumously? Ditto celebrity. Mercifully, acting was a here and now affair, and those who were no longer "here," even if gloriously spoken of like Bernhardt, couldn't compete posthumously, as writers or painters or composers could. William congratulated himself on his choice of career.

"You'll meet some cousins your own age tomorrow," Bayard told him before they went to bed. A picnic at Blue Hills House was planned. House and grounds were closed to the public on Sundays and a special provision had been made to admit the Douglas family to the grounds.

"I won't be coming, just your Nash cousins, Flora and Sally, and Sally's husband. Oh, and Flora is bringing a friend, so there'll be one young woman, anyhow, who isn't kin." He said Albert would set things up and the Frazers would call for William at midday.

3

Studying her image in the full-length mirror, Ginevra Tuttle adjusted the bodice of her strapless cotton dress and reluctantly put on the matching short-sleeved bolero. Then she smoothed impatiently with both hands her short pale crop of hair that tended to frizz and go its own way. Her eyes, set wide apart, had of their own account and without aid from any facial expression, a mildly disapproving look; her brow, partly obscured by an unruly ruffle of bangs, showed nonetheless high prominence.

"I'm looking forward to it even if you're not," she announced defiantly to Flora, who sat glumly on the bed in her stocking feet. "I expect he'll be tall and dark with piercing green eyes. They say your uncle Bayard bought him in Chicago from some gypsies."

"I hear he's minute," said Flora. "And I think we're too dressed up for a picnic. We look silly." She was suddenly engulfed by loneliness. She often felt that way in company, but Ginevra's was generally an exception. Their talks and confidential exchanges over the years had succeeded, like the occasional good book, in getting Flora outside herself—enabling her to jump in and join up—and making a refreshing change from an otherwise circumscribed existence. But now, watching Ginevra's eager scrutiny of her appearance, and the ugly pink flush rising out of the strapless dress, Flora thought her trite and obscurely disloyal.

The two girls had often discussed the male sex and unanimously had deplored the female flirtation and pandering to its sensibilities so ingrained in Southern culture. To their minds the recipients weren't worth it.

"Well there *are* some men on this planet who're worth knowing," Ginevra continued, almost aggressively. "Where's your imagination, your sense of romance? He's played Hamlet for heaven sakes, in London."

"Twice."

"And he's been to Oxford." She pressed the springy hair down again in mild exasperation. "To put it bluntly, Flora, he's the first male our age to come through Nashborough with any worldly credentials. So stop being so resistant—so suspicious of people all the time.

"What's more, he's almost a Hollywood star," she pursued doggedly in the car. They were being waved through the gates of Blue Hills House by the watchman, and Flora, without making any reply, drove taciturnly up the winding gravel drive.

"Oh look," Ginevra breathed.

Under a big oak tree on the lawn, a table covered with a white cloth was laid with silver and crystal and floral porcelain. It glittered and sparkled in the pinpoints of sunlight streaming through the broad tree branches. Beside the tree trunk stood a big blue cooler.

"Wow! I've never picnicked sitting at a table before. You see, we're dressed right after all. Perfectly so, in fact."

"Uncle Bayard is really putting on the dog," Flora dryly observed, "making up for lost time. He must be feeling guilty."

"Are we early do you think?" The table, Ginevra had suddenly taken in, was alarmingly unpeopled. She had envisaged the others in place as she and Flora floated gracefully across the lawn in their pretty dresses, waving a little, like princesses.

Two loud squawks on a horn sounded behind them. Ginevra jumped. Half-turning, she spied the Frazers' station wagon. Small hands were sticking out like hat pins from a big pin cushion.

"Damn, they've brought their children!" cried Flora glancing in the rearview mirror. "They're spoiled rotten and she can't control them."

Flora parked the car at the side of the house so as not to block a view of it from the lawn. Sally followed suit. In the back of the crowded station wagon, they glimpsed a brooding countenance squashed beside two of Sally's boys.

The young women got out quickly, Ginevra smoothing her full skirt and Flora scowling in marked disapproval as the Frazers noisily disgorged. William, of necessity, was the last to get out, which only increased an awkward feeling of suspense, as if they were waiting with some uncertainty for a show to begin.

Flora saw that he was ill pleased and making no effort to hide it. She didn't blame him, and insofar as Flora ever smiled, she smiled in sympathy as they rapidly took each other in.

"Cousin Flora, Cousin William," Jack offered by way of introduction. William still stood by Sally's car, and moving forward, Flora shook hands and introduced Ginevra, who was suddenly very formal and reserved.

William was indeed small, not much taller than the girls themselves, but a lithe elegance pervaded his diminutive being. The slant of almond eyes, the finely sculpted nose, dark skin, and very dark straight hair looked foreign and therefore of enormous distinction. His linen suit had been badly rumpled during the short but riotous journey, and he carried a wide-brimmed hat.

A fixed incuriosity pervaded his manner as he stepped forward for a better look at the house, examined it with a grim and narrow-eyed contemplation, then abruptly turned his back on it.

Not my idea of Hamlet, Flora thought and, remembering the Mongolian spot, wondered if the Chicago gypsies might have either kidnapped him or bought him cheaply from some coolies working on the railroad tracks.

"Now that looks mighty fine!" declared Jack of the well-laid table. "My orders are to tend the bar and Sally'll see to the grub." He turned to his children. "Hey y'all kids. Round up and fall in!"

Surprisingly they did so in a line from big to small.

"I had to bring them," Sally apologized, laughing. "I couldn't find a kennel. But they'll sit down at one end and you won't notice them," she promised as they descended the lawn.

"Hey, this is a swell campsite," said Jack. "Plenty of cold champagne and no mosquitoes. You know it's mighty accommodating of mosquitoes not to eat their dinner till the evening."

Flora saw on William's face the finest hairline of a smile.

"Or Nature is fattening us up for them first," Ginevra rejoined, with a quick sidewise glance at their guest.

As self-appointed hosts, Jack and Sally did most of the talking, punctuated by commands to the far end of the table. "Eat it anyway. Wipe your face. Don't hit your brother so hard." But when William spoke, which was infrequent, everyone, even the children, stopped and listened. Of course they all wanted to hear about Hollywood, but as yet William himself knew nothing, and said so. His beautifully cadenced voice, when he elected to use it, his polish, his evident poise, intimidated as much as it impressed. Not for a second could they think of him as a relation. He was far too exotic and they dull and parochial by comparison.

Or the women thought so. Jack saw a pretty boy in fancy dress, but he was pleased nonetheless that whenever he himself spoke, he got William's full attention.

"A real showhorse," he said later to Sally. "Too prancy ever to pull a plow. I hope he won't run short of oats out there in Hollywood. Even grass is hard tack to a stable-kept specimen like that."

"Oh he does have style and he's very attractive, very sophisticated." Sally was combing out her hair in front of the dressing table mirror. "Something about him makes me uneasy though. He's not trustworthy I think. A woman can always tell."

"Well I'm mighty glad then they don't practice law. Knowing who's innocent and who's guilty without ever going into court, now that would be bad for business."

Having collected their brood for afternoon naps, Sally and Jack had departed after lunch, the two girls promising to drive William home. He looked relieved as the station wagon full of small, scrambling and shouting bodies drove away, merrily honking good-byes.

Then, glasses in hand and smoking cigarettes, the threesome strolled about the grounds. William asked Flora if she had been inside the house.

"Not since it became a museum. I can't remember before that. It was empty for years, you know, after it was confiscated."

William crushed his cigarette under an impeccably polished shoe. "Was Bayard crooked do you think?" he asked abruptly.

The bluntness of the question, its crudeness, pulled Flora up. "Uncle Bayard's no more crooked than that drainpipe over there. He got overextended, that's all. Everybody knows that." Whether true or not, this indeed was the established position throughout Blue Hills, endorsed by one and all.

"I've seen some photographs of inside, taken back in the thirties," William continued, apparently satisfied by his cousin's answer. "I imagine it's much changed." And stepping forward he casually tried a couple of windows, but found them solidly shut.

"You could shimmy up the drainpipe," Flora said deadpan.

William and Ginevra were standing side by side, their faces against the dark glass. The inside curtains were drawn. They had just discovered they were out of cigarettes.

"Mine are in the car," Ginevra volunteered. "I'll be right back."

William and Flora stood waiting uneasily, Flora awkwardly holding an empty glass, William leaning in a posed study against a wooden bench. Suddenly a curious expression lit his face. He stood upright, strode purposefully over to the house, and with a wry almost cocky smile at Flora, peeled off his jacket, dropped it casually on the ground, and, embracing the drainpipe, began to climb it with the ease of an island boy going up a coconut tree.

Reaching out with one hand for a balcony baluster, he let go the drainpipe, grabbed the balusters with both hands, and, hanging perilously, swung back and forth to get momentum. Then in one graceful movement he threw a leg over the ledge and catapulted onto the balcony with the agility of an accomplished cat burglar.

Flora, pale with relief, quickly collected his jacket and was nervously brushing it off when the window beside her flew up.

"*Entrez.*" William was smiling a little.

Hiding her astonishment, she climbed, with his help, inside, still holding on to his jacket.

William shut the window. They were standing in what had been Bayard and Ellen's drawing room, the room where the best breezes of summer were always found, the room where William's arrival in the Douglas family had been announced so emotionally by Clara, her apron over her head, twenty-five years before. But the beiges and pinks and soft, faded blues of the aubusson-tapestried furniture, of Picasso's acrobats grouped serenely over the mantelpiece and staring so inscrutably into space, were gone. The room was now a parlor in the Southern antebellum style, furnished in a mix of Federal and Victorian furniture, and with a big floral-patterned carpet on the floor. Steely blue damask covered the rosewood settees and chairs, their undulating frames adorned with ornately carved displays of flowers and fruit. Blue damask, dripping a heavy icing of fringe, also framed the high windows, the pelmets carefully pleated in great crescent loops. A large gilt mirror replaced the Picasso, and a series of English sporting prints hung where Klee's notorious platter of fish had been on view.

William made a face. "Victorian propriety and gloom. I thought Southern planters led a more riotous and unconstricted life." He had flung himself down on one of the settees, sprawling at an angle to counter its demanding upright lines. His movements Flora had begun to liken to a sleek and prowling leopard. She was fascinated.

"In my day here—all one and a half years of it," he told her, "everything was French. *Grace à Mamma*, it was light and pleasant and elegant. But then Mamma did a bunk." He looked at Flora closely. "*She* must have thought he was a crook."

There was a pause. Flora was without any reply.

"It could be of course she was mistaken," he went on. "She's a highly moral woman is my mother, very finely tuned in that department, impeccable standards. I remember she spanked me once for exaggerating. She said I'd told a lie. That spanking made a big impression, but not the one she intended. I was simply more careful after that. Anyhow, what is a lie? 'Tis but the truth in masquerade,' " he quoted.

Flora wanted to say that Ginevra would be looking for them, but didn't. There was such magic in their invasion of the heavily draped and shadow-laden house, like entering a walled and secret garden. The very act had created a mysterious world preciously suspended in time. Ginevra would have to wait.

William got to his feet with an elastic leap. "Come on. Let's explore.

"To think I might have grown up here," he went on speculatively as they entered the Wedgwood dining room, its color drawn from bisque medallions inlaid in the marble mantelpiece.

Flora still held his jacket, both arms hugging it. The Hepplewhite dining table and once-pawned silver candelabra, on loan from Bayard, stood under a magnificent crystal chandelier, its pendants obscurely glittering like heavy icicles in a sunlit cave.

"I would have been a very different person, I suppose. It's interesting to think about, isn't it: the possibility of other lives. I've been dispossessed of quite a few, you know. Whack whack," he made a sharp scything motion with his arm, then perched lightly upon the dining table.

"Was it so awful to find you were adopted?" She looked at him with great seriousness. "I sometimes feel I was. That this isn't my real home."

"You mean you don't fit. Well I thought I did fit. Illusion number one. I was almost grown and within reach of a title and a fine inheritance when I found out the truth. Yes, to answer your question, I confess I was knocked for six."

"If you'd stayed here, you would have found out earlier, someone would have told you, because too many people knew. Maybe that would have been easier. Nobody would have thought any more about it, and you wouldn't have expected a title. You could have just made the most of what you had."

"Precisely my decision, in any case." He slid gracefully off the table and, moving restlessly about the room, examined the bits of Wedgwood china displayed on console tables and the broad sideboard.

"Would you like to see my birthmark?" he asked her suddenly. "It's the only real credential I possess." Before she could answer he had removed his waistcoat and pulled up the back of his shirt. "It seems I am Chinese."

Flora, still holding the linen jacket, inspected the inky mark, grown so much smaller with time. "Blue blood," she offered gravely, sorely tempted to touch it.

"You think so?" For the first time he gave her a direct smile. "I see you have some imagination, and considerable tact." Flourishing the waistcoat he made a matador-like bow and put it back on, his shirt still hanging out. "It may be I am descended from the emperor of China." Glancing into the overmantel mirror, he stretched his already slanting eyes and bit his lower lip, grimacing to show his teeth. "The last one was deposed you know. His name is Harry Pugh. He was translated into a commoner by the communists. An interesting, inverse fate. I may be his younger brother. The family is now in so much disarray.

"Or else I am simply no one in particular—an impostor, a cuckoo in a nest that in any case is about to disappear. Mind you, there's freedom in that, the freedom to pick and choose. It's the whole basis of my profession. I try on new roles like other people try new hats. I can reinvent myself at will. I can raise the dead, bring kings and princes back to life, and breathe life into people who have never lived. Or I can impersonate the living."

He suddenly struck a limp angular posture, his weight transferred on to his heels. "That's a swell vest you're invested in there, Cousin Bill. Do they wear them thangs all the time over in England? It must git pretty hot, just like we do here under the collar."

Flora laughed out loud. It was a perfect mimicry of Jack. So that was why William had attended him so closely.

"I like him, mind you; he's a decent chap; and I don't like all the chaps I play, though I'm best, I think, with some of the worst. One day I'll play Richard III. I could do wonders with him."

William had stepped forward as though leaving a stage. "So, as you see, ultimately I'm whomever or whatever I choose to make myself. Ultimately I am perhaps a fiction, and that provokes a fashionably existential question. Do I then in fact exist?"

Glancing into the mirror again he casually tucked his shirttail in. "Why am I telling you all this? I think it's because you're so quiet, quite a deep one perhaps. And of course we're cousins. More fiction. You're very pretty you know."

He had seemed so sure of himself and yet his narrative largely belied it. Was his fine self-assurance simply another role, an attitude carefully, strenuously held in place by concentrated effort? Flora understood well putting a face on things, constructing an impromptu mask, and how difficult it was to hold—how stressful, as a result, social life could be.

"When I was little I used to pretend I was a cowboy. I had some big adventures riding across the range on my pony and fighting my enemies— the pony was real. I haven't enjoyed anything so much since." She blushed. The admission not only astonished her, but it sounded so silly, so childishly absurd.

"Come!" He nodded toward the double doors and going out into the hall they went upstairs. Again Ginevra passed uneasily through Flora's mind, to be again suppressed. Amends could be made later on.

The upstairs bedrooms were decorated with bright floral wallpaper, mahagony washstands, and huge highly polished Victorian beds. William thought the house surprisingly small and said so.

How big was Elderest, then, Flora wanted to know. Blue Hills House was one of the biggest houses in Nashborough, and probably in the South.

"Oh ten, twelve, fourteen bedrooms. I never counted. And I won't bother now. When my grandfather dies my mother will be out on her ear, and me along with her. But by then I shall be rich and famous. I'll buy another place like Elderest, so it doesn't really matter. For the present we are poised for transit, so to speak."

William had picked up a little Dresden statue of a lady in a bell skirt, her arms upraised like an actress taking a bow. Next thing it was on the floor, the uplifted arms broken off. He picked the figurine up, pocketing the broken pieces. "She is improved, I think: Venus de Milo instead of a simpering shepherdess. Will anyone notice I wonder?" He replaced the figure on the table. "Probably not."

They trailed back down the famous unsupported staircase spiraling out at the base like an open fan. At the bottom Flora offered him his jacket, holding it up for him to slip into. But pivoting suddenly, he wrapped the jacket backward around her, swaddling her playfully with it; and thus imprisoned, he kissed her on the mouth. "We are, I gather, kissing kin," he said with a small smile, unwrapping the badly creased jacket and putting it on without her help.

Flora had thought of giving him a slap, but sympathy and fascination stopped her. Besides it was part of the play. They were in a playhouse, the excitement and sense of conspiracy uniting them against the common enemy of reality, which, as displaced persons, they both felt some hostility toward.

"Maybe I'll marry you," he cheerfully declared as they exited through the drawing room window. "Then you'd be a double Douglas, and I'd be a bona fide in-law, instead of an outlaw, as now."

Ginevra was sitting on the front steps, her back against a column. She had taken off her bolero and was smoking a cigarette, her mildly critical look having deepened into an unpleasant scowl. She did not move when they rounded the corner of the house. Flora was looking apologetic and William, hands in his pockets, maddeningly nonchalant.

"We managed to get inside," said Flora hesitantly by way of explanation. "William wanted to see the house. He couldn't remember it, so we broke in and made a little tour."

Ginevra looked up at her friend with contempt.

"What about those cigarettes?" asked William cheerfully.

Reluctantly Ginevra extracted the cigarettes from her bag. She did not offer one to Flora, who did not ask; but as William was lighting his, Ginevra looked hard at them both, first one, then the other. Flora, flushed and smiling, was watching William too. Ginevra's scowl blackened.

*   *   *

THE FOLLOWING WEEK was a round of summer parties and dances. It was the debutante season, and William's presence added novelty and excitement in the too-familiar crowd. He was much feted and much flirted with, his genial urbane manner easily hypnotizing his young audience. He could discuss existentialism and quote Byron and T. S. Eliot, which impressed them greatly, and he was the best dancer anyone had ever met.

Nonsocial by nature Flora went along to the parties almost as a voyeur, watching with pleasure as the girls admired William's good looks and polished English style—as they flirted with him so unabashedly.

To her surprise, however, though clearly enjoying the attention awarded him, William announced that he found Southern belles annoying. They were fraudulent creatures, he said, their flirtation an empty titillation, soliciting male attention solely to feed their vanity. They gave small satisfaction to the easily scalped young men.

Madeleine Ames had smiled on hearing this, saying it was all part of the tradition of courtly love and could in fact be very pleasant.

"Then the troubadour's role is not for me," William had quickly answered. "Like these Southern belles, actors prefer getting attention over having to give it. We have our vanity to attend to too.

"Besides, they're all so ignorant," he continued irritably to Flora the next evening, sitting out on the country club front steps, despite the drizzly weather. "They don't read. Most of them have never seen a play. They watch television and go to the cinema. That's about it. Their houses are furnished with great care but their minds are virtually empty—paupers' residences. Yet they're so self-satisfied, so protected by their imagined superiority, so appallingly provincial."

Flora wondered painfully whether he had been rebuffed by one of the girls. She recalled Sally Ann James smirking and whispering to another debutante in a corner of the ballroom. Both had looked over at William, wide eyed and smiling smugly.

But perhaps not, because he surely would have told her. He'd confided that he regarded her as his private diary, where he recorded all his real impressions, communicated to her alone. "We're both of us mavericks," he told her. "Neither of us belongs."

But if neither of them belonged, at least William knew where he was going. He had a fondness for his pretty cousin, so touchingly vulnerable behind her fierce and self-protective wall of Douglas pride. She was witty too in the sad way true clowns are. He had contemplated seduction but instantly perceived the foolishness of blotting as it were the family album and causing embarrassment to Bayard and his mother. There would be plenty of starlets in Hollywood to seduce. In any case, his heart was well sheathed in a shining scabbard of ambition, and he stood inviolable; behind his heavy shield of rational motivation and control.

That Flora might develop a plan of her own however—a desperate battle tactic of the severely beleaguered—that he might be caught off guard, did not occur to him.

Later that same night, Flora came upon him in a private dining room— the door was partly open—locked in the arms of Sally Ann James. A fierce urgency pervaded the encounter. Sally Ann was roughly pressed against the wall. They seemed almost to be fighting.

Turmoil such as Flora had never experienced descended like a thunder-clap, wrecking a tranquil mind absorbed in happy fantasies. She felt bitterly betrayed. It was unreasonable, but then feelings by definition were unreasonable. But her hold on William, she was forced to see, was tenuous at best, their intimacy a single thread among so many in the fabric of his active life. He had told her she was pretty, that she had imagination, that they were mavericks marooned together on an alien isle. Even that he might marry her. Yet none of it bound them or had meant anything much at all. Suddenly Flora was terrified. She was she saw as vulnerable as a slug. And as a further catastrophe her desire awoke. But she said nothing and he had no idea she'd seen him with Sally Ann James, or its effect on her.

Dartania however noticed her daughter's silent preoccupation and rightly guessed some of its cause.

"I like Cousin William," she told her, as they were walking in the back pasture to look at a new foal. "He's been well brought up and he has good manners."

"Good manners!" Flora repeated indignantly. "He's a star!"

"Well, he's certainly handsome," Dartania continued pleasantly. "He's got those gypsy good looks."

Flora perked up. "Some people say he is one."

"He's no more gypsy than I am. He's from a Chicago orphanage," said Dartania, as though the fact established a known lineage.

"He's got a Mongolian spot."

"There are no Chinese gypsies," said Dartania, offering the proof of the pudding. "Besides, he's your cousin now. You were raised in the same family and that makes a difference. But the English sometimes need a little encouragement. The boys and girls go to separate schools, so they're shy with each other."

"How would you know?" Flora replied dismissively, even a trifle rudely. "You never had an English boyfriend."

"Don't say 'boyfriend,' it's so common. Yes, I once had an English beau."
Dartania gave a little smile.

Flora felt somewhat upstaged. "Well, why didn't you marry him then?"

"Why didn't I marry him? I didn't marry him because I was in love with
your father."

"Henry!" cried Flora of her father, in disbelief. Love must be blind indeed.

"Men sometimes need a little encouragement," said Dartania, continuing
her point, "before they'll commit themselves, or take a risk. Going out on a
limb must look like it's worth it, after all." She thought Flora's natural reticence might easily pass for indifference, and a small gesture of personal
interest not go amiss.

"I can tell he likes you," she went on, having decided her daughter needed
a bit of encouragement too.

"Can you?" The tone sounded unbelieving, but Flora felt lifted on air.

"Confidence is the thing," her mother said. "So much in life is a trick of
confidence."

"Where does it come from though?"

"You have to be brave. Just shut your eyes and jump. As I said, it's a trick."

Flora shivered. "I'm not brave," she said forlornly.

"If you want something badly enough you will be." Dartania made it
sound so easy. "You won't have much choice. If you don't risk failing, you
fail anyhow. Better to have tried," she added buoyantly.

Frowning, Flora regarded her mother with a grain of new respect. Her
cavalier style was a bit more "with it" than she had suspected. What she'd
said made good sense; it was even logical. Closing her eyes tight, Flora then
and there made up her mind: She swore that she would jump. If she failed
there was always suicide.

That Sunday, William's last day in Nashborough, Flora and William
returned as a lark to Blue Hills House, taking a bottle of whiskey pinched
from Bayard's cabinet and again breaking into the house, the sash window
having not yet been secured.

Drinks in the Victorian parlor were followed by drinks in the oak-paneled
library, by drinks wandering proprietorily through the house.

In what had been Ellen's shell-pink bedroom, now covered with wallpaper printed with red twining roses, Flora, her heart trembling with desire
and fear, sat down matter-of-factly on the Victorian bed and, methodically
taking off her clothes, stretched out upon it naked.

This was not at all the sort of encouragement her mother had in mind.

And what could William do? As a gentleman, he was morally obliged to
accept so generous an offer, and willingly he did so.

Afterward there were bloodstains on the white bedspread. William was alarmed and for more reasons than one, but Flora, to his amazement, appeared not in the least perturbed. She pulled the cotton bedspread off the bed, casually rolled it up, then scribbled a cryptic note, "At the cleaners," and took the bedspread with them, saying she would send it back anonymously in the mail. At most it would mystify.

They were silent in the car. As he was leaving next day there was little to say, except that he would write to her. There was nothing for her to say except that she wished him success. But having played her hand to the fullest, she would, she believed, be left with an emotional scrap to gnaw in the ensuing famine.

At Bayard's, Madeleine was there, and Flora came in briefly. She was even more silent than usual, and William more ebullient and good humored. So that Bayard remarked to Madeleine a little later how much the boy seemed to have enjoyed himself and been made to feel at home.

Madeleine, lighting a final cigarette, observed offhand that Flora was more than a little taken with her glamorous cousin.

"Nonsense. Flora is never taken with anybody, or taken in by anybody, either. The girl's completely walled in, looking out at life through an *archere*."

"I know a lovesick girl when I see one." Madeleine held on amiably to her point. "They droop like forlorn puppies but inside they are absolute tigers, believe me."

"Well," said Bayard, finishing his whiskey, "I'm glad I never knew it. You women are an untrustworthy lot. I've always said as much."

"We don't want to scare you off by holding up mirrors," Madeleine smilingly replied, adding almost sadly, "but oh dear, we're all such pawns in Nature's relentless reproduction game. Poor Flora. If William hadn't come along, someone else would have. But he has come along and so she has no choice, right now anyhow, but to see it through. Probably she's fighting for her life." Madeleine paused, weighing whether or not to go on with her developing line of thought. Clasping her hands together, she leaned back in the chair.

"And frankly, as attractive and interesting as I find your son, I'm sorry for Flora, because it's my belief he'll make any woman suffer. Adopted children usually do. Having begun life by being abandoned, they can never really trust."

"Oh, Ellen's attentions will have mitigated that, even if mine have not. He's been spoiled rotten at Elderest, treated like an Olympian god."

"My dear, the mark is indelible. Like Cain's it's beyond erasure."

"Then that goddamned inheritance business is to blame. But for that, he need never have known."

"You know, I used to wonder why people compared the world to an oyster, and in such inviting tones. Why an oyster of all things? But now I think it's because, with a bit of grit, there's always the chance to spin one's life into a pearl. I do so hope that Flora succeeds."

"And William is only a bit of grit?"

"Well, dear, he is in Flora's little world, since a pearl is the most that one can hope for, I'm afraid."

4

....

William wrote to Flora three times during the next six months, and on each occasion Flora answered at once, then woke up every morning afterward vainly hoping for another letter on the breakfast table. At least it got her up in the mornings. William's first letter announced his screen test was a success: He was photogenic—in other words, more appealing in two dimensions than in three—and on screen he had looked six feet tall. The upshot was he'd been offered the part he was scouted for in London. The movie would star no less than Gary Cooper. He would play Cooper's son Luke, and his agent was asking for "thousands of lovely greenbacks."

Flora was ecstatic and could think of nothing else. Her dissolute study habits slumped to a new low. She dreamed and dreamed, an unrepining princess in a cloud-bound tower, awaiting, if vaguely, her eventual release.

"Tira lira by the river sang Sir Lancelot." Flora hummed and smiled. Her dreams, wrapped in this cloudy euphoria, were far from specific, dwelling more on visions of William than of the two of them together. She too had enshrined him on a screen. But dreaming was the diet that from childhood had most nourished her.

A few months later William wrote to say the movie was completed. It was "in the can," which was very different from "being canned," or would be so long as it got out, which should happen sometime before Christmas, and to look out for it. He said it was called *Luke*, which was quite a leg up; that they had nearly called it *Luke Comes Home*, but at the last minute thought it sounded too much like *Lassie*. However, some of the studio bosses had liked that: They believed it might sell more tickets.

"Hollywood is pure artifice," he wrote. "Only the movie screen has reality. I am projected, therefore I am." He said she was still his diary (the letter began "Dear Diary"), and that often, in his mind, he told her what was happening, even though he was negligent in putting it on paper. He would stay in Hollywood till the film's premiere, which was going to be at Grauman's Chinese Theatre; then he was off to England for Christmas, but hoped to stop in Nashborough on the way. He was going to write to Bayard about it.

Flora went out and bought a calendar, the type where one sheet is torn off each day to reveal the next. In this way time could be physically disposed of with some satisfaction and the days invested with a useful and definite purpose.

The movie, which came out in November, was immediately a success. Gary Cooper was too great a figure to be overshadowed, but William in the role of a disaffected son whose widowed, ranch-owning father is far too nice, captured in his own right a big slice of the public's imagination. In next to no time a contract had been negotiated with Paramount and William was engaged for three years on what seemed by any standards a stupendous salary. He telephoned Bayard to ask if he might come for Christmas, in between films, as the next one would start shooting in January.

All Nashborough flocked to see Luke. They would have done so in any case, because of Gary Cooper, but William's performance made a profound impression; it was so convincing—and the younger generation was agog at the thought of his celebrity.

Investing in a chocolate milkshake for cover, Flora combed surreptitiously through the movie magazines in Kidd's Drug Store. She found two interviews, some romantically handsome studio portraits, and a picture of William at a party hugging a buxom starlet. Both looked drunk but the caption said that they would probably marry. Flora stopped looking.

Then two weeks before Christmas a glossy Christmas card arrived. Its caption read, "All I want for Christmas," and there was a dotted line on which to write the answer. William had written "to see you, so much to say."

Flora had her hair cut and bought a blue velvet dress, which Ginevra said was definitely not her color. But then Ginevra couldn't be trusted these days. Flora had simply shrugged and turned away, rather grandly, twirling an imaginary train.

"Movie Star in Nashborough for Christmas," the *Echo*'s front page proudly announced. Having said William was the son of Bayard Douglas, and touching cryptically on his English education, the paper said that Nashborough claimed him unequivocally as her own. He was a red carnation in the city's buttonhole.

Local radio and TV stations telephoned Bayard to arrange interviews in advance, but he of course would tell them nothing. He was mightily surprised therefore when, on William's arrival, a scrum of photographers and newspapermen, cameras blazing, blocked the airport gate. Later there was even a man with a camera prowling about in the shrubbery outside Bayard's house.

"My congratulations on your celebrity." There was only the finest irony in the remark, for William's thespian abilities had genuinely impressed his father, and the part of disaffected son had been convincing enough to make him a bit uneasy. No pearls without grit, he recalled, however, mildly congratulating himself.

"What did you think, Albert?" asked William, as they tussled on the stairs with William's wardrobe trunk.

"I ain't seen it yet, Mr. William."

"Then I will get you a ticket tomorrow. In fact I shall reserve a box, if they have any." It had not registered with William that blacks were required by law to sit in the balcony.

"I seen *Bambi*," Albert said, politely deflecting this awkward point with mention of the only movie he in fact had seen. "That was a right sad picture show." They had set the trunk down at the top of the stairs to catch their breath. "And I seen Mr. Gary Cooper on TV. I guess he could play Mr. Bayard right good."

This wonderful connection, with its sliding perceptions of reality, took William a minute to work out. Perhaps at some deep psychological level there was even a truth obscurely buried in it.

TWO DAYS AFTER William's arrival, an equally newsworthy if less triumphant return graced Nashborough's recently enlarged airport.

Shortly before William's movie was released, Seneca had been defeated for reelection to the United States Senate. Courting the Northern black vote, which was now considerable, the Democrats had openly committed themselves to civil rights reform, and Seneca, uniquely, had refused to sign a manifesto of elected Southerners dissenting from this decision. As a result the state welcomed its first Republican senator since Reconstruction, and the revered general and distinguished senator, his presidential bid a pile of ashes, came home, now covertly referred to as a "nigger lover."

Standing in the dogtrot at Longwood, Seneca looked grimly about. The house, unchanged since his marriage except for growing disrepair, seemed suddenly smaller. He felt as if the walls pressed literally inward as he heard the door of this familiar cage clang shut. A prisoner in his own home. What was worse, it was a prison he was largely responsible for building. Despair, at first inchoate, mushroomed into an ugly cloud, while at the same time, failure and dissatisfaction stung like hornets trapped inside his shirt.

Flora, coming downstairs, gave him a cautious kiss. "Eleanor's playing cards," she announced as they entered the shabby gun room. A leak in the ceiling had left a peppery fuzz beside the fireplace, together with a smudged rectangular outline of the portrait that had hung there. The gun cabinet had a broken pane where James had put a broom handle through it. Seneca's old armchair, almost bottomless had been rebuilt by a pile of lumpy cushions. It was covered in animal hairs.

"Out," he ordered the recalcitrant spaniel, pulling it off by the collar and giving the animal a whack.

Flora made her father a drink, and sitting down on the sofa opposite, longed to cheer him up, but could think of nothing to say that would interest him. He was so critical of whatever she said or did, always judging her, finding her wanting and telling her she ought to do better, inferring a discredit to him, that she was all the more stilted and uneasy when around him. Yet she sensed his awful loneliness and was grieved her company gave no relief.

"William's here for Christmas," was all she could find to say, then had to explain who William was.

Seneca recalled the infant in a frilly white dress reposing on Ellen's lap like a piece of overly icing wedding cake. He had not known of William's movie but managed a polite inquiry about it before, his mind moving on to other things, he got up to examine the letters on his desk. The telephone rang and it was Pete Weaver calling to welcome him home.

Wrinkling her nose distastefully, Flora handed her father the receiver. "Your understudy." The law firm's welcome was she knew wholehearted: Seneca drew clients in a way the others could not. Pete had openly admitted that.

Among the letters on Seneca's desk was one from the Reverend Robin Douglas. The two men, now on so much easier terms, had even evolved a sort of first-name relationship, in that Seneca was "Senator" and Robin Douglas "Reverend." Both titles, affectionately applied, retained an inbuilt reserve, requiring only a change in tone to restore professional formality.

The reverend's letter welcomed him home too, and it also had a purpose. "You're going to be a lot more useful to the movement without political handcuffs on," Douglas assured him. "Congress is at last committed to civil rights. They've woken up, so that side will begin to take care of itself. But at grassroots level things are bleak—they are antediluvian in fact.

"Ours is the greatest moral fight this country has seen since the Civil War, and we want you with us, General. You have immense prestige in this state, and now that you can speak out freely, people will listen and allow themselves to be influenced."

Seneca liked, as he knew he was meant to, the implication, in being addressed as general, that he might lead them into battle. But though offered the part of Joshua, he concluded, amused, that Douglas was rightly saving the omnipotent role of Moses for himself.

As soon as Flora left the room, Seneca telephoned Jasmine. He badly needed cheering up. So for that matter did Jasmine, yet for her part, simply hearing his voice appeared miraculously to do the trick. She told him Madeleine had offered to let Dell Cottage, as the former shack was now called, and that with some refeathering, she could live there perfectly comfortably. It would make, as before, an ideal meeting place.

In fact Jasmine disliked Nashborough, she had no occupation, and now she would see a great deal less of Seneca, when for the past six years they had lived more or less together, with considerable discretion, as a couple.

Though she did not say so, however, she did have one good reason to be pleased. She had that morning received a very substantial check. The Museum of Modern Art had bought two of Frank's big paintings, assuring him thereby a firm plantation in the fluctuating climate of contemporary art. Some two dozen other paintings had been sold at the exhibition, and Jasmine was in possession of many more. Their value could only go up, she was advised. Though delighted by this success, she tried never to think of Frank himself, and out of loyalty to Seneca, she had not attended the New York exhibition.

"What's for dinner?" Seneca asked Delphine, drumming up a jovial interest after she had warmly welcomed him home.

"Pork chops and turnip greens."

Not what he was used to, but he had grown up on it, and suddenly it sounded good. He would go to his office next morning, sort the place out, and then he would take stock. At fifty-five, surely he could not have come full circle, his life merely biting its tail, blatantly spelling zero. But if this in fact was all, what could he claim to have accomplished? Well, he had helped to win the war, but then who in his generation had not?

5

*D*addy, this is William." Flora seemed not to breathe, as if a sudden monsoon, inevitable and unstoppable, sweeping toward them across the horizon, made drowning probable.

Seneca had by now heard much—too much—of William Douglas. The newspapers were full of him and even Dartania said what a good-looking and attractive fellow he was. Pete Weaver spoke of him often—and abusively— saying he was a show-off, a lightweight, and probably a drunk. While Jasmine, who had seen *Luke*, deemed him a wonderful actor, "utterly convincing and with true magnetism."

Then a report had come in that made the present meeting, hazardous in the best of circumstances, hugely precarious.

During William's few days in Nashborough, he and Flora had been constantly together, and unable to risk a hotel room, they had made Blue Hills House their private trysting place. Unlatching a scullery window with Flora's nail file made repeated entry easy. They made love in all the bedrooms, they drank a lot of whiskey, they even brought in picnics, sitting down at the Hepplewhite dining table and eating off Meissen dessert plates on special display as at a Christmas banquet; they were always careful to tidy up everything afterwards. They had correctly surmised moreover that by getting *in* the beds no one would discover they had been there, having no reason to look beneath the neatly smoothed-out spreads.

Though Flora willingly followed William into any piece of mischief, being full of invention, she also initiated pranks, so that an element of mutual daring, beginning with William's nimble drainpipe ascent—initially Flora's idea—loomed fairly large in their relationship.

But on the fourth night, fast asleep in their favorite bed, its tall rosewood paneling framed by carved birds poised as for flight, something unforeseen had happened. They were awoken suddenly by a blinding light.

"Git up out of there!" a male voice shouted.

The pair sat bolt upright under the coverlet, pulling it up around them.

"Git up out of there and gitcha clothes on. You got two minutes. You heah me now." The watchman left the room, slamming the bedroom door behind him.

In the dark, they felt for each other's hands and squeezed hard. "We better hurry," Flora whispered, leaping out of bed. Both knew adverse publicity could easily destroy William's fledging career. Hollywood stars could marry a hundred times but they must be known only to sleep with their wives. Nor did they break into houses. If William was prosecuted, there would not only be bad publicity but a plethora of embarrassing innuendo.

"I'm going to buy the fellow off," William whispered hotly, but Flora, buttoning her silk blouse, gravely shook her head. "Don't try it," she gently advised. "He's probably religious."

As they emerged, the watchman again shined the flashlight blindingly into their faces, then switched on an ordinary overhead light. He was an elderly man, hunched and white haired and clearly very much affronted. Flora noted a slight palsy in his movements, and that his uniform fit badly, as if recently inherited from a predecessor.

"You're going straight down to the police station," the old man hoarsely rasped out.

Flora, her hands clasped together, spoke out with quiet dignity. "I'm Mr. Douglas's niece," she said. "Mr. Douglas, who used to own this place. I knew it as a child and I wanted to show it to my friend from out of town. It was wrong of me I know. I'm afraid we had too much to drink, and then we just sort of fell asleep."

"You Senator Douglas's girl then?" asked the astonished watchman.

The reluctance in her acknowledgment could not be missed.

"And who's this here?"

"Just an acquaintance, passing through. But it was my idea to come here. He doesn't know this town; he hasn't ever been here before." Flora decided to go for broke, to focus the blame entirely on herself in order to save William. "I met him in a bar."

She looked into the man's eyes to see whether he believed her. She could tell that he was shocked. He found her behavior scandalous. Her family, highly respectable people, didn't deserve to have such a daughter. But if possible, therefore, they should be spared any humiliating publicity on her account.

"I know we shouldn't be here, and I'm really sorry we've caused you so much trouble. You must have thought we were burglars and had guns or something."

The watchman hesitated, his duty now confusingly at cross-purposes. He scratched the side of his face, looking from one of them to the other, then down at the floor, scuffing one shoe against the other as if thinking it over at both ends.

"I reckon you-all can go on home for now," he said at last, his voice thickened by confusion and disgust. "I got to report this to the committee though. I got to report a breaking and entering. That's my job. They kin decide what they want to do." He shook his head repeatedly going down the stairs. "Shame on you I say."

Walking behind the watchman William again squeezed Flora's hand in gratitude. The business wasn't finished but it would be in the hands of people who would wish to play it down. For Flora however it could still be pretty rough. She didn't mind. She would have entered a fiery furnace to protect him, which, knowing her father's patriarchal rage, she well might have to do.

The members of the committee, which included Madeleine Ames, spoke to each other on the telephone. No one minded about the prank of breaking in, but most of them were appalled by Flora's behavior. The watchman reported she'd picked the man up in a bar somewhere.

"I never heard of such a thing!" Lulu Piper declared. "Have you-all? She must be a nymphomaniac. They do that, and I can't think who else would, can you-all?"

Of course, Madeleine guessed the truth, as did one or two others. But the overriding question was whether Flora's parents should be told. She was, if only just, a minor. They felt obliged therefore to do so, and reluctantly Madeleine shouldered the task, discussing it first with Bayard.

Bayard was as angry as she had ever seen him. He was furious at William's dalliance with his cousin and equally furious he had broken into Blue Hills House. The boy had doubly fouled his nest, and just when Bayard was growing proud of him and had begun to believe that he would come to something.

"Seducing his own cousin. I thought he had more sense," Bayard exclaimed with blistering indignation.

But Madeleine disagreed. "Does one ever? Besides, he may not have been the initiator." Getting William's sympathy would in her view demand a great personal outlaying. The pair were both such self-protective creatures that one of them would have to yield entirely to snare the other, and Flora probably was desperate enough. Madeleine insisted the whole thing was perfectly natural. They were in love, or Flora almost certainly was, and they had to go somewhere. "Why not home, so to speak?" It was a teapot tempest.

Bayard, far from placated, welcomed any conclusion that bypassed an ugly scene with William, which would also be unproductive—and worse, might require his writing to Ellen. "Dartania won't want to know," he rightly opined, having quickly thought the business through. "And I shall pretend I don't." Perhaps Madeleine was right and it was not really serious. And yet it could have been. It still could be.

Madeleine decided the best route to Seneca was through Jasmine, who could inform him tactfully, defusing at the same time excessive paternal ire.

Jasmine found the escapade highly entertaining, openly admiring Flora's daring. The girl seemed so walled up, but if she'd begun to take big chances, then she'd begun to let life in. Jasmine could see nothing to get upset about, but nonetheless Seneca received an edited report.

He was not told the pair had been discovered in bed, only that they had broken into Blue Hills House with a bottle of whiskey, drunk most of it, and got caught, somewhat inebriated, by the night watchman. "Go easy on her," she pleaded. "That sort of prank shows an adventurous streak, a chip off the old block."

Informed so soothingly, Seneca hadn't minded at first. But thinking of repercussions if newspapers got hold of the story, he waxed hotter. "Senator's Daughter Breaks into Museum," was the rubric waving like a red flag in his brain. Would Flora never become a responsible adult: She was nearly twenty-one years old!

"Behaving like a common criminal," was the line he took. "You're damned lucky you didn't go to jail, and you can thank your Aunt Jasmine and Mrs. Ames for that. This boy comes here and is at once an embarrassment to his father."

"It was my idea," Flora had tearfully insisted.

"Then you better stop having them if you can't think clearer than that." He didn't believe for a minute it was her idea, and the intensity of his anger once in flow surprised him. But seeing his favorite child, always so quick witted and full of mordant humor, reduced to such rank feebleness—it got his goat.

Now, two days later, as Flora introduced William to her father at Longwood, Seneca looked him menacingly in the eye. "I remember you on your mother's knee," he said, as if that image were preferable. In fact the boy had looked ridiculous then, cocooned in ruffles and lace, and he looked ridiculous now, his pale waistcoated suit and wide-brimmed fedora, encapsulating some silly Hollywood notion of what Southern gentlemen wore. Far more astonishing however was the pair of six-shooters buckled in a holster around William's waist.

"You need a cigar to complete that getup." Seneca pulled out a cheap drugstore packet.

"Have one of mine," William answered, cheerfully courteous, extracting a Havana corona from the offending jacket.

Seneca took it without the smallest hesitation. Waving aside the proffered cigar cutter, he bit the end off and spit it forcefully into the fire.

"Expecting some trouble?" Nodding at the pistols, he lit the cigar, sucking his cheeks in repeatedly like bellows. "We don't have much of that sort east of Hollywood these days."

The pistols had been a present from Paramount and William hugely enjoyed wearing them when, as now, a fine theatrical opportunity arose. The tough gentleman image had strong appeal, but so perversely did the immediate challenge. Already in disgrace, by provoking further irritation, even derision, he would, he believed, occupy a large emotional space in Seneca's mind. And emotions being inherently volatile, it was relatively easy, once engaged, to lead them where you pleased. By such means one hooked and manipulated audiences; and if it worked with audiences, why not with individuals? William was to a degree experimenting; being already in disrepute, he chose to make the most of it, for he did not lack courage.

"That's a nice pair of Colts—forty-fives, aren't they?" Dartania, entering the room, came to the rescue, speaking admiringly and as if it were perfectly natural to be packing a pair of pistols at Sunday lunch. She liked the boy's refined good looks, his English elegance and cool, well-spoken self-possession. Moreover, being already in the family, his acceptance at Longwood was, to her mind, automatic.

William thanked her with a little bow and smiling narrowly at Seneca said, "Flora tells me you're interested in guns, so I brought these along to show you. They're a special edition."

"Well now, let's have a look," Seneca drawled, showing a mildly better humor. The excellent cigar was helping some, but he still had strong reservations about this fellow—like spotting a patch of ground that might not bear much weight, its weakness capable, therefore, of undermining oneself.

Unbuckling the holster, William handed it over, and Seneca removed one of the pistols. It was a long-barreled Colt, the silver-plated stock busily engraved, showy, but of excellent workmanship. To Seneca's great astonishment, however, it was loaded, the five cartridges plainly visible in the chamber. A damned silly kind of playacting!

Conscious of his daughter's sensitivity, and reluctant in any case to openly reprimand a guest, Seneca reflectively spun the cartridge chamber.

"Let's try em out," he said instead, his manner firm but affable in a way that sent a worrying message to the women.

"We're going to have dinner in a minute," Dartania quickly interjected, "and you all will want a drink. I know I do."

Flora gave her a grateful look.

"Go get those Coke bottles on the back porch," Seneca told Flora. "Get James to help you." His desire to put this jumped-up playboy in his place was now overlaid with the need to save his daughter from entanglement with a charlatan. Pete Weaver had been right; young Douglas was pure celluloid. Any twelve-year-old knew better than to go around packing loaded pistols. By emptying the chambers through contest he was set to kill more than just one bird.

William and Flora brought the Coco-Cola case full of empty bottles from the back porch. With Seneca's help they stood the bottles on the split-rail fence posts bordering the front lawn: five posts, two bottles side by side to a post.

"One point for the bottle that goes down first, and minus three points for missing altogether." said Seneca.

William nodded solemnly.

"You take those on the right. I'll take the left. Go on and call it, Dar."

Dartania, who along with Flora had quickly mixed herself a dry martini, came out onto the gravel drive, to the right of where the men were standing side by side. Flora, looking pale, sat down on the front steps, her chin in her hands, her drink stored safely beside her.

"Fire," shouted Dartania with all the gusto of an admiral ordering from the poop a full assault.

Both bottles on the first post went down, but William's went down first.

The men moved to the right in line with the next post.

"Fire," Dartania called out again, raising her glass and evidently beginning to enjoy herself.

Again two bottles disappeared and again the right-hand bottle went down first.

Seneca's jaw was set firm. The boy was fast and he was not without accuracy. Even if he didn't know gun etiquette, he did know how to shoot.

Not speaking, they moved on, in line with the third post.

"Fire!" A hoarse boyish edge had entered Dartania's voice.

The scenario was again repeated. William had accrued three points.

Flora, suddenly very pale, took a big gulp of her martini. She desperately wanted William to win, but she could not bear it that her father should be beaten. Utterly miserable, she tossed down the rest of the martini, hoping to incinerate thereby the hot pain of divided loyalties.

Surprisingly, on the fourth shot William missed, and Seneca, taking his time, easily demolished the left-hand bottle. In that single round, William's score was reduced to zero and Seneca had accrued one point. His spirits enormously improved, he nodded firmly at Dartania, indicating the final call.

"Dinner's ready!" she called out instead. "We can't keep Delphine waiting. She wants to get off to church this afternoon."

Stunned, Seneca saw that Dartania was making goddamned sure that he stayed ahead. Yet how dare she imagine he might not. A sudden recollection of the shoot-out long ago at Timbuctoo swept across his mind. She had protected him then, as now. A sudden tenderness grazed his heart, and obediently he lowered the pistol.

Flora was looking at William with admiration. "Fastest gun in the West," she whispered as he came up.

"They're fine pistols," Seneca hospitably obliged reentering the house.

That William might have missed on purpose never remotely entered Seneca's head—which was just as well. The patronizing smugness of such an action would have brought hellfire and brimstone tumbling upon them all. Instead Seneca was feeling kindly disposed toward the fellow. But though veering so unexpectedly to benevolence, he could not resist the top dog's primal instinct to stay firmly on top. Removing the remaining bullet he handed the pistol back with a light but clear reproof. "We don't keep guns loaded in this house."

William was replacing his, still loaded, in the holster, and putting Seneca's emptied pistol in as well, he wrapped the belt around both pistols and laid the holster on a nearby table.

The fellow was either deaf or damned impertinent. Again the pendulum swung.

They had to sit at the table for ten minutes before Delphine brought in lunch. When it did arrive, however, in true Longwood style and to Flora's great relief, the meal was short and swift—they ate instead of dined. But attempts at lightness by Dartania failed to dispel the musk of an aggressive excitement generated between the two men, and sitting over coffee in the gun room afterward, a bone of contention was rapidly nosed up and the battle for its possession enthusiastically engaged.

Flora's calling her father Henry caused William to mention he'd played one of Thomas à Becket's assassins in *Murder in the Cathedral.* He said he didn't blame King Henry for having Becket removed. The man was a pious nuisance and Henry was powerful enough to get away with it.

Seneca said that like Sir Thomas More, Thomas à Becket had, when the crunch came, jeopardized his life to stand up firmly for his beliefs. It was a courageous and manly thing to do. He greatly admired it. "They were both of them practical and ambitious men, but when they were forced to take a stand they did so, even though it meant their deaths."

"As both thought they were going straight to heaven, the investment probably seemed worth it," William lightly observed, accepting with a sly smile more coffee from Flora, whose hand had started slightly to shake. "Why else would sensible men risk their lives for mere opinion, unless of course they were fanatics."

"A man, to be a man, must stand up for what he believes." An ominous note of warning hung in Seneca's tone. His sacred credo was being wantonly trampled by this impudent upstart, whose offer of another cigar he now with some difficulty refused.

"It's my view a man should use his head, not lose it," William said, lighting a corona. "It's there to ensure his survival, and acting against survival is crazy, or the result of some pretty extensive brainwashing."

"It's because those men put the public good, as they saw it, before their personal safety, that we're talking about them hundreds of years later." Seneca's cadences had taken on the incantatory beat of a war drum being summarily thumped.

"Any man who gives up his life for that sort of vanity is an ass," said William, drawing on his cigar with obvious pleasure.

"The wish to leave behind an honorable name and honorable achievements, to make one's life serve some worthwhile purpose, is one of mankind's finest instincts, and without men of that caliber there would be no civilization in which to sit here so comfortably puffing on expensive cigars and making frivolous comments about them." The cigar's pungent and enticing aroma was wafting seductively over the room.

"Service to the community, or the world, or whatever, is fine," said William airily in agreement, "but surely service to oneself comes first. Whether people admit it or not, when the chips are down it's every man for himself."

"Millions of men were fools, as you see it, to lose their lives beating Hitler and Hirohito. Well, you ought to thank them for it with all your heart. They left the world a better place, and the next generation, your generation, has inherited obligations because of their sacrifice—obligations to carry on improving the world. Almost every generation owes its forebears a good deal."

Flora could feel "Horatius" moving into her father's mind, but if so, mercifully he repressed it.

"Do you feel no need to contribute something to the world you live in, and which at the cost of so many lives, has nurtured you?" Seneca asked with considerable and undisguised disgust.

"I do," said William, exuding a cool grandeur. "I shall keep them entertained."

"William's name is almost a household word," Flora hurriedly put in, pouring herself a brandy and smiling anxiously over her shoulder at William.

The hit was unintended and in any case missed its mark. Seneca could no more credit serious worth to playacting than he could credit it to play of any kind. He greatly admired playwrights, respected profoundly their abilities, but actors didn't signify. Like tickbirds perched upon the massive shoulders of a rhinoceros, they were useful, but in a completely superficial way. Seneca could afford to be charitable.

"Entertainment is a valuable commodity," said the gracious Titan. "It diverts the mind from stresses in real life and throws some valuable light on them, without making the superstitious demands of a religion."

"People should stick to their families, that's what," said Dartania obliquely, making an unusual entry into debate.

The remark, for William, had its ironies.

Seneca saw that the topic was probably exhausted. Despite acute annoyance and a deep distaste for young William, it had been stimulating. Adrenaline had poured like powerful amphetamines throughout his veins, enlivening, assuring invincibility and a sense of purpose. He was sorry for young people today. Having failed to perceive the importance of social commitment, they went around worrying idiotically about the point of their existence. They were devoid of honor and loyalty, and their spirits, deprived thereby of virtuous enlargement or expansion, were perennially at half mast, becalmed, and going nowhere.

He got up and shook hands, pleading work.

"The play's the thing," said William, courageously meeting his eye.

"Next time you go anywhere with those pistols, unload them first," was Seneca's parting shot.

"THAT GUY IS a bad penny," Seneca told Jasmine later. "He's totally out for himself. He has no social responsibility at all and he thinks people who do are naive. He's for selfish exploitation whenever it can be managed."

"It's odd that artistic people are often asocial." Her mildly critical tone belied the taking up of their defense. "But they do contribute," she went on, as if being vaguely speculative, "and their contributions are sometimes very great, even if they were only meant to serve their egos and imaginations." William's perversity had recalled Frank, who, Jasmine believed, had painted a lot better before he'd got caught up in politics. But wisely she chose to change the conversation's drift. "You know your daughter's in love?"

"I know she drinks too much and moons about all the time. If that means love then I guess you must be right."

"Or starstruck," Jasmine proposed, softening her observation. "Others' love affairs always look so comic don't they, when one's own is so deeply serious."

"Whether she's starstruck or lovesick," said Seneca, "she's boring, and she used to be so quick-witted. Besides, that fellow's no damn good."

On New Year's Eve another episode further ratified this view.

Climbing up on a table at the country club, William, with a burnt champagne cork, had painted a mustache on the serene and benevolent countenance of Robert E. Lee. Then, having given the patriarchal beard youthful streaks of black, he had sketched a pair of trendy sunglasses on the patrician nose.

Older members were shocked by this blasphemous defacement of a hallowed icon, but the club's manager pretty swiftly accepted William's subsequent offer to have the painting cleaned, which in any case it had badly needed. This wasn't the first time youthful shenanigans had been firmly but pleasantly dealt with, especially where Englishmen were concerned.

The incident however increased Bayard's already pronounced unease. There was some complexity at work within the boy, a negative or destructive side to his otherwise ebullient and gregarious nature. But he doubted William's motive had been philistine. More likely a swipe at local gods lay behind it.

Seneca declared it infantile and professed a total lack of surprise, at which Flora again wept, making her father angrier than ever. But Dartania, who loved pranks, thought it was all great fun and told her husband he was being pompous. She said she hoped Blue Hills' old biddies were having conniption fits. It would do them a power of good. "They can do with a good shake-up," she said. "They badly need the fizz."

In fact Blue Hills was more dismayed by Seneca's latest action than by the charismatic William's drunken pranks. The evening paper had prominently reported Seneca's membership in Nashborough's NAACP, the only member needless to say—although the paper did say—who was white.

Seneca had some fine qualities; no one disputed that. His antecedents were the best, his blood as blue as the bonny blue flag, his parents excellent people, and his achievements in the war outstanding. The problem was that he had simply never grown up. Ideals and so on were acceptable, even desirable, in youth, and were to be expected, but they were misguided in the gray ambient light of full maturity. Seneca had failed totally to comprehend the Darwinian mechanics of society. A brilliant general, he was nonetheless in ways extraordinarily naive. But if he thought they were going to allow a pack of ignorant blacks, most of them perfectly happy as they were, to overrun downtown Nashborough and sit all over the buses (not that they themselves ever rode on buses), he had another thing coming. Moreover it was wicked to stir the Negroes up by making them empty promises. They would only be disappointed in the end. If you had an ordained place in life, then you didn't have to push so hard, to climb so high, or to wrestle so continuously to stay on top. Life was easier. This principal tenet of entrenched class systems, so profoundly un-American in character, could not be mooted openly, but everyone knew it was true. They knew it was harder to keep your balance on top of a totem pole than on the bottom, where stability was so solidly strengthened from above. Without question, the Negro was better off as he was.

6

....

*O*n returning to Hollywood, William found that he had won hands down the hotly fought-over role of Mr. Darcy, the proud and arrogant hero of Jane Austen's *Pride and Prejudice*. The part seemed tailor made. The movie's costume budget ominously suggested another costume drama, but large outlays in other realms worked to preserve a balance. The novel had been adapted for the movies by Aldous Huxley and without interference from Paramount's script department. The period sets were being designed by Cecil Beaton. David O. Selznick would direct, and a young actress, newly contracted to Paramount, and whose beauty reputedly rivaled Hedy Lamarr's when young, would play Elizabeth Bennet. Her name was Mary Bowers. In style, intelligent handling, and natural box office appeal, the movie promised to be the studio's proudest achievement that year.

Reading *Pride and Prejudice* for the second time, Flora experienced considerable empathy for Miss Elizabeth Bennet, saddled with her embarrassing family. She saw too that William, as Mr. Darcy, would be perfection. But having incautiously resumed her clandestine perusal of movie magazines, the delicately molded features of Mary Bowers, despite the vapid smile, left her fainthearted with inferiority. Soon the magazines were reporting a hot romance between the two ascending stars. The story of Elizabeth Bennet and Mr. Darcy was being acted out in real life as well as on the lavish Paramount set.

"Rubbish," William told her on the telephone. "Mary Bowers is a cretin for whom the English language appears to be a new and untried vehicle. In that respect at least she makes a perfect foil for Mr. Darcy. But in no way is she an equal." He said that stories of a romance were circulated by the studio publicity department in order to attract an early interest in the film. Movie fans apparently preferred real life and fiction to be seamless. More idiots they.

As predicted, Mr. Darcy was for William a magnificent vehicle. Fan letters poured in and people noticed him in the street, "Look, there's Mr. Darcy," so convincing was he in the film.

This last, however, was unfortunate. Hollywood stars were supposed to make each role a manifestation of themselves, not the reverse. In other words, the part of Mr. Darcy should have been associated with William and not William with the part of Mr. Darcy. As the studio pointed out, nobody said of Clark Gable on the street, "There's Rhett," or of Marlon Brando, "Look, it's Stanley." Both men had assimilated these highly charismatic roles into their own more dominant personalities. They had, as it were, successfully eaten the protagonists alive.

William nonetheless scored a huge personal triumph, though the movie unfortunately did not. Mary Bowers, as beautiful as the dawn, had turned the acutely intelligent Elizabeth Bennet into a suburban bobby-soxer dressed up for a costume ball, and not even Americans wanted that. The film barely broke even.

But in any case, William was bored and mildly exasperated by Hollywood. As a dream machine it was not the stuff *his* dreams at any rate were made of. But he enjoyed the fame and he liked the money. He'd even bought a black Jaguar convertible, suitable to the role of a glamorous Hollywood star. However, he wanted to return to England for a bit. He needed the refreshment, before making another picture, and he suggested that Flora meet him in New York. They would stay at the Plaza for a few days and live like lords—a favorite expression of William's.

Knowing her father wouldn't pay her fare, and that her mother would say going to New York was just a waste of time, Flora visited the old pawn shop off Church Street, carrying in tissue paper her grandmother's diamond brooch, which she had never worn. Coming out of the shop, pleased to have secured her fare and a bit more, she ran smack into Bayard, who, with his beady look, eyed her suspiciously.

"Buying or selling?" he asked, the tone for Bayard unusually intense.

Ever the cool liar, Flora met the question easily, "Oh, I'm buying. This is a great place for second-hand cameras, Uncle Bayard."

Pointedly he viewed her empty hands.

"I'm still making up my mind."

Bayard continued to stand and peer, then said, "Don't, for heaven's sake, go and pawn the family silver."

"Oh, I wouldn't dream of it," said Flora, cool as a cucumber, "though I doubt that anyone at home would notice. Have you heard anything from William, Uncle Bayard?"

"If you need money, you can always come to me. Is that clear?"

She thanked him, didn't move.

"Only through his mother," Bayard volunteered at last. "She says he's going back to England but not stopping here." Again the piercing look . . . "What does he tell you?"

"Oh about the same."

In New York (Flora claimed to be visiting college friends) she noted with feelings of pride mixed with a mild anxiety the looks and smiles that William collected behind his back. Heads nodded and bobbed in his direction and, like royalty—film stars *were* America's royalty—he created a frisson of excited pleasure wherever they went. A bizarre and magical power—as new to him as to her—it was exhilarating and a little frightening. When they dined at Sardi's, necks positively craned, but of course people went there mainly hoping to see celebrities. The Plaza was more restrained, the hotel treating William with impeccable courtesy, their bedrooms discreetly connected by a sitting room, in order to protect, as Flora pointed out, amused, William's reputation, and not hers. Both had received complimentary bouquets of two dozen roses, but William also had a basket of fruit and a box of superior chocolates. A cooler of champagne stood in the sitting room with a card from the hotel manager addressed to William.

William both relished and detested celebrity. He adored applause, but when stopped in the street repeatedly and asked for his autograph, he barely contained his irritation. "In England, people let one alone," he complained. "Americans seem to think that because they know who I am, they don't need an introduction, that because I'm a star, I in some way belong to them." The tail, he perceived, was in danger of wagging the dog.

Flora felt some sympathy for the fans, being herself one of them. Except for Miss Allen she had never loved anyone before with all her heart, and loving Miss Allen had been a miserable business. Flora had felt so sorry for the lonely and deformed old woman. She had been weighed down by Miss Allen's dependence on her, and pinioned by heavy chains of love, she had never before risen felicitously on its golden wings.

But loving William was sometimes very painful too, if in a different way. Now she was always afraid. She had entered a country that was wild and strange, beautiful but also threatening. Yet she had put down roots. Unlike many species, she had only one to put down, one long taproot that grew so deeply, there could never be transplantation. Drought or severe flooding would be the end of her.

William, she knew, felt differently, though he did at least feel something. She must not demand too much. She must learn to be grateful. And when he kissed her good-bye in the *Queen Mary*'s lounge—he was traveling first class and would sit at the captain's table—she waited, meek but undemanding, for some bond or promise.

"I'll let you know when I'm coming back," he cheerfully volunteered. "It depends on the bloody studio."

Flora went home and began again the excruciating but hopeful monotony of waiting for a letter.

"Eat something, child," said Delphine. "Ain't no man worth starving yourself to death for, and that's the gospel truth."

When she knew that she was pregnant, she did begin to eat, in between vomiting. No word as yet had come from William.

Flora debated and debated. Weighing her father's Olympian anger together with William's protracted silence, she solemnly considered an abortion. Neither need ever know. Then she reflected that part of William was actually alive inside her—like an ingested communion wafer becoming flesh and blood of the god—and she changed her mind. Finally, nervous as a cat, she sat down at the gun room desk and wrote to him. The letter was short, a simple, mined document of information, but it made no demand.

"Are you writing to William?" her mother asked offhand, entering the room.

Flora threw her arm across the page, half-turning to face her. "You told me to give him some encouragement."

"That was ages ago." Her mother was searching the room. "Have you had a letter from *him*?" she tacked on casually, looking under some magazines on the coffee table.

"Yes," Flora lied.

Dartania eyed her a little suspiciously. "Men don't like to feel cornered or run after, you know," she cautioned, "and they like to think they're making all the decisions themselves, running the show." Dartania had found her cigarettes. When she reached the doorway however Flora suddenly threw out, "Why did you and Henry run away and marry?"

Dartania was caught off guard. She turned around. "Why what?"

"Did you have to?"

"Why, the very idea! We never *had* to do anything. We did exactly what we wanted. We always have."

And look where it's got you! thought Flora, who said instead, "Eloping is sort of romantic."

Dartania shrugged. "Well it cuts out all the la de da," she answered predictably. "Tell William I said hello."

Flora decided that coming from Eleanor, that was a sizable commission. She felt a little better. She had, as her mother no doubt rightly suggested, left all the decision-making to William.

AT ELDEREST, WILLIAM read the letter over breakfast. His mother sat opposite, while Lord Ferris, now occupying a private scatter world, held on vaguely at the head of the table. Ellen had seen the postmark and her eyes followed the envelope as William picked it up.

"Cousin Flora," he answered her look, cutting the envelope with his butter knife. As he read the succinct note penned in Flora's untutored scrawl, his face maintained its carefully trained composure. "She sends her best to 'ya'll.'" And putting the letter away, he continued with evident relish to eat his bacon and eggs, commenting, not for the first time, on the cold English toast that for some reason always sat on a rack designed for this sadistic purpose.

That afternoon William went for a walk on the hills above the river. It was a fine day, and, looking down on the old stone manor that any time now would cease to be his home, and more important, his mother's, he found many reasons to consider the future. In Hollywood almost everyone was married. Starlets could make such awful nuisances of themselves, and marriage—sequential monogamy they liked to call it—covered myriad possibilities. Certainly he could afford to marry. As to fatherhood, that exceeded his imaginative powers. But there would be much to learn and much that would be useful to an actor, especially as one got older, like Gary Cooper. He was enormously fond of Flora. He had a most tender spot for her. She attracted him and she was a fine companion. In ways, he was closer to her than to anyone. If he failed her now, his mother would never get over it. That disgrace would, despite her devoted affection, hang in the air forever. But mightn't Flora be persuaded to have an abortion? If not, and a gossip columnist discovered there was an illegitimate child, his Hollywood career was finished—not that he minded so much. Except for the money, Hollywood could go to the devil.

Such was his reasoning as he marched along the hilly ridge. A crisp chill was in the air. The darkening greens of late summer suggested the trees were hoarding their energy for a final brilliant show before they died. A flock of sheep grazed on the slope, fat balls of wool and mutton, blithely innocent of their larger purpose, living so comfortably and self-assured in their fool's paradise. How dull was life lived without danger or adventure or decision, merely as munching victims of others' more powerful desires. How sheep-ish. The point was to seize control of one's destiny and make things happen. Any affirmative action was better than nosing along like a sheep.

That evening William announced that in a few days he was off to America. His mother's surprise masked, if poorly, a curiosity that remained politely wordless, as he was counting on. He was not required to give a reason. Silent moral pressure was being laid on him to do so, but he perversely chose to bear it.

DELPHINE BROUGHT THE letter in, suppressing a grin and hiding the envelope under her polka-dot apron. "Now, chile, don't look so glum. That boy's thinking bout you all the time, just like I told you." With a magician's flourish, parallel with a widening grin, she brought the letter out.

Flora jumped up from the table. Her coffee spilled. Her fork fell on the floor.

"You gone white as a sheet. Now stop that worrying. It's going be all right!"

Flora carried the letter upstairs to her room and sat down solemnly on the bed. She opened it slowly, then held the page at arm's length, blurring her vision in an attempt to examine the overall appearance, to take it in by degrees, forestalling a knockout blow. The letter was short, less than a page, which told her only that it contained no long and cowardly list of excuses.

Dear Diary,

Today I decided to propose marriage to a girl whom I believe will make a most excellent and loving wife, should she be unwise enough to accept me. I go to America next Friday on the Mauretania *to find out, stopping at my father's, if he will consent to have me. I don't think he much approves of me if the truth were known.*

Should my proposal be accepted, we shall marry quietly and quickly, away from the glare of publicity and the usual matrimonial hullabalou.

So ends another day in the life of yours truly, and so begins perhaps a new and dazzling future.

P.S. The young woman in question, being already my first cousin, will as my wife make ours a shockingly incestuous union, something no doubt that, among much else, we will both take pleasure in.

Holding the letter fast against her breast, Flora in her excitement ran several times up and down the stairs. She could think of nothing else to do.

Then, believing this might be too much activity for the baby, engaged so energetically in dividing its cells, she rushed into the kitchen and breathlessly hugged Delphine.

"I ain't never seen you so happy, and I bet I know why!" Though she didn't entirely.

TWO WEEKS LATER the young couple drove across the state line and were married in the fusty, velour-draped and overheated parlor of a local justice of the peace.

Parents had to be tackled next and the studio informed.

Flora was terrified. "I'm not a minor, and it's not as though I'm expecting Henry to give me a lot of money. He can cut me off without a cent for all I care. So really it's none of their business." The confrontation appalled her. Her father's anger would gouge a raw wound into her delicately embodied happiness, or else cause her to smother it with the abject misery of a guilty child.

William however was looking forward to the meeting. "I'll take my pistols," he declared, grinning wickedly. "Empty, except for a single silver bullet. Just in case."

She put her arms around his neck and kissed him madly, gratefully.

Seneca's first response, instantly disguised, was relief at being spared the expense of another wedding. But he also felt thwarted, his authority undermined; and when Flora's pregnancy, so predictable, was confessed, he looked so fierce that the poor girl began silently to weep, the tears falling on her gently folded hands without a sound.

"What's the matter, sorry you married him?" Seneca growled, mimicking Hamilton's patriarchal response to his and Dartania's elopement. She had been weeping too he now recalled, and suddenly he felt a sting of guilt, for his bullying and unfairness.

"I'm glad it's William," Dartania quickly interposed, giving her daughter a hug. "I like him, and as he's already in the family, we won't have to put up with a stranger and a lot of claptrap from his relations." She thought William rather a catch and could well understand her child's attraction. That she and her brother would be grandparents to the same infant also gave the situation an entertaining twist.

William said they would live in Hollywood and rent a house. His contract had another year to run, but after that he didn't know. Hollywood was good money but he preferred the stage. He wasn't the right sort of actor for the screen; it was a different technique, and others were better adapted to it than he.

This frank piece of self-analysis went down well with Seneca, almost the only thing that in their short acquaintance had. Convinced the fellow was of paper weight, Seneca still yearned to crumple him in his ample fist and toss him into the wastebasket where he belonged. But unfortunately, he had achieved the status of a legal document.

For the first time Flora's imagination addressed the future. She had never allowed her thoughts to leap so far, and living in Hollywood quite simply had never occurred to her. But as long as she was with her Williams—she called the baby William Too—it didn't matter where they lived. Nothing mattered.

7

January 1955 was unusually cold. A heavy snowfall blanketed the ground, began to thaw, then froze again, covering the bare tree branches with a coat of ice, so that when the sun shone cold and brilliant, the countryside, still snow carpeted, was transformed by trees that glittered like a fragile crystal forest created mysteriously in the dark of night.

Peering out of frost-glazed windows at this exquisite scene, some people recalled the old days, when the river used to freeze and you could skate on it. But that never happened anymore. Generally it was getting warmer. Generally life was getting easier, and Nature, once so dictatorial in her governance of human affairs, was taking more of a backseat. Man was increasing his control at last, and Nature backing down.

But Nature still held firmly to her primal fief, still ruled that unfathomable, apparent awakening called life, and chose with what seemed whimsical insouciance, its removal. She still gave and took arbitrarily. And now she chose to call on Alice Nash.

Alice was ready and waiting. She had been ready and waiting for some time, enduring patiently, but prepared to dissolve her dulled and crumbling self-awareness back into the anonymous material condition. The magic thread that had, like an umbilical cord, connected her so energetically to the conscious world had steadily frayed in the increasing bodily effort to stay alive and, finally frazzling to one ply, had snapped. And that was all.

Arriving with Miss Alice's breakfast tray, Martha found her mistress lying, open mouthed in wonder, her blue unblinking eyes fixed on a hidden world. Martha had seen death before, and sometimes, as now, it seemed a right and proper thing, a wondrous spiriting away, a soul molting into something new and better, leaving behind its empty and redundant shell.

A religious woman, Martha knew Miss Alice now reposed among the angels and that she must be overjoyed after all this time to see the doctor again. And he her. The sheer delight of it. And yet, leaning over her mistress's body, tears rose up unbidden, christening the still warm corpse, as compassion was suddenly mixed with inexplicable fear. For death is always momentous.

Martha felt Miss Alice's brow, almost a formality, before in one light movement closing forever the cornflower blue eyes. Then kneeling down beside the bed, she began to pray, joined before long by Rosetta and Ben, Miss Alice's most intimate acquaintance, keeping the last vigil.

It was agreed that Ben should tell Mr. Nash, should call Mr. Nash's office and tell the secretary it was an emergency, so as to get through. Mr. Nash would guess right away what it was and be prepared when he came on the phone.

"Just say she passed away real peaceful in her sleep," Rosetta urged, still in a whisper. "That's what folks want to know." Perhaps it also was the truth. They were themselves getting near to no-man's-land, and so were anxious to see death, where possible, as a passive and painless event, something as natural as a worn-out pocket watch, beyond repair, and stopping for good, which, in a way, it was.

Ben took in his own the small, cold, freckled hand. She had been a difficult old lady, imperious and short tempered, but generous and laughing, for she loved a joke and was full of feeling and human kindnesses. She and he were closely twined together by time and circumstance, a many-tendriled connection of mixed feelings that included among its winding stems, irritation, frustration, mutual dependence, and an abiding affection. A familial connection.

Picking up the tray where she had left it, Martha just as quickly set it down again. "Oh Lordy, they say death comes in threes!" She looked uneasily about, as if suddenly finding herself in an unwanted game of musical chairs. "Who's going to be the next, I wonder?"

Then, instinctively seeking to breathe in optimistic air, she quick as a flash recalled the fur coat Miss Alice had promised to leave her, a silver fox with broad shoulders, 1940s style. She might even be able to wear it to church on Sunday. Ben would get Miss Alice's old Cadillac, and Rosetta all her clothes and marvelous hats, and there would be some money too.

Death, like everything, had its compensations, and Miss Alice must be so happy where she was, especially if she was growing younger. The Bible wasn't clear on this important point.

Seneca's response was a few direct and practical questions. Then he turned the business over to his secretary, who telephoned the children and sent a telegram to Emma in Australia.

Sally volunteered to make the funeral arrangements, while Flora, heavily pregnant, called her mother from Hollywood. Ought she to come home?

"There's no point now, is there?" Dartania's perfect logic offered the remit her daughter was secretly hoping for. But later on, Flora regretted it and felt sad and guilty to have missed her grandmother's funeral. She had needed the chance to mourn—a thing that never figured in Dartania's rational response and general disregard of funerals' purposes.

Seneca was better acquainted with death than were most men. He had seen more dead bodies and he had seen men dying in horrible circumstances, separated from parts of their own bodies and pleading to be shot. He had been fully expecting his mother's death, even hoping for it as an earned vacation for her that would last. Now, writing out a brief announcement for the press, he became aware of a strange, uneasy-making noise. At first he had to listen hard; then it got louder, a door having apparently burst open so that the sound came so much nearer. Somewhere, a small child was crying its heart out, lost and bewildered in an ominous and empty world. The child's grief was alarmingly invasive. Seneca laid down his pen. The desolate cries were rapidly peeling back layers of armorial encrustation, till raw and terrible, they struck at his chest, affected his breathing, and, rising up out of nowhere, tears smarted in his eyes. "Mama," he said for the first time in his life that he could remember. "Oh, Mama! Mama!"

He gave orders that there should be no calls.

"LORD A MERCY!" cried out Georgia Mason sitting in her wheelchair, opening the evening paper. "Miss Alice Nash is dead."

"Who's that?" asked her grandchild, whom she was minding or who was minding her. The position was far from clearly established.

"That," said Georgia, "was a grand old lady, one of the finest, that's who. Her people settled this country. They had plenty of stuffing, I can tell you, and plenty of courage and get-up-and-go." She wriggled uncomfortably in the narrow chair. "It's damned oversettled now, if you ask me!"

Finishing the front page article, she read the obituary with its flowery description of Cottoncrop's Christmas parties and of the early settlement of Nashborough by the doctor's forebears, followed by Miss Alice's, who had traveled more grandly in carriages from Virginia, their slaves walking behind and, as the paper said, a "spinet piano" in their baggage. The spinet had been burned as firewood by the Yankees. Well, everybody knew that. They also knew Alice's grandfather built Blue Hills House, "now a museum decorated in period antebellum style." Georgia put the paper aside in a gesture at once contemptuous and resigned. "Turn off that awful racket"—she nodded at the TV set—"and get me a bourbon and water. Make it a big one too."

The child regarded her skeptically, but decided to go along with it despite the doctor's orders—as a leverage for the early resumption of TV. Mr. Peepers would be on in half an hour.

Like Hamilton Douglas ten years earlier, Alice Nash had decreed a simple funeral comprised of her immediate family and servants. But this time Blue Hills didn't feel particularly cheated. Cottoncrop's Christmas parties were so long ago, almost another world, and the high importance old families had then, their pride, and the power they so automatically had wielded, now seemed strange, even vaguely absurd. In any case it was ancient history.

Of course, those who had got there first had accrued some built-in advantages, but they were no longer advantages that enough money couldn't buy. Moreover, Nashbrough's newcomers had no wish to knock down the established goal posts and set up new ones of their own. They seemed positively to enjoy that they already were in place, and they were full of eagerness to play the game. They too wanted to live in Blue Hills, to join the country club, to take a private box at race meetings, and to attend exhibitions and private openings at Blue Hills House. It was as good a reason as any for making money.

Suddenly things long taken for granted were fetching enormous prices. The cost of Blue Hills houses rocketed, while the country club, having voted to enlarge its membership, shrewdly quadrupled new members' entrance fees. With enough money and the right sort of manners, which were easy to learn, anyone could enter society now, and they were welcomed. Or was what had been society ceasing to exist? The sheer numbers broke social life into groups. Everyone no longer knew everyone else; instead they knew those with mutual interests or with similar jobs. A solution to maintaining some degree of cohesion had, however, been discovered in charity balls. People, it transpired, were willing to pay a lot of money to be seen in one another's company—in other words, to belong. But to what exactly?

"Our small safe social world is crumbling," Bayard observed to Madeleine, sitting on her beach-house veranda at sundown, his feet propped up on the railings, a scotch and soda on the floor beside him. "But the scramble it creates is good. It keeps things alive and on the boil."

"Yes, but does it get any better? Is it improving?" She knew Bayard invited businessmen and manufacturers to lunch, and listened with interest to what they had to say. But as they knew little outside their business, that subject exhausted, conversation fizzled and the invitation rarely was repeated.

"Ellen used to say Nashborough's cultural malaise stemmed from everybody knowing everybody else too well. Evidently that was not the root of the problem."

"Whatever it was then, I think it's to do with money now." Madeleine had stood up, leaning against the railing, her back to the sunburnt lake, facing Bayard, shielding him from its glare. "Money is becoming an end in itself, when surely how it's spent should count at least as much as how it's made. Don't you agree?"

"I do, emphatically. The Renaissance was financed by a handful of merchant princes—all of whom knew each other, too."

Madeleine smiled. "Now, why can't something like that happen here? Is popular culture so entrenched, so pervasively rooted, that like a riotous weed it can't be beaten down? Is there no room for anything else to grow?"

"Only in certain hothouses it would seem." It was Bayard's belief that high culture would always, almost by definition, appeal to a small minority, though the trickle-down factor was important. "Unfortunately, though long on merchants we are short on princes, to the point of extinction."

"Well, we need another Rockefeller or a Medici, who's loaded with money and will build a concert hall if only as a monument to himself. If one rich businessman does it, others will jump on the bandwagon. They always do, I find."

"Snobbery and egotism are certainly lucrative veins to mine," said Bayard, who thought art in any form widened opportunities for pleasure. Moreover, artists almost never came from the upper echelons—who, for whatever reasons, generally remained art's patrons. It was something to think about, and over the next few weeks, in doing so, he would hit on a solution.

8

....

As so often happens, William Too was a girl, and bringing the infant back to their rented Beverly Hills house—a green-tiled, pseudo-Spanish mansion with concrete Chinese dragons guarding the front door and a swimming pool centered ostentatiously on the lawn—William and Flora still debated a name.

In hospital Wilhemina had seemed the obvious choice.

"Fine in England," William now opined, "but here she'd be called Willie or Minnie, an insignificant appellation."

"Or Minnehaha. Ha ha." Flora made an encouraging face at the blanketed bundle in her arms. "What about Willa?" Reading Willa Cather, the writer's sense of place, of the land taking precedence over its transient occupants, had made a strong impression on Flora, who in any case had refused to have the child named for herself. And William, resorting to the English style of skipping a generation, now suggested Ellen; but Flora thought the name lacked force. Willa had more character.

They were by this time back in the master bedroom, its orange-peel walls relieved by sliding plate-glass doors framing the patio, and dominated by a king-size bed with a bright blue rubbed finish, straight off a Hollywood set.

Lost in the oversized armchair Flora studied the infant's tiny puckered face. "Cleopatra, mighty queen and femme fatale," she addressed the baby. And to William. "She must have started like this."

"They'd call her Pat."

"Too pat."

"Americans want everything cut down to average. It's an unfortunate off-shoot of their democracy: Triviality and vulgarity are inbuilt."

Flora cast her gaze over the bedroom in agreement as their bantering word game continued. Artemis, they decided, would be Arty or Missy; Hatshepsut, Hattie or Sooty; Bodicca, Bobo or Dicky or Ducky. Theodora— "we had a bird named that." In such fashion would history's great queens and goddesses be Americanized. So that in the end they settled happily on Alice.

"Your father might even lash out for a silver spoon," William optimistically proposed.

"It won't occur to Henry and Eleanor to do a thing. They'll expect to have the baby presented for inspection, that's all. And they'll look down on her. Common as pig tracks, Eleanor will say."

Bayard, in keeping with tradition, sent a silver julep cup, while a trousseau of minute hand-knitted garments in white, and representing months of repetitive and laborious work, arrived from Ellen. There was also a blue blanket monogrammed with a *D*.

"Hope springs eternal," William said when he saw it. He was himself perfectly happy with a daughter, but he suspected that Flora, for whom the baby was a sort of adorable pet, would have enlarged the scope of her affectionate interest for a boy.

William, having begun a new film, departed for the studio each morning at the crack of dawn, and Flora spent the day alone. She read, she swam, she knew no one, nor wished particularly to do so. She even dreamed but little; there was so very little to dream about. For the first time in her life, imagination had been overtaken by reality. Moreover, there was a cook and a houseman and a nurse. Everything was taken care of.

And yet something was amiss. From time to time bouts of anxiety seized her, shook her, and left her limp and exhausted—afraid, when there was nothing whatsoever to fear. But then the setting was all wrong. Like an actress in an open convertible, a fan blowing her hair as a painted background rolled past, giving an illusion of movement and reality, so one lived in Hollywood. Neither she nor William wished to stay on any longer than was necessary. They had discussed New York and London, the English countryside, the south of France, even the Horn of Africa; for William said they could live wherever they pleased. Traveling was part of the job, but there were long periods when actors didn't work, even the most successful ones, and if stretches involving suitcases and hotels were tolerable, then they could live almost anywhere in the world.

Sitting beside the pool, nursing the baby, Flora lazily pondered this. The sun shone gloriously down but soon the smog would descend in a dark moist cloud and the heavy air shoot up to roasting temperature. She had read the paper and eaten her breakfast in bed, and another day loomed idly before her, exactly like the previous one—identical, like beads on the add-a-pearl necklace that had marked each birthday with a repetitive and comforting sameness.

But if the days were quiet, the nights contrarily were not. They were filled by a round of parties. Flora, together with other wives and the husbands of female stars, made up a sort of audience at these events, coming on stage themselves chiefly through sexual advances involving the principals. That was a big part of the party. And of course the whiskey flowed. Everyone drank a lot.

William adored parties. He loved being lionized and flirted with, and his being more or less English carried unexpected kudos. Americans couldn't help admiring the English, as he pointed out to Flora. It wasn't only a matter of style, but of content, the content of minds molded by a classical education and furnished in the traditions of a rich, unashamedly elitist cultural heritage. It showed.

Dressing to go out that evening, sitting on the bed as William wrestled with shirt studs at the dressing-table mirror, Flora brought out suddenly, with a small frown, her hands hugging her waist, "What about moving to Nashborough?"

Their eyes met in the mirror. "Can you get this damned thing in for me?" He held out the offending stud. *"Nashborough!"*

But the germ, so casually sown and upon such fallow-seeming ground, had taken root with an incredible speed. Half an hour later, driving down Beverly Hills Boulevard, William, to Flora's complete astonishment, suddenly cried out with enthusiasm, "We could buy Cottoncrop!"

Such a thing had never remotely occurred to Flora, but at once her own imagination started to trot in tandem. Cottoncrop would come cheap, they decided. The servants had retired and the place was shut up. The farm was worked but otherwise a limbo of uncertainty had descended. And though protected by the farm and fifty acres of grove, the house, being on the wrong side of Nashborough and surrounded by poorer suburbs, was increasingly a white elephant.

"Your pa ought to pay us to take it on."

"Don't count on it." Flora turned to the baby. "If you didn't rate a silver spoon, Miss Alice, I doubt Henry's going to give you Cottoncrop."

For William, replacing Elderest with one of the South's most historic if not most grandiose houses made perfect sense. He had a rooted connection in the town—as rooted as anywhere. Nashborough was in striking distance of New York and Hollywood, while London could always be managed. The pieces were falling kaleidoscopically into place, the resulting pattern dazzling in its attraction.

Seneca, though initially opposed, realized the house's immediate future would be solved, and it would stay in the family, something his parents would have wished. He insisted however on a market price. He could not benefit one child at the expense of his other two.

"His children aren't benefiting anyhow," Flora coolly pointed out. "He is." Knowing her father disapproved of William, she was convinced he wanted blood money for the desecration of his living there.

Then Dartania weighed in, keen that Flora should move back to Nashborough where she belonged.

Cottoncrop must be kept in the family, she told Seneca. Anyhow, a market price was meaningless, since a family house was something priceless. The idea of strangers buying it!

"Then you and I should move there," her husband counterattacked, but this proposal backfired, Dartania's campaign on her daughter's behalf being substantially increased by the suggestion.

Jack and Sally were part of Blue Hills now and Emma was becoming an Australian. Flora was Cottoncrop's natural heir, she said. "Are you going to let the place fall down, are you going to sell it, or are you going to keep it in the family, which means letting Flora have it? You're dithering you know; it's not like you."

"I'm going to sell it, and to my daughter, if her husband can afford it. Six hundred acres and one of the finest houses in the South, the place is worth a fortune."

"Then sell the farm and let Flora and William have the house and grove. William's no farmer; nobody is anymore."

Somewhat grudgingly, Seneca accepted the good sense of Dartania's plan. He put all but fifty acres up for sale and made a lot more money than he had expected, which he promised his children they would see one day.

As to the remaining property, hard bargaining ensued. The house's deplorable condition, its unhappy position and so on, were pitted against its real and historical value. But the young couple stuck to their guns and in the end, and with Dartania's help, paid very little, leaving a considerable sum for the ensuing task of renovation.

Cottoncrop's famous rebirth was about to begin.

William and Flora drove across the continent in a state of high anticipation. William would have six months before his next film, and he entertained great plans. He would do Cottoncrop and himself much credit, creating a family seat to take the place of Elderest and at the same time putting the old place back on the map where it belonged.

As so often happened when old people had occupied a house, disrepair was advanced and the amenities antediluvian. The kitchen was on a different level from the dining room, the central heating wasn't central (heating only a part of the house), the electricity had been threaded through old gas fittings back in the 1930s. The roof was in a parlous state, and one column had a bad crack down the side. The bathrooms, primitive and few, were all in the wrong places. Ceilings needed replastering, woodwork needed to be burnt clean and repainted. Who knew what other surprises there might be.

Cottoncrop's furniture bespoke generations of family life never wildly affluent and accumulated haphazardly. It lacked all coherence. The portraits were of indifferent often meager talent and, like the furniture, badly needed repair. The best portrait, one of General Robert Nash in his Revolutionary uniform, and wearing the order of the Cincinnati, had a bullet hole in it (the restorer claimed it had been plugged with mashed potato). Having grown up with such things however the Nashes never noticed.

William understood the sentimental importance of family heirlooms, but he had no wish to live with those of inferior quality. If Cottoncrop was to become a famous showplace, all must be perfection. Draconian decisions were required.

Flora, though bewildered by the immensity of William's plans, was happy to go along with them. She was back home, which for some unreason, was of great importance. She valued her childhood memories of Cottoncrop and she could just about remember the famous Christmas parties; but a compromise was fitting, and William would be occupied and happy.

"Blue Hills will be seasick green!" William declared with relish, looking about, envisaging his plan. Not that he cared a whit, except that Blue Hills filled the immediate need of prospective audience. "We'll have the finest house in the South and we'll give the most magnificent parties. People will come from everywhere, and we'll open the place to the public on a regular basis." This last, an English custom, had no appeal for Flora, who thought it both ostentatious and an appalling invasion of privacy.

William hired an architect from New Orleans and a consultant interior decorator from Charleston's garden district. The decorator was thrilled by the early cherrywood cupboard, he described the wing chairs in the middle drawing room as "rare," the library's plantation desk, of its kind a positive gem, and Miss Alice's tester bed worth real money, were more ceilings high enough to take it. But all the curtains in the house must be replaced, all the sofas and chairs reupholstered, and the walls redecorated to suit the period. The settees in the front parlor needed regilding, but the French touch would make for a pleasant change. However, the three connecting parlors wanted coordination, and all the portraits, should they keep them, must be thoroughly cleaned.

William planned to buy a number of new pictures, but not as a collector. Engaged himself in creating a work of art, they must suit the period and decor, becoming integral in his minutely worked-out creation.

Meantime they camped, renting a small house nearby; and having found a housekeeper, and a nurse for Alice—one of Ben's grandchildren—they made forays to Richmond, New Orleans, Charleston, and New York in search of furniture and pictures. Then, all the work having been set in motion, they returned to Hollywood. William would fly back and forth to see how things were getting on.

Flora was surprised by how talented an organizer he was. He went at things logically, the whole plan worked out in advance: building schedule, decorating schedule, furnishing schedule. He knew exactly what he wanted and he made damn sure he got it. In May he returned to oversee the placement of furniture and the hanging of pictures. Flora did not come with him. She had got chicken pox from Alice.

The completion of William's movie and the completion of Cottoncrop roughly coincided, as they were meant to do. The movie, *The Renegade*, co-starring Jane Wyman, would be the most successful picture in William's career, making him a top star in the younger generation—a generation that, with one or two exceptions, would never attain the godlike status of its predecessors in the thirties and forties. But William was in demand, fans wanted to see him, and, his contract nearly over, strong bids from rival studios could be expected.

In September, his fame greater than ever, the couple decamped from Hollywood to Cottoncrop, the press cataloging their arrival in exuberant detail.

"We're Nashborough's reigning couple, aptly residing in the seat of the town's eponymous founder. It's all falling into place." A note of achievement, as of winning a competition, underlay William's remark. But a suitable event was needed to mark significantly their investiture—a "first night." And soon enough, William found one. He would revive Cottoncrop's traditional Christmas party, unveiling the restored mansion at a magnificent Christmas reception.

News of the coming event, and of Cottoncrop's resplendent opulence, hummed through Blue Hills on top of a rumor that Paul Newman and Joanne Woodward had been to stay. Suddenly the town felt more important—a focal point. Who else might come! For in Nashborough, celebrity was far more glamorous than either money or family, there being almost no means locally of acquiring it. You had to go to New York or Hollywood for that.

Overnight, Cottoncrop's primal social clout was restored. A Christmas guest list found in the plantation desk formed the core of a meticulously updated version, the culling and enlarging of which, with Sally's help, amused William vastly. It was an exercise in power, and the very act neatly gathered into his hands Blue Hills' social reins.

How silly people were over trivialities like invitations, he declared, knowing full well the square of engraved cardboard's inverse significance. Not to receive one advertised social failure, and in Nashborough social failure was worse than business failure. It was even accompanied by physical disability, for only with difficulty did the head remain upright on its stalk.

William's finished list pronounced as could no charity ball Nashborough's social seraphim and cherubim. Two hundred people were invited, and all two hundred accepted, many of whom neither William nor Flora knew. But that hardly mattered; that was not the point.

By noon on Christmas day, the house bulged again with morning coats and brightly colored silks and velvets. The coatracks drooped with mink, and in the library, doubling as a cloakroom, neat rows of gray top hats lined the floor like stepping stones, and children had repeatedly to be kept off them. Ben and Martha and Rosetta had returned from retirement to serve and to oversee the kitchen, and a dozen younger blacks were at hand to underpin their performance, park cars, and help serve food and drink.

"It's just like old times, only more so!" older people exclaimed. For, instead of dingy portraits, cracked ceilings, shabby rugs, and worn upholstery, a perfected elegance greeted the eye, a sense of lightness and space produced by pale colors and meticulous restoration. In the front parlor the Christmas tree, painstakingly decorated by Ben, touched the ceiling, its thickly layered tinsel falling like molten silver in a covering mass. Real candles festooned the branches, throwing a mellow light over the gilded settees covered in Scalamandre silk.

In the pillared hall, family ancestors, freed from their lacquered veils, looked down benevolently upon the throng, who beamed back admiringly, occasionally trying to place a face or two. But the pièce de résistance was in the central parlor: a portrait of Thomas Jefferson as ambassador in Paris painted by Gilbert Stuart. William had outbid the National Gallery for it.

The young hosts stood in the hall to receive their guests and to accept the avalanche of exclamations that commenced upon entry and resounded all morning throughout the humming throng.

"My God, we're all so rich!" cried Georgia Mason from her wheelchair. "It's the nineteen-twenties all over again."

"Let's hope it lasts longer," said Bayard, nearly smiling. He was proud of William's accomplished revival of the rickety old place and wished suddenly that Ellen was there to see it, a thought he quickly banished.

"Your boy's done wonderfully," said Georgia. "But who are all these people? I must be getting out of touch." Her gaze had fixed with some rigidity on two photographers with a great deal of equipment who seemed to be ordering people around. "And what's all that about?"

"That, dear Georgia, is the national press," said Bayard. "One lets them in nowadays, as you see."

"Whatever for?"

"Whatever for? Because the world is an increasingly slippery slope, and much more populated. Small kingdoms cannot exist without allies. We are becoming global and must move with the times."

Dan was surprised how many wheelchairs were about. They had even created a traffic jam en route to the bar. People were living longer and suffered therefore lingering infirmities, but at that moment Dan felt no sympathy, only sharp annoyance at the fact of it. He had no wish to join any group, but most particularly this assembly of *dégringolés* old beans careening drunkenly about the crowded house.

Seneca and Dartania thought the restoration a great deal of nonsense— pretentious nonsense. What was the point of changing a perfectly adequate house and, in doing so, making it a lot less comfortable. "There's no place for dogs or cats, guns or gun boots. It's like a museum," was Dartania's reaction. But out of loyalty to Flora she kept quiet, her views perfectly understood only by her husband, who was in complete agreement. But they were pleased to see the old servants and to find the eggnog and country ham the same.

Seneca, cornered by Chloe, sat his drink down on the ormolu table where twenty years earlier, sitting on it himself, he had fallen passionately in love with Red Mason. Now he made no connection. In fact, he made no connection with any previous Christmas. He thought the present business artificial and a great bore, and he wanted to get home as soon as possible and go hunting. Chloe, searching as usual for a snaring topic, asked about Sputnik and if the Russians really were a threat. Seneca found the question rhetorical and coolly suggested that she ask her husband. But he was taken aback by her whispered confidence that Stark was going to run for the junior senate seat. He decided to review his reaction to that one later on.

Across the room, Jasmine smiled with understanding. "Isn't Chloe *captivating*," she would say with mischievous irony when next they met. But today they had made no effort even to speak, relations being well beyond the need for desperately snatched moments.

Seneca noted that Dartania and Jasmine kept a distance between them. He put it down on Jasmine's part to guilt. But on Dartania's? Well, perhaps he'd imagined it. He looked at Martha and Rosetta, trays in hand, smiling and whispering so pleasantly together. Ben deserved a medal or the women did. Seneca felt he was himself always walking on eggs.

"My, what a magnificent home," exclaimed a female voice. "And way out here in the middle of nowhere." The voice lowered, "Surrounded by rednecks and nigras!"

"Rednecks and Negroes do not cohabit," an irritated voice corrected.

"Well it's out in the boondocks anyhow, isn't it? Just think what this place would be worth if you could carry it over to Blue Hills."

Flora had come into the middle parlor. She looked vaguely about, smiling slightly, replaced her empty glass with one from a circulating tray, and went out again. Pete Weaver signaled to her, but Flora had drifted out into the hall, then disappeared upstairs. When a little later she came down again, the baby's nurse called out softly to her from upstairs as she descended, and Flora, turning to hear, slipped on the stair, taking a tumble down the last few steps.

Happily, prominent doctors were on hand to bind the not too badly twisted ankle. But afterward Flora stayed upstairs, not wishing to draw attention to herself, she said, lying on the chaise longue in what had been the doctor's bedroom, now Flora's boudoir, adjoining the couple's pink damask-draped bedroom.

Below, the pros and cons of stair carpets and the dangers of floor wax were briefly taken up, and accounts of several plunges, accidental and intended, vividly recounted. But Ginevra Tuttle, who knew Flora better than almost anyone, opined the accident's true cause. "She's smashed!" she whispered to Pete Weaver, as he lit her cigarette.

"Well who isn't?" Pete gallantly came to her defense. "It's Christmas." He was busy watching William, who, having come downstairs, had sat down at the ormolu table and begun to sign his autograph for a crocodile of eager, excited children. A number of teenage girls unashamedly joined the queue, giggling shyly and eyeing William with ambitious reverence. When seventeen-year-old Margot Piper, her black eyes full of suggestion, dropped her fountain pen on the floor, William, picking it up, invited her to accompany him to the bar.

"I've seen all your movies!" she was heard to say ecstatically.

"I've only made three."

"I've seen them over and over again," Margot not unwisely persisted.

A photograph of the Christmas tree glittering above the throng of guests appeared in Sunday's *New York Times* magazine, captioned "An American Christmas." It was to be the first of several such pieces in the coming months. In March, *Town & Country* magazine featured the house and its new owners, the couple posing for the cover in front of the fireplace, under the Gilbert Stuart.

Then the gossip columnists took over, finding much to report in the uninterrupted flow of lavish entertainment. At some of which Flora and William never even appeared, or only perfunctorily. But like court life, the parties went on, arranged by a meticulous majordomo whom William had found in New Orleans.

Before long, vague rumors of drugs and sexual promiscuity began to creep out. A party was reported in which car keys were pooled and guests who drew them paired off with the owners, but it was never verified. The heady cocktail of celebrities, multimillionaires, and European nobility drew an addicted audience, however, fascinated by the louche glamour of rich café society. This was not the cultured elegance William had intended, by example, to impose on the philistine South, but it made for a lot more publicity.

Flora, who occasionally lunched with Jasmine, never mentioned the couple's social life and seemed oblivious to it. Jasmine found her increasingly vague. She did not tell Seneca his daughter drank too much, a lot too much, and all those riotous parties didn't help. After all, what could he do about it? There was an underlying sadness about Flora that had always been there. She had everything. Yet something that not even Flora probably could put her finger on, it appeared, was missing—if not in her environment then in her makeup perhaps.

By the end of the year William had still not renewed his contract, nor had he signed a new one. Hollywood could go to the devil, he said. He was busy designing a garden.

9

．．．．．．．．．．．．．．．．．．．．．．

I hope the reverend isn't going to get his head blown off," Jasmine cheerfully declared, climbing into Seneca's old Chevy. They were headed for
Mountain Springs, a small town at the eastern end of the state, the venue of
a civil rights rally. Robin Douglas had argued strenuously for Mountain
Springs. Barnstorming notoriously intransigent areas attracted publicity—
and the civil rights movement needed all the publicity it could get. Besides,
Robin had argued, mountain people deserved a fair chance at enlightenment and, only through contact with other points of view and ways of seeing things, could they possibly get any.

Seneca called it a red flag pure and simple. He said a market town, where
some support usually existed, would bring better results. Backwoods people
weren't going to change, or allow themselves to be influenced one iota by
outsiders. Trying to make them do so right now was a waste of time. They
would be fishing in a bathtub.

Mountain people had narrow views out of ignorance, Robin had insisted.
But they weren't *bad* people, only badly misled. They were devout Christians, a God-fearing people, whom, he believed, could be preached to as
middle-class whites could not. Preaching was a powerful instrument of
communication, underrated by most whites; but it was highly effective
among minds attuned to its traditions. He earnestly believed he could get
through to them, and he was longing, even morally obliged, to try.

When Martin Luther King agreed to speak in Mountain Springs the deal was automatically clinched. It also made it safer, as the local people, finding themselves under national press surveillance, would be better behaved.

So Seneca had settled in philosophically with the plan, much as he had settled in by degrees to Nashborough existence generally. He told himself that on balance life was pretty good, that one of the results of repeated abrasions was that with constant rubbing, life eventually took on a fairly attractive patina. His reputation in court was unsurpassed, he was making a lot of money, though he had few uses for it, and the civil rights movement satisfied his deep-felt need for dedicated work. Even Stark's unexpected election to the United States Senate, though a complete surprise, had by no means disheartened Seneca. He was glad to be out of politics. The affairs of state, so noble sounding, were, he had discovered, mostly muddy waters, where causes and ideals, instead of making ripples, sank like deadweights straight down to the bottom. Everything involved doing a deal, making a compromise. In the army, by contrast, where decisions were often unilateral, things got done quickly and efficiently, if you could stomach the responsibility. It was no wonder that even well-intentioned men—of course, all men believed themselves to be well intentioned—needed firm restraint not to seek dictatorial powers in politics. If they desired to do great things, it was a sore temptation.

Seneca had even come to accept the austerity of Longwood's domestic amenities, much as he had accepted them in the army. He no longer complained or expected any improvement. The condition was a fact of life and he must live with it. But of course the condition wasn't what had irritated so, it was the principle of the thing. Now, however, letting the issue drop, turning his back on it, domestic life was noticeably easier. Resentment had withered away, and he and Dartania rubbed along in their harness without much kicking or biting.

Moreover, the challenges of the civil rights movement suited Seneca's maverick nature. In addition to the movement's humanitarian side, and the fact that there was much of real importance to accomplish, it was a battle waged against a well-entrenched majority, of which ironically he was himself, socially speaking anyhow, a part. It helped him to keep that distance so desirable to a maverick, and thereby continue to be his own man.

Since the miserable business over at Little Rock the year before, school integration had become the movement's most immediate and pressing challenge. The subject was wildly inflammatory. Rousing deep-seated emotions, it apparently posed for whites the ultimate threat—that of miscegenetion.

Robin had pointed out the extraordinary irony of this phobia. It implied that, given half a chance, the races were sure to get along, and that deep down in their souls everybody knew it.

But the South was glowing red hot, and some cool heads, black *and* white, were needed to keep the "dis-ease," as Robin was fond of calling it, in check. "You're our token white," he reminded Seneca in a show of light humor he sometimes allowed himself. He had long maintained that a man of Seneca's prestige, openly mixing with blacks, gave whites something to think about. It opened up a chink in their resistance, because prejudice was entirely a matter of attitude. That was the nut they had to crack—the attitude nut.

Jasmine smiled at Seneca and patted his hand. Being his civil rights assistant gave them useful cover and much to talk about. But today she had special news, good news, and she positively bubbled with it. Grinning at him, she rolled the window down a bit, holding her news back in suspenseful pleasure.

"Bayard's come up with *the* most amazing scheme! He told me about it last night."

Seneca made no reply, a tactic he knew brought quick results.

"He says cultural ignorance is Nashborough's biggest weakness, that we're a bunch of philistines and always have been. But he's going to try and tackle it head on. That, he says, is where the best contribution to the community can be made."

"Well, it's one," said Seneca, who held it tertiary to his own concerns.

Jasmine, still hoping for a dramatic impact, lit a cigarette, exhaled the smoke slowly, and waited till the traffic light had changed; then, unable to restrain her news any longer, she came out with it. "He's going to will his entire collection of pictures to Blue Hills House—and a lot of the furniture that was there in his day too. Apparently it's in storage. We always wondered. He says Ellen fully agrees—that she wants to keep the collection together. And since William's as rich as Croesus, he can buy pictures for himself. So he's behind it too."

She frowned quizzically at Seneca who seemed not to appreciate the affair's importance. "It'll be one of the finest collections in this country! People will come from everywhere to see it. Why, Blue Hills House will be a modern version of the Frick Museum in New York. The Bayard Douglas Collection, they're going to call it."

At this, Seneca laughed out loud. "That guy's just as shrewd as they make em!" he said, shaking his head in admiration. "He's been broke for forty years, he was once within an inch of going to jail, and he hasn't done a lick of work since he was thirty-five—just enjoyed himself. Now, in one stroke, he inscribes his name for posterity, and the state will pay to keep up the monument. I take my hat off to him!

"It's a shame that with his abilities he never did more with his life," he could not refrain from adding.

"Well he *has* enjoyed it." Jasmine, like most of the Douglases, could see no harm in that. "Dear old Bayard, it's true, though, he's always had a nose for a good deal."

They were nearing the East Nashborough neighborhood where Robin Douglas lived. The one-storey houses, their short ends to the street, stood close together, the materials obviously shoddy, the paint on the wooden verandas a little flaked. But an overall neatness—trimmed hedges, well-washed windows, and carefully weeded flowerbeds—proclaimed the black middle class.

"Bayard's asked me to donate some of Frank's pictures—to remind people that he lived here once and make them more familiar with his work. He says there are tax advantages. Should I do it do you think?"

"He's probably right about the tax advantages."

"I think Frank would have approved, if only as cocking a snook."

Artists being the bugbears in Seneca's philosophy, he was pleased to learn that Bayard was going to make some profitable use of them. Like a man sitting on top of a loaded hay wagon, the crop grown and harvested by others, Bayard was going to town, riding high and ready to draw top dollar. It would be quite a spree.

They stopped in front of a low maroon brick bungalow with a green asbestos roof, set in a small, newly mown yard. A child was playing with a terrier, throwing it a yellow plastic ball, which the animal eagerly retrieved, begging each time for a repetition.

"Blue Hills House and Cottoncrop are both getting to be so famous!" Jasmine continued, watching this.

"They are, but in different ways." Seneca disapproved of Cottoncrop goings-on and the increasing notoriety it attracted.

"Yes indeed. One's alive and the other's dead," Jasmine countered pertly. "While poor old Timbuctoo is buried in concrete, so to speak."

Robin Douglas had emerged. He was wearing a dark, well-tailored suit. A sober tie fronted an immaculate white shirt. It was a notable change from Robin's usually drab ministerial garb, having been specially chosen with a view to impressing backwoodsmen and raising thereby the Negro's image in their minds.

"My, you do look elegant!" cried Jasmine, abandoning the front seat so that the two men could work on their strategy during the trip.

Robin politely protested. "I don't mind sitting in the back of *cars*," he quipped, clearly in a high good humor.

"Best to let folks see you in the front," Seneca rather coldly returned. He disliked the whole enterprise. He knew hill folk—he had hunted with them and politicked among them—and Robin Douglas did not.

Jasmine waved at Douglas's wife, standing in the doorway, the lines of anxiety showing behind a bravely enforced smile. A young girl was peeking shyly, almost flirtatiously, from behind her. The woman waved back, then as the car moved off, called out to the little boy.

"This isn't going to be like bringing the gospel to a bunch of New Guinea tribesmen, you know," Seneca continued solemnly as they approached the new interstate highway. "You want to look out for these fellows. They're great haters, believe me."

Douglas smiled patiently. He, unlike Seneca, was completely relaxed. "They're godly people too, devout Christians who know right from wrong," he asserted pleasantly.

"They're godly people, all right, and there never was a more intolerant bunch than those Old Testament guys. With respect, Reverend, religious prejudice is every bit as bad as racial prejudice. To my mind they run neck and neck."

"With respect, Senator," Robin smilingly corrected, "religious belief is not a prejudice." He could be prickly at times, the chip on his shoulder dangerously evident, but he was used to Seneca's iconoclastic swipes and sometimes they appealed as brainteasers to debate.

"What's the difference then? I'm damned if I can see it."

"The difference is religious belief is intuited, while prejudices invariably are instilled."

"You mean to say if nobody had told you about Jesus Christ, you'd have intuited his existence. Now that's a pretty impressive feat."

Douglas gave a knowing grin at Jasmine in the backseat. "I mean that intuition would have acquainted me with God's presence in my soul. We are all of us endowed with that ability, even if in some it has been willfully suppressed."

"Well, if religious folks would just sit back and enjoy all that when it happens, and not try to press it on others, the world would be a whole lot better place. This biting need to convert others, by your definition to prejudice them in fact, has caused as many wars and killings as anything on this earth."

"I admit it and I confess I don't see a solution. It seems to be part of human nature, part of being a social animal, to want neighbors to have the same values as oneself. It's really nothing to do with religion, only religion gets caught up in it." He paused, then with a light shrug of acceptance added, "And homogeneity does cause less friction. Those New Guinea tribesmen you mentioned are indeed my brothers, and their lives are deeply bound up in religious practices. But it would be impossible to live beside them. It's just too different."

"Yet here," he gestured in a broad sweep across the windscreen, "despite our having the same culture, the same religion, the same daily nourishment as other Americans, white people still refuse to accept that we are like them. They think we are like the New Guinea tribes. Not because we have different values and our behavior is therefore threatening, but because our skin is a different color. This is prejudice of the worst sort, for it serves no useful social purpose."

Seneca, used to Douglas's quasi-preaching mode, and largely agreeing with him, peered through the not very clean windscreen. "Them thar hills." He nodded at the gray feathery outline rising on the horizon ahead of them. "Luckily most of your pals, coming along the southwest route, won't be obliged to cross them."

But Robin's thoughts continued on their own line. "Of course, the need to convert our white brethren is, whether we like it or not, a mission, and we ourselves are therefore missionaries, actively involved in prejudicing others. But there it is," he ended almost gaily, "realpolitik."

The rally was set to begin in the town square at three o'clock, and Jasmine had packed a picnic lunch, as stopping at a café en route was out of the question. It was also illegal. Soon after they left the interstate, therefore, and had reached the hill country, Seneca pulled off the road, a few miles short of Indian Falls. There was a pretty clearing in the woods he knew about, on a bluff rising above a stream-bottomed ravine. On the opposite side, Indian Falls dropped into it like a silver thread unraveling into the white-water rapids below. A cooling breeze issued across the ravine and they were well sheltered from passing traffic on the road.

Laying out a cloth, Jasmine began to unpack the plastic cooler, and Seneca, pulling out his Swiss pocketknife, uncorked a bottle of Chianti. Robin would have proferred a Coca-Cola, but consented out of politeness to the proferred tin cup.

"I believe prejudice *can* be got over in a jiffy, given half a chance," said Jasmine, returning to their earlier topic as she peeled the foil off a square of butter. "When I was a girl in Paris, I once saw Josephine Baker. She was stunning—so elegantly turned out. She had such *presence*. She was coming out of Mainbocher, the couturier's, and instead of walking a poodle like chic French women were doing in those days, she had a leopard on a leash. She was applauded in the street, a thing I've never seen before or since. I was thrilled. Everyone was thrilled. And whatever color prejudice I had, and I did have some, because I'd only known poor and uneducated Negroes, fell away. I wish others had similar opportunities."

"They will," said Robin, "they will." Pleased to receive evidence that this strategy worked, he in return complimented Jasmine on her chicken and potato salad. "Of the picnics I've had—and they are legion I can tell you," he said, inferring the necessity when traveling, "this is one of the best."

Seneca, having finished, lay stretched out full length on the grass, his jacket hanging on a tree branch, his hands behind his head, the wine bottle stashed conveniently alongside. "This is fine country," he told them, "it's great huntin country. Deer, possum, squirrel, even bear. But it's no place to hold a civil rights rally. I've campaigned in these parts and you can't change these people, politically or in any other way. Politically they're dyed-in-the-wool Republicans and that's that. Always have been. A lot of them even fought with the Yankees, but they weren't fighting to free Negroes—you can take my word for that. They're a law unto themselves pure and simple.

"Why only last year, a fellow I used to hunt with over near Mountain Springs, Ephraim Gates, was found shot through the head. They said it was suicide. His shotgun was laying there beside him. But he would have had to pull the trigger with his toe to have accomplished it, and why would he do that? The fact is, he was sleeping with his uncle's young wife. Everybody knew it but nobody told it to the police. To them the police are just another bunch of outsiders."

"And the worst outsiders of all are Negro outsiders," Robin genially supplied. "I have got the picture, Senator." He smiled. "But if it comes to that, Dr. Martin Luther King is a bigger fish to fry than me." The mordant wit, at once so pragmatic and so unchristian, delighted his two companions, who exchanged mutually wide-eyed gazes of amusement.

"A little irreverence from the reverend is a healthy thing," said Seneca reaching for the Chianti bottle.

"You know, Senator," Douglas went on, "your lack of faith puts you in an exposed position I myself don't feel. Faith is a wonderful refuge. No castle is more strongly built. Its sense of security is, I sometimes think, one of religion's finest gifts."

Seneca raised his head slightly, mainly to accommodate the bottle. "I hope to God it works, Reverend, and that's a prayer. But if we do run into any trouble, just sit tight: Put your faith in God, but let me handle it. I know these people." He did not think for a minute the reverend's head was fixed as firmly on his neck as did its trusting owner.

Robin, pouring out more coffee, recapped the thermos. "It's a deal, General," he said, exchanging another complicit smile with Jasmine.

AT INDIAN FALLS a single traffic light marked the junction with the town's main street. Men in faded denim overalls and women in shapeless cotton-print dresses were gathered along the arcade of connecting porches that lined the street. Thin raw-boned people whose lives clearly had not been easy or refined. A few older men sat in straw-bottomed chairs leaning on two legs back against the wall. They and others passing along the arcade stared hard at the car, their expressions grim, unmistakably hostile. One old fellow, sitting in a chair, spat his tobacco pointedly against a tire.

The light stayed red for what seemed an interminable time, and Seneca, without moving his head, glanced peripherally at Robin. He was looking straight ahead, his hands flat on his thighs, attempting beatific calm. Clearly he knew better than to return looks from the street. Eye contact provoked reaction, as it could never be ignored.

When at long last the light changed, they moved forward as in no particular hurry. Some graffiti scrawled on the general store's brick wall a little farther along read "Niggers, get off this mountain!"

"Your publicity people have been on the job," said Seneca. "I see folks are expecting us." He had himself made a point of eye contact with several bystanders, and a few eyes had dropped to the pavement in response. But he could feel their self-protecting anger, their sense of threat and outrage, of invasion. If the great world wasn't to swallow them up or cast them down, they had to keep to their ways and take some pride in them. They were a proud people; they always had been that.

In the rear-view mirror Seneca saw a few men move out into the street behind the car, watching their dust.

"My God, the looks those women gave me!" Jasmine however wasn't in the least alarmed. They were all so sad and run down. But she had been made to feel uncomfortable—a flaming Jezebel who ought to be stoned was what their expressions vehemently declared.

"Disintegrate the Niggers!" a surprisingly witty sign proposed, stuck on the back of a battered pick-up truck parked outside the town's drugstore.

A couple of miles farther along the road, they came upon two men on mules headed in the same direction. Seneca slowed down so as not to frighten the animals. As they came abreast, slowly passing the riders, he saw shotguns lying across the animals' withers. The men did not look at them. When the car had passed however they broke into a trot. Clearly in a hurry to get somewhere.

A little farther on, Seneca spotted a boy perched up in a tree beside the road. He believed he almost certainly was a lookout. As the car passed underneath, a rock descended. Narrowly missing the windscreen, it hit the top of the car. The boy began to vigorously wave his hat in great sweeping motions in the direction of the bend ahead, evidently signaling.

Again Seneca said nothing. Nor did anyone else. They all behaved as if it was nothing special.

The road wound downhill in sharp bends as they descended the mountain prior to ascending its neighbor. A stillness that in other circumstances would have been sublimely peaceful, now loomed uncanny and faintly alarming. Calm before storm. There was no traffic on the road at all, not in either direction.

Suddenly a car appeared at great speed from behind, a bespattered old Ford, a raccoon tail flying from the aerial. The car came up close behind, ominously tailgating. But after a minute or two it pulled out, roaring past them on a dangerous curve. There were three or four men in the vehicle. One of them, his arm out the window, pointed significantly at the raccoon tail. Despite the winding curves, the Ford continued along the center of the road for several minutes, its mudguards studded with glittering red lights that caught the sun. Till suddenly, gunning the motor, it disappeared at a furious pace around a bend.

"Those boys must be in a hurry to get to the rally, Reverend." Seneca was aware that the occupants must know the road was empty.

"How much farther is it?" asked Robin, with apparent calm. It was the first time he had spoken since Indian Falls.

"Only about five minutes as the crow flies. It's right over that mountain. It'll take us a good half hour I guess."

They had begun the final ascent. The curves in the road were less pronounced, snaking in longer spirals than the hairpin bends previously traversed.

Robin looked at his watch. It was 1:45. "Right on schedule," he said lightly.

The countryside was indeed beautiful, much of it virgin forest. Cottonwood trees and flowering dogwood covered the mountainside like a light spring snow. The air was as fresh and cool as it was quiet; and all along the road, spectacular pink and red blossoms adorned the dark and glossy rhododendron bushes. A woodpecker, ignoring the passing car, continued tapping its Morselike code repetitively on a roadside tree.

Rounding the next bend there was a short straight run, the ground flattening out before the next ascent, tall young trees bordering both sides. But at that moment, a hundred yards in front of them, like a mirage mysteriously projected onto the stilled landscape, shadowy figures emerged from both sides of the road, making a line across it. They were dressed as hunters, wearing wide-brimmed hats and carrying shotguns and rifles. Seneca counted four.

Slowly he brought the car to a stop some twenty or thirty yards in front of them. He was gauging it carefully: not too close not too far. Turning off the ignition he did not look at Robin Douglas, nor did Robin look at him, but Jasmine had leaned forward, her hand gripping Seneca's shoulder from the backseat, communicating protectively her alarm.

"Just sit tight," he told them firmly, his voice that of the experienced general commanding his troops. As he opened the car door he was thinking quickly, sizing the thing up, improvising a viable strategy.

"I'll come with you," Robin volunteered. It showed remarkable bravery.

"No point in setting the pigeon down among the cats," said Seneca lightly, repeating in a firmer tone, "Now just sit tight and let me handle it."

He got out, standing for a moment beside the vehicle, his full six foot three inches impressively erect, looking straight at the row of armed men forming a roadblock across the gray tarmac. Then with solemn dignity and a clear show of determined purpose, he strode toward them. His first goal was to stop the men getting anywhere near Robin. Happily, the angle of the sun obscured the windscreen, making a potshot useless.

The men held their guns underarm, barrels pointing at the road, as experienced hunters always carried guns before the prey was sighted. As Seneca came closer, one or two barrels lifted slightly in warning.

About ten feet away from the men Seneca stopped. "You fellows doin some huntin?" he asked casually in the local laconic drawl.

At first there was no response, then, "Yeah, mister, we sure are. Coon huntin." It was the man on the left. He had a brown mustache.

A snigger escaped from his smaller neighbor. The two other men frowned and said nothing.

"I got a meeting to go to over at Mountain Springs. Now, you fellows move back a bit and let me get this car through." As he said this, Seneca looked at each man carefully, sizing him up. They were all middle aged. Two of them had rifles, the man on the left, an old Kentucky rifle that must have been in his family for generations. They were still used in the mountains to hunt squirrels and small game. The other two had shotguns, one of them twelve bore.

Then, unaccountably, Seneca had a piece of luck. The man on the right was busy pulling his hat brim down, covering what was in fact a vaguely familiar face.

"Don't I know you?" said Seneca. "From over at Mountain Springs."

"I ain't studyin nothin bout that." The embarrassed man shrugged, not anxious to be recognized or won over.

"Mrs. Kane's brother. Isn't that right?" When his brother-in-law Robin's marital affairs were being worked out, Seneca had come to Mountain Springs to see Myra Kane's parents, and one of her brothers had come in lugging the biggest deer Seneca had ever seen in the state, twelve beautiful points. They'd had quite a chat about it.

"I ain't got no quarrel with you, General," the man burst out. "But we don't want no niggers on this mountain and that's that. If ya'll'll just turn that car round and git back where you come from there won't be no trouble. That meetin over at Mountain Springs gonna git bust up as it is."

"Give us the nigger," the man on the left suddenly demanded, spitting his tobacco contemptuously on the road.

If they had started with a unified agenda, it was crumbling.

"The man in that car is a preacher. He's a man of God. Now all of you were raised on the Bible, you first heard it sittin on your mama's knee. And you know that preachers are good men whatever color they are."

"Jes give us the nigger and git!" the man repeated.

"I'm taking Reverend Douglas to Mountain Springs." There was iron determination in Seneca's voice. "And if he isn't there in the next twenty minutes, state troopers are going to be sniffing over this mountain like a pack of hounds."

To drive forcibly through the line of men would he knew seriously tempt fate. Even if they did move back they almost certainly would fire at the car, aiming at Robin Douglas, or worse perhaps, shooting the tires and rendering all of them helpless and at their mercy. Already one or two wanted to go further than what appeared to be their brief. But having noted this, Seneca sought to drive a wedge between the factions, to divide and conquer.

"Mr. McArthur"—he had miraculously retrieved the family's name—"you're a man of intelligence, and you and I are sort of kin. Now I want you to persuade your friends here to stand back and let this car pass. I want you to help them stay out of some very serious trouble."

"Then leave that nigger ri'chere," the gangly man with the mustache insisted, raising his old rifle slightly. "Ya'll kin go on yore way, like Rufus here said. We got no quarrel with you less'n you git in the way."

The other men shuffled uneasily.

Seneca turned toward McArthur. "Your friends here are in real danger of going to jail for the rest of their lives, and causing this mountain to be occupied by U.S. Federal troops, a large number of whom *are* Negroes, who have submachine guns, and would like to use them."

McArthur glanced glumly at his cohorts. "Maybe we better let his one go, Wiley," he said.

McArthur's neighbor looked his agreement. "I ain't got no special grudge," he said, "but we don't want no niggers and that's that."

Seneca's strategy was working. "Up here a man's word is his bond just as sure as if his hand was on the family Bible," he said. "Now I'll give you my word that by sunset there won't be one Negro left on this mountain, that as soon as this meeting's over, things'll be back to normal. Unless you stop em."

"I reckon I could go with that," said McArthur. "Me and Jake."

"Well then, let's shake on it." Seneca stepped forward, holding out his hand, purposefully ignoring the other two. They could fall in once the bargain was struck.

"Don't come no closer." The man called Wiley raised the long barrel of the flintlock threateningly, though he still held it underarm.

Seneca moved forward anyhow.

When the flintlock's firing pin moved into half-cock, Seneca looked over at the man, looked him in the eye. Wiley's eyes, narrow and downward slanting, looked mean, through fear rather than determination. Fear was trickier, being unpredictable.

Seneca's gaze returned to McArthur. Again he stepped forward, his senses alert, calm, in full self-control, lit by that special awareness, that superalertness, superliveliness of a brave and able man approaching a rattlesnake. It had the edge of a developing thrill.

When Seneca heard the firing pin's second click as the rifle was fully cocked, he did not duck down or attempt to run, but turned his body slightly to the right, at an angle, to deflect the bullet's impact.

At the shot Jamine thought it had come from somewhere in the woods. The scene in front of her remained unchanged for what seemed a long time. Seneca stood there quite still, then he took another step toward McArthur, but instead of moving forward, he sank down, bending forward slightly, his right hand to his stomach.

"Jesus!" McArthur cried out in what sounded like true anguish. "You done shot a United States general. That there's General Nash. You done shot a war hero!"

Wiley stepped back looking nervous, defensively aggressive. "I tole him not to come no closer. I tole him twice." The magnitude of his action was sinking in. "I done tol him twice."

The car door had burst open and Jasmine was running forward. The other door opened, too.

The four men exchanged quick looks; mainly they looked at Wiley. In a minute, without full-scale carnage, their identities would be known.

"Let's go!" said McArthur. "Let's git out quick."

Robin was running forward, too. Another shot sounded, of warning or of final mad intent. The bullet whizzed by him, and struck the open car door, as the men dissolved into the woods, evaporating as quickly and silently as they had appeared.

Seneca half sat, half lay on the ground. There was no blood on his jacket, to Jasmine's vast relief, not even on the white shirt where his hand was gripping his stomach.

"Darling!" she cried out, stooping down beside him. On her knees she threw her arms around him. Her hand went to where his own lay against the white shirt. Beneath it was a small stain. Of course he had been hit. She knew that but she had been pretending otherwise.

Seneca looked up, his eyes a little vague.

"It's not bad, is it?" she cried, looking desperately around as Robin squatted down beside Seneca. He was reaching for Seneca's pulse.

"We must get you to a doctor," he said. "Is there much pain?"

"I can feel it," Seneca said. In fact the pain was intense.

"We'll have to get you into the car. It's going to hurt, I'm afraid."

Hurriedly bringing the car alongside, Robin got out frowning. There were only two doors. Access to the back seat would be extremely difficult.

"I've got to get you in that car," he repeated with intensity, half to himself. He had pushed the passenger seat forward, making narrow access to the back. Now he tried to pick Seneca up, his arms under Seneca's shoulders.

Seneca's lips shut tight in a thin line. He motioned with his hand to let go. "Leave me be," he said. He knew there was no hospital at Mountain Springs. The nearest one would be at Grafton, fifty miles away. Too far.

"But darling, we've got to get you to the hospital!" Jasmine desperately echoed. And yet they dared not chance moving him roughly. That could do deadly damage.

"There's an ambulance at Mountain Springs!" Robin suddenly recalled. "We're prepared there for emergencies."

Robin and Jasmine exchanged quick serious looks. Her leaving Seneca was out of the question. Robin must drive to Mountain Springs alone and at top speed. But at least the ambulance would be there. Jasmine praised God for Martin Luther King.

She had stretched Seneca out very gently, laying his head on her lap. Robin stooped down again. He touched Seneca's arm. "That bullet was meant for me." His voice was grave, apologetic, but there was no time for things that needed saying.

Seneca motioned dismissively with his hand, saving his breath, perhaps collecting himself for the ensuing battle, for the pain was fierce. He had been looking into the middle distance. Now he looked hard at Robin. "The Lord's got plenty of work cut out for you, Reverend," he said, the general's command even now uppermost in his tone. "See that you get it done."

"Darling!" cried Jasmine, leaning forward, searching his face. The implication was terrifying. And yet there wasn't much blood, almost none in fact. It didn't look that bad. But who could tell about internal bleeding?

In fact Seneca could tell. He was used to gunshot wounds. He also knew the power of a Kentucky rifle at ten paces.

"I'll be back in no time. Just hold on." It was both plea and promise.

"Get that flask," Seneca whispered hoarsely to Jasmine as Robin got in the car.

Robin pulled the whiskey flask from the glove compartment. As he drove off at top speed, Jasmine uncorked the leather bottle and raised it carefully to Seneca's lips. Seneca made an awful grimace, but it seemed to bring back energy.

His head still cradled in Jasmine's lap, he lay gazing up at the sky, framed by a slender circle of treetops waving gently, like medieval pennants around a jousting ground, he thought. Higher up, tufts of clouds were moving smoothly across the sky in tiny regular clusters. Blue had never been bluer or white whiter. He ached with the perfected splendor of it. He wanted to reach up and pull the clouds down to him, to feel their pure moist softness against his face. A moment of ecstasy. The pain had miraculously evaporated, according a glorious suspension.

As the shock deepened, jumbled thoughts came and went with the pictorial clarity of morning dreams. On his pony when he was four or five. The pony had broken into a mad gallop. At first he was afraid, then he had loved it, loved the thrill, the utter freedom, until he landed on his bottom on the ground. But the bump had been worth it. He always remembered that. And military school, when he won the class medal. Standing on the platform, the medal pinned on his breast, life had unfolded before him like a silken carpet being laid down, inviting a special destiny. He knew he had the energy, the intelligence, and the willpower to succeed and to enjoy it all as a supreme adventure. His life would be particular; he would make it so. Above all it would not be wasted. The mysterious forces that had invested in his assembly would, he vowed, be fulsomely repaid. And yet . . . how very strange . . . could it really, so suddenly so unexpectedly . . . be coming to a stop? The pain surged up again.

"Ashes . . ." Seneca murmured a few minutes later, and something about fathers, or was it gods. Jasmine couldn't hear it exactly. She feared he might be raving.

"Darling," she whispered gently, "the ambulance will be here very soon. Any minute now. The doctor will get you all patched up. You remember that trip to Oregon? We'll go there in August and sleep out under the stars and look at the lakes and rivers and flowers and trees. And the night will cover us like a velvet blanket, and the birdsong wake us up every morning, and . . ."

As she spoke, the images passed almost as reality before his eyes, carrying him into other territory, into an immensity of landscape that left the human scale behind. Life was such a pinprick in the vastness of time, almost a joke, a bad joke. And yet he held it so dear, pulled it so covetously to his chest. Life was everything. And suddenly he was being threatened with nothing. That it might go on without him seemed both obvious and incredible. A great surge to keep alive, to hold at bay the black void of oblivion possessed him. He tried to sit up.

"Don't move," said Jasmine, "don't move, darling. They'll be here soon. Very soon." Desperately she looked at her watch. Twenty minutes must have passed. How useless, how frail and impotent she felt. Could the wound really be serious? She had no way of knowing. Surely, with so little loss of blood, he could not be bleeding to death.

But he was. Every moment was falling like final grains into the bottom of an airtight jar.

Hurry, prayed Jasmine. Oh hurry, Robin, hurry!

Seneca felt for Jasmine's hand. He squeezed it, a protection against the void and nothingness. The human scale had returned, and with it ineffable sadness. The terrible prospect of rupture and separation. And yet he must not fear what every man must face. So very many had gone before—in the war, his mother and father. But he did fear it, feared it dreadfully. He must survive! There was so much more living left to do—so much more to accomplish. He could do more, much more, given the chance. He was sure of it. But he must seize that chance, for it would not again be given. A supreme act of will was needed, and reaching into the depths of his being, he summoned it up, refusing categorically defeat. Here was the ultimate challenge, and by God he was up to it! With a tremendous effort he raised himself, overriding pain, willing its abolition. He was going after those clouds.

"You can do it!" he seemed to hear Dartania say, and he almost smiled.

ROBIN DROVE IN a crucible of self-righteous fire. The familiar portage of a heavy cross had given way to that of a battle flag, borne triumphant, recklessly, behind the enemy lines. God must indeed protect him now, if only to preserve another's life—the loss of which Robin himself would bear responsibility for. At that thought something more devastating and insidious than fear possessed him. Guilt. If Seneca died, God in his infinite mercy would forgive, but being only a man, he would never be able to forgive himself.

As he pulled into Mountain Springs, the hostile, astonished stares began.

"Where's the doctor?" he shouted, rolling down the window. The man turned his back, kept on going, refused to see him.

The town square was ahead. It was virtually empty. Bleachers had been erected at one end, facing a raised wooden podium. A microphone was in place. On one of the square's benches sat a lone reporter, his feet encircled by pigeons nibbling the remains of his sandwich. He was reading a newspaper, a camera round his neck.

Robin leaped out of the car. "A doctor. I need a doctor. There's been an accident. Where is the ambulance?"

The reporter looked with some interest at this black man coming out of nowhere and alone. He didn't seem in need of a doctor, though.

"Everybody's in the cafeteria." The reporter nodded toward the neon sign behind him. WHITE'S CAFÉ. It flickered innocently.

As Robin entered, the buzzing hive offered a sudden, stunning silence.

Desperately he searched the room. "Where is the doctor, please!" he demanded nervously of a young waitress carrying coffee cups on a plastic tray.

She looked confused, scanning other faces hurriedly for direction.

"*Please,*" he said again. "I need a doctor, quickly."

When they saw that he wasn't going to try and sit down, it was a little easier.

The reporter, having followed his prey, stood just behind him, and Robin, now frantic for help, instinctively made a bargain. He traded his story. "It's Senator Nash," he whispered urgently. "He's been shot. Please, please help me to get the doctor! I know there's an ambulance here somewhere."

"Yeah, there is." The man glanced at his watch. Martin Luther King was arriving by helicopter in ten minutes. He was supposed to get that story and a photograph. This one was probably better, he decided. "OK, but I'm coming with you."

He approached the pretty waitress and whispered in her ear.

"That's the doc over there," he told Robin. "The ambulance driver's with him. Looks a right sawbones, don't he?" he added of the lean, hunched-over figure.

For the first time in his life, Robin was overjoyed to have a white man's company. He wasn't sure he could have persuaded the doctor, or even have found him in the crowded room.

Now, as the man arose from his lunch, there was silence again, faces agape with curiosity.

"We must hurry. *Please.*"

"What if something happens to Dr. King?" the ambulance driver wanted to know as they crossed the square.

Robin Douglas didn't give a damn.

FROM MORE THAN a mile away, Jasmine could hear the ambulance siren, its eerie wail rising and falling like that of a banshee as the vehicle careened along the winding mountain road, nearer and farther, nearer and farther, urgently racing against time.

Jasmine sat stroking Seneca's brow, his head still in her lap, half listening as the vehicle sped frantically in their direction along the winding road.

The first thing Robin saw was that they were exactly as before. Seneca's head still lay in Jasmine's lap, the pleats of her white skirt remained spread out about her on the ground, her head scarf, half untied, still covered her head.

But as they came into full view, she did not look up or move. She was looking intently at him, her head bowed, her arms spread slightly, as if gently holding his body. They were both so pale, so still. Suddenly a vision of the marble pieta he'd once seen in Rome, the madonna's hands spread out in such futility and despair, passed before Robin's eyes, and as the ambulance came to a halt, he began silently to pray.

10

....

$\int$eneca's death, its violence, and the wanton murder of so eminent a man, bewildered the nation. It seemed so pointless, a wild and random act, like being mown down by a drunken driver. A white man murdered by other white men; for what reason? Because a black preacher was in his car? It was out of all proportion. It didn't make any sense. Even among rabid segregationists, uncomfortable feelings stirred. The press therefore took many views. Some said it showed that guns should be controlled, others whiskey, others that it could only have happened in the backwoods, and a few that if it was racial then clearly there had been an awful foul-up.

The funeral, held three days later at the Episcopal cathedral on Shiloh Avenue, was packed. Television cameras whirred as U.S. senators and congressmen, Pentagon generals, the state governor, the head of the antigun lobby, and Martin Luther King, together with NAACP leaders, entered what *Newsweek* would describe with deprecating irony as the state's first integrated assembly. But every Southerner knew that was untrue. Black servants often attended white family ceremonies, and occasionally the reverse. This time, however, Cottoncrop and Longwood servants were standing with the family, the many dignitaries, black and white, crowding the pews behind; and Blue Hills was relegated perforce to a backseat.

The funeral speech was delivered by the Reverend Robin Douglas, a thing unheard of in the South. Seneca would have wanted it, Jasmine had insisted, and Dartania, for whom funerals were meaningless, had consented.

The lilting rhythmic oratory beloved by Nashborough's black Baptists was muted to a subtle undertone in Robin's speech, the deity never once invoked, the civil rights movement, an ever present undercurrent, mentioned but indirectly. Robin spoke in strong and solemn cadences of the man who had served his country devotedly as a general and a senator, and who had been sacrificed to it—a man who deplored among all vices that of cowardice, and who had fallen prey to one of its most virulent forms: racial prejudice.

"That bullet was meant for me," he told them with a sudden intensity, pausing so that the import would sink in. *"That life saved mine. I stand here at the expense of another man's life.* That knowledge is a heavy burden to bear—a heavy burden. But it is also an awe-inspiring responsibility, a mark to live up to for the rest of my life. Never ever will I give thanks for my delivery, but I can at least serve faithfully at the altar on which that life was sacrificed, and to that aim I am most willingly indentured." He paused again, the gravity of his position printed unmistakably, perhaps indelibly, upon his face. Then, gazing out upon the crowded congregation of mourners, he moved without notes into the more formal traditions of funeral oratory.

"Fellow citizens, we are here to bury a hero, a man who with high courage performed repeatedly in his life tasks that in spite of mortal danger, he believed must not be shirked. Heed him. I beg you, heed him closely, for there are not many of this great breed left. The heroic age is long past and its resplendent heroes fewer and fewer. In our era they are rare indeed. Yet it may be that soon they will no longer be needed, that having done their work, we are brought to the brink of another, a very different era, with its own distinctive lines of personal responsibility. The world is changing. We are changing it; it is changing us; and this new age already is upon us. It is young and fresh and full of promise. It is the Age of Ordinary Man.

"That does not mean, nor must it breed, mediocrity. The age of ordinary man enshrines a shared destiny, it bespeaks equality and consideration towards our fellow men. That is its voice and we are all familiar with it: We have heard that voice before. We have heard it in the aspirations of our founding fathers, in their hopes for an enlightened America, a higher expression of civilization than the world has known before. But what is civilization? The word turns on a single axle: that of civility. And humanity, which is its begetter, defines the exercise of the humane.

"As the great human qualities that have forged and adorned one era sink with their possessors into the clay that is part of us all, our responsibility grows. It grows to achieve, through our civility and our humanity, those goals our predecessors have so eloquently envisioned. To forge a society where education and security and self-respect exist in sufficient quantities that those fears that cause men to shield themselves within the heavy and restricting armor of prejudice can be discarded.

"In America the hour and the opportunity have joined hands, but the bargain must yet be struck. Should we fail, no doubt we must again seek the protection of heroes and fathers on this earth, whether dictatorial or benevolent, and we must continue to endure the cramped and suffocating armor of prejudice.

"Here then is the challenge of this new age. We must give generously of our humanity to accept that challenge, to nourish it, and to make that great vision on which our nation was founded into reality. If we succeed, Senator Nash will not have died in vain and we can write large as an epitaph: 'A life that forged the way.'"

Parts of the speech were played voice-over as TV cameras followed the funeral cortege leaving the Episcopal cathedral and assembling in a train of cars behind the flower-laden hearse, en route to Cottoncrop. Though some had found the words too preachy, others, caught up in the lilting rhythm, had felt themselves lifted briefly as on air by the offered vision.

Either way, Robin Douglas, as an emerging figure in the civil rights movement, was overnight known to all America.

AFTER THE BURIAL at Cottoncrop, Dartania went straight home. She had spoken to almost no one, and knowing her desire for privacy, everyone let her go, sparing her their needful offerings of condolence.

Arriving at Longwood before the servants, she changed quickly, went out to the barn, and saddled up old Molly. She rarely rode nowadays, but suddenly motion of some kind was necessary. Whether its effect was the equivalent of a cradle rocking, or a race well run, or simply something happening, moving along, wasn't clear and didn't matter.

At a walking pace she made her way along the badly rutted track beyond the long wood, the reins resting loosely on Molly's neck as the old mare plodded along, half asleep. It was a fine late-spring day, the dogwood still in bloom, the young leaves confidently uncurling on the oaks. Along both sides of the track, patches of russet sage grass stretched, alternating with a brambly undergrowth, blanketing the corrugated furrows of redundant farmland.

Farming was a thing of the past. The midwestern plains had seen to that, and locally the land, always so quick to erode when cleared, was returning with an extraordinary rapidity back into the forest from which it so laboriously had been pulled. All trace of the hard repetitive toil that for 150 years had imposed man's signature and will was disappearing, and in the long wood deer had recently been spotted.

But Dartania wasn't looking at her surroundings. Hers was an inner vision, if it could be called a vision, more of an innerscape, which she took in intermittently, like rubbing a frosted window and peering briefly through before it iced up again. Not one to examine her feelings, she could not have said what she felt, but numbness would probably have described it best, the rubbed window offering moments of unwanted clarity, making her glad when it froze up again.

That Seneca was dead, that she would never see him again or hear his voice, had not arrived. They had been apart so often—the war, Washington, his many trips. The void, if it was a void, had been there a long time, their feelings for each other such a complex tangle, though recently they'd simply rubbed along, not feeling much of anything really. Always however there ran the subterranean tie—the same as a family tie, part of the same innate connection, and though so often dormant, becoming in extremis absolutely primal.

Whatever his feelings for her—and he had loved her deeply in his way—he also had tremendously admired her. She took great pride in that. His admiration had been aimed at her best self, and for a man like Seneca, it formed the highest tribute. And yet he had wanted her, in addition to what she was, to be another sort of woman, a mothering sort of woman. It had always seemed to her unmanly for a grown man to continue to need and want a mother. She felt it was a weakness, and it had caused ambivalence. Robbie too had suffered from it.

Poor Robbie, now very ill, but devotedly looked after. Each month Dartania sent his wife a check. Nobody, not even Seneca, had known that. She used her own money. At first she'd sent the check to Robin, but eventually his wife had written, begging her to desist, as he spent most of it on drink. So Dartania sent it to his wife instead, and snippets of news came back in the woman's simple notes. Robbie could not last much longer, she had written.

And Seneca was dead.

Dartania looked straight ahead. Summoning the present, she looked hard for the first time that day at her surroundings. The old Tebbit cabin loomed ahead, its roof caved in; the once sun-silvered tin, rusted and twisted, lay strewn about outside like fallen leaves. The screen door hung on one hinge; the door itself stood open. The Tebbits were in Nashborough somewhere, swallowed in the anonymity of town life, in what Cal's son had called with so much pride, the age of ordinary man. The Tebbits had been poor here, locked in an incessant struggle to survive; but they had belonged somewhere, pulling a strong identity from the land. Who, in their opinion, she wondered, were they now?

Dartania dismounted and tied Molly's reins to the porch post. Then she sat down on the porch edge. Just sat there. Somewhere down near the pond—that at least remained as a landmark—they'd had a picnic: she and Seneca and Robin. Robin had just become engaged and was exuberant, perhaps exuberant to have made a decision. And Seneca too had been in high good spirits, waving a coonskin at them in welcome, bristling with energy and purpose. How young she now saw they had been, and how happy and uncomplicated her life. When and how had it gone off the rails?

Until now, except for Robin's disappearance, there had been no momentously reshaping tragedy or event, no serious reversals to health, or even fortune, despite the war and the Depression. Was it merely the perversity of time and flux? She had tried so hard to keep things as they were, to resist change, and to preserve the life they had. But all the time, secretly, she was also waiting—a lady in waiting, she smiled wryly at the thought—waiting for her chance in life, for her vindication of it, waiting for some piece of heroism to come her way, her chance at last to perform great deeds, to feel again as she had felt the time that Seneca shot a lemon from her hand. Keeping free for it, eschewing the normal life of women, with its small concerns, its ordinariness—which lacked all appeal, she had envied Seneca his war, his maleness. She herself would willingly have died a hero's death. That would have vindicated all.

But women married and could not, in Nashborough anyhow, combine two lives. Besides, she had no training or education or money of her own, or even anything specific that she wished to do. Unlike Jasmine and her painting. Though that had come to nothing. But Jasmine had so joyfully fled the family nest. Was it cowardice that she herself had not? For her, uprooting would have removed the very ballast of her being, the connections that defined and grounded and made her who she was. In history, exile was punishment on a par with death. It was a kind of death, and so it would have been for her.

And yet the Prince of Wales had done it—abandoned his golden cage, even welcomed his exile. She had admired that at the time, but recently she'd seen a photograph, taken at some nightclub in New York, and he looked miserable. A displaced person, tumbled into another, foreign, cage. It was the same with Robbie. He had found a mothering woman, but he remained in other ways a displaced person, foundering, ultimately at sea. Perhaps for some people that was always so. They were unable to cut their roots. Transplantation did not mean freedom, only isolation, pointlessness.

As a woman she had expected, it was true, to be looked after, had taken that for granted. It was part of the tradition in which she had been reared. But at the same time she had refused to take up the conventional wifely role that was perhaps its price, refused, she now admitted, to see it as the price. She had taken everything as her due—a tribute to her spirit and beauty, which were much acknowledged. But if she had refused to pay the price, why then shouldn't Seneca have sought compensation for her lacunae elsewhere? In fairness, she could hardly blame him, and the opportunities were always there. Women threw themselves at him. Her own sisters. Jasmine at the funeral had looked so pale. Dartania had pondered that relationship, deciding long ago that Jasmine, whatever her inclinations, was, like herself, too loyal to actively deceive a sister. But if not, maybe Jasmine had done her a favor; maybe she had given, not taken, filling in for her sister's lapses. Maybe she ought to be thanked. In truth, it was easier all round not to know. Let sleeping dogs lie she had firmly told herself, recalling her seething anguish over Red Mason, which, in retrospect, now seemed a kind of madness, corrosive and totally useless.

Chloe too had always had a crush on Seneca. You could see that a mile off. But Chloe hadn't pined or hung about. She had taken what life served up and made the best of it. People were even saying that Stark might be the next vice-presidential candidate. Chloe was dull but she had iron in her soul. Her head was definitely screwed on.

While she herself—the window thawed again and this time Dartania baldly confronted the truth of what she saw—while she herself, at fifty-five, had now nothing to show for it. She had been making do. Keeping free of ordinary concerns, minute and shallow and mundane, she had floated along, marking time and waiting. But her eagerly anticipated hour had not arrived, the niche where her particular genius could unfold had remained empty, its location never uncovered.

And Seneca was dead.

With a sharp edge it arrived, and with it the thought, searingly painful, that he had probably done the best by her he could. A surge of devastating longing possessed her, a desperate urge to compensate, to put things right. And oh, suddenly she missed him! She had taken so much for granted, had taken him so much for granted, as a rock to lean upon—for she had leaned—refusing at the same time that he should do so in return. There was the rub. She dared not look any closer. She must turn away from it, for nothing could now be changed. She stood up nervously. Her throat felt parched and dry; she would have dearly loved a drink.

Nothing could now be changed.

The Tebbits' well was just visible among the brambles, its bucket still there, the dipper hanging on its peg. Carefully Dartania picked her way through the thorny undergrowth and, leaning forward over the dark hole, let the bucket drop. The rope whirred, followed by a sharp echoing splash as the pail hit the black water below. There was something appealing in the sound, definite, familiar. She began to hoist the pail. The rusty pulley made it difficult, but the effort concentrated thought, concentrated reality, obscured the hovering precipice, the fact that *nothing now ever could be changed; it was all too late, over with. Seneca was dead.*

When at last the bucket surfaced, to her surprise, tiny spouts of water were pouring in minute waterfalls from all sides. Someone must have used it for target practice. Quickly Dartania retied the rope and unhooked the metal dipper. Filling it she raised it to her lips. The water was fresh and cold. It tasted good even if it quenched little. She must steady herself, marshal her thoughts, keep away from the precipice, from the thoughts edging in upon her like thick fog. Loss, regret, emptiness, failure—a deadly apocalypse coming through the fog, coming unavoidably into full view, set to trample and crush.

Stubbornly she refilled the dipper and drank again, this time more slowly, focusing on each swallow. Then, her back to the ruined cabin and encroaching wood, she stood, the dipper dangling from one hand, and watched, through misted eyes, the bucket empty, the water showering back into the well from holes too small to see.

11

....

Six months later, on a September afternoon, Jasmine knocked briefly at the apartment door that she knew was never locked. "Danny?" she called out softly from the vestibule.

He had wheeled halfway across the studio as she entered it. "Well, this is an unexpected pleasure!" It was the first time since Seneca's funeral that they had met.

She looked remarkably well, he thought, a little drawn perhaps, the gray line at the part of her dark bobbed hair carelessly unrepaired. And aware that she would not have come without some special reason, added to a general desire to see him, his curiosity enlarged.

"You certainly can keep an eagle eye on Blue Hills from up here," she cast off lightly, rhetorically, looking out at the panoramic view. "Very lofty, yes indeed." Her eyes roved the book-lined room and the desk covered with an untidy manuscript. "Am I the person from Porlock? What have I interrupted?"

"Oh, just bringing the family history up to date."

"Are you still at it, after all these years? Good God! And is it accurate? That could be sort of embarrassing."

"I don't know if it's factually accurate; I hope it's artistically so. People walk and talk. I've put words in their mouths."

"Well, why not. Picasso once said that art is a lie that makes us see the truth."

"And Nietzsche, that we have it so as not to perish from the truth."

Jasmine shrugged and let it go. Although it was only five o'clock, she readily accepted a martini and sat down on the white sofa, her back to the huge bay window. Or rather she perched, nervously upright, unsupported by several inviting cushions.

"You'll never guess what!"

"No, I won't." It appeared there was to be no beating about the bush; she was going straight to the point.

"I've stopped smoking. Given it up. Just like that."

"Oh?" So there was to be some beating about the bush.

"Yes, they say it gives you cancer." The triumphant note usual to any announcement of achievement was absent. "But I have to do something with my hands, so—this will astonish you, Danny—I've started painting again. After all these years. Sunday painting: That was always my level you know; why I would never touch it in the past. I was an awful snob, wasn't I? I don't know how you all put up with me. I thought creativity so superior—that was the upper crust I wanted baking into! But now I think toothbrushes are more important than paintbrushes, and art is just a pastime, like any other."

Dan fell headlong into this one. "Still, art does have special value, I think, even if it is a kind of play. We can live more intensely through it, risk empathy, and learn a thing or two without bringing danger to ourselves, which living through such experiences would do." He sliced the air with his hand. "Lord, excuse the pedantry. How are you, Jasmine?" The question was full of quiet significance.

"Me? Oh I'm fine, just fine." She had got up again. "In fact, I'm remarkably well." She sat down. "I'd kill for a cigarette though."

He made another opening. "You look surprisingly well."

"Do I?" Still she hesitated, then . . . "You're going to laugh at me, Danny, but the fact is I have this extraordinary feeling that Seneca is with me all the time, that he's right over my shoulder, as it were, guiding me along. I talk to him constantly, and my feelings for him have never been sweeter or more tender.

"There's such extraordinary happiness in it—in my heavenly haunting," she added by way of an embarrassed joke.

It was the first time she had openly admitted the relationship to her brother, and after so much open secrecy, that it was easier to confess a fantastic posthumous version—though in some ways safer—privately amused him.

"You sound lucky to me," he said with some sincerity.

"Yes, I think so, too." She smiled vaguely and again reverted to irony. "Dabbling in the spirit world. It's a bit like getting religion, isn't it? And as I could never believe in any of that, why this, I ask myself. Why am I so firmly convinced of this?"

"If it helps . . ."

"If it helps, why be intellectually rigorous you mean? Oh I agree. Robin says it's my innate religious instinct, finally put to some use."

"Robin?" He looked surprised.

"Black Robin." She laughed and went on. "I work for him three days a week now at the SCLC. Seneca would approve of that. But he'd say my heavenly haunting is a crutch. Yet, how can one be sure? It *seems* so real—and stranger things have happened." She twisted the worn strap on her shoulder bag. "Have you ever believed in the possibility of spirits?"

"The human spirit is about my limit I'm afraid."

"But when you think how indescribably complex the universe is, and to have only five miserable senses with which to comprehend it—five isn't much. Maybe all sorts of other things have, or would have, a reality, if only we had faculties to perceive them. Maybe on that scale, by comparison, we're deaf and dumb."

Dan was eyeing her archly.

"All right, I'm flailing about, I know it, but the fact is I'm just not able to let him go. Not yet. I can't do it, Danny. Maybe over time it will all just fade away, or get pushed out by something else. I don't mean *someone* else; there's no chance of that. But become less necessary." She looked him mournfully in the eye.

"We're getting old, Danny. That's what must be faced next. That's the next course: dessert—our just desserts. God, I sound like Flora. She's always making puns. But this is a precious interval and we should give thanks every day for it. I know that's true but I can't *feel* it. A connection's snapped. Oh dear, I didn't mean to bang on about myself. You bring it out, sitting there like some priest with his ear to the confessional grille. And then you go and put it all down in that book of yours. But the fact is, I'm worried about Dar. Have you seen her?"

He suspected Jasmine had reached the point of her visit. "No, have you?"

She shook her head.

"Did she know about you and Seneca?" Dan was surprisingly blunt.

"I don't know. I don't think so. But I'm glad to learn it's not just me she's not in touch with. There's been a sort of veil between us. No more than that. We've always loved each other, you know. But yes, I admit I've been afraid to call her. Well, what could I say? Dar would hate my mentioning anything direct, I mean my mentioning Seneca at all. You know that. You can't talk to her. It's partly because she doesn't know how to reply."

"But you think she may have started to examine things?"

"Oh, Dar's never examined anything in her life. She hasn't the patience. But her instincts are as swift and sure as an animal's. Anyhow, I thought you might know something. Not much misses you up here. Or that if not, maybe you could call her and sound her out. Or we could even drive over to Longwood together."

"Sally says she's become a hermit, if that's any comfort. Never comes into town, never plays bridge anymore."

"But it's so unlike Dar to avoid society. She used to love it so. You see, Danny, I'm afraid she's drinking. It's the family tonic after all. Look at Robbie. And Flora's headed down the same road, I can tell you." She shrugged again, abruptly shifting the breathlessly delivered speech. "It's so odd, isn't it—living I mean. Some people take to it like a duck to water, and others don't or won't or can't. Just look at our family—we've had everything really, all sorts of advantages. But have we made much of it, built on them? Some of us have even fallen behind the starting post. I believe Papa would be disappointed in us."

Dan smiled patiently and suddenly Jasmine saw she had been gauche.

"Well, I mean, poor Robbie's a lost cause, and Bayard hasn't done anything for years, and I'm a Sunday painter with a two-bit job. You're the one exception, with your books. Oh I'd give anything for a cigarette!"

In the end, suspecting they might not be warmly welcomed, they drove out to Longwood unannounced.

Delphine, limping and bent over with rheumatism, met them at the door. Dartania was at Miss Flora's for the night, she told them. They were going to get the little girl a dog. Mr. William was up in New York, or across the waters somewhere.

"I'm so glad we came," Jasmine insisted on the way home. "I feel so much better. At least we know she's getting out a bit, taking an interest in things. Dar is a real survivor, you know. She never lets things get her down. She cuts them off, blocks them before they get too close. That's her way. But Flora has always been her favorite; I only wish the poor girl could be made to believe it."

SITTING TOGETHER AT one end of the long, finely polished dining room table, Flora and her mother ate dinner in an unselfconscious silence, then went to their rooms—Dartania to the ornate guest bedroom downstairs, where, having thrown the embroidered silk coverlet on the floor, she got into bed with her book. She lay there for a minute, propped up by goose-down pillows, staring reflectively at nothing, a deep melancholy taking possession of her delicate features, veiling them in silent misery. Then with a look of conscious determination, she picked up her book.

Flora had returned to her boudoir in the doctor's old bedroom. Like her mother she had felt no need to make a social effort. She readily accepted, even envied to a degree, her mother's isolated hermitage at Longwood. Life at Cottoncrop, at least when William was there, was so enormously public; the parties, the continual stream of house guests, the comings and goings of photographers and journalists. Even passing strangers, if they rang the bell, were allowed to see the house.

Keeping to her boudoir, as now, Flora managed in a show of overt serenity to float through it all—to keep afloat. Yet increasingly she was ill at ease and anxious, depressed and obscurely frightened, and without any reason. Since her father's death it was worse, sometimes edging over into panic. She seemed to grope in a miasmic fog, to flounder in a muffled suffocating vagueness that eradicated what was tangible. When she examined her anxieties however they proved to be distorted perceptions, without any basis in reality. She was in fact enormously secure. She loved her husband and her child. Her roots were deeply in place, and life made no unpleasant demands that could not easily be escaped. Strange that a mysterious shadow world could blot this out like an eclipse and the shadows assume thereby such convincing reality!

William's recent news, so eagerly awaited and so devoutly wished for, had made these baffling and obscure anxieties the more intense. William was to play Richard III on Broadway, the youngest actor ever to do so. But then King Richard, as William pointed out, was only eighteen at the battle of Tewkesbury, and thirty-three at his death. His scheming and ambitious calculations were those of a very young man whose knowledge of life was limited by inexperience. He was dangerously unripe. It would be a novel interpretation. Rehearsals had begun and the play was due to open in six weeks. If it was a success, said William, they could take a suite at the Plaza and live like lords for the duration.

This happy and long-anticipated news had come fast upon the heels of an announcement of a very different stamp. For months William had been using his clout as a celebrity, and also making donations to Catholic charities, when out of the blue it suddenly had paid off. A registered letter had arrived from his Chicago orphanage. Signing for it, William had stuffed the envelope casually into his pocket and tucked himself away to read it in private.

"It transpires that I am not Chinese. Nor am I descended from Genghis Khan, as you so romantically have supposed." Having flung himself into the old rocking chair in Flora's boudoir, he stood up again, so lightly he seemed suspended on strings, and placed himself upon the small stage of the hearth, "You see before you a descendant of one of America's oldest families." He paused, a twist of bitter irony lit his words.

Flora was all ears.

"Daddy, it seems, was an American Indian. Perhaps part of the Chicago World's Fair exhibition. Or a cigar-store specimen," he added with a blister of deep anger. "But Mama's family, being up-and-coming, I suppose, hadn't raised their daughter to squaw in some reservation wigwam. Or perhaps there was already a greasy, blanket-covered squaw in residence. So, into the orphanage with the embarrassing debris. They refused to give names, said that might embarrass my progenitors. Pretty illogical in my view, but not that it matters; I've no desire to look them up, I can tell you."

Flora had been delighted by this pedigree. That little Alice was a quarter Indian, she found charming, though she could find no high cheekbones or the square shoulders she imagined to be typical, on the little girl. But William appeared to feel he'd lost another inheritance. Whatever he had expected to find, this wasn't it. A surprising moroseness had descended, to be miraculously, instantaneously dissolved by the announcement of his Broadway role—and its collateral: the imminent assumption of another character.

Now, sitting in the rocking chair after dinner, reading Thackeray's *Vanity Fair,* Flora reflected that England's class system had left unfortunate marks on William, just as it had on Becky Sharp, turning them both into unrelenting and ambitious conquerors. Her father too had been a conqueror and ambitious, but it was balanced by a sense of social fairness into which such instincts had been channeled, or largely so. No, she would not think about all that.

Letting the book slide to the floor, she stood up and wandered over to the French doors of the balcony. She could see the moon beginning to rise, malformed and lumpy—a gibbous moon, if you were a poet. She watched as it moved toward her over the rows of little houses in the surrounding subdivisions, before disappearing suddenly into the black magnolia tree at the foot of the lawn.

She noticed that the light was on in her mother's room below, and she wondered if she was secretly mourning, perhaps was wretched even. If so she would never show it. But some of her old verve was gone if you looked closely enough. That she might in fact be miserable, sunk in a wordless isolating sorrow, caused Flora a wrenching dismay, for her mother was not a woman who could be comforted.

At that, Flora went into the bathroom and, taking the julep cup that doubled as a tooth mug, opened the little refrigerator in William's dressing room and poured out a large shot of vodka. Then she returned to the rocking chair, lit a cigarette, and, rocking gently, watched with closer interest as the moon, having pulled free from entanglement in the magnolia, began to rise like a half-filled helium balloon, handicapped but triumphant, in the sky. She was waiting for the arrival of her quiet time, when the detritus of everyday life would fall away, sloughed off like a shabby suit of clothes, and with it her growing and ever-present disquiet. She was waiting for bliss to roll in—so gently, so mysteriously—and cover her like a warm and soothing counterpane, at the same time reuniting her with the universe, melting her into its bosom.

It was getting harder and harder to achieve. There was so much distraction, so many petty things to think about. The house overwhelmed her. This room was really her house, and sitting in it, rocking, smoking, and sipping the warming strident vodka, had become a quasi-religious ritual—the act of communion needed to achieve her own personal little nirvana. Peace and euphoric tranquillity. But another shot would be necessary, at the very least—a need that was soon fulfilled.

Standing again before the balcony, idly studying the patch of lawn lit by her mother's bedroom light, suddenly Flora perceived that someone was out there, near the magnolia tree, just beyond the bedroom's throw of light. Someone was standing very still, watching the house. They were being spied upon. Startled, she drew swiftly back, then peered at the lawn more closely from a protected angle. She and her mother and little Alice were alone in the house and she couldn't remember if she'd locked the door. Probably she had not, and yet Cottoncrop's constant publicity could so easily have attracted burglars. Why had she never seriously thought of that!

Nervously Flora began a cautious vigil of her own, but it was difficult to maintain. Fifteen minutes passed and still the figure had not moved—she would have discerned any movement, given the patch of light, even from within the shadows. But the figure was as immobile as a statue, gazing with such immensity of concentration at the house. It was uncanny.

So uncanny that suddenly a spreading frisson of excitement took possession of her. It could be that it was the Indian. Yes, oh yes, surely it must be him! She was almost certain of it. The protracted and unearthly watch, such absorbed scrutiny and patience—from whom else could such things emanate? Instantly the threatening presence was converted into a comforting sentinel, though she could not have said why. Never once had she speculated on the Indian having any particular character or purpose. His rare and ghostly presence had always been enough—it had delivered wonder. But now, standing so still, so patiently; what on earth could he be waiting for?

Flora drew the rocking chair up to the French doors, and sitting down, continued to gaze with fascinated curiosity into the lugubrious shadows. Reflectively she sipped her drink. Of course she *had* been thinking of Indians, but still . . . She peered again more closely, hoping to prove the reality of her prodigious insight. But at that moment her mother's light went out, and like a theater curtain ringing down, darkness blanketed the lawn. The show, it seemed, was over, the sole remaining audience being the pale lopsided moon, its head, so strangely cocked, still gazing from above with eerie contemplation, continuing inscrutably the watch.

DARTANIA AWOKE FROM a muddled dream about maimed horses. A furious scratching sounded at the bedroom door. It took her a minute or two to figure it out. Flora's cat.

She was about to get up and let the animal in when the scratching ceased. But a few minutes later it began again, together with a high-pitched mewing.

Dartania got up and opened the door. "What is it, Ftatateeta? Do you want to come in? Well come on then."

But the cat shot off.

Mildly annoyed, Dartania was closing the door when, having followed vaguely the animal's direction, she saw with astonishment what looked like a heavy cloud suspended strangely at the top of the stairs. It was as if the sky had fallen in.

Smoke! How could she not have smelled it!

"Flora!" she shouted out.

Holding up her flannel nightgown, Dartania rushed barefoot up the stairs, frantically calling her daughter's name.

An eerie light glowed on the landing like a beacon seen through dense fog, investing it with a rosy glow. "Flora! Flora!"

Someone was coughing, gasping for breath, and crying.

Little Alice. The nursery was opposite.

Holding her breath, her long plait held masklike across her face, Dartania hurried across the smoke-filled hallway and into the nursery. She pulled the child from her crib without a word. The little girl might have been a bundle of clothes. Where the devil was her nurse! All her thoughts were fixed on Flora.

"Flora, for God's sake, wake up!" Dartania shouted, leaving the nursery. "Flora! Flora! *For God's sake, please wake up!*"

But there was no reply.

Suddenly she could hear the scream of distant sirens. Someone must have sounded the alarm, seen flames. Perhaps the roof was on fire.

She would have to get Alice, gasping frantically now for breath, downstairs, and then come back. She would have to hurry. Her own eyes were watering badly and it was harder and harder to breathe.

As she sped downstairs, the cat hard on her heels, the floorboards, suddenly warm under her bare feet, felt oddly comforting.

Outside, massive red fire engines were pulling up. Men were shouting. There was the sound of breaking glass.

"Here, take this child!" she ordered a tall young man in boots and black slicker jacket, about to enter the house.

The young man could only comply, and the child, fascinated by such a spectacular fireworks display, went easily into his arms, almost without noticing.

Now tall ladders were going up, flat hoses unwinding, filling with water. A powerful stream arched in a sudden burst toward the upstairs window, where flames poured out so fiercely, they too seemed to desperately seek escape.

Dartania ran back into the house. She could hear men shouting at her. Upstairs the whole front of the house was now ablaze. A fierce determination possessed her. There was no wavering, no thought for herself, she was driven by a single purpose. Only the faintest sensation under her fears for Flora suggested that she was edging toward something momentous— something approaching vindication.

At the bottom of the stairs an older fireman stepped forward, blocking her ascent. "You can't go up there, lady."

"Get out of my way," she shouted. "My child is up there! You come too," she ordered him. "Front bedroom on the right."

Though taken aback, the fireman, who thoroughly understood his job, resolutely held his ground. "They'll get her out with ladders," he said firmly. "There's too much smoke up there. The roof may come down any minute. You get out now, ma'am. Don't worry. We'll see to it." But he was shocked to learn someone was still up there, as it almost certainly was too late.

Dartania pushed contemptuously past him.

The fireman, at a loss for a minute, quickly recollected himself. Without hesitating, he grabbed her by the forearm and pulled her forcibly back.

Wheeling on him, Dartania with the other arm struck out with all her might. It was a heavy blow. The fireman almost lost his balance on the step, almost let go. But he knew now that he had no option. He returned the blow with force.

Dartania sank to the floor and was carried unceremoniously outside.

"Better sedate her," the fireman advised the young doctor gazing in rapt awe from beside the ambulance. "There'll be some bad news, I'm afraid."

IN THE SURROUNDING subdivisions, people watching from their lawns in fascinated horror the sky glow red with flames, pulled their dressing gowns more tightly about them as the house that had always dominated their horizon, glowed incandescent, like a great fireball descended from above. Over in Zion dawn seemed to be rising early and in the wrong direction. And even in far-away Blue Hills a faint tint on the skyline could have be seen in Dan's bay window, as the historic old house, so magnificently and painstakingly refurbished, was incinerated.

By midmorning only the brick walls remained, but debris was still burning and a few casual looters skipped furtively among the smoldering remains. One of them carried a Sevres sugar bowl hidden in the frayed remains of an old sack, or what appeared to be an old sack. "One for all," heavily smeared by soot, was stitched on it. The rest had fizzled away.

"Movie Star's Historic Mansion Burns," the morning *Echo* blazoned. It had gone to press too early for any pictures.

William was on his way back from New York, and as other members of the family were yet to be informed, Flora's death for the time being was discreetly unreported.

By afternoon however television cameras, showing the smoking ruin, panned over the blackened walls and skeletal remains of charred and broken beams. There were interviews with firemen and neighbors who had seen the blaze, and across Nashborough possible causes of the fire and its horrific results were authoritatively discussed. An electrical fault was suspected or more likely a chimney had caught fire, or else a gas main had erupted. Hadn't an explosion been reported? The inevitable sprinkling of paranoid people suggested arson by envious neighbors or, more vehemently, Zion Negroes. Some even gave names to the police. But a cigarette, dropped from the hand of a sleeping woman who had had too much to drink, was never mooted—or if it was, never openly so.

12

....

*D*artania repeatedly insisted she could have saved her daughter. Her failure to do so haunted her obsessively. She had dreams of saving her—of Flora standing trustingly before the flames as Dartania made her way to her through heavy smoke. Or anxiously tapping her sleeping daughter's shoulder, and Flora arising trancelike from the canopied bed and gliding faithfully behind her mother down the big staircase. At which point Dartania always awoke, feeling, like Orpheus, that something had gone dreadfully wrong.

The funeral had been horrid. Untimely deaths were always horrid. But the blackened skeleton of Cottoncrop, rising ominously beyond the family graves, underlined with graphic versimilitude the realities of ruin, decay, finality, and ultimately man's frail grasp on his own circumstances.

William had been grim and dignified, keeping aloof and speaking to almost no one. Only Sally had wept, but her generation did that sort of thing. Dartania, hating words as useless and ceremonies as absurdly empty, looked nervous and impatient, even angry. Obviously exhausted, she was the first to leave.

"Poor Flora! She couldn't have lived," Jasmine, standing beside the open grave, whispered to Madeleine. "She *had* everything, but she lacked the essential equipment. This living business isn't for everyone, you know."

"You're quite the sibyl." Madeleine smiled indulgently.

"I am quite the survivor," Jasmine corrected, her tone suggesting a prison sentence unavoidably being served.

"Dar's in a dreadful state," she added sadly. "She gets that angry look when she's really down. It means she's fighting hard; and she's been crying her eyes out too. Did you see how red they were? Of course she'll never let on."

As the others departed Jasmine, lingering on, wandered over to Seneca's grave. It was marked by a simple headstone. So too the graves of all the Nashes, whose husks lay beneath the ground, the more recent ones too well encased by modern technology ever to become a part of it. The headstones, simply engraved with a name and dates, movingly bespoke a futile human longing not to vanish utterly from the earth. Stone outlasted flesh.

A gentle awe arose as Jasmine mused upon this eloquent statement of the human condition, its innate tragedy of transience and curtailment. Yet death was, paradoxically, not only the price of life, but without its accompaniment, life wouldn't really be worth living. That was the extraordinary thing, that was the joker in the pack. Death gave to life its edge and, together with its sadness, its essential sweetness and value. It was individuality that made death so terrible, for there was always renewal, the genes kept on going, the chemicals re-formed into other matter; life went on. Only the individual disappeared. But the individual was becoming more and more important, and death in consequence the more terrifying and outrageous. Family life, communal life, the tribe were vanishing. Men increasingly were islands, and evidently by their own choosing.

Beyond the thicket of headstones, some of them wafer thin, she saw William leaving. A chauffeured car waited to take him back to the airport. His play was due to open in five weeks, and he fully intended it should do so.

THERE REMAINED UNSETTLED, however, the question of little Alice. Ellen had volunteered to take the child, even to come to Nashborough for her. At which Bayard was politely mute, and Madeleine put her reaction into a single raised eyebrow.

But all agreed it was the only solution. The child could not live in hotel rooms with her father, and in a year or two she would have to go to school. For the present she and Janey, her new nurse, had moved to Bayard's, which was cramped, and intruded on his established routine and general mode of living. On Thursday, traditionally the servants' day off, Bayard was completely at a loss. Who was going to look after the child?

In desperation he telephoned Dartania. As a grandmother she, too, must make some contribution. At least come by and look after Alice for two or three hours while he went to a meeting. It was an important meeting: shaping Stark's bid for the vice-presidential nomination. They might see Stark in the White House yet—and Chloe with him. The odds were damned good.

Dartania instantly jibbed. She had never looked after a child in her life. (On Miss Allen's days off mercifully the chore had fallen to Delphine.) Besides, she had other things on her mind, and she could no longer adapt to sudden arbitrary demands. Her resilience, or what was left of it, had been incinerated in the fire. Flora's death had simply flattened her, turning the world on its ear, so that leaving Longwood right now was out of the question. She simply wasn't up to it. Too much had happened of late, and she was literally prostrate with fatigue.

But Bayard stuck to his guns, so that by two o'clock his sister sat fidgeting in his elegant living room, crossing and recrossing her legs and nervously taking short puffs on a cigarette. Little Alice, wearing a blue pinafore, sat opposite, staring at her like the stranger she was.

Dartania decided, as so often these days, that what she herself needed was a good stiff drink. "Would you like a Coca-Cola?" she politely asked the child. "*Coca-Cola?*" she repeated as to a person new to the country and its language.

Alice nodded solemnly. She had her mother's round saucer eyes and mop of short curly hair, though both were darker than her mother's. Black as a skillet. Where had Dartania heard that phrase? She pushed it to the back of her mind and put the glass of Coca-Cola down beside the child. Then she poured herself a large scotch and took it back to the chair beside the fire.

Again grandmother and granddaughter silently confronted each other.

"Have you had your nap?" Dartania optimistically inquired.

The child nodded. She seemed very subdued. Three-year-olds purportedly were unmanageable. They climbed bookcases, kicked the furniture about, and stuck their fingers into electrical sockets. But Alice had hardly moved, had hardly even blinked.

Dartania lit another cigarette and gratefully sipped her whiskey, but the pressure to create some form of entertainment mounted distressingly.

"When I was about your age," she blurted suddenly between puffs and recrossing of legs, "I had a little dog named Elf. He followed me home one day from our front gate. He was black, part terrier, and he was no ordinary dog. He had magical powers. In fact he was only part dog I think . . ."

The child fixed unblinking eyes on her grandmother over the rim of the glass.

Dartania rambled desperately on, ad libbing, the effect on her audience ultimately unreadable. But having always been a performer, once she got into it the story unraveled as easily as if it had been true, which parts of it more or less were.

"And then Elf climbed up into the tree and there I was hanging upside down by my apron strings and he gnawed right through the cloth and down I came into Mrs. Eliot's carrot patch. Elf was so pleased with himself. He leaped down out of the tree into the carrot patch beside me, and in a jiffy he had turned himself into a rabbit, just for a while, and he ate all the carrots. I was eating one, too, when Mrs. Eliot . . ."

"Was he haunted?" the child suddenly asked.

"Haunted?" Dartania thought for a minute. "Well I suppose in a way he was. Because of his special powers. That can be a kind of haunting."

"Mama said I could have a puppy."

Dartania visibly flinched, recalling the expedition that had in fact brought her to Cottoncrop. Something wrenched alarmingly, deep inside. Did the child know her mother was dead? How could she? She didn't know what death was. Yet she had not asked for her. It was as if she were being discreet, aware something was wrong and sparing the grown-ups more embarrassment than they already showed.

"Well!" Dartania suddenly brightened, she looked at her watch. "I'll tell you what. Why don't we go and get one, right this minute?" The opportunity of filling the next hour loomed appealingly. "We can drive to the pound," she said, standing up.

Already the little girl was slipping from her chair.

"Have you got a coat?"

"I have a mackintosh."

Dartania smiled. "Well, you had better bring it."

BAYARD RETURNED HOME that afternoon to be greeted by a brown rampaging puppy. "Say hello to Elf," Dartania commanded airily. Granddaughter and grandmother were sitting cross-legged on the living room floor playing cards. "Slap jack!" cried Dartania, slapping her hand on the jack that Alice had just laid down.

"Good God, Dar, he's peed all over the floor. Where the devil is Albert?" he demanded, forgetting it was his day off.

A bowl stood on the hearth, most of its contents spilled on to the hearthstone. The bowl was Minton, one in a complete set of rare soup plates. His sister had never been a responsible person. She had simply never grown up. He knew that. But these were positive signs of retardation. The child's blue pinafore had a dark stain down the front. Were both of them drinking his claret!

Her brother's discomfiture amused Dartania. He had a stuffy side if you looked hard enough. Well, he could take over now. She jumped spryly up.

She had done her bit. "Over to you, brother dear. I hope Janey isn't delayed," she added mischievously, then turned brightly to the child. "Bye bye, Alice, sugar. Give your grandmama a kiss," she cheerfully recommended.

The little girl stood up looking dazed and did as she was bid.

Dartania picked up her jacket, which had been thrown over a chair, and followed by a disapproving Bayard, headed for the entrance hall, mildly pleased with herself for having survived the afternoon without disaster. On the whole, in fact, the thing had been a success, and she felt better than she had for some time.

As she opened the front door, however, Alice, rushing wildly across the room, was suddenly upon her, clutching her skirt, begging her not to go, not to leave her. *"Please. Please. Don't go Dardar! Please don't go?"* Weeping pitifully.

Dartania, as Bayard later said, was like a pillar of salt melted into a help-less puddle by a rain of tears. No one had ever cried after her in her life, or even remotely depended on her. The child's utter vulnerability, her sore need of protection, her resemblance to Flora, all of it honing to a sharp point, went straight into her heart. And the poison was honey sweet. No ambiguity was attached. In a child vulnerability was right and proper. And vulnerability was Dartania's Achilles' heel. Moreover, that Alice clearly believed she was being abandoned again was searingly painful.

Dartania looked helplessly at her brother, and the two grown-ups exchanged a quick understanding. "Now, you go with your grandpapa," she said gently as Bayard stepped dutifully forward to dislodge the clinging infant. "Janey will be back soon and Albert will give you a delicious supper."

Falling in love only takes a minute, as even the most reasonable of philosophers knows. That is the mystery and the wonder of it. So, too, Dar-tania learned. Through a pinhole pricked in her strong armor of defense, a flood of gentle protective tenderness had rushed, washing her whole being in a golden warming light, removing an emptiness she had been unaware was there.

The child had stopped crying but still she clung to Dartania's skirt, as to the edge of a raft in choppy seas, her anguished silence more profoundly affecting than her tears.

Dartania did not hesitate again. As always, pure instinct carried her for-ward. "I'll take her back with me," she said, not looking at her brother. It sounded offhand, casual, the easiest of decisions. "James can bring Janey and her things over in the morning.

"Where's your mackintosh, sugar?"

Rapidly the little girl retrieved it, and, helping her to put it on, stooping and buttoning it for her, Dartania then stood up, shouldered her bag, and took her suddenly smiling granddaughter by the hand.

Bayard watched speechless. The scene, so prosaic and yet so full of significance, so surprising, yet so matter-of-factly enacted, amazed him utterly. Then, recovering his old style, always driest when at his merriest, and staring hawk-eyed over the half-moons of his spectacles, he erupted crisply. "Don't forget that dog!"

AT THE COUNTRY club's bridge tables, the ladies smiled and shook their heads. Dartania was out at Longwood playing Slapjack and Old Maid. Late love evidently brought on a type of senility.

Maybelle Collins reported that Dartania had refused outright to let Alice go to England. There might even be a legal tussle. Dartania had insisted she was Alice's grandmother in blood, and Ellen, by comparison, an impostor. What's more, Alice's roots were in Nashborough, and that was where she belonged.

Whatever his reaction to this tug of war, William, unlike Solomon, did absolutely nothing. His play had opened on Broadway and his dark anger at the dictatorial hand of fate, which had repeatedly wiped out his world with such completeness, was brilliantly channeled into King Richard's overwhelming desire to work the world and to master fate.

"A Richard for our time!" the *New York Times* triumphantly declared. "A young man jettisoning honor and loyalty for the freedom to dominate, to impose his personal will. An existential Richard who understands too late that utter isolation is the price of utter freedom. That is his tragedy."

"I did the same when I was young—well, in a mild sort of way," Jasmine cheerfully insisted, reading the review Madeleine had brought back with her from New York. The two women were finding more and more in common. "But now I think of everything as God's will, just like those Russian peasants do, sleeping so comfortably on their stoves in winter. And yet I'm not religious. Seneca would say I'm going soft in the brain."

In New York, William had told Madeleine he was going to stay there, perhaps also buy a house in England. Nashborough had taken back all that it had given, and he was through with it. Alice could stay on if she wanted. It was up to her. Even his mother, he felt sure, would quail at fighting Dartania. That misplaced Amazon, she called her; what did she know about children, or even civilization.

As to Cottoncrop, rumor had it the insurers were going to have to pay a fortune. But then a fortune had been spent on the old place. And there was its historic value to boot, if conceivably you could put a price on that. Already, too, a pack of hungry developers was hovering on the scene, waving lucrative proposals. East Nashborough needed shopping centers, it needed housing, it needed a football stadium, a bigger Baptist church.

What William needed, however, was tax breaks, and taking legal advice from Nash and Polk, he soon reached a decision. The following week the *Herald* announced William's plan to donate Cottoncrop's remaining fifty acres to Nashborough for a public park. Upkeep of all the graves and preservation of the garden, as he had planned it, were part of the deal.

William openly scorned the town's proposed name of Cottoncrop Park as debasing the English language. Nash Park was worth consideration. With Seneca's death, the eponymous surname, alive in Nashborough for two hundred years, was gone. Even so, reasoned William, the family already had a town named for it, a fast-growing one, too. So that in the end a mild perversity ruled. Why shouldn't his own antecedents be remembered?

The following September, William appeared briefly in Nashborough for the formal opening of Escali Fields, his celebrity adding to and at the same time dwarfing the occasion's high civic purpose. There was a famous actress with him, and the pair was trailed by a swarm of fans and autograph hounds, following them from the airport. They hardly seemed to notice. They were used to swarms. People looking for gods, as William coldly described them.

The legend of Escali, part of Nashborough folklore, was widely revived by the opening of the park. And as time went by some people claimed that of a morning—out walking their dogs early, when the mists were lifting—to have seen a mysterious figure standing sentinel on the edge of the woods, beside the old Indian graves. Others were sure they had seen an Indian family, the wife pulling a travois across the fields, away from the splendid gardens, and toward the woods, not looking to left or right, as though great plains and forested hunting grounds were being left behind, and they were coming home.

But as Dartania so often said, people will see what they want, and there's no stopping them. To which she would later add, watching Alice and Elf play Space Invaders around the old log house, and why not?

Epilogue

+-+

I am sitting in my penthouse eyrie, in front of the bay window, and looking out at the panoramic view of Blue Hills with its green, well-
watered lawns, and beyond to the tall, new office buildings of
downtown Nashborough, glittering in the sunset like rows of gold bars
upended on the horizon. In so many ways it is a changed world from what I
can first remember, but in other ways, not yet, significantly, so.

Oddly, I am almost the only leaf of my generation left fluttering on the
family tree, and, after so many years, I await the onset of winter without, I
confess, a great deal of regret.

Only last month, dear Dartania died. She was eighty-nine and had lived
alone for years, after Alice grew up, the old place tumbling down around
her. But I believe she was not unhappy. She had brought Alice up, and,
according to Bayard, it was the making of them both. I think myself that he
was probably right.

Bayard died nearly ten years ago—back in 1980—and his collection, as
Jasmine rightly predicted, has become one of America's most celebrated. It
has put Nashborough, if superficially, on the cultural map and inscribed for
future generations the Douglas name. But the living Douglas name too
remains firmly on the map—Robin and William having both become so
famous. The only true Douglases in name, however, besides myself, call
themselves Kane, and nobody knows where they are. Somewhere out there
on America's streets. There were I believe quite a lot of them.

Jasmine is in a nursing home and becoming very forgetful. She told me
recently when I visited that she and Seneca were off to France together. I
suppose she never did let him go. Or conveniently he comes and goes. Jas-

mine could always work things to some personal advantage, and that powerful instinct, even in senility, has survived. She also paints. Always it is the same picture: a picture of a wood, or I think that's what it is, with a sort of waterfall in the background. And every time it is admired anew by the nurses and other inmates alike.

I told her Timbuctoo was going to be pulled down to make way for a shopping center.

"I suppose that's progress," she replied, and let it go. But I'm glad Dartania hasn't lived to see it. To her it would have been the obliteration of her roots in an erased grave.

Alice came back from California for Dartania's funeral. She is a biologist at the University of California. She married another biologist, but was pretty quickly divorced, which seems to be the fashion nowadays.

"The world is going to be a very different place," she told me confidently when she came by for a drink. "As a means of change, evolution is too primitive; it's so haphazard and it's way too slow."

The future, it seems, is to be a race between geneticists and computer engineers, one of which will produce a perfected species.

"No one will comprehend how protopeople like ourselves lived with pain and death, and just accepted it," she said. "We're taking over from the gods now, so to speak; correcting their shortcomings, adding finishing touches. We know what we need." Her round eyes sparkle with the assurance of professionalism, of a proper training. She is the new woman. Her mop of dark hair, cut short like a boy's, frames an angelic face without makeup, and she was wearing coveralls.

"Your family history will be interesting archaeology one day, Uncle Dan. The way things were, I mean. Because there won't be any families then, just people, and everybody is going to live forever. We're getting there, you know. It's going to happen!"

List of Characters

Frazer, Jack ....Ex GI, from Mississippi.

Mason, Eddy ....Son of Herbert Mason, member of hunt staff.

Mason, Georgia ....Wife of Herbert.

Mason, Herbert ....Master of foxhounds, Nashborough Hunt.

Mason, Johnny ....Son of Herbert, member of hunt staff.

Mason, Philip ....Younger brother of Herbert, works for Ford Motor Company.

Mason, Red ....Wife of Philip Mason.

Nash, Alice ....Wife of Edward Nash.

Nash, Dartania, née Douglas ....Born 1901, married to Seneca Nash.

Nash, Dr. Edward ....Descendant of Nashborough's founder. Owner of Cottoncrop.

Nash, Emma ....Second daughter of Seneca and Dartania.

Nash, Flora ....Youngest daughter of Seneca and Dartania. Born 1931.

Nash, Phoebe ....Third daughter of Seneca and Dartania.

Nash, Sally.............................Eldest daughter of Seneca and Dartania. Born 1923.

Nash, Seneca ....Only son of Edward and Alice. Born 1899. Owner of Longwood.

Noland, Frank ....Iconoclastic painter.

Piper, Jack ....Young man with chip on shoulder.

Prince of Wales, Edward ....Later Edward VIII.

Sayle, Harry ....Cotton broker who enters politics.

Spencer, Maybelle ....Young socialite.

Stein, Gertrude ....Writer and art collector.

Tebbit, Mattie ....Longwood tenant.

Tebbit, Sammy........................Mattie Tebbit's son.

Toklas, Alice B. ....Companion to Gertrude Stein.

Webster, Mary Ann ....Schoolteacher interested in politics.